...when she received 'The
Call' in 2012. Maya lives in England with her husband,
kids and an endless supply of books. Contact Maya:
mayabauthor.blogspot.com
twitter.com/mayablake
facebook.com/maya.blake.94

Fiona Brand lives in the sunny Bay of Islands, New
Zealand. Now that both of her sons are grown, she
continues to love writing books and gardening. After a
life-changing time in which she met Christ, she has
undertaken study for a bachelor of theology and has
become a member of The Order of St. Luke, Christ's
healing ministry.

Award-winning author **HelenKay Dimon** spent twelve
years in the most unromantic career ever – divorce
lawyer. After dedicating all of that effort to helping
people terminate relationships, she is thrilled to deal in
happy endings and write romance novels for a living.
Her books have been featured in *Cosmopolitan*
Magazine and E! Online. HelenKay loves hearing from
readers, so stop by her website at helenkaydimon.com
and say hello.

Bachelor Bosses

Bachelor Bosses:
The Ex Appeal

MAYA BLAKE

FIONA BRAND

HELENKAY DIMON

MILLS & BOON

First Published in Great Britain 2022
By Mills & Boon, an imprint of HarperCollins*Publishers*, Ltd
1 London Bridge Street, London, SE1 9GF

www.harpercollins.co.uk

HarperCollins*Publishers*
1st Floor, Watermarque Building,
Ringsend Road, Dublin 4, Ireland

BACHELOR BOSSES: THE EX APPEAL © 2022 Harlequin Enterprises ULC.

The Boss's Nine-Month Negotiation © 2017 Maya Blake
A Tangled Affair © 2012 Fiona Gillibrand
Reunion with Benefits © 2018 HelenKay Dimon

ISBN: 978-0-263-30466-4

This book is produced from independently certified FSC™ paper to ensure responsible forest management.

For more information visit: www.harpercollins.co.uk/green

Printed and Bound in Spain using 100% Renewable electricity at CPI Black Print, Barcelona

THE BOSS'S
NINE-MONTH
NEGOTIATION

MAYA BLAKE

To Carly, for making my stories shine!

PROLOGUE

NOTHING HAD CHANGED in six years.

Emiliano Castillo was mildly surprised at himself for entertaining the thought, even for a second, that things would be different. Wasn't 'the old way or no way' one of the endless tenets forming his family's foundations and beliefs?

Wasn't that rigid clinging to tradition one of *his* reasons for turning his back on his family?

He kept his gaze dead straight, refusing to turn his head to glance at the miles of rolling paddocks that usually held his family's prized thoroughbreds and foal training ground. Even then, he couldn't help but notice, as his chauffeur drove him towards his ancestral home, that the normally teeming landscape was now curiously empty, the dozen or so gauchos usually in each corral nowhere in sight.

He brought his wandering thoughts back under control. There would be no indulging in nostalgia on this visit. In fact, Emiliano intended the trip to the renowned Castillo Estate just outside Cordoba, Argentina, to be as brief as the summons that had brought him here.

He had only come out of respect for Matias, his older brother. Had Matias been in a position to speak, Emiliano would've made sure his brother relayed his refusal of the summons he'd received in London loud and clear to their parents.

Sadly, Matias wasn't in a position to do any such thing.

The reason for that tightened his jaw, even as a brief tinge of sadness assailed him. Thankfully, there was little time to dwell on it as the car drew up in front of the extensive luxury villa in which several generations of proud, intractable Castillos had lived.

Oak double doors opened as he stepped out of the car.

Emiliano tensed, for a moment forgetting that neither his father nor his mother had deigned to open doors of their own accord for as long as he could remember. Not when they had servants to do it for them.

Mounting the steps, he nodded curtly at the ageing butler's greeting. This particular member of staff wasn't one he remembered and for that he was marginally thankful. He wanted no more memories triggered, or to go down the lonely, dismal path he'd done his best to try to forget.

'If señor would like to come with me, Señor and Señora Castillo are waiting in the drawing room.'

Emiliano allowed himself the briefest of glances at the walls that surrounded the home he'd grown up in, the sturdy bannister he used to slide down as a child, the antique cabinet he'd crashed into and earned himself a long-since-healed fracture on his collarbone.

He'd had time to do all that because he hadn't been the firstborn son. His time had been his own to use or misuse as he pleased, because only one person had counted in this household: Matias. But it was only as he'd entered his teenage years that he'd grown to fathom exactly what that meant.

Securing the button on his single-breasted suit, he refocused his gaze and followed the butler into the wide, sunlit reception room.

His parents were seated in twin wing-backed chairs that wouldn't have been out of place in the throne room at the Palace of Versailles. But, even without the heavy accoutrements and almost-garish displays of wealth to punctuate their success, Benito and Valentina Castillo carried themselves with near-royal pride.

They both eyed him now with equal expressions of hauteur and indifference— both expressions he was used to. But Emiliano glimpsed something else beneath the brittle exteriors.

Nerves. Desperation.

He tucked that observation away, walked forward and kissed his mother on both cheeks.

'Mama, I hope you are well?'

Her expression twitched only for as long as it took for her to give him a once-over, before settling back into prideful superiority. 'Of course. But I would be better still if you'd bothered to answer us when we first reached out to you. But, as usual, you choose to do things in your own time, when it suits you best.'

Emiliano gritted his teeth and curbed the urge to remind them that it was the legacy of forgetful indifference they'd bestowed on him which had dictated his actions. Instead he nodded to his father, received a curt nod in return and selected an armchair to settle in.

'I am here now. Shall we get on with why you summoned me?' he said, then refused the offer of a drink from the butler.

His father's mouth twisted. '*Sí*, always in a rush. Always, you have somewhere else to be, don't you?'

Emiliano slowly exhaled. 'As a matter of fact, I do.' He was in the middle of a bidding war for a revolutionary social media programme back in London. The programme's creators were being courted by at least half a dozen other venture capitalists. Despite his company being the biggest and most powerful of them all, he reminded himself that he'd been the underdog once, before a daring move had set him on his way to stratospheric success. This wasn't a time to take his foot off the pedal.

He also had to approve the finishing touches for the birthday celebration his event planner had put together for Sienna Newman.

His vice-president of Acquisitions.

His lover.

Thoughts of the woman whose intellect kept him on his toes by day and whose body thrilled his by night fractionally allayed the bitter memories of his childhood. Unlike his past liaisons, she hadn't been an easy conquest, her reluctance even to give him the time of day beyond the boardroom was a challenge that had fired his blood in the months before she'd even agreed to have dinner with him.

In his quiet moments, Emiliano still silently reeled at the changes he'd made in his life in order to accommodate his lover. The few who presumed to know him would agree— rightly, in this instance—that this behaviour wasn't like him at all. His own disquiet in the face of the reservation he sometimes felt from Sienna made him question himself. But not enough to disrupt the status quo. Not yet, anyway. Although, like everything in life, it, too, had a finite shelf life. It was that ticking clock which made him even more impatient to be done with whatever this summons was all about and get out of this place.

He stared at his parents with a raised eyebrow, letting the silent censure bounce off him. He'd long ago learned that nothing he said or did would ever change their attitude towards him. He was the spare they'd sired but never needed. His place would be on a shelf, fed, clothed, but collecting dust and nothing else. So he'd left home and stopped trying.

'When was the last time you visited your brother?' his mother enquired, her fixed expression breaking momentarily to allow a touch of humanity to filter through at the mention of Matias.

The question brought to mind his brother's current state. Comatose in a hospital bed in Switzerland with worryingly low signs of brain activity.

Emiliano weathered the punch of sadness and brushed

a speck of lint off his cuff. 'Two weeks ago. And every two weeks before that since his accident four months ago,' he replied.

His parents exchanged surprised glances. He curbed the urge to laugh. 'If this is all you needed to know, you could've sent me an email.'

'It isn't. But we find it…reassuring that family still means something to you, seeing as you abandoned it without a backward glance,' Benito stated.

The fine hairs on Emiliano's nape lifted. 'Reassuring? I guess it should be celebrated that I've done something right at last, then? But, at the risk of straying into falsehoods and hyperbole, perhaps let's stick to the subject of why you asked me here.'

Benito picked up his glass and stared into the contents for a few seconds before he knocked it back and swallowed with a gulp. The action was so alien—his father's outward poise a thing so ingrained it seemed part of his genetic make-up—that Emiliano's jaw threatened to drop before he caught himself.

Setting the glass down with a brisk snap, another first, Benito eyed him with fresh censure. Nothing new there.

'We're broke. Completely destitute. Up the proverbial creek without a paddle.'

'Excuse me?' Emiliano wasn't sure whether it was the bald language that alarmed him or his father's continued acting out of character.

'You wish me to repeat myself? Why? So you can gloat?' his father snapped. 'Very well. The polo business, the horse breeding. Everything has failed. The estate has been sliding into the red for the past three years, ever since Rodrigo Cabrera started his competing outfit here in Cordoba. We approached Cabrera and he bought the debt. Now he's calling in the loans. If we don't pay up by the end of next month, we will be thrown out of our home.'

Emiliano realised his jaw was clenched so tight he had to force it apart to speak. 'How can that be? Cabrera doesn't know the first thing about horse breeding. The last I heard he was dabbling in real estate. Besides, Castillo is the foremost polo-training and horse-breeding establishment in South America. How can you be on the brink of bankruptcy?' he demanded.

His mother's colour receded and her fingers twisted the white lace handkerchief in her hand. 'Watch your tone, young man.'

Emiliano inhaled sharply, stopped the sharper words that threatened to spill and chose his words carefully. 'Explain to me how these circumstances have occurred.'

His father shrugged. 'You are a man of business...you know how these things go. A few bad investments here and there...'

Emiliano shook his head. 'Matias was...*is*...a shrewd businessman. He would never have let things slide to the point of bankruptcy without mitigating the losses or finding a way to reverse the business's fortunes. At the very least, he would've told me...' He stopped when his parents exchanged another glance. 'I think you should tell me what's really going on. I'm assuming you asked me here because you need my help?'

Pride flared in his father's eyes for a blinding moment before he glanced away and nodded. '*Sí.*' The word was one Emiliano was sure he didn't want to utter.

'Then let's have it.'

They remained stoically silent for several heartbeats before his father rose. He strode to a cabinet on the far side of the room, poured himself another drink and returned to his chair. Setting the glass down, he picked up a tablet Emiliano hadn't spotted before and activated it.

'Your brother left a message for you. Perhaps it would explain things better.'

He frowned. 'A message? How? Matias is in a coma.'

Valentina's lips compressed, distress marring her features for a brief second. 'You don't need to remind us. He recorded it before his brain operation, once the doctors gave him the possible prognosis.'

Emiliano couldn't fault the pain in her voice or the sadness in her eyes. And, not for the first time in his life, he wondered why that depth of feeling for his brother had never spilt over for him.

Pushing the fruitless thought aside, he focused on the present. On what he could control.

'That was two months ago. Why are you only telling me about this message now?'

'We didn't think it would be needed before now.'

'And by *it*, you mean me?'

His mother shrugged. Knowing the iron control he'd locked down on his feelings where his parents were concerned was in danger of breaking free and exploding, he jerked to his feet. Crossing the room to his father, he held out his hand for the tablet.

Benito handed it over.

Seeing his brother's face frozen on the screen, the bandage around his head and the stark hospital furniture and machines around him, Emiliano felt his breath strangle in his chest. Matias was the one person who hadn't dismissed him for being born second. His brother's support was the primary reason Emiliano had broken away from the glaringly apathetic environment into which he'd been born. He knew deep down that he would've made it, no matter what, but Matias's unwavering encouragement had bolstered him in the early, daunting years when he'd been floundering alone on the other side of the world.

He stemmed the tremor moving through him as his gaze moved over his brother's pale, gaunt face. Returning to his seat, he pressed the play button.

The message was ten minutes long.

With each second of footage that passed, with each word his brother uttered, Emiliano sank further into shock and disbelief. When it was over, he lifted his gaze and met equal stares that were now less indifferent and more... concerned.

'Are you... Is this for real?' he demanded.

'You're hearing the words from your brother's lips and still you doubt it?' his father asked, a trace of shame lacing his stiff demeanour.

'I don't doubt what Matias is saying. I'm questioning whether you truly gambled away millions that you knew the company couldn't afford!'

His father slammed his hand on the table. 'Castillo is my company!'

'It's also Matias's birthright! At least, that's what you drummed into him from the day he was born, was it not? Wasn't that the reason he all but broke his back to make it a success? Because you pressured him to succeed at all costs?'

'I am no tyrant. What he did for Castillo, he did willingly.'

Emiliano barely managed to bite back the swear word that hovered on his tongue. 'And for that you repay him by frittering away the profits behind his back?'

'The deal we made with Cabrera was supposed to be a sure thing.'

'A sure thing? You were duped by a man who spotted an easy score a mile away.' He stared down at the screen, still unable to believe the tale Matias had told. Bankruptcy. Destitution for his parents. Absurd promises made. Regret that the burden now fell on Emiliano's shoulders.

The naked plea in his brother's eyes and solemn tone not to let the family down.

That last entreaty, more than anything else, was what

kept Emiliano from walking out the door in that moment. Even though what Matias was asking of him—the request to honour the deal his parents had struck with Rodrigo Cabrera—was so ludicrous, he wondered why he wasn't laughing his head off.

Because every single word was true. He could tell just from looking into his parents' eyes.

'You really are serious, aren't you? You struck this bargain that Matias would marry Cabrera's daughter if the deal went south and the loans became due?' he rasped with renewed disbelief. 'Isn't she still a child?'

A brief memory of a little girl in pigtails chasing around the ranch during family visits flitted through his mind. Matias, as usual, had been patient and caring with Graciela Cabrera, but Emiliano, fully immersed in dreams of escape, could barely remember her, save for a few exchanges at the dinner table.

'She's twenty-three years old,' his mother supplied. 'She may have had a few wild escapades that have left her parents with more grey hairs than they wish, but she is more mature now. Matias was her favourite, of course, but she remembers you fondly—'

'I don't care how she remembers me. What I care about is that none of this set-up rang any alarm bells for you!' He seethed, unwilling to rise to the subtle dig. 'From a supposed family friend!'

For the first time, his father had the grace to look embarrassed. But the expression didn't last long. He regrouped, as was the Castillo way. 'We are where we are, Emiliano. The burden of our family's fortunes now rests with you. And don't bother taking out your chequebook. Cabrera has made it clear he wants only one thing. You either marry Graciela Cabrera or you can sit back and watch your mother and me lose everything.'

CHAPTER ONE

SIENNA NEWMAN STEPPED out of the shower, finished drying off and eased her black hair from the tight bun it'd been in all day. Swiping her hand across the steamed-up vanity mirror, she couldn't resist smiling at herself.

Sister Margaret from the orphanage where Sienna had spent most of her childhood had often told her to count her blessings. Of course, counting those blessings while smiling goofily at herself in the mirror would've been met with a frown. The orphanage matriarch certainly wouldn't have approved of the illicitly carnal thrill that went through her as she smoothed expensive and luxurious lotion over her skin, her senses revving up in anticipation of what the evening ahead held for her. It was a good thing therefore that Sister M, as the children had referred to her, wasn't here to see this tiny fall from grace. Because, even with the old biddy's beady eyes on her, Sienna didn't think she could've stopped smiling.

Today, her twenty-eighth birthday had started in spectacular style. Four giant bouquets of calla lilies and white roses, her favourite flowers, had been delivered to her desk on the hour between nine o'clock and midday, each time with a jaw-dropping present wrapped in white silk paper and black velvet bows. The stunning beauty of the diamond tennis bracelet delivered at eleven o'clock had only been topped by the magnificent sapphire teardrop necklace with matching earrings at midday. But even more special than all the presents had been the handwritten notes from Emiliano accompanying each gift. The scrawls had been as bold and domineering as the man, nowhere near flowery, but the intimate words of desire and felicitation had touched her deeply.

The afternoon had taken a different but nevertheless incredible turn, with culinary delights from edible-gold-dusted chocolate to caviar to a single pink-and-silver frosted cupcake with a lit candle for her to wish on and blow out.

She'd made a wish all right. One that had stealthily sprung into her heart and taken root about three months ago, around the time it had dawned on her that she'd been in a relationship with a hitherto unattainable man for almost a year.

Extreme self-preservation born of painful past experiences had fuelled her need to ignore the growing wish, but with each day that passed she'd began to hope rejection wasn't on the cards for her this time, as it had so often been.

As Sienna re-entered the bedroom, her smile dimmed a touch.

The only slight downside to her fantastic day had been the need to once more be evasive in the face of interest from colleagues about her love life and the knowledge that, although his extravagant birthday surprises had been thrilling to experience, Emiliano had once again run roughshod over her need to keep their relationship private.

The last time she'd touched on the subject, they'd rowed, Emiliano's Latin temper erupting in a torrent that had included his adamant refusal to 'skulk around in shadows' or 'pretend I'm not into you when we're in public.'

After a heated back-and-forth on the subject they'd retreated to the not-so-neutral zone of their bedroom, where he'd expressed his extreme displeasure passionately.

Sienna blushed in recollection, but her smile remained elusive, her heart skidding again as a different issue interrupted her happiness.

Another thing that would've made her birthday perfect was Emiliano's presence. Or, barring that, a simple phone call.

All she'd received was an email wishing her happy birthday and a single line to say he was aboard his plane, flying back home from Argentina. Although she'd been relieved that the unexpected extension of his overseas trip by four more days was finally over, she'd yearned to hear his voice. So much so, she'd called him straight back the moment she'd got home, only to have her call go to voicemail. Same as most of her calls the last three days. The one time he'd picked up, he'd been brusque to the point of monosyllabic.

She curbed the tiny spurt of anxiety and pulled on her underwear before sliding on the dress she'd shopped for for hours before discovering it in a tiny shop in Soho. The blood-red sleeveless gown showed off the slight tan she'd gained from their recent weekend away in St Tropez. Fastening her new necklace and earrings, she brushed out her shoulder-length black hair and stepped into black stilettos. The added height would be nowhere near Emiliano's six-foot-three-inch frame, but the confidence boost was nevertheless welcome.

Exhaling, she pushed away the insidious voice that wouldn't remain silent, reminding her that everything in her life—bar her career—thus far, had been ripped from her. That what she had with Emiliano would follow suit. After adding the finishing touches of perfume, clutch and wrap, she headed for the door.

She didn't want to, but Sienna couldn't stop the nerves that assailed her, or the equal amounts of excitement and dread that fluttered through her stomach at the notion of going out in public with Emiliano tonight. Even though they'd never resolved their argument, he'd grown increasingly possessive of her in public recently, his bold caresses almost baiting her to protest. Unwilling to provoke another disagreement, she hadn't, and in her quiet moments even admitted to enjoying those displays. Nevertheless, the butterflies in her stomach grew, their wings beating so loud she almost missed her phone buzzing with a text message.

Her heart skipped a beat when she saw Emiliano's name on her screen.

Slight change of plan. We'll dine at home. Restaurant delivery is taken care of. Let me know if that suits? E.

Her smile burst forth anew, her heart squeezing with happiness as she quickly answered.

That more than suits. Can't wait to see you! XXX

Hitting Send, she stared at the little faint bubble that said her message was being read. Then waited. He didn't answer.

Swallowing, she returned her phone to the clutch and left the bedroom.

The restaurant they were supposed to dine at was a mere two miles away from the Knightsbridge penthouse she shared with Emiliano. And, if Emiliano had already contacted her favourite chef, then the meal was most likely already on its way.

She walked down the stunningly decorated hallway and through the vast sitting room to find Alfie, their young live-in butler, setting the table in the dining room.

He looked up and smiled when he saw her. 'Good evening, miss.'

She returned his smile and nodded at the table. 'Looks like Emiliano has given you the heads-up on the change of plan?'

'Indeed. He's also given me the night off,' he replied

with a grin. 'I'll just wait for the delivery to arrive then I'll leave you two alone to enjoy your birthday.'

She fought the blush that threatened, recalling the butler's wry comment months ago about how he'd become the grateful recipient of many sudden nights off since she'd moved in with Emiliano. 'Thanks.'

Alfie nodded and went back to laying the table. Not wishing to intrude, she drifted back into the living room. Decorated with luxury and deep comfort in mind, the slate-coloured sofas, matching tables and the white walls were interspersed with dark-gold throw pillows and rugs that added welcoming warmth to the large room. A dominating fireplace was aglow to complement the November autumnal weather.

Sienna strolled to the mantel, picked up the single picture adorning it and stared down at the selfie she'd taken of herself and Emiliano three months ago. It had been a rare moment of throwing caution to the wind and all the more special for it. On a late-afternoon stroll in the park across from the penthouse, after a morning and afternoon spent making love, she'd confessed to sadness at not having photographic mementos of a childhood spent in foster care, no matter how wretched. Emiliano had insisted she seize the moment to make a memory. And, even though he'd refused to look into the camera, his years of avoiding the glare of the paparazzi's lens deeply ingrained, he'd posed for the picture. The end result was Emiliano staring at her while she looked into the camera, flushed and self-conscious from his brazenly hungry scrutiny.

He'd taken a look at the photo, pronounced himself satisfied and promptly printed and framed it for the mantel.

Sienna stared at the profile of the man who commanded her days and nights, the boss who'd changed his own company's rules, despite her many blithely ignored protests, in order to date her. Her heart skipped another beat, and with it the secret wish lurking in her heart.

Emiliano Castillo had done more than amend his company's rules. He'd gone on to trigger a few more firsts, as she'd found out in the months following the start of their relationship. For a start, he hadn't been one for *relationships*. Certainly not one with a vice-president of his venture capitalist firm. Most of his liaisons only lasted a couple of months. He'd also never lived with a lover. And he'd certainly never lived with one for going on six months!

Which was why Sienna was daring to believe that theirs was more than a supercharged physical affair. It was why she'd found herself hoping for more. They had never talked about a family, largely because the subject had been strictly off-limits for both of them, save for unavoidable instances that filtered through their lives.

As far as she knew, his relationship with his parents was strained at best, but she'd seen his devastation when his brother had been seriously injured in a car accident four months ago. And, with each trip she'd accompanied him on to the state-of-the-art medical facility in Switzerland where Matias was being cared for after his brain surgery had left him in a coma, she'd witnessed Emiliano's distress and sadness.

Hers was a different story. She had no past to discuss, so she never did.

The desolation she'd learned to live with overpowered her for a single moment before she pushed it back into its designated box. Today was her birthday. She was lucky she had a date to celebrate. But she'd also worked hard to make a life for herself, and she was determined it wouldn't fall victim to rejection and heartache.

So celebrate she *would*.

She returned the picture to the mantel in time to hear the penthouse door's electronic lock disengage.

Expecting it to be Alfie, taking delivery of their food, her heart leapt into her throat when Emiliano walked in.

He was supposed to have been gone for two days. He'd been gone for six. She hadn't comprehended just how much she'd missed him until he handed over the food boxes to Alfie and walked tall and proud into the living room. A rush of longing and happiness overtook her as her gaze met his.

At six foot three, with a powerful but streamlined physique, Emiliano Castillo gave the term 'tall, dark and handsome' full, visceral meaning. But he also carried an extra edge that ensured that heads, and hearts, turned whenever he graced humanity with his presence. His wasn't a flawless face, to start with. A scar sustained along his right jawline from a horse-riding accident as a teenager evoked a sense of illicit danger, if you just looked at him. Bold slants of jet eyebrows over brooding, dark, coppery eyes and a full and sensual mouth sculpted for long, steamy lovemaking nights made him very difficult to look away from.

So she stared, transfixed, heart slamming against her ribs, as he walked slowly towards her. He stopped several feet from where she stood. Electricity crackled through the air as they stared at one another. Then slowly, his eyes traced her body from head to toe, lingering, *possessing*, and back again.

Expecting him to stride forward and sweep her into his arms in that overwhelmingly possessive and blatantly male way he employed, she braced herself, her every sense leaping with excitement.

But he remained where he stood.

'Happy birthday, *querida*. You look exquisite.' His voice was deep, laced with the Spanish intonation he carried proudly. But the words, despite being felicitous and complimentary, were a touch grave. As were the hands he shoved deep into his pockets instead of using them to reach for her as he normally did when they'd been apart this long.

Her heart skittered, but Sienna pushed away the fizzle of anxiety. 'Thank you. It's great to have you back,' she replied, with her tongue lightly slicking lips gone nervous and dry.

His eyelids descended for a moment, then his head tilted slightly, dark eyes resting on her, seeming to absorb her every expression. 'Have you had a good day?' he asked.

The reminder of how her day had gone brought a smile. His breath seemed to catch as her smile widened. 'It was wonderful, Emiliano. I'm not sure how you planned everything without my knowledge but I loved every second of it. Thank you so much for these…' She caressed her necklace and earrings. 'I should be angry with you for forcing me to field questions, though.' She deliberately infused lightness into her tone, but her reluctance to incite another row didn't mean she was damping down what was important to her.

'No doubt you found your usual diplomatic way to deny my existence despite it being an open secret,' he returned with a distinct edge to his tone.

Sienna's breath snagged in her lungs. Yes, the subject was definitely still a sore one. But one she intended to tackle soon. Maybe tonight…

'I've never denied your existence. Merely not fuelled workplace gossip. There's a difference.'

His upper lip curled slightly, his jaw flexing a touch. 'If you say so.'

She floundered for a moment, the ground beneath her feet shaking a little. Was her continued denial of their relationship outside the privacy of their penthouse causing more damage than she realised?

Inhaling deeply, she widened her smile.

'I do say so. And it would've been perfect if you'd been

here, regardless of who knows about us.' Sienna knew she was offering a tentative olive branch, while subtly digging for answers to questions she wasn't completely certain were wise to pursue, but the worry that had taken root between her ribs was growing by the second.

'I'm sorry. The situation couldn't be helped.'

She wasn't surprised at the slightly cryptic answer. The enigma that was Emiliano Castillo operated at optimum capacity, always. She'd learned the hard way that to gain his attention she had to meet her lover and boss toe to toe. It was what had brought her to his attention in the boardroom. It was why their chemistry remained sizzling hot in the bedroom. A chemistry that had stunned and bewildered her in the beginning and continued to overawe her even now. It was the reason she checked herself now from leaving the safety of the mantel to close the seemingly yawning distance between them, even though every muscle strained to be in his arms.

Denying herself the pleasure, she remained where she was, sensing the deep, puzzling tension within him as a muscle jumped in his shadowed cheek. But even from a distance she experienced the jolt of electricity that lanced through her when his eyes remained fixed on hers. 'You didn't elaborate on what was going on. Is it Matias?' she asked.

A shadow drifted over his face. 'In a way, yes.'

'Is he okay? Has there been any improve—'

'His condition remains unchanged,' he interrupted.

Her gaze dropped, drifting over his lower lip. He inhaled sharply, gratifying her with his reaction. But his hands remained in his pockets.

'So you spent all six days with your parents?'

Another clench of his jaw. *'Sí.'* The word was chillingly grave.

Her heart dropped. 'Emiliano…I… Is everything okay?'

He finally breached the gap between them and grasped her hand in his. Lowering their linked hands, he stared at her upturned palm for several seconds before he released her. 'No, everything is not okay, but it's nothing that won't resolve itself eventually.'

She opened her mouth and started to demand more information. But he'd turned away.

'Come, the food will be getting cold.'

She followed him into the dining room and pinned the smile on her face as he held her chair and saw her seated. Again she anticipated his touch on her bare shoulders, a drift of his sensual mouth across her temple. She received neither.

She watched him take his own seat, the neutrality of his expression underlined with a grimness that lodged a cold stone in her stomach.

'Emiliano...'

'I belayed ordering oysters. I didn't want them to be ruined in transit. We'll have your second favourite.'

She waved him away as he opened the first of the specially packed gourmet dishes. 'It's fine. I don't care about the food. We can have oysters some other time.' Her blush at the mention of oysters and the special significance they held for them was suppressed beneath the blooming disquiet. Even then she couldn't help but be disturbed that he'd made the order without speaking to her first. 'Tell me what's going on.'

His firm mouth thinned for a split second and the eyes that met hers were closed off, bordering on cold. '*Querida*, I don't wish to upset your birthday celebration.'

She frowned. 'Why would telling me how your trip went ruin my birthday? What happened?' she pressed.

His gaze swept away from hers, back to the dish in his hand. Shutting her out. 'My parents happened.' He looked up, tawny-gold eyes piercing her. 'And since they come under the numerous subjects we don't discuss, perhaps we can drop it?' he drawled.

The statement hurt a little, but Sienna couldn't deny that it was accurate. There were swathes of their private lives they avoided, their common threads of familiarity were business and the bedroom. Again she experienced the ominous sense of shifting sands, prompting her to go against her better judgment.

'Maybe…this one time we can make an exception? And, before you bite my head off, I only request it because I can see that whatever happened is affecting you, Emiliano.'

'You are kind, *querida*, but I would also caution you against making those sorts of statements. There are some things you can't take back. Besides, I believe you're exaggerating things a little.' He dished the seafood salad starter onto her plate, served himself and poured them both glasses of chilled white wine.

'You think I'm exaggerating things?' She hated herself for the tiny catch in her voice and the needy words that spilled in the bid to make her point. 'Then why haven't you kissed me since you walked in the door? Usually, you can't keep your hands off me, yet you haven't so much as touched me. And, if you clench your jaw any tighter, it'll snap.'

'I've told you, you look breathtaking. I've wished you happy birthday. I showered you with presents all day, even in my absence. Perhaps I'm saving the rest for later. I know how much you love the anticipation,' he drawled before he raised his glass to her and took a large gulp.

Sienna caught a glimpse of the banked desire in his eyes. Her heart resumed its erratic thumping, but she couldn't dismiss the other, more terrifying feeling residing beneath her breast. Because there was something else lurking in his eyes. Something cold, bracing and soul threatening.

'Six days of anticipation is more than enough. "One day

is too long." Isn't that what you said last month when you returned from that two-day business summit in Athens?' That she had to remind him of that was even more shocking, the unusual recounting of gestures received but never spoken about making her reel.

'Careful, Sienna, or you'll have me thinking these declarations you've previously led me to believe are over the top are in fact secretly yearned for.'

A flush crept up her neck to stain her cheeks but she didn't drop her gaze. 'As I said, perhaps I wish to make an exception.'

His shrug was almost...bored. 'There is no need. I've had a long and turbulent flight, *amante*. Right now, I want to relax and see you sated with food. Is that too much to ask?' His voice held a definite bite. A warning to leave well enough alone.

She shook her head, convinced more than ever that something was seriously wrong. 'Whatever it is that's bothering you, I...I want to help.' Throwing caution to the wind, she abandoned her glass and, in a first move that made her insides quake, she initiated touch by placing her hand over his.

He tensed, his nostrils flaring as he gazed down at her hand.

Then he removed his hand from under hers.

Her heart stopped as another thought sliced through her mind.

'Emiliano? Is it me?'

The eyes that held hers were completely devoid of emotion. 'Sienna, leave this alone...'

'Oh, God, are you annoyed with me for finalising the Younger deal without you?'

'What?'

'You gave me carte blanche, remember? You said I should go ahead and offer whatever we needed to land the deal. And that's what I did. I know it was another five million more than we initially agreed, but I did the figures and judged that it was worth it.'

His brow clamped in a frown as he yanked his tie loose with his free hand. '*Santo cielo*, not everything is about business—' He ruthlessly checked himself and drew in a breath. 'Rest assured, I'm not annoyed with you about the deal. Without your quick thinking and acting, we'd have lost it. I believe I had Denise send you an email commending you for it today.'

She'd seen the email from his executive assistant, and again wondered why Emiliano hadn't contacted her himself. 'Okay, but—'

'You want further commendations from me? More flowers? More accolades on top of the presents you've already received? Is that what this show of neediness is about?'

Shock and anger scythed equal swathes of pain through her. 'Excuse me?' Despite having called herself the same only minutes ago, the label stung badly.

He drained his glass and set it down with more force than necessary. Charging to his feet, he rounded the table. His impressive height and bristling demeanour would've made a lesser woman cower. Hell, she'd seen grown men wither beneath the look displayed on his face now.

But she'd never been one of them.

Surging to her feet, she faced him, their untouched food abandoned. 'Did you just call me *needy*?'

'Am I wrong? Now that we're behind closed doors, where your precious reputation isn't at risk, do you not *need* something from me? Have you not been full of *needful* words since I walked in the door?' he accused.

'Don't twist my words. I just want to talk to you, find out what's—'

'I don't want to *talk*, *querida*. You're usually adept at

picking up simple cues like that. Has my absence affected you that much, or is there another agenda going on here?' he taunted.

The tightly furled subject she'd tentatively intended to broach with him tonight knotted harder, congealing into stone that chafed against her heart. Incisive eyes dragged over her face, probing her expression and then widening upon witnessing the evidence she couldn't quite disguise.

'*Sí*, another agenda,' he bit out. 'Do I get three guesses or shall I strike for gold and deduce that you're breaking your *unique* mould to broach the predictable "where do we go from here?" conversation women feel the *need* to have at the most inappropriate times?'

Sienna wasn't sure whether it was his uncanny acuity or the abrasive tone that alarmed her more. 'You're turning this around on me, Emiliano. We were talking about you.'

'A subject I've clearly expressed my abhorrence for. Now, are we to go around in circles, or are we going to eat?'

She lifted her chin, the distress and foreboding she'd staunched so fiercely blooming into life within her chest. 'I've lost my appetite.'

He took another dangerous step closer, swallowing the gap between them, extinguishing the very air that sustained them until only pure, sizzling electricity remained. Soot-coloured lashes swept down and paused, the heat in his eyes branding her mouth for endless seconds before his gaze rose again.

'For food? Or for everything else?' His voice was thicker. Deeper. His nostrils flared in blatant, carnal hunger.

'Why are you so angry with me?' she whispered, unable to stem the dread crawling over her skin.

An enigmatic expression blanketed his face for a blind second, his eyes blazing with a light she couldn't fathom. 'Perhaps I'm tired of being compartmentalised in your life, of being put on a shelf and taken down and dusted off only when your needs get the better of you.'

She gasped. 'What? I've never—'

The firm finger that drifted over her lower lip stemmed her answer. 'I wish to get off this merry-go-round. So I ask you again, what have you lost your appetite for?'

Lust, need, anger and hurt strangled her in equal measures. With a few pithy words, he'd reduced her to a needy female eager to sink her talons into a man she wanted to possess. With one label, he'd reminded her of the one thing she'd vowed never to be again.

Dependent.

They'd had disagreements before, but nothing like this. Sienna couldn't catch her breath, couldn't stem the hurt that flowed like a bloodied wound. But with each second that passed, with each intake of his breath and exhalation of hers, a different emotion surged forth. Familiar. Overwhelming. Devastating.

A deep tremble seized her, shaking her from head to toe. He saw her reaction and triumph coated his features, his eyes darkening as he watched. Waited.

'Emiliano...'

'*Sí*, Sienna?' he whispered against her mouth, but holding himself a breath away, taunting her with his proximity.

Her breath shook out. 'Something's going on. Don't make me think I'm crazy or that I'm overreacting. Please, just tell me—'

'Stop. You know better than to push a closed subject. You're an expert on closed subjects, after all. So do not let tonight be the moment you change your tune, *querida*, hmm?'

Another bolt of shock went through her. Her gaze collided with his. The hunger was still there, but everything else was just...wrong. 'Who *are* you? Why are you speaking to me this way?'

'You're the one who insists on incessant discourse,' he bit out at her.

'You don't want me to talk? Fine!' She grabbed his tie and pulled it free. One vicious twist of her wrist sent it flying across the polished table. Then she attacked his shirt. Buttons turned into tiny missiles launched across the room, the depth of unbelievable hurt and lust tearing through her and making her irrational.

Her actions felt surreal, an out-of-body experience that sent shockwaves through her other self, the one observing what she was doing from a safe distance.

The live, breathing one initiating hot-headed moves swallowed hard at the first sight of Emiliano's tanned, chiselled chest and gave a helpless groan, her body weakening and surging with desire at the same time.

Emiliano's breath hissed out when she reached for his belt buckle. *'Querida—'*

'No! If I don't get to talk, neither do you,' she insisted, probably because she was terrified that talking now would force her to think about what she was doing, and the possible reason behind Emiliano's behaviour. Which was wrong, but she couldn't help it. Not in this instance. Not when a mere hour ago she'd felt on top of the world.

Her fingers gained renewed power. Tugging the belt free, she jerked it away and heard it whistle through the loops on its way across the floor. Her fingers brushed the powerful erection behind his fly and a powerful shudder rocked him.

'Dios mio, Sienna…' His voice was thick, his arousal present and potent.

'Unless, of course, you're going to tell me I'm crazy to think you want me?' She kicked away her shoes and reached for the zipper of her dress. Lowered it. Watched the tops of his sculptured cheekbones flush with raw need.

His lips parted, his breath emerging in shallow pants

as he watched her dress loosen and drape, secured only by her heaving breasts.

But, as quickly as the alien bravado had risen, it died, leaving her once again flailing, distraught.

What on earth was she doing?

Dropping her hands, she hiked up the skirt of the gown and took one step back, then another. He followed, tracking her with the calculated steps of a ravenous predator.

They moved like that, locked in their erotic dance, out of the dining room. Somewhere along the way, the top part of her dress dropped, exposing her.

Emiliano stumbled. Then cursed under his breath. At any other time, Sienna would've smiled a wicked, teasing smile. Not now. Now each breath was weighted with desire, yes, but also with a fearful heaviness that left little room for hilarity.

'Am I crazy, Emiliano?' she pressed, even though part of her desperately urged herself to remain silent.

Long seconds ticked by as he prowled after her. Her back touched the bedroom door, swinging it open. Momentarily, his gaze flicked past her to the king-sized bed they'd shared insanely passionate moments in for six months. The eyes that returned to meet hers were heavy with need and regret. Whether it was for their argument or for something else, she didn't know. Although, with the ache in her chest she couldn't quite shift, she suspected the latter.

CHAPTER TWO

'No, you're not crazy.'

The strained admission restored a little of her hurt. As did the slightly desperate aura about him as he nudged her backwards into the bedroom. Whatever else was going on, Emiliano still wanted her. It was by no means anywhere near what she ultimately wanted from him, but the knowledge soothed and settled the wild alarm racing through her veins. A little restored feminine power would sustain her. For now.

Tomorrow. She'd revisit the subject again tomorrow. Once they'd slaked far more immediate and urgent needs. Even though it went against her nature to leave a problem untackled, she would refrain from pushing for answers tonight.

With that thought, she let go of her dress. It pooled to the floor a mere second before Emiliano pounced, lifting her out of it to stand her naked except for her thong and his jewels. His arms dropped back to his sides, and she watched his hands clench with electric tension for a ragged second, then jerk towards her, beckoning her forward, his eyes burning gold. 'Come here, Sienna.'

Invitation of the most sinful nature. Invitation she grasped with both hands, stumbling forward into his arms.

Hard hands plastered her against his body and tangled in her hair, holding her still before she could satisfy the urgent need to kiss him.

He stared down at her, eyes endless pools of shadows, secrets and passion. But between one second and the next, she once again caught a glimpse of something that made her heart clench.

'Emiliano...'

He nudged her even closer, heat from his body chopping off her words, the disturbing look in his eyes resolutely erased. 'Take what you need, my little wildcat,' he breathed against her mouth.

With a moan, she rose on tiptoe, her hands sliding around his neck as her mouth pressed gloriously, ravenously, against his. Her eyes slid shut, the better to savour what she'd missed, what she'd craved so desperately, these past six days. Her senses sang when his hands wrapped tighter, mercilessly, around her, his deep groan relaying his mutual feelings.

Tongues meshing, relishing, devouring, the kiss deepened, their ragged breathing the only sound in the room as he walked her backwards on plush carpet, his aim the wide bed which was their personal haven.

Sienna gripped him tighter as he swept her off her feet and placed her on the bed. When he attempted to move, to shed the rest of his clothes, she stopped him, the idea of letting him go bringing a fresh wave of alarm.

If her unusually possessive hold on him registered, he didn't give an indication. Instead, he rolled them sideways, still delivering hot, pleasurable kisses as he impatiently shucked off shoes and trousers. His briefs followed and her breath caught all over again at the heat of his girth against her thigh.

Greedy hands closed over his steely hardness. They both groaned. Oh, how she'd longed for this.

'I missed you. So much!' she gasped between kisses, once again letting go of the tight hold she usually held on her emotions.

His body grew tauter, the carnal tension whipped through him, making muscles and sinew rock-hard beneath her touch. She expected him to reply with something wickedly decadent. His clever tongue would usually by now be whispering erotically charged words in her ear.

He remained silent even as his hands moved feverishly over her body.

Her often vocal, always possessive lover was choosing mute seduction, delivering his pleasure through his hands and mouth, ruthlessly dragging double bliss with harder kisses and rougher caresses. Sienna thrilled to the exchange even as she pushed back the million *whys* that demanded answering.

His tongue slid over her skin, tasting her nipples, sucking, teasing, melting her thoughts, to leave only pure sensation. A firm tug at her hips ripped free her panties, then he was there, at the centre of her need, delivering even more potent bliss. She sank her fingers into his hair, her cries growing louder as pleasure piled upon pleasure. Until it culminated in endless waves of ecstasy.

Sienna was still floating when he parted her thighs wider, filling her senses with his presence. Prying her eyes open, she stared at the god whose intellect and charisma left her in awe, whose touch lifted her from ordinary to extraordinary.

Who was staring at her with narrowed eyes even more shadowed than they had been minutes ago. Before she could attempt to voice her quaking thoughts, he slanted his mouth over hers and penetrated her in one smooth, urgent thrust.

Flung straight back to nirvana, Sienna could only hold on as she was completely, utterly possessed. Nails bit into flesh, cries turned into screams. Emiliano pushed her to the brink over and over, slowing down just before she reached her peak. As if he wanted their lovemaking to go on for ever. As if he wanted to be imprinted on her very soul.

As if he wanted the experience to be unforgettable.

Why?

The word blazed across her mind again, larger, louder. Her hands shook as she framed his face, searching his eyes.

'Emiliano…please…' she whispered.

His jaw turned to stone beneath her fingers. With a thick grunt, he pulled out of her body, flipped her onto her stomach and surged back into her. Brushing her hair out of the way, he sank his teeth into her nape, roughly tasting her, branding her. Raw pleasure ploughed through her, leaving her clawing at the sheets as another orgasm surged high.

Behind her, she heard his rough breathing, his own impending climax bearing down on him. She wanted to hold him in her arms, look into his eyes and be reassured that everything was all right between them. Or as near enough as possible.

Because, although it had hurt to have him point it out, she knew their relationship had a few inescapable flaws. Flaws that seemed to gape wider with each passing second. Flaws she needed to address.

But he had her pinned, six feet three inches of superior masculinity spread all over her delivering sensation she never wanted to end. So, closing her eyes, Sienna gave in, diving headlong into pure heaven as stars exploded across her vision.

Endless minutes later, when their bodies had cooled and their breathing calmed, he slid off her and gathered her in his arms.

Strong fingers slid into her hair, the movement unusually jerky. His gaze was hooded when it met hers, hiding his expression.

'Happy birthday,' he rasped.

'I…' She floundered for a second, wondering whether to go back on her resolution and tread the dangerous waters swirling beneath her feet.

'Emiliano…'

'These look exquisite on you.' He pulled her closer, his fingers slipping down to trace the skin beneath the diamond necklace even as the forbidding force of his stare punched holes in her resolve.

Tomorrow, she decided once again. 'Thank you,' she murmured.

Tilting her head up, he placed a hard, short kiss on her swollen lips. 'Sleep now,' he ordered.

In the aftermath of bliss and even with her mind churning, Sienna couldn't hold back the drugging effect of that command. So she gave in.

What felt like only minutes later, she jerked upright, her heart hammering. Beside her, Emiliano was lost in slumber, one muscled arm curved over his head. Heart twisting, she studied him, vainly trying to decipher what was wrong. In sleep, his breathtakingly handsome face was less forbidding, his jaw slightly slack and his forehead smooth. She didn't deem him any less intimidating but at least she could stare at him now without the bracing force field that usually surrounded him. She even dared to lift a hand to his full lower lip, tracing the velvet-smooth skin. He exhaled harshly in his sleep and she froze. Withdrawing her fingers, she lay back, knowing sleep was out of the question with her mind once again in churn mode.

Half an hour later, she gave up and rose from the bed. At 5:30 a.m. in early November, it was still dark outside. Going for a run outside in the dark without Emiliano would incur his displeasure, as she'd found out on the one occasion she'd attempted to do so. In fact, he'd completely banned her from running outside without him. But she needed physical exertion to prevent her from waking him up and demanding to know what was going on.

Quietly tugging on her running gear in the large dressing room adjoining the master suite, she silently let herself out and took the lift down to the basement, where the top-line gym reserved for the exclusive use of the penthouse owners was located. Plugging in her earbuds, she hit the treadmill, running at her top speed for a solid hour before her leaden legs forced her to slow down.

When she stepped off the machine, her resolution was firmly back in place, her mind no longer racing. Emiliano valued her professionally because she wasn't afraid to go after tough, seemingly unattainable deals. It was what had seen her rise from junior fund manager to junior vice-president in the three years she'd been with his venture capitalist firm.

While privately her lack of sexual experience placed her somewhat on a back foot, she'd never let Emiliano cow her. She was also brave enough to admit her new but secret emotions also factored in whatever situation was brewing between them. Which was why she would tackle it now.

Setting down the bottle of mineral water she'd rehydrated from, she left the basement via the stairs. She would pick up the newspapers and magazines they had delivered to the penthouse to prevent their talk from being interrupted by the concierge.

She reached the ground floor and crossed the polished marble foyer to the concierge desk. Exchanging a greeting with the manager, she accepted the stack and crossed to the lift. The other tiny secret she'd been harbouring for several weeks lightened her heart a little as she entered the carriage and pressed the button.

Having witnessed the pleased light in Emiliano's eyes whenever she'd responded in Spanish to a simple question, she'd embraced the idea to take it further.

She hadn't divulged her attempt to learn Spanish to Emiliano because she'd wanted to approach the outskirts of proficiency before she told him. Privately, she'd devoured Spanish newspapers and magazines in her spare time in the hope of quickly learning her lover's mother tongue, and even admitted that it had become a guilty pleasure to gorge on all things Argentinian.

Unfortunately, it was the reason the headline screaming from the front page of the glossy celebrity magazine made perfect sense to her once she fished it out of the pile.

Stumbling out of her lift, she froze to a halt, her heart dropping to her toes. Unable to catch her breath, she stared, first at the photo, then back at the headline.

A Castillo-Cabrera Union!

The rest of the papers fell out of her hand, her useless limbs unable to hang on to anything but the evidence of all her *whys* spelled out in bold white letters. Her shocked eyes dropped to the smaller print.

The Polo Match Made in Heaven!

Emiliano Castillo to Wed Graciela Cabrera.

There were other words, such as *wedding of the year... Dynastic union... Valentine's Day wedding...*

But her vision was blurring, her heart refusing to pump properly. She was going to pass out. She was sure of it. She wasn't sure whether to view her present state as a blessing. What she did know was that she wanted to block out the sight of Emiliano and the drop-dead gorgeous caramel blonde sitting at the intimate candlelit table, her hand on top of his, her smile holding a thousand delicious secrets as she stared at him.

And he stared back at her.

He wasn't smiling—Emiliano *never* smiled in the presence of a camera, especially one wielded by a paparazzo. Most of the time he glared at the intrusion. He wasn't glaring this time. The expression on his face was even...accommodating. Fond.

Lungs burning, Sienna forced herself to take a breath. Turn the pages. Her world turning to ash, she stared at glossy page after glossy page of Emiliano and his new *amor.* On the fifth page, she stared, tears surging into her eyes, at the ring on the finger which announced Graciela Cabrera as the brand new fiancée of Emiliano Castillo.

To add insult to injury, her heart tripped to a stop when she saw what Emiliano was wearing. If there was even a shadow of a doubt that this picture was a terrible, cruel hoax, it was wiped clean when she saw the tie. She'd gifted that tie to him on his birthday two months ago— had packed it in his suitcase herself exactly one week ago, when she'd sent him off with a kiss on his lips and hope in her heart. She was world-wise enough to know sometimes the tabloid media regurgitated old photos and manipulated images to suit their headline. The evidence of the tie confirmed these pictures weren't fakes.

Finally, *everything* about last night...about the past few days' silence...made sense.

She stumbled forward, the scattered papers forgotten as she made her way back inside, absently wondering how she was able to put one foot in front of the other when she felt so numb.

Time and space ceased to make sense until she was standing before the bedroom doors. Her hand shook as she raised it to the handle. She clenched her fist tight in a desperate bid to retain some control. She had to confront this, in spite of what the outcome would be.

Had to.

She jerked at the forceful wrench of the door from the inside, stealing away the control she'd barely summoned. Emiliano stopped short before her, his face in a deep frown.

'Sienna, what are you doing standing...?'

She stared at him. He was right there in front of her. Powerful. Magnetically charismatic. Drop-dead gorgeous.

Bastard.

She didn't want to look at him. Dear God, it hurt just

to lift her gaze to meet his. Because even now she wanted desperately to cling to the hope that she'd got it wrong. That the pictures in the magazine clutched in her fist, his lack of emails, his coldly forbidding expression upon his return, even his silent lovemaking, had all been in her imagination.

But she met his gaze. And knew she was clinging to false hope.

'Is it true?' she tried asking anyway. One last time.

Tawny gold eyes hardened a touch, the coldness returning. 'Is what true?'

A bolt of anger freed her frozen limbs. 'Don't play games with me, Emiliano. It's beneath—'

She'd been about to say *us*. Except there was no *us* any more. Had there ever been? Her frantic brain raced, desperately sifting, analysing every gesture, every word, wondering if everything she'd lived, revelled in and hoped for during their relationship had been based on a colossal lie.

'This!' She shoved the magazine into the bare steel torso draped with the navy blue shirt he'd been about to button. *'Is it true you're engaged?'*

Ripping off her MP4 player and earphones, she dropped them onto a nearby dresser and turned, watching him flip through the pages before tossing the magazine aside.

The eyes that met hers were arrogantly unapologetic. 'Yes.'

The last minute's anger had fooled her into thinking she was strong, that she could withstand whatever was coming her way.

She was wrong.

The punch to her solar plexus from his words robbed her of breath and weakened her knees. Shaking her head, she stared at him. Waited for him to continue. He didn't. He just stared back at her, his expression icily neutral.

'"Yes"? That's all you're going to say?'

He braced strong hands on lean hips, his stance cold and withdrawn. 'You're in no condition to hear any more right now—'

'Are you serious? So what, you expect me to just…go through my day until you *deem* me ready?' Incredulity rendered her voice hoarse and shaky.

'I would prefer to have this conversation with you when you're not emotionally high-strung, *sí*,' he rasped before raising his hands to begin buttoning his shirt.

Inhaling long and slow, Sienna fought for the control she was so good at attaining in the workplace. Except this wasn't work. This was so much more. 'You owe me an explanation. Right now. Or are you too much of a coward to grant me one?'

He froze, hard eyes lancing into her with the brutal force of a scalpel. 'Watch your tone with me, *querida*,' he warned.

'Do not call me that! You just told me you're engaged to another woman. Engaged! And you dare to call me your *darling*?'

A puzzled expression flicked like lightning over his face, as if he didn't understand her objection. Then it was gone and he was back to the stranger who'd walked into their penthouse twelve hours ago.

Her green eyes flashed. 'Were you seeing her behind my back?'

A black frown clamped his forehead as he secured the last button. 'I do not cheat.'

'No? You've never cheated? What was last night, then? Weren't you cheating on *her* with *me*?'

'You're my lover. She knows of our association. She understands that it needs to be taken care of.'

'Oh, how very accommodating of her. And is that what you were doing last night? *Taking care of me* before you dumped me?'

He jerked back, as if she'd struck him. 'Sienna, you need to calm—'

'You couldn't resist one last tumble between the sheets before you handed me my marching orders?'

He had the grace to look uncomfortable. 'It was your birthday…'

Hot pins stabbed her until she was a whisper away from howling. It was too much to take standing still. So she paced. 'How decent of you. I was the poor, pathetic soon-to-be ex-lover you couldn't stand to disappoint on her birthday, so you waited for me to find out what you'd been up to from the press?'

He slammed the cufflinks he'd picked up back onto the dresser. '*Basta!* This wasn't how I intended to break the news.'

'How very inconvenient for you!'

He pinched the bridge of his nose and inhaled deeply. 'I'm heading to the office now—I have a conference call scheduled with Norway which has been postponed twice. But let's catch up later. Maybe this evening? I don't mind if you take the day off to absorb the news. Then, tonight, we can talk about this rationally.'

'About the fact that you were going on a trip to see your parents but went and got engaged instead?'

His jaws gritted together for a second. 'Amongst other things, yes.'

She forced herself to stop. To face him. 'Fine, let's have it. Surely I'm worth five minutes of your time right now?'

'I don't think—'

'I do!'

Taking a deep breath, he stared at her. 'Sienna, it wasn't supposed to happen this way.'

'What wasn't? Please spell it out fully so I understand.'

One sleek eyebrow rose as if he was seeing her in a new

light. In that moment, Sienna wasn't sure she wanted to find out what he saw as he stared at her.

'The way you're reacting right now, I'm almost tempted to believe your career *isn't* more important to you than this thing between us, whereas I know for a fact that, if I asked you to choose, you wouldn't even blink before choosing the former.'

She inhaled sharply. 'First of all, if we ever found ourselves in the position of you asking me to choose, then we'd be in serious trouble, especially when I know how many female, family-orientated executives you employ. Which makes me think this would most probably be some sort of test. Why would you need to do that, Emiliano?'

He shrugged, but the gleam she'd witnessed in his eyes last night burned even brighter this morning. 'Perhaps the idea of coming second best doesn't sit well with me. Perhaps I'm thoroughly bored of it.'

Shocked laughter spilled from her lips. '*Second best?* How... When...have you ever allowed yourself to come second best? You win at absolutely everything!'

His lids swept down, his mouth twisting. 'That is where you're wrong.'

'Fine. Maybe we don't know each other as well as we should, but I guess you not even bothering to give me any option speaks volumes!'

He slashed a hand through his hair. 'I was going to give you... *Dios*, this wasn't how...I have to do this.'

She stilled, the combination of Emiliano struggling for words and the choice of those words unsettling her. 'You *have* to?'

'*Si*, I gave my word.'

'Your word? To *who*?'

He huffed, a breath filled with icy frustration. 'It's a family thing. I don't know enough about your own family circumstances, since you've never felt quite like sharing, so I will forgive you if you don't understand.'

That cut her off at the knees. 'How dare you?' She gasped, raw pain hammering her from heart to soul. 'You've equally withheld your own background from me. Don't punish me for thinking I was respecting your wishes. And, whatever my circumstances, you can't assume that I don't understand the concept of family.' Being an orphan had triggered a yearning for a family of her own, a wish she held dear in her heart, the fulfilment of that dream a hope she refused to give up.

Emiliano's mouth thinned. 'You mistook my meaning.'

'Looks like I've mistaken a lot of things. Things like you neglecting to tell me you've been *promised* to somebody else all along.'

'I'm not. I wasn't.'

'Then what is this?' She indicated the paper. 'Don't insult my intelligence. You know her. There's a familiarity there, so something must have been going on.'

'Our families are...connected. I've known her since she was a child.'

'And they needed a marriage, so you agreed to step in?' she mocked with a pained laugh.

Laughter that dried up when he nodded.

'Yes, something like that.'

She gasped. 'You're serious.'

He didn't blink. 'I'm serious.'

Her mouth dropped open, but no words emerged. Shaking her head, she tried to clear the buzzing growing louder.

'I'm going to go out on a limb and mention that there is another scenario I was thinking about for us in light of this news.'

He stared at her, a touch of something she absurdly wanted to label uncertainty flashing across his face before it disappeared. When her vocal cords refused to work, he continued, 'If you want our…liaison to continue, I'm willing to discuss how we—'

A punch of rage freed up her vocal cords. 'I sincerely hope you're not about to suggest I be your bit on the side while you're married to someone else!'

His face hardened into a rigid mask of fury. 'Please refrain from putting words in my mouth.'

She folded her arms. 'Okay, I'm listening.'

He started to speak, then clenched his jaw again and shook his head. 'Perhaps discretion is the better part of valour here. I'll be speaking to my lawyers this morning. You can keep the penthouse and everything in it. I'll have the requisite deeds drawn up. Also one of the cars. Pick whichever one you please. If you want anything else, let me know. I'll try and accommodate—'

'Are you discussing *possessions* with me, Emiliano? I want to know why you're engaged to another woman when you're supposed to be mine!' She was shouting, her pain raw and unfettered, her dignity in shreds. But she couldn't help it.

And with each word she flung at him he grew colder, withdrawing into a block of marble. Retrieving his cufflinks, he slotted them into place with calm, precise movements. 'I thought there could be a…negotiation…but it's clear I was wrong.'

Her hands splayed out in a bracing gesture, appealing for understanding in a world gone crazy. 'A *negotiation*? What on earth are you talking about?'

'It doesn't matter now. I didn't take this decision lightly, but it's done, Sienna. For the immediate future there'll be no changing it. It's clear that dissecting it wouldn't be productive to you. Not in this moment, anyway. Perhaps not ever,' he stated with a finality that chilled her to the bone.

'So that's it? I'm dumped with no proper explanation?'

He stared at her for endless seconds. 'Whether we want

to admit it or not, we were both aware this thing between us was bound to run its course sooner or later. Maybe it's better that it's sooner.'

Then he picked up his jacket and walked out the door.

CHAPTER THREE

THE NEXT FEW hours were spent in a semifugue state. Sadly, Sienna wasn't numb enough to remain painfully unaware of what was happening.

Her voice was hoarse as she called out to Emiliano. His stone-cold silence as he left the penthouse. Her cracking voice as she instructed her secretary to push her appointments to later in the day.

The deep concern on Alfie's face when she refused breakfast and asked him to procure packing boxes, and the endless waves of bewildered agony as she stuffed her belongings into boxes and suitcases, organised storage facilities and booked herself into a hotel.

Tears. So many heart-shredding, despised tears as she stood in the shower in a soulless hotel room, hating herself for not being stronger, excruciatingly aware she'd let herself slide into the danger zone of false hope based on useless foundations. But, as she dried off and dressed, she also recognised the slow build of anger. Of determination.

She'd put every safeguard in place to protect herself, yet she'd let herself hope, just as she had as a child staring yearningly out of the orphanage window for something *better*, when she'd known better should first and foremost come from herself. From *within*. She'd allowed herself to forget her history, to be lulled into disabling the locked-in belief that abandonment by those she let close was a thing of the past. She'd let herself indulge in fantasies built around a man who'd made it clear from his previous relationships that he would never settle down.

But he had settled.

What was an engagement, if not a precursor to the ultimate commitment?

But he didn't choose you, remember? Like your own mother chose a different life without you.

She tried to fortify herself against the savage pain the reminder brought. But she felt it like a raw wound exposed to salt, and couldn't stem the harrowing memories of growing up in an orphanage, the heartbreak each time a hoped-for foster family rejected her or, even worse, gave her the initial promise of a family only to yank it away weeks or months later.

She should have been used to rejection by now. Should've kept her steel-plated armour securely fastened in place. Instead, she'd let Emiliano in.

The ramifications of her stupidity held her hostage as she left the hotel and hailed a cab to what had once been a place of pride for her achievements and was now the secondary scene of her downfall.

As she walked through the grand, breathtaking marble-and-glass lobby of the Castillo Tower in the city, Sienna couldn't help but feel that, despite her staunchest effort to keep her private life under wraps, every gaze directed her way held a degree of mocking judgement of the poor choices she'd made.

Her secretary's furtive gaze and normally exuberant but now-hushed tone told Sienna her disguise had failed.

Or was it because news of Emiliano's engagement had already filtered through? Of course. Castillo Ventures, no matter how progressive a work place, was still a hotbed of interoffice gossip. She didn't doubt that every single member of the five-hundred-strong workforce would know the truth by now, although her stellar but straitlaced reputation would mean no one would say anything to her face.

Fresh pain battered her as she walked into her office and shut the door. On shaky legs, she approached her desk and sank behind it. Fingers trembling, she pulled up the requisite programme, typed a brief, succinct letter and sent it.

Ignoring the loud pings of emails that dropped into her inbox, she calmly set a notepad and pen on the desk before her and got on with planning for her future. For as long as she could remember, having a plan in place had helped keep her focus true. She'd only abandoned that plan when a dynamic, drop-dead gorgeous Argentinian had set her in his sights and piled on relentless pressure, leading her to imagine mistakenly that he was her future.

It was time to relocate her compass.

Ignoring the phone when it began to ring, she meticulously set out her to-do list, starting with finding a place to live.

Ten minutes later, she heard the soft rap on her door, followed by her secretary's entrance. When she didn't immediately speak, Sienna forced her heavy head up, frowning when she saw Laura's visible distress.

'Yes, what is it?'

'Um… Mr Castillo wants to see you.'

Her heart stuttered, then dropped to her stomach. Somehow, she managed a tight smile. 'Please let him know I'm busy. I have work to do.'

'I… He said you're to drop whatever you're doing and report to his office right away.'

'Tell him—'

'I'm sorry, Sienna,' her secretary interrupted, naked apprehension on her usually cheery face. 'I know you said you don't want to be disturbed, but he's been calling you for the last five minutes. He made it clear he wants you in his office. He said to let him know when you're on your way. And that he will hold me responsible if you don't come right away.'

Rage boiling in her gut, she surged to her feet just as her phone rang again. She didn't need to look down to confirm the caller's identity. 'It's okay, Laura. I'll deal with it.'

Her secretary was barely out of the door when she snatched up the phone. 'I'd thank you not to threaten my secretary.'

'She's my employee. If you didn't want her put in this position then you should have picked up your phone when I called.'

'What do you want, Mr Castillo?' She strove for a calm, poised tone and shut her eyes briefly in relief when she achieved it.

At the end of the line, Emiliano didn't respond for a few terse seconds. 'What I wanted when I called ten minutes ago. You, in my office. Now.'

'I'm—'

'Not as busy as you say. You forget I have access to your diary. Come now, Sienna. Or I'll come down there. My office affords us more privacy than yours, but either way you and I will be doing this face-to-face. The location is your choice. You have three minutes.' The line went dead.

Her hands shook as she hung up. Anger still rumbled in her belly, but the thought of seeing him again so soon meant a different kind of emotion—pain and loss for what she'd never really had superseded that anger, holding her immobile in her chair for a long moment before she forced herself to move.

Hushed whispers and quickly muted conversations trailed her as she made her way to the lift. For a wild, absurd second she wished she'd relocated her office from the twentieth to the thirtieth floor at Emiliano's bidding two months ago. But she swiftly conceded it would've been ten times worse to be in her situation now.

Either way was no consolation. So she put one foot in front of the other until she stood before a set of misted glass double doors. Emiliano's trusted PA was nowhere in sight. Whether by coincidence or by design, she didn't give herself time to dwell on it as she turned the handle and pushed the door open.

He sat at his smoked-glass desk, the iconic vista of the financial heart of London sprawled out behind him. He'd shed the jacket to his bespoke suit. Or perhaps he'd never worn it. His pinstriped tie was loosened, the top button of his shirt undone and his hair sexily dishevelled, as if he'd run his hand through it several times.

Not quite his usual impeccable, well put-together self. But the package was no less impactful. A direct hit to her severely flailing senses, especially when he raised his arrogant head, locked those gold eyes on her and tracked her approach.

She stopped a good distance from his desk, stepping deeper into his orbit, breathing him in... No. Better she stay where she was for her self-preservation, which was way past overdue for reinforcement.

'You wanted to see me. Here I am.'

Narrowed eyes tracked her from head to toe. 'Why are you wearing black? You know how much I hate it when you do.'

She refused to allow memories surrounding discussions of her clothes to intrude. Most of them had taken place in their once-shared dressing room when they'd been naked. 'You didn't summon me to discuss my work gear. That would be a colossal waste of both our time.'

'I asked you here to discuss this.' He waved a large, expressive hand at his computer screen, his jaw as tight as the pellet-hard words falling from his lips. 'What is the meaning of it?'

'If you're referring to my resignation letter, I would've thought it was self-explanatory.'

'Considering your dedication to your career, this is a

trigger response you *will regret* in the very near future,' he snapped. 'I'm willing to overlook it if you are.'

'No, thank you.'

He looked askance, genuinely puzzled. 'Excuse me?'

Sienna took a moment to breathe. 'I'm not going to debate the matter with you. Thankfully, my employment, like my attire, is no longer a subject you have a say on. The copy I sent you by email was unsigned. I believe this makes it official.' She took the requisite steps forward to place the signed resignation letter on his desk before retreating to her position in the middle of the room.

He took his time to scrutinise her face, probing long and deep with penetrating eyes, before he deigned to pick up the piece of paper. After a cursory glance, he flung it back on his desk.

'I do not accept this.'

'You have very little choice in the matter, Mr Castillo,' she replied, her voice less than warm.

His jaw flexed and his nostrils flared. 'You forget that I have to approve this ridiculous "with immediate effect" resignation. And give whatever future employer you choose a worthy reference.'

'If you're under the misconceived notion that I intend to bow and scrape to remain in your good books for the sake of a so-called *worthy reference*, consider this a heads-up that it's not going to happen. I've had assurances of my pick of the top five hedge funds for the last six months should I ever choose to leave Castillo Ventures.'

His head snapped back, his mouth thinning into a line of displeasure. 'You've been courting other companies behind my back?'

Unexpected laughter scraped her throat raw. 'Please let's refrain from flinging accusations of what's happened behind whose back.'

His face tightened. 'I can still make things difficult for you. You know this.'

She deliberately relaxed her limbs, returning his gaze with contrived boredom. 'To what end, though? Besides the rank display of sour grapes on your part, I know one or two CEOs who will hire me simply to get back at you for deals you snatched from right under their noses.'

His eyelids swept down and his fingers formed a steeple on his desk, both signs that his clever brain was ticking over, finding another angle of attack. Sienna braced herself.

'The requisite notice period for someone in your position is six weeks, or have you forgotten that clause in your contract? I can compel you to stay by law.'

Her insides hollowed. 'You would have me stay, be the subject of pitied whispers and lunchtime gossip?'

Indomitable eyes locked on her. 'It only affects you if you allow it. I still maintain that what goes on between us is nobody's business,' he hissed.

Words she'd heard before, the last time whispered against her mouth in this very office, right before a kiss that had made her whole being sing. Words that now made her insides bleed. 'You're wrong, first, to imply there's an *us*. There isn't. I'm beginning to think there never was. Second, you made it everyone's business by taking out a front-page spread about your engagement to another woman!'

He jerked to his feet and rounded his desk, striding towards her. 'I didn't take out a spread. These things just happen!'

She backed away several steps, already fearing her hastily stitched-into-place façade was crumbling. 'I'm sure they do in your world. I want no part of it. I'm leaving. Let me know who you decide to pick as my successor. I'll stay for the rest of the week to bring them up to speed on my projects. I have two months' accrued vacation. If you insist on me working my notice, take that.'

'That's not how it works.'

'Too bad. Sue me if you have to, but on this subject, and on everything else not directly pertaining to Castillo Ventures business, you and I don't have anything more to say to each other, Mr Castillo.'

'Damn it, stop calling me that!' The sharp words were accompanied by a savage shove of his fingers through his hair as he eyed her from the charged space between them.

The unexpected score of needling him should've soothed the torrent of despair inside her. Instead, rough anguish only dug its talons deeper. 'I will *never* call you by your first name again,' she replied in a ragged whisper. 'If you insist on prolonging this farce, I *will* find other names for you, though.'

He shoved his fists in his pockets, his unwavering stare drilling holes into her. 'You really insist on doing this? On throwing your precious career away?'

'How arrogant of you to believe I'll only be a success with you,' she returned with a scornful glare. 'How insufferable of you to imagine I won't thrive with anyone else but you.'

He sauntered towards her with slow, measured, predatory steps. 'You think anyone else can offer you what I have, *querida*? Fire up your intellect or stimulate you the way I do?'

She stared at him, a part of her still reeling and running for cover from the events of the past twelve hours. The other traitorous part wanted to unfurl itself at the warmth of the memories he was callously evoking, to bask shamelessly in bygones.

Brutally, she superimposed her to-do list onto the memories, reminding herself that she had a purpose far away from this man and this place. That she was worth more than this humiliation.

'You are far from the unique gem you imagine yourself to be, Mr Castillo. Don't worry about me. I'll be fine. I'm looking forward to the challenge, actually. Now, if we're done here, I think I'll take you up on that offer of a day off. I need to go apartment hunting.'

Emotion akin to shock flashed briefly through his eyes. 'You're moving out of the penthouse?'

'Moved. Past tense.'

'Why? The papers are drawn up, Sienna. It's yours, free and clear.'

'No, thanks. I don't want *anything* from you.'

Not entirely true. What she'd wanted, he'd cruelly made clear would never be hers.

His eyes darkened to hard stone. A muscle ticked in his cheek as he closed the gap between them.

'Are you quite sure, *querida*? You will not have a chance to change your mind.'

'One hundred per cent,' she replied through clenched teeth.

For endless seconds he stared at her while her heart hammered a wild tattoo against her ribs. Then he jerked his square chin at the door behind her.

'Go, then. Forget me…if you can,' he taunted.

She turned on her heel, forcing herself not to take that one last, desperate fill of him. Her hand grasping the door handle, she paused. Because she needed to say this, as much for herself as for him.

'I *will* forget you. With pleasure.'

There weren't many parts of the world she could go without memories of Emiliano dogging her. But she tried, rewarding herself the moment she left Castillo Ventures a week later with a plane ticket to South America.

The Inca Trail to Machu Picchu served a dual purpose of being an Emiliano-free zone and a physically taxing enough trek to aid her to dreamless slumber in her tent each night.

But any numbness she'd managed to wrap herself in fled the moment she landed at Heathrow four weeks later and turned her phone back on to floods of texts and emails. Sienna forced herself to ignore them as she settled into the back of her taxi and recited her to-do list.

Unpack and settle into her new flat.

Find a job.

Find a way to stop desperately missing the man who'd cruelly rejected her.

She clenched her fist when her heart lurched in that irritatingly dramatic way it did whenever she thought of him.

She had the rest of her life to get on with. Thankfully, the taxi journey to her new address in Chelsea was short. Sienna wasn't ashamed to admit she'd chosen to live on the opposite side of the city to where Emiliano's penthouse was located in East London. She had even contemplated moving out of London altogether. Except that would mean he'd won. She still had some pride left.

Pride that wobbled when she walked into her two-bedroom flat and saw the seven meagre boxes and three suitcases that formed the sum total of her existence. She'd never felt the lack of belonging as acutely as she felt it in that moment.

Angrily, she swiped at the tears that spiked her eyes and got to work. Two hours later, new furniture ordered and boxes unpacked, she tackled her emails.

The only communication from Emiliano was via his HR department. Her severance package was exactly what she was owed and not a penny more. Sienna had insisted on it. So, subject to a few final forms to sign and return, she was officially free of Emiliano Castillo.

Ignoring another squeeze of her heart, she scrutinised the job offers the headhunter had sent. She was about to respond to the one that looked halfway appealing when her mobile phone rang.

A quick check of the screen and she was berating herself for the jolt of disappointment. Pulling herself together, she answered.

'You're back. Thank the Lord! My phone has been ringing off the hook with offers. I have… Wait for it… *Six* hedge funders dying to talk to you.'

David Hunter, the aptly named headhunter who'd made it his business to call her at least once a month for the last year in an attempt to steal her from Castillo Ventures, was as relentless as he was charming. She'd met with him briefly twice before leaving for South America. At their second meeting she hadn't failed to detect the personal interest in his eyes. The warmth in his voice now was a welcome balm to a loneliness she didn't want to admit to feeling, even though she had no intention of entertaining that interest.

'Wow,' she murmured half-heartedly.

He laughed. 'Um, maybe try that again, with feeling?'

Sienna chose to view the small smile that curved her lips as progress. 'Sorry. Jet lag.' It wasn't completely a false statement. Her twelve-hour journey and her frenzied attempt to make her flat habitable had sapped the last of her energy reserves. Her head felt heavy and she wanted to sleep for a week.

'I'll let you go if you agree to have dinner with me tomorrow to discuss the offers,' he pressed.

'I'm not sure, David. Can I let you know?'

He paused for a beat before replying, 'Okay, here's my mini pitch. You're in a unique position to choose your next job, Sienna. Everyone wants you. Castillo is a market leader, sure, but there are other equally exciting opportu-

nitics out there for you. They won't stay on the table for
ever. I don't want you to miss out on them.'

The vice around her heart squeezed painfully at the
mention of Castillo. And as with every time it happened,
it also brought a tiny spark of anger. She couldn't mope
for ever.

'Okay, dinner tomorrow.'

'Wonderful. Do you have a cuisine preference?'

She thought for a single second before she named her
favourite restaurant. As with every corner of her life, it
was time to root Emiliano out of this one, too.

'Great, shall I pick you up at seven?'

Because that smacked too much of a date, Sienna shook
her head. 'No, it's fine. I'll meet you there.'

His response remained enthusiastic, even if his tone
held a touch of disappointment. Finishing the conversation, she made herself a cup of tea and slice of toast. Half-
heartedly eating her meal, she took her first shower in her
new apartment, then fell into bed.

Twelve hours later, she woke, refreshed if a little listless.
Finding herself with next to nothing to do in the middle
of a work week was a strange sensation. On a whim, she
dressed, snatched up her handbag and caught the Tube
to King's Road. After buying a few practical items she
needed for her flat, she splurged on a bright bouquet of
flowers and a new dress.

She hated that everything in her wardrobe had an Emil-
iano-sized reminder tag on it, but throwing it all out and
starting anew was one step too far. The new emerald silk
dress was chic enough for a dinner while projecting a professional air. And, when the time came to get ready, she
teamed it with black slingback shoes, black pearls and a
matching bracelet. After sliding on her favourite red lipstick, she picked up her clutch and made her way outside
to the waiting taxi.

Zarcosta was a Michelin-starred restaurant, which specialised in European dishes with a distinct Mediterranean flavour. The owner, Marco Zarcosta, was effusive and temperamental, a short, bespectacled character who either loved or hated clients on sight. Sienna had been lucky enough to be enfolded in the former group and she was met with a hug and a kiss on both cheeks when she entered the intimately lit restaurant in Fitzrovia.

'A shame about this relationship business, *cara*,' the Italian murmured in her ear. 'Such a shame. But Marco is here for you, eh?'

Pulling back from the embrace, she nodded and plastered on a smile, while wondering if coming here had been a wise choice. But David, having spotted her, was rising from the table and making his way towards her.

With his gelled blond hair, sparkling silver-grey eyes and a flashing smile, it wasn't a stretch to picture David Hunter as a surfer, the only thing differentiating him from that carefree lifestyle being his three-piece suit and the look of determination in his eyes. Determination that morphed to intimate interest when his eyes met hers. A quick once-over of her body and his smile widened.

'Glad you made it. You look fantastic.'

'Um, thanks.'

Although she was a little taken aback when he cupped her elbows and repeated Marco's version of kissing her hello, she wasn't altogether surprised.

What did surprise her, though, and what sent a tectonic jolt of electricity through her as she cast a gaze across the full room on her way to their table, was the sight of Emiliano Castillo staring at her with chilling eyes.

CHAPTER FOUR

SHE STUMBLED. She *actually* stumbled.

Cringing and hating herself for the telling action, she plastered an even wider smile on her face as David caught and steadied her.

'Hey, you okay?'

'Of course, why shouldn't I be?' The question emerged a touch more aggressively than she'd intended.

His eyes widened a little before he offered her a sympathetic smile. 'Sorry if I came on a little strong yesterday,' he said as he pulled out her chair and saw her seated. 'Landing you will do wonders for my account,' he said shamelessly. 'Not to mention my street cred.'

Her laugh was a little forced, her nerves screeching with horror to find that her every sense was attuned to the man across the room. The one whose piercing gaze she could feel boring into her skin.

'Well, I do need a job, so let's hear what's on the table.'

'Excellent. First, I'll order us some wine. Or would you like champagne? We might have something to celebrate at the end of the evening, I expect. You don't think I'm jumping the gun, do you?'

She gave a carefree wave of her hand. 'Not at all. Go for it,' she replied with enthusiasm that echoed patently false inside.

His smile brightened. Thankfully, he was not picking up on her act. Their waiter arrived. David ordered their drinks and she ordered her favourite meal. Simply because she wasn't about to give in to the voice mocking her about her situation.

The moment they were alone, David started raving about the offers.

She listened. She nodded. She even managed one or two pertinent questions.

But they all sounded boring. Nothing as intellectually stimulating as the work she'd done at Castillo.

You think anyone else can offer you what I have, querida?

His voice was as clear as a bell in her head. So much so, her head snapped towards the man in question. His stare was direct and unapologetic. Cold and arrogant. His dinner companions, a male and female she didn't recognise, were making conversation. He nodded and said something back. All without taking his gaze off her.

Sienna grew hot. Then cold. Hot again. As if her body didn't know what to make of the circumstances.

Warm fingers drifted over the back of her hand. 'Hey, I'm not losing you, am I?'

She started, looked down at David's hand on hers. Then absurdly, because a part of her remained a glutton for punishment, she glanced back at Emiliano.

His already-hardened face had grown tauter, his jaw clenched in steel as his gaze dropped to take in the caress. The look in his eyes when their gazes reconnected was no longer Arctic cold. It was furnace hot with censure.

She wanted to laugh but she was sure the action would strangle her. So she turned away, focused her gaze on her dinner companion and smiled.

'No, you're not losing me. In fact, I want to hear more about Chrysallis. They sound like they could be a great fit.'

Their starters arrived. She ate without tasting a morsel while David dove into his role with even more gusto, pausing only when their plates were cleared away.

Needing a breather because the weight of Emiliano's regard was unsettling her more by the minute, she placed her napkin on the table and picked up her clutch.

'Would you excuse me for a minute? I need to visit the ladies' room.'

'Of course.' He rose immediately and solicitously came round to pull back her chair. Before she could step away, he leaned down towards her. 'And I know it's a little awkward having your old boss in the same room while discussing your next job. Sorry about that.'

Startled, she turned to look at him. Sympathetic grey eyes met hers and, for some absurd reason, a lump rose in her throat. 'It's not your fault, but thank you for understanding.'

He nodded, then stood back to her let pass.

The much-needed composure gathering took five long minutes of pacing the empty ladies' room, water splashed on her hot wrists and reapplication of her lipstick. Reminding herself that she'd been through worse adversity—because what was worse than being rejected by four different foster families within the space of a year when you're eleven years old?—she squared her shoulders and pulled open the ladies' room door.

To find Emiliano leaning against the wall, feet planted in patent aggression.

The look in his eyes hadn't changed. In fact, he looked even angrier, his every breath evocative of the dark rumbling of a volcano before it erupted and destroyed everything in its path.

Sienna reminded herself that they were done. She didn't need to engage him, even though every fibre of her being insisted on straining towards him.

Forcing her gaze from his tall, sleek body, she took a step away from him.

One hand shot out to grip her waist, long fingers imprisoning her.

'You really want to play it like this? You want to pretend I don't exist?' he snarled at her.

What his deep voice did to her insides, she didn't like. Not one little bit. 'You don't exist, not to me. You challenged me to forget you, remember? This is me forgetting you.'

'By bringing another man *here*, on your first date?'

'Why, did you think this place would stop being special to me because you dumped me? Why should I stop coming here? The food is great, the ambience is excellent and the company sublime. And what makes you think it's a first date?' she threw in with a raised eyebrow.

Leonine eyes glinted pure danger. 'How many times have you seen him?'

She sighed. 'Why do you care? It really is none of your business.'

He opened his mouth then clamped it shut again when a trio of women came down the hall. His hold moved lightning quick from her waist to her wrist, taking it in an implacable hold and using it to compel her through another door. Between one moment and the next, they were outside in a quiet alley, the sound of dining guests and cutlery cut off abruptly.

'How many?' he growled again.

A dart of apprehension lanced her that had nothing to do with the cold temperature and light falling rain. But with it came a dose of something else: excitement.

She hated herself for it. He'd left her. Rejected her in the worst possible way in favour of something better. *Someone* better. Just as her mother had done. Just as all the potential foster families had done. She didn't owe him the time of day, never mind this conversation. But she would answer him. If nothing else, there was the matter of her pride. The silent treatment never worked with him. She'd learned very early in their relationship—their *ex*-relationship—that Emiliano was arrogant enough to think he'd won an argument whenever she chose silence instead of answering.

'This is our third date.' She proffered the lie coolly, keeping her gaze squarely on his. She knew what her answer would mean to him. Was morbidly curious to see the effect it had on him.

Because Emiliano never forgot.

He went marble-still, his chest barely rising and falling. Sienna knew what it meant. She'd struck a very raw nerve. Part of her rejoiced. Even as a greater part of her curled up and died for that rejoicing. Because what did that say about her? That she was so hung up on him, she wanted to get a rise out of him for delivering information that was sure to remind him of them? That would remind him that they'd made love for the first time after their third date?

'Your *third* date?' he repeated ominously.

She raised her chin, shivering despite the volcanic atmosphere between them.

He spotted her reaction and started to shrug off his jacket, the way he'd done numerous times in the past when she'd needed an extra layer of warmth.

She stepped back quickly, unable to bear the thought. 'What do you think you're doing?'

He paused. 'You need to ask?'

She shook her head emphatically. 'No, thank you.'

Jaw clenched, he shouldered the jacket back on, his frown turning blacker. 'Answer me, Sienna.'

'Yes, *third* date. And it's going very well, even if I say so myself. I've just ordered the oysters. If you haven't had your main yet, I suggest you try them. Marco's outdoing himself tonight.'

He took a single, predatory step towards her, his face a mask of frozen fury. 'Who is he, Sienna, hmm? This guy you're eating oysters for?'

She affected what she hoped was a half-decent indifferent shrug. 'He's the guy who may or may not know what the significance of a third date with me means. He's witty, charming and intelligent, and we have oodles in common, so I'd say his prospects are—'

The single, filthy curse was her only warning before Emiliano grabbed her by the arms and slammed her against the wall. To anyone witnessing the action, it might have seemed violent, but it was a practised move perfected in their time together that ensured her no harm. The reminder sent everything inside Sienna screaming with mingled horror and sheer delight as electricity rushed through her. It was the most natural response in the world to start raising one leg in preparation to have him hitching her up. But the assist never came. And in the dark alley, the cold wind reminded her that it was over between Emiliano and her.

That this conversation should not be happening.

'You will *not* sleep with him,' he pronounced darkly, his thinned lips white with restrained fury.

She laughed. It was either that or succumb to something else—such as tears. 'Do you need a reminder of how I react to orders, Mr Castillo?'

His face tightened further at her deliberate formality. 'Unless you were seeing him behind my back, you barely know the guy. For all you know he could be—'

'What? Someone else who leads me along for over a year then dumps me for his fiancée?'

He had the grace to drop his gaze, to blink, but it was the only give in an otherwise rigidly unforgiving but breathtakingly striking face.

'Sienna, things aren't what they seem. I told you why I'm doing this—'

'Let me go. Go finish your meeting. Then go home to your fiancée. I'm not sure exactly what you intended by cornering me this way. But if somewhere in your twisted imagination you thought you were looking out for me, then don't. We both know I've never been the feeble, cuddly type. You hurt me, but as you can see I didn't curl up and die. I don't intend to. I've moved on.'

She placed her hands on his chest and pushed. For a moment, he didn't budge. Then he stepped back. Sienna wished he'd stayed a moment longer. And cursed herself to hell and back.

She moved from the wall and ran damp hands over her dress. When she raised her head, he was regarding her with icy mockery.

'I thought you many things, but I never thought the day would come when I'd think you a petty fool.'

Her mouth dropped open. 'Excuse me?'

He shrugged. 'Deny it if you will, that all of this was staged for my benefit. You didn't hope I would see you with another man and immediately come running back?'

She forced her mouth closed and raised a hand casually to flick her long hair over her shoulder. A sliver of satisfaction came with witnessing the trace of hunger on his face as he followed the movement.

'You have a particular word in Argentina for a donkey's behind, don't you, Mr Castillo? I'm sure I heard you use it once or twice, usually when things weren't going your way. Well, guess what? You're being a giant one right now.' She stepped close, even though her every instinct screamed at her to flee in the other direction, and she continued, 'The only thing I want you thinking about me tonight, when you get home and are enjoying your favourite cognac, is how much I appreciate everything you taught me in bed during our time together. And how much I'm going to be enjoying sharing all that gorgeous, decadent knowledge with David. And then I want you to raise that glass to yourself, because you truly deserve the kudos—'

'*Cállate!*' Grasping her arms, he pinned her back against the wall, a feverish light glinting dangerously in his eyes. 'Shut the hell up!' he repeated in English. With each snarled word, he moved her higher up the wall until he was eye level with her. 'You want a reaction from me, *enamorada*? Well, your wish is about to be granted.'

The kiss was hell. And heaven. And everything in between. The edgy hunger and fury with which Emiliano kissed her, devoured her, robbed her of thought in a single second. All she could feel, breathe, hear, was the riotous, ecstatic thundering of her senses.

With a helpless groan, she opened her mouth and welcomed a kiss that should not have been happening. Whether it was the illicit nature of it or, because contrary to what she'd been telling herself he continued to be vital to her very being, Sienna was too afraid to find out. All she could stand to entertain in that moment was that he was here for a brief moment in her arms. The man who had taught her the finest art of passion was in her arms. And she didn't want to let him go.

His moan echoed hers as the kiss deepened, their strained panting echoing in the dark alley as the rain intensified, hands roving, touch reacquainted. Her hands slid over his shoulders, locked into the vibrant hair at his nape and scraped over his scalp.

He jerked against her, the imprint of his powerful arousal a primal force at the cradle of her thighs. She couldn't help it, she moved against him, her tongue sliding sensuously against his in blatant, desperate need as her body melted. He shifted, placing a little distance between them.

Sienna whimpered and started to close the gap. Felt the mist of rain on her face. Then it all came rushing back.

Emiliano stepped away, eyes blazing but face frozen once more.

'Go now, *querida*. Return to your *date* with my touch all over your body. Go to him and tell him I was the one who made you wet, who caused that glazed look in your eyes and your swollen lips. Tell him how I could've had you right here, right now, against this wall if I wished. And if he wants you after that—' he shrugged '—try telling yourself he's still the charming and intelligent man you want.'

Anger swiftly followed shock and shame. 'You…you're disgusting. I hate you!'

'Be truthful. You don't hate me. You hate yourself because your little game has been turned back on you.'

Thick, gulping tears threatened. Sienna battled them back through sheer grit. But even after she got herself under a modicum of control she couldn't speak. She stared at him, the man she'd allowed to mean more to her in their time together than had been even remotely wise. She'd paid heavily for that gross misjudgement. Was still paying. As she gazed into his powerfully gorgeous face, she shook her head.

'You're right. I don't hate you. What I feel is sadness for you—that you feel the need to do this just to prove a point. But I don't hate myself for trying to move on. You can do your best to belittle my efforts—it's not going to stop me. You can either move on, too, or waste your time trying to corner me in dark alleys. No matter what you do or say or try to prove, all you'll get is me, walking away from you every time.'

A cryptic expression washed over his face, followed by another, before his mask slipped back into place. 'Great speech, *querida*, but perhaps if you'd stop for a minute you can hear what I have to say.'

'I don't want to hear it. You and I had nothing to talk about when I left you last month. We have even less to talk about now.'

He lifted a lazy hand and passed a finger over her tingling lower lip. 'Our kiss said otherwise.'

She jerked away. 'The kiss I'm already incredibly ashamed of, you mean?'

His face darkened and his hand dropped. 'Excuse me?'

'You're not deaf. You're engaged to another woman, and yet here you are, kissing me. Don't you have even a shred of decency?'

He shook his head. 'Sienna, it's not going to be like that—'

'No! Enough. And stop saying my name,' she snapped. Prying herself off the wall, she started walking away.

'Come back here,' he bit out. 'We're not finished.'

She hurried her steps, almost fearful her feet would disobey her and rush back to him, to hear him out if it meant hearing his voice, seeing his face for a few more precious minutes. She heard him behind her and quickened her steps.

'*Dios mío*, stop!'

She broke into a run, catching a sob before it slipped free.

'Sienna, slow down!'

She saw a mound of snow swept to one side of the pavement, she heard voices from pedestrians at the entrance to the alley and ran faster. The urgency to get back to civility, away from Emiliano's captivating presence, rushed through her. What had she been thinking? He belonged to another woman. He was no longer hers to kiss, to touch, to make love with…

The sob broke, horrible and pain-filled. Tears surged into her eyes, blinding her. She rounded the corner at full speed. She never knew whether it was a body or an object she bumped into. But she felt her heel slide over the icy sidewalk. Felt her body wrenched sideways as she lost her balance. Saw the ground rush up to meet her. Heard Emiliano's guttural shout from behind. Then felt excruciating pain as her head cracked on the side of the kerb, her braced arms doing nothing to halt her fall.

She moaned as stars exploded across her vision. Hands turned her, cradled her. Her vision cleared for a second and she saw golden eyes filled with concern blazing down at her. Then another rip of pain.

Then the blissful succumbing to nothing.

CHAPTER FIVE

'MISS NEWMAN? SIENNA?'

She turned her head a fraction towards the sound but kept her eyes closed. The effort it took to move even her eyeballs was too much.

'Hmm…?'

'Don't try and speak, Miss Newman. Take it easy. Open your eyes when you're ready.'

Miss Newman? Was there someone else in the room with her? Was the voice speaking to someone else besides her? She would much prefer it because having someone engage with her would mean she had to respond. She would have to speak. She turned away from the voice. She didn't want to speak. She wanted to sink back into the harmless abyss where there was no pain, only oblivion. Where there were no voices murmuring, drawing closer to where she lay.

'We need to take your vitals, find out how you're doing. You've been out for a while.'

Out? Where?

She tried to turn her head again, felt the restriction across her forehead and paused. She was wearing some sort of a cap. Tentatively, she lifted her hand to her head.

'That's your bandage. It needs to stay on for a while, I'm afraid,' a kind female voice supplied. 'Can you open your eyes for me, dear? The doctor needs to examine you properly.'

Doctor. She was in a hospital. But… Why?

Dropping her hand back onto her stomach, she carefully cracked her eyes open, then winced at the bright lights overhead.

'Nurse, turn down the lights, please?'

The lights dimmed. She opened her eyes a little wider.

Two faces stared at her. The male doctor wore glasses behind which dark eyes gleamed with serious intelligence. The nurse's face was kinder, more maternal.

She smiled broadly now, almost as if her patient opening her eyes was a personal triumph for her.

'I'm Dr Stephens, this is Nurse Abby. Can you tell me the last thing you remember, Miss Newman?'

She brought her attention back to the doctor. She blinked tired eyes again, casting a look around the room to make sure he was talking to someone else and not her.

He couldn't be addressing her.

Because she wasn't Miss Newman. Or Sienna.

Her name was…

It was…

She shook her head, trying to clear her brain of the thick fog.

'I…' she croaked. Her throat was raw and painful. Her voice felt disused. Raising her hand to her throat, she massaged her skin, then froze when she saw the needle inserted into her vein. Examining the back of her hand closely, she saw several puncture marks. For some reason, the sight of the tiny bruises struck fear into her heart. Her eyes sought the health professionals staring down at her. 'I… How long…?'

Dr Stephens scribbled on a sheet before he pulled out a pen light. 'You've been unconscious for a little over two weeks. The bandage on your head is because we had to perform a minor surgery to reduce the swelling on your brain.'

'Brain…*surgery*?'

'Yes.' He stepped up to the bed and held up the light, the question clear in his eyes. When she gave a small nod, he shone it in one eye, then the other. Then he stepped back. 'Can you tell me the last thing you remember?' he asked again.

A series of fragmented images flashed through her brain, like strobe lights in a dark room, on and off, before she could form a proper picture. Shaking her head again, she tried to concentrate, to capture one solid image. Her mind remained a dark, blank space.

She saw the doctor and nurse exchange glances.

'Please...' She stopped when her throat protested. The nurse stepped forward with a glass of water and straw. Gratefully, she sipped, relief pouring through her when the pain eased. 'What's... What happened?' she managed. 'Where am I?'

'You're at North Haven,' Dr Stephens replied. 'We're a private medical facility just outside London. As for what happened, you slipped on ice outside a restaurant and hit your head hard enough to cause a little brain bleed. You don't remember?'

She shook her head. 'No.'

'Do you remember going to the restaurant?' He stopped and checked his notes. 'I believe it's called Zarcosta?'

Again she shook her head, fighting the surge of panic. 'I don't...remember.'

The doctor fell silent for almost a minute, his professional mask slipping briefly to exhibit his concern. 'Miss Newman, can you tell me your date of birth?' he pressed gently.

She probed her mind desperately, and found only black space. Her throat clogged. She swallowed, refusing to succumb to tears. 'No,' she whispered. 'Is that my name— Newman? Sienna Newman?'

Dr Stephens nodded solemnly. 'Yes, it is. Do you know what you do for a living? Or where you live?'

'I don't know!' This time she couldn't stop the rise of

tears or the twisting of her hand into the sheet for something, anything, to hang on to. 'Why can't I remember?'

'I can't give you an answer yet. Not until we run a few tests.' He put away his pen light and attempted a smile. 'Try not to worry. We'll know what's going on very shortly.'

He turned and spoke to the nurse in medical jargon she couldn't decipher.

She looked down. Her hands were trembling. In fact, her whole body was trembling as confusion and panic rose in steady waves.

Sensing her emotions, Nurse Abby patted her hand. 'The technicians and I will run the tests the doctor needs, then we'll take it from there, okay?'

She couldn't do much else but nod and watch with climbing despair as they left the room. Then, forcing herself to calm down, she probed her mind again, searching every corner until tears spilled down her cheeks and exhaustion weighed her down.

She could barely summon the energy to take interest in what was happening when the nurse returned with two other medical staff. Blood was taken and her vitals recorded before she was wheeled away and placed in an MRI machine.

Time passed. Then she was returned to her room, by which time oblivion was a welcome relief. So she gave in. The sunlight outside her window had turned to night when she woke up. Her room was bathed in soft light and a breathtaking bouquet of flowers—calla lilies and white roses—stood on the dresser across the room.

The pain in her head still throbbed but she was getting used to it, enough to be able to recall the conversation with the medical team.

Even though a practical voice prompted her that panicking would bring no answers, she couldn't stop the fear squeezing her heart.

She'd had brain surgery. And now she couldn't remember her own name.

She was still grappling with the million questions teeming in her mind when Nurse Abby walked back in.

'Have I… Have there been any visitors? My family?' she blurted, the question seeming to come from nowhere.

The nurse cast a furtive glance at her before busying herself with checking the intravenous drip. 'We weren't given details of any family members to contact, but we called your…' She paused, unnecessarily straightening the sheets. 'Your friend. He's on his way.'

'My friend?' she repeated, hope momentarily robbing her of breath.

'Yes. He says he was with you that night. You're very lucky to have him. He's been here every day since your accident. He's had a bunch of those lovely flowers delivered every day, too,' she said, with a trace of envy in her voice.

Sienna—the name was still so alien to her—returned her gaze to the flowers. They were her favourite. She didn't understand how she knew, but the knowledge wasn't one that needed probing. That tiny revelation of self eased the panic threatening again. Not enough to keep her from going on a desperate hunt for her memory once again, though, and experiencing the hollowness in her stomach expand when she found nothing. Retreating from her mental flailing, she latched on to the only real thing available.

'My friend… What's his name?' she asked.

'It's… Oh, here he is now! We have our share of celebrities using this facility, but none of them arrive by helicopter,' she divulged in an excited whisper as she peered out of the window.

Although Sienna couldn't see the spectacle capturing the nurse's attention, she heard the distinct beating of rotor blades, the sound growing louder as the aircraft flew overhead.

As she absorbed the news that she had a friend who owned a helicopter, a buzzer sounded in the room. Nurse Abby dragged her attention from the window, reached into her pocket and withdrew a miniature tablet.

'Perfect timing. Your test results are ready. Dr Stephens will want to see them before he talks to you both.'

'Both?'

Nurse Abby paused by the door. 'I'm not one to gossip, but your man isn't the kind to take no for an answer. He's demanded to know every detail of your progress. And, with us not being able to contact any family members, we've had to rely on him to give medical approval. Which is a good thing, because his consent saved your life. It's clear he cares a great deal about you.' Again, Sienna caught wistfulness in her tone that told her Nurse Abby was a romantic at heart.

'So he knows I have a…um…memory issue?'

The older woman's face softened in sympathy. 'Don't worry about that, my dear. Everything will be all right. I just know it.'

Her tablet buzzed again. She was gone before Sienna could voice any of the questions burning on her tongue. And for the next twenty minutes they grew until she heard voices approaching.

Dr Stephens entered, a file in his hand. Paralysed with fear as to what that file contained and what her diagnosis was, she didn't immediately acknowledge the other presence in the room, not until she felt the tingle from the power of his stare. Not until her heart began to flutter wildly, from reasons that had nothing to do with the sorry state of her mind.

Her reaction to the man partly obscured by Dr Stephens's advancing form was so visceral, so primitively electrifying, her fingers locked on to the sheets and her breath strangled in her throat.

'Miss Newman, I have the results of your tests. Before we continue, Nurse Abby informs me she's told you of Mr Castillo's involvement in your medical care.' He rounded to the side of the bed, stepping out of the line of sight of the man behind him. The man who stood tall, imposing. Frozen at the sight of her. 'You won't remember him, most likely, but this is...'

The buzzing in her ears stopped her from hearing the rest of Dr Stephen's words.

From the tiny pieces of useless, broken memory, a single one began to form. Not a whole picture, but enough fractions coalesced to make her heart skip several beats. To make her whole body tremble into wakeful, joyful awareness when the piece held.

Enough to make her stare at the man whose face, like a blazing comet through the night sky, was beautifully real and infinitely magical to her.

'Emiliano...' Her voice emerged as a hopeful rasp. When he didn't disappear, when he remained a solid, towering reality before her, she struggled upright. 'Emiliano!'

He took a single step towards her then froze again, his face losing several shades of colour. 'You remember?' he rasped, a peculiar note in his voice as he stared with watchful, almost-alarmed eyes.

'Yes! I remember you. Oh, God!' Her gaze darted excitedly to the doctor and back to Emiliano. 'I remember!'

He still hadn't moved. Why? Did she look that horrific? She knew from the brief and cringe-making self-examination she'd conducted earlier that she'd lost weight. There were hollows not just on the inside of her but also on the outside.

But Emiliano had nursed her through a horrific flu and chest infection recently without batting an eyelash. And she was sure she'd looked worse then.

Realising she'd just had another memory, she gasped. 'The flu! I had the flu around a month ago,' she said.

Dr Stephens glanced at Emiliano. His jaw flexed for a second before he shook his head and they both stared at her.

'What?' she demanded.

'Your flu wasn't a month ago. It was in late September.'

'And?'

'And it'll be New Year's Day in three days,' he said, his deep voice curiously flat.

Her heart lurched, then thudded anew with dread. Before it could take complete hold, Dr Stephens cleared his throat.

'Miss Newman, can you tell me what your relationship is with Mr Castillo?'

She glanced at Emiliano, her panic receding a little as his eyes met hers. 'We're lovers,' she said, blushing when his eyes began to darken. The word *lover* had always felt a little too intimate to share, but she couldn't think of a better term to describe the relationship between her and Emiliano. 'We've been together for nearly ten months.'

A rough sound emerged from his throat. He must be worried about her. He hadn't liked it when she'd got her chest infection. She couldn't imagine what the last two weeks had been like for him. In a reversed position, she would've been out of her mind.

Tentatively, she reached out her unencumbered hand to him. 'Emiliano, I'm okay. I'm sorry if I worried you.'

After a tense little moment, he moved towards her. The hand that enfolded hers was warm, strong. Stimulatingly electrifying. Her breath caught all over again when she raised her head and saw their touch was having the same effect on him.

They both turned when Dr Stephens cleared his throat again. 'Mr Castillo, can you corroborate that?'

'No. It's been longer than that. About a year, to be exact,' he said.

'A *year*?' She searched his eyes.

'Si,' he confirmed.

Thrown into confusion all over again, she struggled to breathe. 'What's wrong with me?'

'You're showing all the signs of retrograde amnesia,' Dr Stephens said. 'Your head trauma has caused you to lose chunks of your memory. Can you tell me your earliest memory of you and Mr Castillo?'

She frowned, sifted through the jagged pieces. 'I… We were in Vienna…at the summer opera…in June?' She glanced up at Emiliano. He nodded.

'And the last?' the doctor asked.

'Um… It must be October, then. A client meeting in Vancouver, followed by dinner. I was feeling much better by then.' She couldn't stop the flow of colour into her cheeks as other memories burst forth. The tightening of his hand on hers told her he was recalling the hastily made excuses after the deal had been struck, the abandoned meal, the frenzied kiss in the lift, Emiliano lapping vintage champagne from her naked body.

He'd murmured thick, charged words to her in Spanish as he'd made love to her. Words she was beginning to understand. Words that had sparked the belief that she wasn't just another transient body, warming his bed for a finite spell.

'So you remember what you do for a living now?'

She nodded. 'I'm his… I'm the vice-president of Acquisitions at Castillo Ventures.'

Dr Stephens's gaze flicked to Emiliano before it returned to her. 'Anything else? Your age? Family? Favourite soccer team?'

She held her breath and delved deep once more, her hand grasping Emiliano's tighter as she came up empty.

Swallowing, she shook her head. 'No, but I know Emiliano's birthday is in September.'

The doctor nodded. 'Okay. Let's move on to other things—'

'Wait. What… When will I get my memories back? Is there anything I can do?'

Beside her, Emiliano shifted, his free hand sliding over her nape to gently direct her gaze to him. 'Dr Stephens stresses the importance of not forcing your memories to return, *querida*. Isn't that right, doctor?'

There was something in his voice. The bone-deep authority stamped into each word and deed was nothing new to her refreshed memory, but there was underlying terseness in there.

Dr Stephens nodded. 'It's better to let the memories return on their own. Unfortunately, there isn't a time frame of when that'll be. Your brain is still healing itself after the trauma. My recommendation is for the complete absence of stress of any kind, especially considering your other condition.'

She felt Emiliano tense as her own anxiety spiked. A quick glance at him showed his darkly questioning stare levelled at the doctor. 'My other condition?' she asked.

'You said she was healing,' Emiliano accused icily.

'She is. I don't mean that.' His gaze returned to her. 'Since the time frame of your relationship is right, I'm going to assume it's okay to share this information with Mr Castillo, as well.'

'What information?' she demanded.

Dr Stephens consulted the file one last time, then closed it. 'The result of the blood test we took when you were first admitted two weeks ago revealed you are pregnant.'

Her heart somersaulted into her stomach. 'I'm… *What?*'

The hand on her nape had tightened almost to the point

of discomfort, but she didn't mind too much. It was the only thing keeping her grounded.

'Yes, doctor. Repeat that, *por favor*,' Emiliano commanded through clenched teeth.

'Obviously with the gap in her memory we won't be able to determine how far along she is, but the scan shows she can't be more than three-months pregnant.'

'How is that possible? She never missed taking her pill.'

'And you? Did you use protection?'

Emiliano replied without embarrassment. 'No. We preferred it that way. We both got blood tests to prove we were healthy.'

'She mentioned the flu and an infection. Did she take a course of antibiotics?'

Emiliano nodded tersely. 'Yes, but she got her period after that. She's as regular as clockwork.'

'But the effectiveness of the pill may have been compromised by the antibiotics. It only needed to be disrupted briefly for pregnancy to occur. And menstruating in the first month of pregnancy isn't uncommon.'

Dr Stephens carried on speaking. Emiliano fired more questions at him.

'Is the baby okay?' she asked when a lull came in the interrogation.

'Yes, we've been monitoring you closely and, besides the head injury, your body is thriving.'

Sienna exhaled in relief and turned her hand within Emiliano's, needing even more of his touch as her senses went into complete free fall. First came shock, then panic. Then...utter elation. Something in her heart, an emotion she didn't completely understand, cracked wide open, spewing endless joy through her at the thought of the baby growing inside her.

But all she could do was stare at her lover, her insides singing with happiness.

'Emiliano…' she murmured softly, a tiny part of her afraid that, like her absent memories, her new joy would disappear if she spoke too loudly.

He heard her and stopped speaking to stare down at her. His deep shock was clear in his eyes. As was a tumble of other unfathomable emotions. Emotions she was confident they would work through eventually.

'Yes, Sienna?'

'Emiliano…I'm… We're having a baby,' she whispered in wonder.

His eyes blazed with a fierce light that turned her insides molten. His gaze left hers to track down her body. It paused at her still-flat stomach and stayed, the stamp of possession unmistakeable.

His eyelids descended, temporarily veiling his expression. '*Sí, querida.* It seems we are to be unexpectedly blessed.'

Turning her head, she raised their joined hands and on impulse kissed the back of Emiliano's hand before resting her cheek against it. She heard his sharp inhalation but she refused to be embarrassed about the public display of affection.

Silence reigned for a handful of seconds before Emiliano eased away.

'Rest now. I need to speak to Dr Stephens about when you can be discharged.'

She settled back into bed, her mouth curving in a smile. 'Oh, yes, please. I can't wait to go home. Alfie must be bored out of his mind with just you for company,' she teased.

He didn't return her smile. But her instinct told her that wasn't new. 'He wouldn't dare admit it to me, but I have a feeling he will be pleased to have you back,' he offered dryly. Then he walked out.

Despite the huge obstacles she was sure awaited her

future, Sienna couldn't stop her smile stretching wide as her hand drifted down to rest on her stomach.

Some of her memories might have been temporarily taken away, but while she waited for time to heal her she would revel in what she knew in her heart was a true blessing.

CHAPTER SIX

'YOU'VE KNOWN SHE was pregnant for two weeks and you didn't tell me?' Emiliano demanded the moment the doctor shut the door behind them. He wasn't sure why his blood was boiling so high. Nor did he welcome it. The shock he'd just sustained needed to be treated with cold, calculated precision. Not this frantic pacing and hammering heartbeats.

Sienna was pregnant. The woman who he had very little doubt hated the very ground he walked on was carrying his child. The same woman who'd told him coldly two weeks ago that she'd moved on from him, and who'd blatantly flaunted another man in his face.

His gut clenched hard, the punch of that statement nowhere near dulled despite the passage of time.

The situation with the Cabreras was nowhere near resolved, despite his best efforts to find a solution. They were intent on the son paying for the sins of the parents. And they were wealthy enough not to be influenced by the offer of financial compensation.

Only Emiliano's agreement to wed Graciela Cabrera had sufficed. He'd gone along with it, thinking he would find a quick alternative solution while they were temporarily appeased.

Emiliano would've consigned the whole situation to hell by now had it not been for Matias's plea at the end of his video message and his own meeting with Graciela.

It was clear the young girl was desperate to find a way out from beneath her father's oppressive thumb, her wild behaviour and risqué media courting simply outbursts of a cornered, bewildered victim. Emiliano wasn't ashamed to admit empathy had forced him to stay at the dinner that had been photographed by the paparazzi.

Even then, he'd been all set to walk away. Despite his brother's entreaty, he'd known he needed to find another way to honour Matias's wishes. Until Graciela's blatant plea for help, for him to go along with the ruse for a short time just to buy her some time. His agreement in that moment had been to buy *himself* more time.

What he hadn't expected was for the whole situation to blow up in his face even before his feet had touched the ground properly. In light of Sienna's accident, a different powder keg had been activated, a situation that needed to be dealt with very carefully.

As for the news that he was to be a father...

He pushed that to the bottom of the list. He was pragmatic enough to accept that, whether he liked it or not, this was his new reality. Sifting through his feelings to find the correct descriptive right now would serve no useful purpose.

Neither would dwelling on the fact that this was the last thing he would've wished for, given the choice.

His question, however, needed answering. He focused on the doctor, who shrugged. 'You're not my patient. She is. I shared those details that were pertinent to her continued health with you because I needed your consent to treat her head trauma. Her pregnancy didn't fall into that purview.'

'It wasn't up to you to decide what to share and what to withhold. I'm the father of her child!' The words felt alien and almost...alarming coming from his mouth. What did he know about parenting? His own experience had been beyond abysmal to the point of non-existent.

The thought triggered a deep unsettling inside him and he had to tighten his gut against letting it rule him.

'The history you gave me when she was admitted left

room for questions. I had to do whatever I could to treat her trauma, but I couldn't share confidential information with you, because you'd told me you two were no longer together. I had to consider the possibility that someone else was the father.'

A part of him understood the doctor's reasoning. A greater part of him raged maniacally at the thought of Sienna sleeping with another man, never mind taking his seed into her body and carrying his child. He'd seen her on a date with David Hunter and he hadn't reacted well. In fact, he'd go as far as to say he'd been ashamed of himself for the way he acted. That didn't diminish his rage. Or the guilt dogging him.

Telling himself his possessive instincts had spiked and remained fiercely active when she'd walked away from him was true enough. He hadn't been anywhere near ready to let Sienna go despite his growing misgivings about her. Having the decision taken out of his hands while he'd been in retreat and regroup mode had stung.

None of that changed the fact that he was the reason she was laid up in a hospital bed with gaps in her memory. Gaps he couldn't fill without causing further damage. To her or the child.

His child.

His responsibility.

Again he experienced a bolt of bewilderment and shook his head, everything that had happened recently making him ball his fists in silent fury.

'Give me the raw prognosis. And a way forward that enables me to come clean with her about our relationship.' He abhorred the thought of lying to her.

Dr Stephens shook his head. 'My recommendation still stands. Any further trauma, even emotionally, could have a severe adverse effect on her health. Remember, it's not just her in the picture now. If she's going ahead with the pregnancy—'

'*If?*' Icy waves of disbelief washed through him, followed closely by a total rejection of the very idea. 'Why would she not want the baby?'

The other man shrugged. 'She's an independent woman, who from all accounts seems to be blocking out the last few weeks of your relationship and the break-up. You need to prepare yourself for every possibility once her memories return.'

The stark words kicked him square in the solar plexus, rocking him back on his heels.

Normally, Emiliano prided himself on seeing every angle of a problem. Spotting an opponent's strategy, being half a dozen moves ahead, picking at the flaws and beating them at their own game had seen him walk away with life-changing deals before he'd turned thirty. At thirty-two, he'd made himself, and every single one of his elite clients, unimaginably rich in the process.

But it seemed, the moment he'd set foot back in Argentina, everything had gone wrong. He'd thought himself immune to anything to do with his parents. But, when it'd come down to it, he hadn't been able to walk away. Especially not when Matias had pleaded with him on their behalf. But hard on the heels of Matias's plea on behalf of Graciela had come words which had made it impossible for him to walk away.

You owe me. And I'm collecting.

Those six words had ultimately stopped him from walking out.

He'd lost his touch. He'd lost his woman.

Now, he was faced with the very real possibility that he might lose his child. Unbidden, the scene in the alleyway played through his mind. While he'd been grappling with the increasingly demanding Cabreras and his parents, Sienna had been busy moving on, *dating* another man.

Another man she might well go back to when her memory returned. Only now she would be walking away with something that was rightfully his.

Unlike the bewildering confusion surrounding his impending fatherhood a handful of minutes ago, his thoughts were crystal clear now.

His child would be going nowhere. He might not have the first clue about how to be a parent, but neither was he prepared to take a back seat in his child's life the way his own father had done with him.

Setting his jaw, he stared at the doctor. 'When can Sienna be safely discharged?'

'I'd like to monitor her for twenty-four hours, make sure there are no setbacks.'

'And after that? What does she need to ensure she and the baby remain healthy?'

'Complete rest for a few weeks, then she can resume normal activities as long as she doesn't overdo things. I'll make sure you have a detailed aftercare programme.'

The urge to pace once again attacked him. Glancing at his watch, he realised the late hour and forced himself to curb the rest of the questions firing through his brain. 'I'll be back to collect her tomorrow. In the meantime, if she so much as twitches in discomfort—'

'You'll be my first call,' Dr Stephen finished wryly.

His walk back to Sienna's private room was a little less agitated than when he'd made the last journey. Hell, he wasn't ashamed to say that, even with this unexpected news, the vice tightening his chest had eased.

Regardless of the unwelcome emotions she'd triggered in him by attempting to walk away, *again*, from him that night, watching her fall and injure herself had been an experience he never wanted to repeat.

Knowing now that she'd taken a fall while carrying his child...

Emiliano paused outside her door, clamped a hand that was less than steady and breathed deep.

Possessiveness of the things he valued was a trait he'd recognised and shamelessly embraced very early on in his life. He hadn't needed a psychologist to tell him it was a result of having been patently *valueless* to his parents that had driven him to surround himself with material things, even sycophants, in his early adulthood. It had brought him a modicum of satisfaction, hell even a sense of belonging after long years of having been placed on a shelf and consigned to second-best status. In later years, he'd grown very selective of the things he placed value on.

Loyalty and hard work from his employees.

The growing closeness between Matias and him.

A woman in his bed who knew the score and would quietly exit his life when her time was up.

Nowhere on that list of desirable possessions had there featured a child. Not for the foreseeable future, if ever. Simply because he didn't have the right tools to forge a father-son bond.

And yet it was all he could think about now as he raised his hand and pushed the door to Sienna's room open. In the space of an hour within which the news of his impending child had been placed before him, then immediately potentially threatened, all Emiliano could think about was how to protect it. *Possess* it.

The voice that warned him against making so bold and intractable a claim was ruthlessly suppressed.

His brain working a mile a minute, he entered and crossed to the bed.

She was asleep, her long lashes fanned out against her skin. Her complexion was paler than he was used to, but she was no less breathtaking now than she'd been the first time he'd seen her across the interview table at Castillo Ventures. Now, as then, the sight of her elicited a powerful response in him, the majority of which was sexual, he admitted. But there had always been something else, something *more*, to his relationship with Sienna.

He'd never liked puzzles. His area of expertise was strategizing. Somewhere along the line he'd satisfied himself with the sound rationalisation that he would've parted ways with Sienna once he'd solved the puzzle of why she triggered this unknown...*craving* within him.

That was before other factors had stepped in and brought things to an unsatisfactory conclusion.

They'd had unfinished business before her accident.

Now they had something...different altogether.

'Emiliano?'

His gut clenched at the sound of her voice. Mere weeks ago, she'd sworn never to say his name again. Hearing it brought a peculiar sensation he couldn't quite name. Whatever it was, it wasn't enough for him not to crave hearing it again.

'*Si*, I'm here.' And he intended to be here for the foreseeable future. For the sake of the child he hadn't known existed but now could not put out of his mind.

She raised her head a fraction off the bed, the silky black hair not restricted by the bandage sliding on the pillow. 'Are you... Is everything okay?'

He drew closer, reached out and caressed her cheek. The gesture soothed her, which was supposed to be his aim, helping her remain stress-free. But he couldn't deny that he really liked touching her. 'Everything's fine. Sleep now, *querida*.'

She smiled drowsily and turned into the caress. 'I love it when you call me that.'

He tensed. He needed to stop calling her that. The endearment had slipped out without thought. But it seemed breaking habits when it came to Sienna wasn't as easy as he'd imagined.

For one thing, he'd yet to fill the position she'd vacated at Castillo Ventures. In the weeks after she'd resigned, he'd sat in on interview after interview, discarding one application after another, until one of his subordinates had suggested that perhaps the void left by Sienna was immutable.

Emiliano had snarled his disagreement. Then cancelled all following interviews.

Now his brain ticked over. Perhaps he'd been wise to keep the position open. He would have to proceed very carefully because this game could only have one outcome.

But that didn't mean he couldn't arm himself with as much ammunition in his arsenal as possible.

Whether that included leaning down to brush his lips against the cheek of the woman who subconsciously hated him was a thought he wasn't content to dwell on.

At all.

What he did concentrate on was having Sienna's belongings relocated back to the penthouse as soon as possible. The moment that task had been achieved, he called North Haven. By early evening the next day, he was landing his helicopter on the extensive lawn of the private hospital.

Discharge papers were produced, which he signed, along with a very large, very gratefully received cheque. Emiliano knew he was buying expediency, which was gratifyingly supplied. Within half an hour of landing, Sienna was being wheeled out, her suitcase carried by a porter.

Her bandage had been removed, the two-inch patch of skin where her operation had been performed replaced with a plaster and half-disguised by her long, loose hair. The shapeless hospital gown had been replaced with a cashmere jumper dress, the navy blue colour highlighting her stunning green eyes.

Eyes that now smiled at the staff who'd lined up to say goodbye.

Emiliano watched, hiding his impatience as she took the time to thank the nurses on duty before handing Nurse Abby her calla lilies and promising to stay in touch.

When she requested yet another stop to thank yet another member of staff, he put his foot down and steered her to the lift.

'No more stops. We're leaving before you wear yourself out.'

'I'm being wheeled around in the Rolls Royce of wheelchairs. I'm fine,' she replied, a grin tugging at her mouth.

Emiliano dragged his gaze away from the appealing fullness of her curved lips and stabbed at the call button. 'You've been in a coma for two weeks. Save the meet-and-greet for when you're stronger.'

She gave a mock salute. A feeble one. 'Yes, boss. Anything you say,' she said, her voice turning smoky and husky as she cast him a glance from beneath her lashes.

His gut clenched hard as he fought his libido's eager response. The last time she'd used that term, he'd bent her over his desk and showed her in no uncertain terms who was boss.

The blush staining her cheeks suggested she recalled the incident, too. The lift arrived. He stooped low to mutter in her ear as he wheeled her in, 'Behave yourself, we have an audience.'

He caught her tiny shiver before her gaze slid to the porter trailing them. It would've been an easy job to take the suitcase and dismiss him but Emiliano welcomed the buffer. It would stop him from smoothing her hair back behind her ear or leaning in to inhale her perfume.

Somewhere in the middle of the night, when he'd been polishing the finer details of his plot, he'd concluded that physical distance was crucial in order to make this madness they were embroiled in bearable. He could provide what Sienna needed without further compromising himself. Or her.

She might be forming new memories now based on half-formed foundations, but even the half-truth didn't justify succumbing to their mutual desire for the sake of her peace of mind.

The tiny darts of regret that had stabbed him last night when he'd accepted his own decision returned, sharper this time. Sucking in a breath, he looked down to find her gaze on him, one shapely eyebrow curved. Before they'd met, he hadn't been one for public displays of affection. That had quickly changed with Sienna. The relentless need to touch her, to establish ownership, was an unquenchable fire that burned within him.

Finding that Sienna hadn't shared his new-found need to embrace his ownership had...unsettled him. Truth be told, it had been one of the many out-of-the-norm things that had disconcerted him about their relationship. That still did.

But he intended to handle it.

He saw the question in her eyes now triggered by his withdrawal. Before he could formulate an acceptable response, the lift doors parted on the ground-floor lobby. He wheeled the chair to the edge of the lawn then scooped her up in his arms.

Her breath caught lightly before her hands curled around his neck.

'Are you okay?' she breathed against his ear.

'I should be asking you that.'

'I told you, I'm fine. Whereas you seem...agitated.'

There was a little lingering teasing in her tone, but her face had turned serious.

'Look at the situation we find ourselves in. I think a little bit of agitation is warranted, don't you?'

'*Situation*... You mean the baby?'

He froze to a halt three feet from the chopper. 'The baby is one factor, of course, but I meant you, too.'

She made a half-comical face. 'Am I the first lover of yours to literally lose her mind?'

'Your attempt at hilarity is noted. And rejected.' He stepped into the aircraft and placed her on the back seat. Joining her there, he buckled her seat belt before nodding at his pilot.

When he went to secure his belt, her hand covered his. 'I wasn't trying to make light of the situation. I just...I may not have all my faculties intact, but I can tell you still brood over things. I don't want to be one of the things you brood over. I'm not fragile.'

He couldn't stop the bitterness that twisted inside him. 'Trust me, I already know this.'

'Emiliano—'

'No more talking, Sienna. There will be plenty of time for that. For now, just enjoy the ride.'

At that time of the day there wasn't much to see, save moving headlights on the motorway and then a spiderweb of lights as they flew over London. But she complied, curling her body against his as they headed to the penthouse.

As they swung east, her gaze tracked the iconic landmarks of the Shard and the Gherkin.

'It'll be good to be home,' she murmured.

Even though a bracing gust of guilt blew through him, he concluded that he was doing the right thing. '*Sí*, it will,' he agreed.

Except it wasn't. Alfie, alerted to the situation, showed his concern without giving the game away.

Not so much the large bouquet of flowers that was delivered half an hour after they walked in.

Emiliano's hackles rose the moment he spotted the over-the-top floral display the concierge manager was handing to Alfie. Unfortunately, Sienna spotted them at the same time, too.

'Oh, how pretty,' she gushed to a wary-looking Alfie. 'Are they for me?'

The butler nodded slowly and opened his mouth. Emiliano's single shake of his head had him clamming up, depositing the vase on a nearby table and walking away.

She approached the flowers and began to dig around for a card. Emiliano, close on her heel, found it first. A brief glance confirmed what he suspected about the sender. A wave of anger rising in his chest, he crushed the card and shoved it in his pocket.

'Are you going to let me read the message or tell me who they're from?'

His jaw clenched. 'No.'

'Oh, come on. Somebody's gone to a bit of trouble. The least you can do is—'

'Nothing! He's a nobody. Forget him.'

His harsh condemnation echoed around the room.

Her eyes widened. Then she frowned.

'You're overreacting. You don't normally overreact. Don't ask me how I know. Unless it's a new habit? Or this is more than just flowers? It's the person, isn't it?'

Emiliano realised her probing was unravelling him, reminding him of everything about their relationship—*Dios mio*, when had that word even become normal for him to utter?—that needled him beneath the surface. He sliced his fingers through his hair, the vow he'd made not to hide the truth from her as far as he could suddenly seeming like the worst idea he'd ever had. Still, he toyed with not answering.

Not until she walked up to him and laid a hand on his cheek. 'Tell me,' she insisted with a quiet firmness.

His skin jumped beneath her touch, a hunger flaring in him he had no right to feel. And yet…

'If you insist on knowing, yes. The sender is a head-hunter. According to you, he's made it his mission to poach you from me many times.'

'He's *tried*? That means I haven't entertained him. He's probably just trying to get under your skin.'

He turned away, his lip curling. '*Dios mio*, he's succeeding.'

She gave a startled laugh.

'What?' He frowned, failing completely to see the funny side.

'I never thought I'd see the day you'd admit to being anything but totally invincible.'

He shrugged. 'We all have our faults, *querida*. Some of us are better at hiding them than others.'

A puzzled line appeared on her smooth forehead. 'I'm not sure that's a good thing to boast about.'

'Boast or not, it's the simple truth. If your vulnerability or circumstance is constantly exploited, you learn to hide them. And, with everything that comes from frequent practice, you wake up one day to find you excel at it.'

'And in your case it's basic survival?'

'*Was.* I'm invincible now. Remember?'

She laughed, then sobered after a minute. 'Did I know this about you before? You're not telling me something I've forgotten, are you? Because that would upset me.'

Emiliano was hit by a bolt of shock at her naked admission. 'Why would it upset you?'

'Because, if I don't know this about you after a year, then what have we been doing all this time?'

He had a ready answer for that, but to do that he would need to reach into a box he preferred to keep shut for the sake of sanity. 'Rest easy, *pequeña*. This is a revelation of sorts for us both.'

'Wow. And all from a simple bouquet of delphiniums and baby's breath,' she murmured, reaching out to touch the nearest petal.

He scooped the vase out of her reach, curbing the urge to throw it across the room. 'You hate delphiniums. Baby's breath, too.'

She dropped her hand. 'Now you're exaggerating.'

'No, I am not. You're very particular about the flowers you love. These aren't on your list.'

Her eyes widened. 'I have a list?'

Despite his black mood, his mouth twitched. 'You have a list for everything. These flowers didn't make the cut. Which is why they're going in the bin.'

He derived a certain childish satisfaction in trashing the flowers before tracking down his butler. A three-minute revelatory conversation worsened his mood.

David Hunter had been in touch with his concierge several times in the last day, seemingly after an extensive search for Sienna. He had to give the man credit for his investigative skills. But that was where Emiliano's tolerance started and ended. Hunter had balls, sending flowers to a woman at her lover's apartment.

Ex-lover.

Whatever.

Emiliano had been hustled into letting her go before he was ready, not that he doubted he would have done so eventually.

Whereas Hunter was overstepping. Unless he felt an entitlement towards Sienna that extended beyond just hopeful interest...

Emiliano's teeth clenched tight as the possible answers to that question reeled through his mind.

Questions he couldn't ask.

Exhaling to restore much-needed control, he issued a new set of instructions to his butler, one that included prohibiting David Hunter from coming anywhere near his building, and returned to the living room.

'I've decided,' he announced, his thoughts sifting through pros and cons and demolishing every obstacle in his way.

Sienna turned in a graceful movement, her slender body drawing and keeping his attention.

'What?'

'A change of scene will do you good. Tomorrow, we're going to take the jet, head to Paris for New Year, then we're going island hopping around the Caribbean until you get disgustingly homesick and beg me to bring you back.'

Her full lips parted in surprise, then a light frown marred her forehead. 'But... What about work? You can't just take off.'

'I'm the boss,' he said. 'I can do whatever I want, work from any continent I choose.'

'What about me? I can't just—'

'Yes, you can. I decree it, so you're signed off indefinitely. Besides, it's the holidays. And you love the islands at this time of year. It made the top of your list, I believe.'

Her smile was wide and blinding, tugging at him in places he didn't want tugged. But still, he stood in place as she swayed towards him and rose on her bare feet to slide her arms around his neck.

'Okay, then, if the boss decrees it...'

'He does.'

'Then I'm all yours.'

He tried to keep his face and voice neutral, despite the thick pounding in his veins. '*Sì*...you are.' The possessive punch in his tone was to do with the child nestling in her womb he told himself. Nothing more.

'But I bet you get homesick before I do.'

'Care to put your money where your mouth is?'

Her gaze dropped to his mouth and he fought to suppress a groan. The eyes that met his were a darker shade of green. And the voice that responded was a sultry one that dared. 'Bring it.'

CHAPTER SEVEN

'EMILIANO?'

'Hmm?' His voice was a deep, sexy rumble that drew a delicious shiver through her.

Before her, Paris was spread out in stunning electric light, the hour before the year ended and a brand new one began filling the cold night air with palpable excitement. From their bird's-eye view from the top of their magnificent five-star hotel, it truly felt as if the world itself was laid out at their feet.

She had no recollection of previous visits to Paris, although Emiliano had informed her there had been a few. It disturbed her not to remember, but the idea of falling in love all over again with the romantic city wasn't too bad, so she embraced it.

The discreet terrace heater nearby was designed to keep the worst of the chill out of the air, but Emiliano had draped a cashmere blanket over her shoulders a moment ago, then stayed close when she'd tucked his arms around her. On the low wall in front of them, her glass of sparkling water stood next to his flute of champagne and behind them, in the living room of their presidential suite, soft sounds of French Christmas carols lent even more magic to the night.

Her sense of contentment should've been complete, but she couldn't dismiss the disquiet blooming within her.

'What is it, Sienna?' he pressed after a minute had gone by.

She hesitated, unwilling to taint the night with unwelcome conversation, but she couldn't hold it in, so she blurted out the question that had been looming large in her potholed mind for the last twenty-four hours. 'Why weren't the hospital staff able to locate any of my family?'

She felt him tense and for a second she regretted voicing her question now instead of later.

His breath stirred the top of her head and he pulled the cashmere blanket tighter around her. 'Don't worry about that right now.'

She shook her head, turning in his arms to look up into his face. 'Tell me, please. Otherwise I'll imagine the worst…' Her words drifted off when she caught sight of the regret in his eyes. 'It *is* bad, isn't it?'

'Sienna…'

'Are we estranged? Was it my fault? I can't imagine falling out with every member of my family, though. Unless my family is small. Even so, it's New Year's. Why would they not want to see me at—'

'Stop.' His voice was firm. 'No, there is no estrangement. There is no abandonment because…' He stopped, his jaw flexing for a moment. 'Because there is no family. Not one I could find, anyway.'

Pain and shock robbed her of breath for a moment. 'What? Why? Did…something happen?' She almost dreaded asking as much as she dreaded the answer.

His arms tightened convulsively around her. 'This is not the type of conversation I envisioned to usher in the New Year.'

She braced her hands on his chest, shamelessly taking strength from the steady beats of his heart. 'Then let's finish it quickly.' She saw the obstinate look in his eyes and pressed harder. 'Please, Emiliano.'

'I had my investigators look into your past these last couple of weeks.'

She frowned, her disquiet growing. 'You mean, I never told you?'

His face tightened, a neutral expression sliding over his features.

'You might as well tell me everything, Emiliano. My life is one giant question mark right now. I can't help that, but I don't want to bring this one into the New Year, either.'

He remained silent for so long she thought she'd lost the argument. His chest rose and fell beneath her hands. 'We never shared our pasts with each other. We preferred it that way. So, no, I don't know enough about your history to tell you why I couldn't find any family for you.'

The words, although stated evenly, still landed with cold brutality, probably because, contrary to what she'd imagined, she was nowhere near ready for them. 'I... Oh, God... What if I don't have any?' She didn't realise she'd swayed and slumped against him until he swore under his breath and gathered her even closer.

'This was a bad idea,' he stated grimly. That peculiar note was back in his voice again, but when she stared up at him his expression remained unreadable.

She shook her head. For several minutes she couldn't speak, the sheer starkness of her existence almost too much to bear. 'I, well, I'm glad you told me...'

A rough sound rumbled from his throat. 'Are you?'

She nodded despite the abject news. 'I don't want secrets between us.'

His jaw clenched for a taut second before his arms tightened around her. 'And I don't wish anything to stand in the way of your recovery, so I reserve the right to veto any questions or demands. *Si?*' The demand was domineering.

She wanted to say yes, but a knot inside her refused to unravel. 'I can't help but think, if you hadn't been there for me when I was in hospital, I would've been alone...'

His grip tightened a fraction. 'But you are *not* alone. You are here. With me.'

She heard the words, wanted to bask in their possessive warmth, but she couldn't shake the confusion as to why she would keep secrets from this man who made her heart beat with wild desire every time he looked at her. She couldn't imagine he would let her keep something so important from him.

Unless he wasn't interested?

The question came from nowhere, slammed with force into her and left her floundering. She watched his nostrils flare, felt a new restlessness tinge the atmosphere. 'Why didn't I tell you about my past?'

He shrugged. 'Family isn't a subject either of us likes to dwell on. I left you to your reasons. Mine were…inconsequential.'

'Inconsequential?'

'*Sí*, and enough about this matter, too. I've answered your questions. Just bear in mind that, whether you do have family or not, it isn't uncommon to feel completely alone even in the largest of so-called families. It might look rosy and whole from the outside looking in, but appearances are often deceptive.' His tone held a trace of bitterness that brought her up short and bruised her heart.

She'd been firing questions at him with no regard for his own circumstances.

'Emiliano…'

She stopped when a muted roar rose from street level. Turning her head, she saw the countdown clock superimposed on the Eiffel Tower.

Thirty seconds until the old year was put to bed and a new one ushered in.

Firm hands touched her cheek, redirecting her focus to the powerful man in front of her. 'You're carrying my child. A child whose needs should come first. This is what should be at the forefront of our minds. Are you prepared to do that?'

'Of course. I want this baby. More than anything.'

'Then no more dwelling on the past, *si*? From this moment forward, we look to the future. Agreed?'

'*Dix, neuf, huit, sept, six...*'

Sienna held her breath as the clock counted out the last seconds. Exhaling in a muted rush, she nodded. 'Agreed.'

Fireworks burst into the night sky, drenching the heavens with colour as a loud cheer cannoned across the city. Eyes of dark gold held her captive, bore into hers, before drifting over her face to rest on her mouth.

'Happy New Year, *querida*,' he murmured huskily.

Her heart lurched wildly then banged hard against her ribs. 'Happy New Year, Emiliano,' she replied, her voice equally hoarse, draped with unvoiced hopes and desires. Catching one of the hands binding her, she linked it with hers and pressed them gently against her belly. 'Happy New Year, Baby Castillo.'

Emiliano inhaled sharply. After a moment, his hand freed hers to splay over her belly in a display so potently possessive, she would've protested had she not completely revelled in it. In the tumult of the past couple of days, many questions had plagued her. One she hadn't been brave enough to confront was how Emiliano felt about this unplanned pregnancy. With his words, his touch, a part of her settled. They needed to have a more in-depth conversation at some point down the line, but she was prepared to rest her mind on that score for now.

Caught in the maelstrom of emotions she couldn't name, she raised her gaze to his. One desire in particular rose to the fore, the need pounding through her as forcefully as the pyrotechnic display thundering overhead. Locking her fingers at his nape, she pressed herself against him. 'Kiss me,' she begged.

A strangled sound emitted from his throat a second before he shook his head. 'No, Sienna.' His voice held pained reluctance.

Had she not felt the evidence of his formidable need against her belly, or the blazing hunger in his eyes, she would've thought he didn't want her. She could only conclude that his reluctance stemmed from somewhere else.

'It's okay. I'm not fragile. I passed all the tests the doctor put me through this evening.' Despite her protests, Emiliano had refused to leave London without a doctor and nurse accompanying them on his private jet to monitor her every twinge. After much negotiation, they'd agreed on a check-up every twelve hours.

A grimace tautened his face. 'Nevertheless, I don't think you should—'

'A kiss isn't going to harm me, Emiliano. Not when it'll make me…happy.'

A deep shudder shook his frame. *'Dios mío. Esto es el infierno.'*

This is hell.

She didn't stop to ponder how she understood his words. Or why a simple kiss was so hard for him. It probably had something to do with the fact that nothing between them felt simple. All she knew was that he was still denying her a kiss. And she was being consumed by the desire for it.

'Please. Isn't it tradition to kiss the one you're with at the stroke of the New Year? I won't break, I promise.'

A short bark of self-deprecating laughter rolled out before he inhaled deeply. 'You don't know what you're asking.'

'Yes, I do. And I'm not taking no for an answer.'

She'd barely finished speaking when he gave a pained groan, spiked his hands into her hair and slanted his mouth over hers. Hot, potent and more exhilarating than the fireworks still echoing around them, Emiliano's kiss was intensely thrilling and completely addictive. With a deep, thankful moan, she opened her mouth beneath his, granting him the possessive entry he sought without hesitation.

He kissed her with an expertise that resonated all the way to her toes and back up again. When his tongue danced with hers, the flames—already stoked high with anticipation—rose higher, threatening to consume her.

Breasts aching, sensitive nipples peaked with shameless arousal, it was all she could do to whimper and hold on as sensation soared. Sienna wondered if it was the hormones raging through her that made this kiss more special than any she'd shared with Emiliano before, but by the time the need for oxygen drove them apart she was trembling from head to toe. Trembling and on the point of tears.

'Sienna?' A thick vein of alarm threaded his voice as he stared down at her.

Chagrined, she brushed away a tear. 'It's…I'm okay. Hell, I don't even know why I'm crying.'

'Maldición,' he swore thickly before he swung her up in his arms.

Striding through the opulent suite fit for a king, he entered the master bedroom.

Tugging the blanket from around her shoulders, he crouched before her and slid off her stone-coloured platform shoes. Her cream wrap-around dress, secured by a simple tie, came loose with a single pull. Sliding it off her, he tossed it onto a nearby chaise before striding into the dressing room and returning with a silk nightie.

In the bathroom, he stood next to the vanity, watching with eagle eyes as she brushed her teeth.

By the time they re-entered the bedroom, irritation was beginning to take hold.

'I can put myself to bed, Emiliano. And you can stop beating yourself up about the kiss, too. This…' she indicated her drying tears '…is just pregnancy hormones.'

He paused a second before he carried on his self-imposed task of disrobing her. 'It wouldn't have been triggered if I'd kept my hands off you,' he stated grimly.

'You've had your hands on me in one form or another since we left the hospital. You take my hand and walk me to a chair when I enter a room. You tuck my hair behind my ear when I'm talking to you and you can't see my face properly. And who dressed me tonight, despite me saying I was quite capable of putting my own dress on?'

A wave of shock washed over his features before his brows clamped in a dark frown and his features shuttered. 'You have my apologies. I'll be more careful in the future.'

She let out an exasperated breath. 'I don't want you to be careful!' Pulling back the sheets with a little more force than necessary, she slid into bed. 'I'm fine with all of it, Emiliano. I just don't want you treating me like I'm made of delicate glass because we kissed.'

'Calm down.'

'I am calm,' she said, then took another steadying breath, the corner of the luxurious bedspread twisting between her fingers. 'The way you treat me…I feel as if I'm missing something vital, which is ironic, considering I only have a fraction of my mind working correctly.'

'Your mind is fine,' he stated in a tone that said he wouldn't welcome challenge on that declaration.

She sighed, a thread of weariness weaving into her limbs despite her protest. 'We'll agree to disagree. For now. But I reserve the right to resume—and *win*—this point.'

One corner of his mouth twitched even though the forbidding expression remained. 'I don't doubt it. Your superb cognitive skills were the reason you were my vice-president of Acquisitions.'

She frowned. *'Were?'*

He froze for an infinitesimal second. '*Sí*, before your accident.'

'Oh. Right. I suppose I can't return to work now with my mind the way it is.'

His jaw clenched. 'You can't return to work because

you've been through a trauma. From which you're recovering while carrying a baby. You won't be gracing the inside of a boardroom with your presence anytime soon.'

'Is this my boss or my lover talking?' Her challenge was half-hearted, the warm sheets seducing her into sliding deeper, pulling the duvet to her chin.

'It's the man who has a vested interest in your wellbeing. The man who also intends to win his argument, and a few more besides, when the time comes.'

She didn't want to start another argument, or delve beneath the somewhat cryptic remarks, simply because her eyelids were growing heavier by the minute. And also because she'd become painfully aware that Emiliano was making no move to undress and join her in bed. He'd taken to sleeping in the adjoining bedroom, while Alfie and the medical staff slept in the suite next door.

It was a situation she'd hoped would be altered come New Year. But it seemed her hopes were to be dashed when he stared down at her for a long moment before he stepped back with a resolute expression.

'Sleep well, Sienna.'

He was gone before she could respond in kind. As, she discovered an hour later, was the sleep she'd thought would be quick in coming.

Changing positions for the umpteenth time, she replayed the evening in her mind, including the kiss, memory of which still glowed like embers inside her. Sienna wished the heat of that kiss could erase the cold reality of the past Emiliano had divulged.

There was no record of a family out there.

For all intents and purposes, and until her memory supplied her with the information, she only had Emiliano, the man she would be connected to for ever through their baby.

The man who consciously didn't want to touch her. Telling herself her condition was very much a factor and that it was early days didn't soothe the tiny prickles of anxiety within her.

Something was wrong. And, if she couldn't rely on her memory to supply her with the *whys*, she'd just have to find another way.

Emiliano threw back the cognac he'd poured for himself before settling in his study chair to place the call. He didn't dread it—he was too much of a pragmatist for that—but he wasn't relishing it, either. All he knew was that it needed to be done. The twinge of guilt that lanced him for letting Matias down was ruthlessly suppressed. He would find another way to help Graciela and make it up to his brother if...*when*... Matias emerged from his coma.

He entered the number from memory, surprised he still retained it. It was answered on the third ring.

'It's about time you called,' his father said by way of greeting.

Emiliano barely managed to stop his lip from curling. 'You forget that I am the one coming to your rescue. A little appreciation wouldn't go amiss.'

His father hesitated a moment before he spoke, and Emiliano was gratified to hear the less belligerent tone. 'We haven't heard a word from you, save a call from your assistant to say you'd be in touch. That was a week ago. We were...concerned.'

'My life doesn't stop simply because yours is in free fall.' He didn't see the need to mention his own life had been in free fall, too, from the moment he'd returned from Argentina.

He heard his father clear his throat and refocused. 'Rodrigo Cabrera has been expecting your call. He feels insulted to be kept waiting. He's being hounded by the press for an official announcement.'

'He should've thought of that before he planted his tabloid hacks to create a relationship that doesn't exist.'

'A relationship you agreed to.' He heard the definite note of panic in his father's voice.

'My only agreement was to have dinner with his daughter in the hope of convincing her to talk some sense into her father and get him to drop this whole ridiculous situation before it went any further. What I should've done was walk away then.' If he had, he wouldn't be in this situation.

'But you didn't.' The panic was much more pronounced. 'You made promises, which Cabrera wants you to honour now.'

Emiliano's hand tightened on the handset, the knowledge that he wasn't as immune to his father's distress as he'd like to be making his jaw clench. 'That is not going to happen. We need to find another way to deal with the matter of your debt.'

'Impossible. I have an agreement with Cabrera.'

'An agreement that had neither my knowledge nor consent. An agreement you forced on Matias. Did you stop to think how your selfishness would impact on him, or did you blithely sign away his life the way you're attempting to sign away mine?'

'What are you talking about?'

'Do you even know where Matias was going when he crashed?'

'Of course I know. He was on his way to conduct Castillo business—'

'No, he was on his way to the airport after ending things with his girlfriend. He destroyed his relationship with her in order to save your skin.'

The irony of the full circle his family seemed to have come would've been laughable if it wasn't so eerily spine-chilling. Except, this time, he wasn't the one who'd fallen into a coma. It was the mother of his child. The woman whose presence in his life hinged on the absence of her memories. The knot that had resided in his gut for far longer than he cared to contemplate threatened to unravel. Ruthlessly, he grappled it into place.

'Your brother understood the true meaning of family and sacrifice, whereas you don't seem to have second thoughts about breaking your—'

'Save it, old man. You lost your right to guilt me into submission a very long time ago. And don't speak of Matias in the past tense. You may have written him off, but I haven't.'

'Have some respect, boy,' his father bristled. 'You wouldn't exist without me.'

He wouldn't exist. The words struck a deep chord within him, causing his fingers to fist on his desk.

Yes, his father was responsible for bringing him into the world. Just as he himself was now responsible for another. Only, Emiliano didn't intend to be little more than a biological footnote in his child's life.

He would be more.

He didn't know how, but would be *better*. He wouldn't fail or ignore his child as he had been failed and ignored.

'Are you listening to me?'

His attention refocused, sharpened until his intent was as clear as the finest crystal. 'I'm listening and I'm hearing you, but I don't think *you* are hearing me. The deal with Cabrera as it stands doesn't work for me. He can accept my financial terms, or I'm prepared to hear him out if he has an alternative that suits me. But marrying his daughter is irrevocably off the table.'

'Why?' his father demanded.

'Because I'm getting married to someone else.'

CHAPTER EIGHT

'*BUENOS DÍAS, CARIÑO.*'

'*Buenos días, guapo. Has dormido bien?*'

Emiliano froze in surprise and stared at the woman bathed in sunlight on the terrace of his villa.

'You speak Spanish?' he asked.

A light flush tinged her cheeks before she responded hesitantly, '*Un poco, pero estoy tratando.*'

He carried on walking towards her, his senses reeling a little as he pulled out the chair and joined her at the breakfast table. In the typical style of the woman who'd managed his acquisitions with exemplary intelligence, she'd perfected the nuance and intonation of his mother tongue, and even found a way to thread sensuality through the words. 'You're more than trying,' he responded, noting the gruffness in his voice. 'You excel at it.'

She grinned before a plump segment of mango found its way into her mouth. Watching her tongue dart out to lick a drop of juice from the corner of her mouth lit an instant fire in his groin. Combined with the white bikini set clinging to her body, its existence poorly disguised by the see-through mesh sarong, he knew the next half hour would be a true test of his control.

They'd been on his private island off the coast of the Bahamas a little over a week. Each day had brought the challenge of seeing her in a different swimsuit and wrestling with the increasingly uncontrollable urge to touch her. It also hadn't gone past his notice that her costumes were getting skimpier with each passing day.

It was the reason he'd banished the villa's employees to the staff bungalow yesterday. Only Alfie was allowed into the main residence without express permission, the fact that he was gay barely giving him a pass.

'How long have you been keeping this from me?' he asked, concentrating all his efforts on pouring steaming black coffee...slowly...to take his mind off the satin-soft skin on display.

Her smile widened, still blindingly beautiful, her green eyes lighting up. 'I woke up this morning and the memory just appeared. I remembered I'd been listening to tapes, although I can't remember where I got them from or how long I've been learning. I'm guessing from your reaction that you didn't know, so... Surprise!'

The rigid tension charging through his body made him wonder how he was managing to set the coffee pot down without breaking it. 'No, I didn't know. And, yes, it's a wonderful surprise.' He paused a beat, then asked off-handedly, 'Did you remember anything else?'

Her smile dimmed then switched off completely. A vice tightened viciously around his chest. He wanted to pre-empt the words that she was about to utter with...something. But none were forthcoming. So he sat and awaited the falling axe.

'I...I know now why no one came to see me at the hospital. Besides you.'

His gaze probed her face, noted her distress. 'Tell me,' he encouraged, the need to know overcoming whatever consequences lay in his future.

Her gaze dropped. He fought the urge to nudge her delicate chin up and watched her.

'I remember my childhood. I'm an orphan, Emiliano. I was left with nuns at a children's mission in Surrey when I was a baby. My first name was folded into my baby blanket. The nuns gave me a last name.'

She gave a laugh that sounded surprisingly similar to the one that coughed up whenever he thought of his own childhood. 'I was abandoned by a mother who only stopped long enough to scribble a name she thought was appropriate for the child she didn't want to raise before disappearing.'

Her hand dropped to her stomach and her face twisted in anguish for a brief second. 'So that's my history. And now you know.'

Despite her words, the eyes that met his held a touch of vulnerability that had him going against his better judgement and capturing her chin in his hand.

'And it changes nothing. You are who you are, regardless of the mystery of your birth. Even armed with full knowledge of one's birth, there are never any guarantees of affection or acceptance.'

She blinked, her full mouth trembling for a few moments before her head rose and the strength and determination he'd glimpsed many times across his boardroom table powered her spine straight.

Nodding, she said, 'I remembered something else.'

Emiliano swallowed hard. And again. *'Qué?'* The question was a rough croak.

'Switzerland.'

'What about Switzerland?'

Troubled eyes rested on him. 'I remembered that your brother is in a coma. We went to visit him on the way back from Prague. In July...?'

It was a disgrace to feel the enormous relief that punched through him. But he'd never professed to be perfect. Relief tingling through his extremities, he picked up his cup and took a gulp of coffee. *'Sí,* that's correct.'

'Is he... Has there been any change?'

Recalling the last time she'd asked him the same question, Emiliano schooled his features before he shook his head. 'I visited him two weeks ago. There's been no change. The doctors are debating whether to try an experimental procedure to wake him.'

Her breath caught. 'Is it risky?'

'Every procedure carries an element of risk, but they think he can withstand it. His brain activity is promising. The doctors believe he should be awake by now.'

'So are they going to do it?'

He took another sip of coffee before he answered. All he tasted was bitterness. 'If I had my way, they would do it tomorrow. Matias needs to wake up and live his life. Unfortunately, my parents have to provide consent. They're... debating the matter.' The raw anger eating through him that Matias's life was wasting away because of his parents' indecision mounted.

'What? Why? I would've thought any parent would jump at the chance to see their child well.' Her genuine puzzlement and response settled something inside him he hadn't even been aware needed tending.

Or perhaps he had. His own silent floundering about his ability to be a father had also thrown up questions about the mother of his child. He didn't doubt Sienna would rise to the challenge of motherhood with the same vigour she'd brought to his company...should she choose to, once her memory returned.

And there was the other conundrum. Sienna might be excited about the pregnancy now, but what would happen in the future, when perhaps she would conclude that he fell short of the task of being a father?

Emiliano knew first-hand that love for one child didn't necessarily transmit to another. For the longest time, he'd tried to unravel that particular puzzle in his own circumstances, until he'd realised he was wasting his time.

Warm fingers touched the back of his hand, bringing him back to the present and her questions.

'Because keeping Matias the way he is now keeps him alive and safe, which is an appropriate action any parent would consider on behalf of their child. But their indecision also serves the dual purpose of elevating me to the position of temporary firstborn, which means his responsibilities become mine.'

Her eyes had been growing rounder with consternation with each utterance. 'Are you saying they're using him as a *pawn*?'

A few weeks ago, he would've given an unequivocal affirmation. 'Perhaps not deliberately, but I can't hide from the evidence that their indecision plays to their advantage while keeping him in a glass box,' he ground out through the tide of fury blanketing him. He'd yet to find a way to circumvent the current impasse with his parents. But he would. His brother deserved better than the hand his parents were dealing him.

'Has it always been like this between you and them? The distance and the…bitterness?'

'Until Matias's accident, I hadn't seen or spoken to them for over ten years. I left home the day I turned eighteen.'

'Why?' she asked softly, passing him a peeled orange before reaching for a warm croissant.

He took his time to chew and swallow, certain the dull ache in his chest was residual anger from the situation with Matias. His history with his parents was dead and buried. 'I realised very early on in life that Matias was the chosen son. That I was merely the spare, brought and paraded as and when I was needed, but otherwise there was very little use for me.'

There was no trace of a smile on her face now, only naked anguish. For him. 'Oh, Emiliano. I'm sorry,' she murmured.

Her voice soothed him. *She* soothed him. So he found himself continuing. 'I don't think they even noticed the day I left.'

Her green eyes turned stormy dark. 'That's not true. I'm sure they did.'

A long-forgotten conversation with his brother un-spooled in his mind. 'Perhaps. Matias told me once they asked about me. But they didn't care enough to pick up the phone. Not once.' He shrugged, but the gesture didn't quite flow.

'Did Matias ever try to talk you out of leaving?'

He nodded, the recollection opening a new vein of pain he'd thought healed. 'Many times in the weeks before, when I told him of my plans. I think it hurt him more to admit he was our parents' favourite. When he realised my bags were packed, and that I would leave with or without his help, he gave up.'

Her face pinched in deeper sympathy and for several moments Emiliano wondered why he hadn't told her this before, why he was choosing now to tell a story that he'd buried so deep.

It wasn't as simple as not having other things such as work or sex in the way. No, sex was very much on his mind. *Dios mío*, he only had to catch a glimpse of her chest rising and falling to feel his temperature soaring. And ever since he'd walked onto the terrace his fingers had been itching to sink into her thick, luxurious hair and kiss her the way he'd done at New Year.

But he admitted there was an openness to this version of Sienna that appealed to him. It made talking to her easier. Made him want to reach out to her... Hell, maybe be a better version of himself, too?

He mentally shrugged, took the buttered croissant she'd set in front of him and took a large bite. For a few minutes they fell into easy silence as they mulled over his revelations.

She picked up another pastry and buttered it for herself but didn't eat it. Instead, she glanced back up at him through long lashes. 'So, where did you go? What did you do after you left?'

'I'd planned on staying in Buenos Aires, finding whatever job I could. But Matias had other ideas.'

'Oh?'

'He drove me to the airport and handed me a ticket to London. He'd enrolled me in night school so I could continue my education and got me a paid internship at a financial institution.'

'Oh, my God, that's amazing.'

His throat clogged for a brief moment. '*Sí*, he was...*is*... amazing. The only thing he wanted in return was that I wouldn't forget our family, and that I would offer my help should he need it. He didn't ask for over ten years.'

'So we were both abandoned, in our own way, by those who should've cared for us,' she mused quietly, her croissant now in shredded pieces on her plate.

He hadn't taken the time to make that connection, but now he nodded, a swell of feeling widening inside him as he stared into her eyes. 'But we have risen above it, *sí*?' Her nod wasn't altogether convincing. And, when her green eyes clouded over again, he leaned towards her. 'What is it?'

'I can't help but wonder if our scars will affect our child somehow.'

He was shaking his head before she'd finished speaking, everything inside him rejecting the possibility of that notion. 'We will do better for our child, *querida*. On this you have my full promise.'

He cursed under his breath as her mouth gave the faintest tremble before tears filled her eyes. 'You're crying again.' God, he was becoming a master at stating the obvious. In his defence, he'd never been faced with a tearful Sienna in the year they'd been together. He grimly admitted that this was yet another thing that pushed him right out of his comfort zone.

She waved him away before swiping at her cheeks. 'I'm

fine. I told you, my emotions are a little heightened, that's all. And, yes, this time it's definitely your fault.'

'For throwing my unsavoury skeletons at your feet?'

She rolled her eyes, rose from her chair and slid sinuously into his lap. Emiliano stifled a desperate groan as her arms wound themselves around his neck. She smelled of lemongrass sunscreen and pure, intoxicating woman. And he was drowning in the hunger that shook through him. 'For easing my fear that this baby isn't going to regret having me as a mother one day.'

Another knot unravelled. 'Your concern means you care, so he will be lucky to call you Mama,' he replied gruffly, the hands he'd ordered to stay at his sides somehow finding their way up her thighs and over her hips.

She bent forward until their noses were almost touching. '*She* will be equally blessed to have you as her father,' she whispered, another well of tears filling her eyes.

He gently brushed them away with his thumb. 'Enough with these tears, *querida*. I don't like them.'

'Okay, Emiliano, I'll do my best not to bother you with my unsightly tears,' she said, her breath washing over his lips. The plump curves of her mouth were a lesson in raw temptation. As were the nipples peaking beneath her flimsy bikini top.

'There's nothing unsightly about you, *guapa*.'

'The scars on my skull tell a different story, but I'm prepared to let you win this argument. *Gracias, hermoso.*'

Emiliano decide there and then that, with her soft voice echoing in his head, he would encourage her learning so she would only speak to him in Spanish. He also decided for the second time since he sat down that he was fine with not being perfect. Because *not* kissing her right then, denying himself the pleasure of her soft lips, was one ask too far.

So he lowered his head and tasted the sweetest nectar

known to man. Her response was unfettered and immediate. As if, like him, she'd been caught in the talons of hunger for far too long. He took her mouth the way other, more ravenous parts of him wanted to take her body.

She whimpered, moaned and pressed closer until a red haze of arousal overtook his entire world.

He needed to stop before things went too far. He'd come out here to discuss their future with her. A discussion that required delicate handling. Following the words he'd spoken to his father—words he hadn't realised had been on the tip of his tongue before he'd spoken them, but had known immediately that he would act upon—he'd been biding his time until Sienna was stronger. The week on his island had worked wonders for her, a brief bout of morning sickness lasting a few short days before abating.

He'd thought long and hard about waiting for her memory to return before going ahead with his plans, but the doctor had reiterated that they were dealing with a piece of string of indeterminate length where that was concerned.

And, with each day that passed, Emiliano was losing the conviction that waiting was the better option. Whatever the future held, they were having this baby. And, before the issue with his fake engagement had broken them apart, they'd been content together. He wasn't willing to accept that that was gone for ever.

So he kissed her, infusing his need into the act until she was breathless and pliant against him. Only then did he pull away to look into her desire-drugged eyes.

Yes, he was doing the right thing.

'I have to touch base on a few things this morning, but come out on the boat with me this evening,' he invited, after taking another all-too-brief kiss.

A smile lit up every dark place inside him. 'Where are we sailing to this time?'

His hands moved from her hair to her shoulders, down

her warm, silky skin, and it was all he could do not to pick her up and find the nearest bed.

All in good time.

'It's a surprise.'

The package he'd requested had arrived from Turks and Caicos late last night. The rest of the preparation would be underway soon enough. Before then, he needed to step up his investigations on Cabrera, find a weak spot to use to his advantage.

He rose with Sienna still in his arms. It disturbed him that she still weighed much less than he was used to, but the staff were under strict instructions to reverse that situation. And so far she wasn't objecting to being fattened up.

'Where are you taking me?'

He didn't miss the slightly breathless anticipation in her voice. He nearly altered his course, only the stern voice warning him to do this right keeping his compass true.

'To your second-favourite spot on the island.'

Although she made a tiny face when he rounded the terrace and made a beeline for the pool, she laughed. 'And my first is?'

'A certain king-sized bed, of course. Your happy snores shake the whole house at night.'

She thumped his shoulder playfully as he set her down at the lounger next to the table which had been set up with a cooler of drinks and several snacks. He knew Alfie would be out like clockwork every hour to make sure she didn't want for anything.

Taking a step from him, she untied the knot and dropped her sarong.

'Madre de Dios, tener compasión.'

Her very shameless, very feminine grin as she caught her hair up to secure it in a loose bun atop her head told him she relished her effect on him and wasn't interested in the mercy he pleaded for. Her gaze dropped to the very visible, very inconvenient evidence of his arousal before rising to his. He was gratified to see her quickening breath.

'*Hasta la vista, cariño.*'

She bit her lip as she turned away and spread her delicious body out on the lounger. He needed to leave, head back inside, but he stayed for one more look. And, as his gaze paused on the barest hint of roundness at her abdomen, that well of feeling in his chest expanded.

Yes, he was doing the right thing. All he had to do now was to secure her agreement.

At the stroke of six, Sienna heard a light knock on her bedroom door. She turned away from the mirror, loving the way the loose white sleeveless dress floated around her body before the hem dropped to her ankles. On her feet, she wore gold flip-flops, her deeper desire to go barefoot overridden by common sense. The path around the villa to the jetty where the launch would take them to Emiliano's yacht was a little gravelly. She couldn't risk twisting an ankle or falling on her behind.

Flipping her hair over her shoulders, she quickly secured the gold hoop earrings and answered the door.

Alfie stood on the threshold dressed in a smart white tunic and dark trousers.

'I've come to escort you to your date,' he said, offering his arm.

Although his smile was easy now, she'd caught a questioning look in his eyes in the past week which she'd shrugged off. She knew he and the rest of the staff had been given an abbreviated version of her illness and instructed to take special care of her. They weren't intrusive and every assistance offered to ensure she took care of her baby's health was welcome, so she didn't mind.

He conversed easily with her as they went down the long hallway to the grand staircase leading to the stunning hallway. Solid light oak floors polished to the highest gleam beautifully complemented whitewashed walls decorated with nautical blues and greens that gave the extensive luxury villa a fresh vibrancy. Every glass door and shuttered window was built to slide aside during the day to let in the salt-tinged breeze from the sea. According to Emiliano, the first time she'd set foot on Castillo Island, she'd remarked that the inside of the villa made her feel as though she were walking on sunshine and she couldn't help but smile now as she walked outside and inhaled the fresh, clean air.

Along the path that led past the garden to the beach, small flame lamps had been positioned to guide their way. Crickets chirped among the colourful plants, and palm trees swayed softly overhead. Although her gaze touched on and absorbed the heady paradise surrounding her, her senses leaped eagerly, fast-forwarding to the evening ahead.

To Emiliano.

She'd spent most of the day outside but her thoughts had dwelt very much on the innermost secrets he'd revealed to her and the secret hope in her heart that she wasn't afraid to admit to herself any longer.

She wanted Emiliano. Wanted to be with him, to claim him in the most primal way possible. It had nothing to do with the baby and everything to do with the fact that she recognised and accepted her deeper feelings for him.

She didn't know whether she was ready to put a label on how she felt or even probe it past mere acceptance. For now, she was going to acknowledge its existence. Maybe nurture it with care and attention.

Emiliano stood waiting at the end of the twenty-foot-long jetty. He wore casual white trousers teamed with stylish loafers. The sleeves of his open-necked white linen shirt were folded back to reveal strong muscular arms bronzed by the sun. At some point the breeze had ruffled his hair, lending him a raffish air that threatened to blow her composure to smithereens.

Intense eyes tracked her progress from path to launch, his hand extending to her as she reached him.

He took both of her hands in his and kissed each cheek. Her heart tripped over itself as he shamelessly inhaled her scent before tucking her hair back to rasp in her ear, *'Buenas noches*, Sienna. You look breathtaking.'

Suddenly tongue-tied, she smiled and murmured, 'Thank you,' as Alfie readied the launch.

They didn't have far to go, only a mile or so to where Emiliano's superyacht was anchored in deeper waters. The vessel was a stunning masterpiece, its sleek white-and-silver lines spotlighted by coloured lights that magnified its beauty in the early-evening sun. She'd been on board twice since they arrived and each time she hadn't failed to be awed by the craftsmanship.

She hadn't made a 'wow' list yet, but she was sure the yacht would make the top ten. Of course, the item that would top that particular list would be the man whose hand rested on her waist to guide her up a short flight of stairs to the middle deck. There at the open-air end a candlelit table had been set, complete with crystal goblets and sterling silverware.

A member of staff hovered nearby. At Emiliano's nod, he stepped forward with a tray holding two coconut drinks. Accepting the drink, she sipped, giving a pleased little moan as exotic flavours exploded on her tongue.

She was about to take another sip when she felt a slight jolt. They were moving. About to ask where they were headed, she remembered it was a surprise. So she followed Emiliano when he took her hand and walked her to the railing, enjoying her drink as they sailed towards the setting sun.

'It's so beautiful here,' she murmured in hushed awe.

'Yes, it is.'

She turned and looked at him. His gaze was on the horizon, but it met hers a second later, his lips curving in a smile that tugged wildly at her heart.

'I take it then that you're not homesick yet?'

The urge to blurt out that she would never be homesick as long as she was with him was caught back at the last moment. Her feelings were still new and untried. She didn't want to risk exposing them to scrutiny yet.

'No, not yet. But I have been wondering about having a scan, though.'

His gaze sharpened. 'Is something wrong?'

She shook her head quickly. 'No, but according to the pregnancy books I'm due for one about now.' Since learning that, she'd been quietly excited about hearing her child's heartbeat for the first time.

Emiliano's fierce expression eased a touch. 'If that's what you want, we don't have to leave. I can have that organised for you here.'

She grinned. 'Careful, or you'll have me thinking you want to keep me barefoot and pregnant here for ever.'

Tawny eyes raked her from head to foot before he shrugged. 'The idea isn't unappealing.'

She laughed. Although he joined her, she caught a serious look in his eyes that twanged a brain cell. Unbidden, she was thrown back to their night in Paris, when she'd sensed an undercurrent in his mood. After searching his expression and seeing nothing but heated interest, she shrugged off the feeling.

As they finished their drinks, they settled into easy conversation, which continued when they sat down to dinner. Chilli-and-lemon-flavoured grilled calamari sharpened her appetite for the chicken and rice dish that followed.

She looked up in surprise when Emiliano stood after their plates were cleared away.

'Don't look so disappointed, *belleza*. We're having dessert over there.'

She followed his pointing finger to a deserted beach where a wide picnic blanket was illuminated by two tall, flaming lamps. Below them, Alfie was readying the launch. She held on to Emiliano's hand as he guided her back downstairs and into it. A few minutes later, he was swinging her into his arms and treading shallow water towards the beach. Alfie deposited the cooler he'd carried ashore before returning to the yacht.

Sienna turned in a circle, looking for other signs of humanity.

'Why do I get the feeling we're all alone?' she asked Emiliano.

One corner of his mouth tilted upward. 'Because we are.'

'Who owns this place?'

'I do.'

'You own two islands in the Bahamas?'

He shrugged. 'I own five, but who's counting?' Reaching into the cooler, he extracted a single item.

She lost interest in the subject of islands and rushed to the blanket. 'Oh, my God.'

He gave a low, sexy laugh. 'I thought the ice cream would capture your interest.'

She grabbed a spoon, impatiently waiting as he tore off the top of the ice-cream tub. 'I don't know how I'm going to live without these when we go back.'

Again she caught a hint of something in his eyes before it disappeared again. 'You won't have to. Everything you crave, you only have to ask for and it'll be yours.' He held out the mango-and-caramel concoction to her and she dove in.

They ate in silence until she couldn't manage another mouthful. After setting the cooler to one side, Emiliano pulled her close.

All evening, she'd been secretly terrified that he would reintroduce his no-touching policy. Relief had her melting into his arms.

'Thank you for tonight. It's been wonderful.'

'De nada, querida.'

Sensing the quiet tension in him, she raised her head to meet his eyes. 'But there's something else, isn't there?'

He nodded. 'Yes.'

A vein of apprehension threatened her bliss. 'What is it?'

'We agreed today that we both wanted the best for this child, *sí*?'

She nodded a touch warily. 'Of course.'

'In that case, I think we should make the ultimate commitment.'

Her heart swan-dived from dizzying heights before taking up extreme drumming lessons against her ribs. Telling herself to keep breathing, she pulled away to look deeper into his eyes, make sure her ears weren't deceiving her.

'The ultimate commitment?'

His eyes darkened as he nodded, the flames from the lamps leaping in the gold depths as he reached into his pocket. The black velvet box bore a distinct, portentous logo. But she was more interested in the words falling from his lip. Words that made her jaw drop.

'Yes, Sienna. I'm asking you to marry me.'

CHAPTER NINE

'MARRY YOU?' SHE didn't need clarification. Not really. She just wanted to make sure she wasn't dreaming.

'Yes. Unless the idea is unsavoury to you?' The tension hadn't left his body. In fact, he was even edgier.

Sienna frowned. 'Of course not. At least, I don't think so. God, I really hate that I can't remember...'

He stared at her for a handful of seconds before he gave a decisive nod. 'Ask me what you want to know and I'll tell you.'

She rose onto her knees on the blanket and faced him. 'Have we ever discussed marriage before, even in passing?'

His jaw flexed for a second. 'No.'

Her gaze fell to the box clutched in his fist. 'So this... is really for the baby?' The drumming in her chest slowed to a dull thudding.

Emiliano's expression shuttered. 'It's for us. A united front going forward.'

'That sounds more militaristic than...'

'Than?'

She affected a careless shrug that was purely for show. 'Than I don't know... A romantic union?'

His hand dropped and his eyes narrowed. 'You've found this lacking in some way?'

Thinking about the whole evening up till now, she answered truthfully. 'No, it hasn't been lacking.' But something didn't sit right. With her memory still on vacation she didn't know how well to trust her gut. The Emiliano she could remember wasn't an openly affectionate guy, although this last week he'd shown her a different side to himself. A side she liked even more than the previous version. And, as proposals went, she was sure very little could top the magical production he'd put on for her this evening. And yet...

'You require more flowery words, perhaps?' His tone had a tight clip to it that sent a tiny shiver through her.

'Not unless they are meant, no.'

He expelled a rough breath. 'I thought we were on the same page this morning.'

'We were. We *are*. But this...'

'Your future doesn't accommodate such a commitment to me?'

'Don't put words in my mouth, Emiliano.'

He shoved his free hand through his hair. 'We are compatible in and out of the bedroom. We're dedicated to doing the best for our child. Every other obstacle can be overcome.'

Put like that, Sienna had no counterargument. Except the reality of the feelings locked within her heart. But they, like this new facet of her relationship with Emiliano, were new and untested. Didn't she owe it to herself to nurture them and see if they blossomed into something worth treasuring? Especially if her child stood to benefit, too?

Her gaze fell to the jewellery box, her heart resuming its wild hammering. Slowly, she licked her dry lips, the step she was about to take thrilling and terrifying all at once.

'Sienna?' he asked, mirroring her stance and rising onto his knees.

'What if I regain my memories and remember that you snore louder than I do?'

She expected him to laugh or shrug off her joke. But his eyes remained dark and intense. Cupping her elbows, he stared down at her for a long moment, before sliding his hands up her bare arms.

'When your memories return I hope you will give me

a chance to offer up my better qualities and plead my case on any faults you find.'

She opened her mouth, ready with an answer, because she couldn't think of any further reasons not to take the next step that promised more of everything she found enthralling about him. 'Okay.'

He seemed to stop breathing, his hands gripping her tighter as he drew closer. 'Say the words, Sienna. I need to hear you say the words.'

Swallowing, she rested her hands on his solid chest, taking strength from the heart thundering beneath her touch. 'Yes, Emiliano. I'll marry you.'

She should've known Emiliano would move with lightning speed once he had his answer. She should've known the kiss he'd delivered after she'd said yes would rock her to the foundations of her soul. She should've known the ring nestling in the box would be one of the most beautiful things she'd ever seen.

The impact of all three had her still reeling two days later as she stood in the master suite, a simple, sleeveless white gown draping her body, and two attendants who'd been ferried in from Miami fussing over how to put up her hair.

In the gardens below her bedroom, a beautiful wedding arch had been set up and a celebrant waited to perform her wedding.

Her wedding.

Emiliano's answer to her half-hearted request to wait had been, 'What for? There's no one besides Matias I wish to have at my wedding. And I am all *you* need.' The arrogant but true statement had knocked the wind out of any argument. The knowledge that he stood as a solid buffer between her and abject loneliness warmed her heart.

Enough for her to give her agreement when he'd pressed for an immediate wedding.

Now, she stared at the stunning engagement ring adorning her finger. Contrary to his denunciation of flowery words, the ring spoke volumes with its huge heart-shaped diamond and similarly shaped gems set in cascading layers on either side of the platinum band. She hadn't been able to stop staring at it since Emiliano placed it on her finger. And, within the hour, an even deeper symbol of commitment would be joining it.

She dragged her gaze from the sparkling gem and huffed beneath her breath. 'Leave it loose.'

The attendants stared at her. 'What?' the older one finally asked.

'Emiliano likes my hair loose so let's just brush it out and be done with it.' She tagged on a smile to hide her impatience.

The women exchanged glances, then they both dove into their bottomless bag of tricks and emerged clutching a delicate filigree diamond tiara.

At her nod, a hairbrush was produced and her long, black hair coaxed into a gleaming waterfall before the tiara was set into place. A touch of eye make-up and lip gloss and she was ready.

Butterflies sprouted motorised wings and beat wildly in her stomach as she descended the stairs, two long-stemmed calla lilies bound together with white velvet rope clutched in her hand. Their familiar scent calmed her a little as she walked through the living room and stepped onto the terrace, but nothing could suppress her see-sawing emotions for very long.

She was joining her life with a powerful, formidable man primarily for her baby. But she couldn't deny that she was emotionally invested, as well. And that investment seemed to be growing with each passing day. It was that knowledge that rattled her the most as she stepped onto the lawn.

One look at him and everything fell away. No, not fell away. It was more like a complete overtaking of her senses. Even from across the wide expanse of green grass, his eyes hooked on to her, holding her captive, claiming her with an implacable will that reduced all her feeble fears to nonsense.

Predatory eyes gleamed, mesmerised and pulled her close as if compelling her to the altar by his sheer will alone. Seemingly between one breath and the next she was by his side, relieved of her bouquet, ready to say the words that would join them for ever.

For ever with Emiliano Castillo.

Dressed in a dove-grey suit and a white shirt, his feet planted firmly apart, he looked larger than life... An alpha in total control of his kingdom.

Her breath shuddered out. He sent her a narrow-eyed glance then caught her hand in his. Whether his touch was meant to be reassuring or to stop her from fleeing, she wasn't sure. And she wasn't given time to dwell on it.

The celebrant was clearing his throat, his Bahamian lilt marking the start of her life-changing journey. Traditional vows were exchanged, rings slid onto fingers and blessings offered.

A deep tremble overtook her as Emiliano closed the gap between them and slid strong fingers into her hair. 'You're mine now, Sienna Castillo,' he murmured against her lips, a deep relish in his tone that escalated her trembling.

'As you are mine,' she replied, somehow noting the importance of establishing equal ownership.

'*Sí*, that is exactly so.' His voice throbbed with possessive satisfaction, binding her even more strongly than the new ring on her finger.

His mouth closed over hers, hot and demanding, uncaring that they had an audience. Over the pounding in her ears, she heard applause from the gaggle of staff and attendants. Her hands found Emiliano's waist, to hold on to and to touch him.

A mere second and an eternity later, he freed her, the feral hunger in his eyes promising the main course to the starter he'd just delivered.

Champagne was poured, a glass of sparkling mineral water handed to her, congratulations offered and received. Then she was strolling beside Emiliano along their private beach, another spectacular sunset robbing her of the breath not already captured by the man whose hand imprisoned hers.

Her husband.

His jacket had been discarded a while ago and his shirtsleeves rolled up. Despite his casual attire, he remained a powerful, magnetically handsome force, commanding her attention with no effort at all. The sense of bewilderment snapping at her heels finally caught up with her in the form of a tiny hysterical giggle.

Emiliano stopped, his bare feet digging into the soft white sand next to hers. 'You find something amusing?'

She shook her head in wonder. 'I can't believe I'm married,' she said in a reverential whisper.

He circled round to face her, lifting her chin with a firm finger. 'Believe it. You're married. To me. And tonight I will make you mine again.'

This time her shiver was pure decadence coupled with anticipation of the highest kind. Desire flamed through her, setting the secret place between her legs alight.

She couldn't help the moan that broke free. He heard it. One corner of his mouth lifted in an arrogant smile. 'Are you ready, Sienna?'

'Sí, mi esposo,' she replied.

He jerked as if a powerful charge had jolted him. Catching her hand in his, he stalked up the beach. He stopped at the edge of the lawn and instructed her to lift her gown. Then, sinking low before her, he grabbed the water hose and washed the sand off her feet. Sienna didn't know if Emiliano's touch on her feet had ever felt this electrifying or whether the new dimension to their relationship was lending this night an extra enchantment. Whatever the reason, the urge to touch him grew too strong to contain. She slid her hand over one broad shoulder to his nape, then she snaked her fingers through his silky hair. He paused in his task, his head snapping up. Their gazes met. Meshed. Need pounded between them.

The hose was cast aside. Then he was on his feet again, tugging her after him once more.

White rose petals greeted their path when they stepped onto the terrace, and were crushed beneath their feet as they hurried down the hallway. At the foot of the stairs, Emiliano swept her into his arms. Effortlessly, he carried her into her suite. *Their* suite.

He stopped in the middle of the large, opulently decorated room. The French doors leading out to their private terrace had been pulled shut, but the last rays of sunshine streamed in, basking them in an orange-gold glow.

Letting go of her fingers, he stepped behind her. She felt a slight tug in her hair as he removed the tiara and set it aside. Moving her hair out of the way, he placed a single kiss at her nape, the breath feathering her skin and sending a delicious shiver coursing through her.

Hands drifted over her shoulders and down her arms to circle her wrists. Slowly, he lifted her arms above her head.

'Stay,' he commanded, tracing his fingers back down.

She stayed, her heartbeat frenzied, her every sense poised in wild anticipation.

He found and slid down the side zipper securing her

dress. The satin sheath pooled at her feet, leaving her in a silk strapless bra and matching lace panties.

Behind her, his breathing altered and turned choppy.

'*Madre de Dios*, you're so beautiful.'

'I feel beautiful. Right here. With you.'

'You're beautiful, always,' he insisted. He recaptured her hands, kissing the back of one, then the other, before he let them fall to her sides. A single tug and her bra was undone and at her feet. In the next breath, Emiliano resumed his position before her, his eyes ablaze with feral hunger as his gaze moved over her.

Sliding his fingers into her hair, he planted kisses on her forehead, her eyelids, cheeks. Everywhere but where she needed him most.

Fastening her arms around his waist, she strained towards him. 'Kiss me. Please.'

He teased the corner of her mouth. 'Ask me again. In Spanish,' he ordered in a guttural voice.

'*Bésame, por favor,*' she begged.

He granted her wish and more, strong arms wrapping her in heated muscle and hot desire as he tasted, devoured and mercilessly fanned the flames of her need.

The sun had dipped beneath the horizon by the time he lifted her off her feet and placed her on the bed. Retreating, he turned on bedside lamps. Eyes never leaving hers, he deftly undid his buttons, baring his toned, bronzed chest to her everlasting delight.

Suddenly nerves overtook her. Her recollections of making love with him were a little fragmented, the memory of how *he* made her feel more sharp than the reverse. What if he found her a disappointment? Hands twisting in the sheets, she swallowed as he kicked his trousers and boxers away and prowled onto the bed.

He became absorbed in the hand he drifted down her

body, following each caress with a kiss that almost defused the troubled questions in her mind.

Almost.

Licking her lips, she cleared her throat. 'Emiliano?'

His mouth brushed against her collarbone as he answered. *'Sí, querida?'*

A moment of silence passed when words failed her.

He raised his head and frowned. 'You look troubled. Why?'

'I'm not... Show—show me...how to please you,' she stammered.

His nostrils flared with his sharp inhalation. 'You already know how. Here—' he touched his lips to her temple '—and maybe even here...' His mouth drifted down to kiss the space over her heart. 'But rest assured in the knowledge that, if you do this to me—' catching her hand, he kissed her palm then lowered it to settle over his groin, shuddering deep when she gripped his thick, impressive length '—then you're halfway there.'

He renewed his caresses, his kiss even more passionate, his strokes a touch more rough, taut cheeks flushed with arousal as he raised himself over her body. Mouth drifting over her skin, he kissed every inch, lingering over the rosy flush of her ultrasensitive nipples.

She cried out, one hand tangling in his hair to hold him there for a little while longer. Need crested high. Higher. Just when she believed she'd lose her mind if he tugged on her one more time, he freed her to continue his erotic exploration.

His hands stroked reverently over her womb, his eyes taking on a glaze of wonder as he lowered his head to place a kiss on her abdomen.

Tears she'd sworn not to shed filled her eyes. Quickly, she blinked them away, unwilling to spoil the moment. Impatient hands drew off her panties, then she was bare before his heated eyes. Parting her wider, he stroked her, growling in blatant hunger, before lowering his head to deliver the most intimate of kisses.

With his skilled tongue and deft fingers, Emiliano brought her to completion. She was still basking in delicious aftershocks when he kissed his way back up her body. She read the naked intent in his eyes, but she didn't want this to be one-sided. Raising herself onto her elbows, she nipped his firm lower lip, then used his momentary surprise to reverse their positions. His raised eyebrows nearly eroded her nerves.

But his potent scent drew her, tempted her to lower her head to his washboard torso, to attempt to deliver a fraction of the pleasure he'd just bestowed on her.

She dropped an open-mouthed kiss on his pecs. Warm and faintly salty from the sea breeze, he tasted like vitality itself. Next, she flicked her tongue over one flat nipple.

He bucked wildly against her. *'Dios mio,'* he cursed thickly.

She froze, her breath stilling with alarm. 'Did I do something wrong?'

He gave a rough groan. 'You did something right, *belleza*,' he rasped. 'So very right.'

Flush with feminine power, she repeated the caress, again and again, until not-so-steady hands bore her back onto the bed.

The eyes that met hers were the stormiest she'd ever seen. They held hers captive. Parting her thighs, he guided himself to her heated entrance.

Slowly, inch by delicious inch, absorbing her every gasp and shiver, he entered her. Fully seated inside her, he held himself there, their breaths mingling.

'Amante, you feel sublime.'

She wanted to answer. To say more. So much more. But

the indescribable feelings cascading through her robbed her of breath. That was even before he started to move.

He possessed her completely, each thrust stamping his ownership of her. Sienna could only hold on, senses and heart soaring as pleasure mounted.

She crested the wave first, but Emiliano was hard on her heels. A series of rough groans preceded hot Latin words that touched her soul and prolonged her bliss.

He was still murmuring low, deep words to her when her body cooled and she drifted off to sleep, curled up against his warmth.

Sienna wasn't sure what prompted her awake. Perhaps it was the tension vibrating off Emiliano's frame even from across the room. Or maybe it was the disturbing dreams where she'd tried repeatedly, futilely, to cling to his hand as they weathered a storm.

Whatever it was, her heart was hammering with a very different sensation from the one she'd gone to bed with when she sat up suddenly.

'What's wrong?'

He jerked around, the fingers he'd been spiking through his hair dropping to his side.

He didn't answer immediately. She got the feeling he was trying to find the right, precise words.

'Is it Matias?'

He shook his head. 'No. There's a situation in Argentina. One that I need to deal with personally.'

His parents. 'When will you return?'

Dark brows furrowed. 'Return?'

'I'm assuming you want to go on your own?'

The statement seemed to take him aback. Slowly, he walked back to bed, shedding his briefs along the way. Sliding into bed, he pulled her into his arms, tunnelling his fingers into her hair. 'On the contrary, I think it's time we faced the world. Together.'

CHAPTER TEN

THEY LEFT THE island three days later, Emiliano taking the time to make sure the information he'd received regarding Rodrigo Cabrera and his business practices was accurate. He wasn't ashamed to admit he'd deliberately delayed triple-checking his facts because, having finally allowed himself the ultimate indulgence of making love to his wife, he hadn't been in a hurry to abandon his marriage bed.

But the debt he owed his brother needed to be fulfilled. And he was done with his parents and Rodrigo Cabrera imagining they could call the shots on his and Matias's lives. They needed to be dealt with, quickly and decisively.

He ended the conference call on his private jet and re-entered the main lounge.

Sienna was curled up on the large sofa with a cashmere throw tucked around her. The book she'd been reading was propped on her chest, her delicate lashes resting against her cheeks as she slept. Disposing of the book, he took the seat next to her, his hand reaching out almost of its own accord to tuck a swathe of hair behind her ear.

For a moment, he wondered whether he'd worn her out with his lustful demands since their wedding night. Then he recalled with satisfaction her equally fervent responses.

If anyone had told him three months ago that they were capable of achieving another level of carnal intimacy, he would've dismissed it out of hand. The past three days had proved conclusively otherwise. But, while he was more than pleased with their activities in the bedroom, Emiliano was becoming aware that intimacy was creeping in elsewhere. He felt unsettled when she was out of his sight;

her laughter made his heart race in ways he couldn't quite describe.

Last night, when a nightmare had disturbed her sleep, he'd lain awake with her, talking long into the night about their hopes for their child. In the past, his conversation with Sienna had mostly circled around work and broad outside interests.

Those quiet hours together had brought a certain…contentment. One he wasn't used to. One he wasn't sure he could trust not to get in the way of logical thinking in future.

Because there was still the matter of the weeks they'd been apart to deal with when her memories returned. He might prefer this softer, more open version of Sienna, but there were no guarantees she would remain the same woman. No guarantees that her feelings would remain mutual. His child's legitimacy was safeguarded—not really necessary in this modern world, he knew, but still a firm foundation on which to build a life. And Emiliano was certain that a little foundation was better than none. Without Matias's support underpinning his own attempt at a new start in life, Emiliano wouldn't have been the man he was today.

Which meant that while he could lose himself in his wife's arms every now and then, getting used to it—or, worse, imagining he could rely on any unknown feelings she might have—was dangerous.

'You're thinking far too hard, *cariño*,' her sleep-soft voice murmured.

Despite the severe caution he'd just placed on his floundering emotions, Emiliano experienced a buzz at the effortless endearment and an even deeper thrill when sultry green eyes connected with his.

'I'm strategizing,' he replied. 'Go back to sleep.'

She made a face and sat up. 'Your game face just scared

away any notion of sleep. Tell me what you're strategizing about. Maybe I can help.'

He forced his body not to tense, and again momentarily wished he hadn't been so hasty to let her leave the insulated safety of his island. Looking away from her face, he chose his words carefully.

'My parents got themselves involved with the clichéd unsavoury businessman who was supposed to be a friend. They entered a deal with him hoping to make maximum profit with minimum output. Elite polo outfits are difficult to break into in Argentina. Rodrigo used his family friendship with my parents to gain a foothold, then cut them out, giving them the option to buy in again at a steep price. They embezzled from their own company to save themselves from bankruptcy.'

She made a disgusted sound. 'That's the definition of a recipe for disaster.'

'Exactly. My father would deny it to his last breath, of course, but he doesn't have the first clue about business. His strategy for dealing with this problem has been wrong from the very start.'

Intelligent eyes rested on him. 'But you have a way?'

'Of course. There is always a way, if you take the time to look.'

Her laugh was low, sexy, incendiary to his senses. 'I'm glad I'm not facing you across the boardroom table.'

He rose from his seat, crossed to the sofa and slid in next to her. 'It would be a delight to have you facing me. I could savour the thought of what I would do to you once I won.'

One sleek eyebrow curved upward. 'Really? By the time I *let* you win, you'd probably be too worn out to follow through.'

Something swelled in his chest, the way it did lately whenever they were immersed like this in conversation. 'Is that a challenge to my manhood?'

Faint colour tinged her cheeks as her gaze dropped to his thighs, but she tried to project an air of nonchalance. 'I'm just stating a fact. I don't need my memories to tell me I'm no slouch in the boardroom.'

He wisely conceded the argument. 'You're no slouch anywhere.'

A wide smile transformed her face. 'Thank you.'

From then, it seemed the most natural thing in the world to lean in and kiss the full, tempting mouth. And carry on kissing her until a throat cleared nearby.

He turned to find Alfie, hovering with a tray.

Sienna groaned half-heartedly. 'Between Alfie and all the cooks you have stationed at your residences, I'm going to get hopelessly fat.'

'It's a privilege to care for you while you care for our child.'

Had he not been totally absorbed by the sunlight slanting through the window onto her face, he would've missed the bruised hurt that momentarily clouded her eyes.

He frowned inwardly, wondering where he'd made a misstep. But then her gaze swept up and she was smiling at Alfie as he set out her meal.

Excusing himself, because he wanted every single cog in place before he landed in Buenos Aires, he returned to the conference area. The last time he'd flown to his homeland, he'd been woefully unprepared, and that had cost him. He didn't intend it to happen a second time.

For the next four hours, he worked. But, although his business brain sifted meticulously through facts and figures, his subconscious couldn't dismiss the look he'd seen in Sienna's eyes. His mention of the baby—had that been wrong? He didn't think so. They'd talked openly about their child. They'd talked about him. About Matias. But not about much else... Not about her.

The pen he'd been bouncing in his hand froze. Did she

feel neglected? In a bid to follow the doctor's orders—
and, yes, perhaps selfishly to keep the problem-free status
quo—was he in danger of making her feel the loneliness
she thought was behind her?

Frowning, he rose from his desk and stood at the entrance of the short galley that led to the living area. She
was still seated on the sofa, legs curled underneath her,
her book back in her hand. Beauty and sharp intelligence
shone from her face and that peculiar sensation in his chest
grew as he stared at her.

Sensing his gaze, she raised her head. Smiled.

Although the smile transformed her face, Emiliano
caught the shadows in her eyes. He wanted to tell himself it was nothing, but the fine hairs prickling his nape
told him it was something. *Something* that needed to be
dealt with.

But first, he needed to come clean. Ensure their marriage held no secrets.

Sienna was strong. Had been growing stronger still
with each passing day. They would talk things through,
he would admit his faulty choices and they would move on.

'Emiliano?' Her head was tilted and she was staring at
him with questions in her eyes.

He started towards her, then cursed under his breath
when his co-pilot emerged from the cockpit to announce
they would be landing in fifteen minutes.

Taking his seat next to her, he ensured they were both
buckled in. 'Later, *querida*. We'll talk later, when this is
all over, yes?'

Her nod was wary, the shadows under her eyes a little
more pronounced. The nightmares she'd experienced in
the last two days had clearly taken their toll. Or could it
be something else?

Yes, it was most definitely time to clear the air once and
for all. But first, he had to deal with Cabrera.

What he'd planned might take a little time, depending on how obstinate his opponent chose to be.

He planned to be quick and merciless, but he didn't intend to be in Argentina one minute longer than necessary. He had a life to live and a wife to plan it with.

The mansion in Cordoba—rarely used, according to Emiliano—had its own lake and man-made waterfall that dropped dramatically onto rocks in enthralling fashion. The orange-roofed, whitewashed residence was large enough to house several families, two additional wings having been added when he'd purchased it.

The whole property seemed to go on for acres and acres, even from the bird's-eye view of the helicopter circling to land on the manicured lawn.

'Why did you want to make it bigger?' she asked him.

To her surprise he seemed a touch embarrassed, but the look was quickly replaced by his customary self-assured shrug. 'I was newly successful and a little cocky and, yes, I wanted the world to know it. Contrary to popular belief, size does matter.'

She searched his face and saw the emotion he was trying to hide. 'You wanted your parents to finally see you, witness your success and acknowledge their shortcomings,' she offered softly, having discovered that talking with him about his past helped ease the bitterness she sometimes glimpsed in his eyes.

She also selfishly used their talks to work through her own emotions about her mother's motivation for abandoning her. She would never know the true reason, but she was beginning to accept that not everyone was cut out to accept the huge responsibility of caring for another life, even one they'd brought into the world. Emiliano's parents hadn't abandoned him, but they might as well have. That new kinship between them strengthened her even more than before. Where she'd been brave enough to face the world on her own, and thrive, it warmed her to know she didn't have to face every single obstacle on her own.

But it didn't stop her heart aching for Emiliano, for what he'd been through, every cell in her body wishing she could take his pain away.

His jaw flexed for a second before she got another shrug. 'Like I said, I was cocky. And misguided.'

'You were reaching out, the best way you knew how. Don't regret that you tried.'

His gaze searched hers for several heartbeats, before he exhaled and nodded. 'Enough about that. Come, I'll show you around.'

There was much to show. Swimming pool, stables, an internal courtyard with meticulously tended potted plants, an extensive wine cellar, countless bedrooms, a tennis court and even a tiny stone bridge over the narrowest part of the swan-inhabited lake.

To one side of the large outer patio, there was a *quincho* complete with double barbecues and roasting pits. Vintage saddles hung on the walls along with old black-and-white photos of gauchos. The wear on the saddles indicated they'd been well used at one point. Everywhere she looked, she saw evidence of past care and present attention. Emiliano hadn't bought a property to flaunt in his parents' faces, he'd invested in a potential home bursting with history.

It broke her heart that a place clearly intended to be lived in and loved had been left maintained but essentially abandoned. 'When was the last time you came here?'

'It's been two years. But Matias used it when he visited the city.'

She smiled. 'I'm glad. It feels wrong somehow for this place not to be lived in.'

He sent her a puzzled glance before leading her back

inside. Ochre tiled floors perfectly balanced white walls and arched windows.

Their suite repeated the same theme with a massive four-poster bed made of dark oak and laid with a rich, multihued spread.

Tugging her to where he stood, he began to undo the buttons of her yellow sundress. She thought about protesting that she could take care of her own undressing, but the wide yawn that overtook her put paid to that.

Once his own clothes were taken care of, she followed him into the bathroom, keeping her ogling to a few dozen stares. In the shower, she braced her hands on the wall and let him wash her, wrap her in a warm towel and lead her to bed. Her eyelids were drooping by the time he stepped back. 'Dinner will be served after you've had your rest. I'm not sure when I'll be back. Don't wait up for me.'

She nodded drowsily, the sleep that had eluded her for the past few nights determined to drag her under now. 'Go slay 'em.'

Cool arrogance glittered in his tawny eyes. 'I fully intend to,' he replied, his voice attaining an edge of steel. Bending, he touched his lips to her temple. 'Sleep well.'

She didn't.

In fact the pattern continued for nearly a week. With Emiliano fully immersed in the situation with his parents, she was left pretty much to her own devices. She would swim, visit the horses in the stables and potter around the herb garden that the housekeeper, Blanca, tended with meticulous care. All activities designed to provide the exercise she needed and, hopefully, grant her a good night's rest.

But barely an hour after going to bed she would jerk awake, sharp, dark images piercing through her subconscious and transforming into physical pain. On the seventh night in a row, she lay in the dark, her heart hammering as she tried to breathe through the ache in her head. After endless minutes, the pain began to subside.

Rising, she shrugged on a dressing gown and made her way to the kitchen. Emiliano was out at yet another meeting and the staff had retired.

Fetching a glass of water, she sipped as she wandered through the house, gratefully noting her headache had retreated to a dull throb. She eventually ended up in the inner courtyard, taking a seat before the low firepit that warmed the cool night air. When Alfie found her a few minutes later and offered to bring her a snack, she shook her head.

She had no appetite. And she was finding it increasingly difficult to shake off the sense of déjà vu crawling over her. Realising these past few days was the first time she'd been on her own without Emiliano nearby sent a jolt of alarm through her.

She'd already acknowledged that her feelings were getting troublingly intense when it came to her husband. The idea that craving him was manifesting in other ways made her heart lurch before she pursed her lips.

No. She wasn't a feeble, wilting flower unable to function without her man by her side. She didn't need to be told she'd risen to the position of a vice-president at Castillo Ventures through anything other than sheer grit and determination.

All this…anxiety bubbling beneath her skin was just a natural reaction to readjusting to the real world. Castillo Island had been a perfect, heady paradise. But not a place she could realistically stay for ever.

With that thought in mind, she rose and followed the sounds of crockery to the kitchen. Alfie turned at her entrance.

'Did you need something?' he asked.

'A pen and pad, please, if you have any handy.'

His smile widened as he opened a nearby drawer and took out the items. 'Is it time for a new list?' he asked, then he visibly checked himself. 'I'm sorry.'

She shook her head. 'Don't be. Emiliano has already told me about my list-making habits.'

She noted the relief on his face as she pulled out a stool at the kitchen island and sat down. Her first list consisted of baby names divided into male and female columns. It didn't escape her notice that the top ones were Spanish.

Next she made a list of things a baby would need.

At some point, Alfie slipped a plate of food in front of her. The grilled chicken cutlets and herb potato salad was half finished by the time she'd finished her third list.

Somewhere in the house, a clock chimed eleven o'clock. Her mind started to drift to Emiliano. Resolutely, she pulled it back.

But her husband was intent on making his presence felt despite his absence. Because on the pad in front of her, his name was written in bold letters and circled beneath it she'd written 'don't fall in love.'

She was back in bed but wide awake when she heard the crunch of tyres on gravel. Pretending she was asleep was childish and beneath her, although she did contemplate it for an absurd second.

The truth was she'd been craving elusive oblivion since her subconscious had blurted what her heart feared—that falling in love with Emiliano would be her undoing. Her panic that it may already be too late, that she was in all probability more than halfway there, was what had kept her body poised on the brink of full-blown panic.

Footsteps approached. She sat up, an intrinsic vein of courage stopping her from cowering away from her fears.

Emiliano entered and froze at the sight of her. For a few charged seconds, he stared at her, then a slow smile curved his mouth, the palpable tension blanketing him easing a touch.

'I meant it when I said don't wait up. But I do like the idea of you waiting up in bed for me.'

Despite his easy words, grim lines bracketed his mouth. Gleefully pushing aside her own disturbing emotions, she focused on his.

'Did everything go according to plan?'

The muscles in his neck bunched as he tossed his head in a purely Latin motion of vexation. 'Cards were laid on the table. A few threats tossed in. I expect compliance to be forthcoming in the next twelve hours.'

'How did you do it?' she asked. She'd been probing him on the subject since they arrived, but he'd remained tight-lipped about his dealings.

He hesitated for a moment then he prowled forward, shrugging off his jacket and discarding it on a scrolled seat. The innate sexiness of his every movement dried her mouth and spiked her heartbeat. It was all she could do not to lunge for him when he dropped onto the bed and slid one hand over her thigh.

'Men like Cabrera operate on greed and tend to spread themselves thin in the hope of making multiple paydays at any one time. I targeted his most lucrative companies and convinced a few key shareholders to part with their shares for a considerable markup. Then it was just a matter of making it clear that I would take pleasure in making his life hell if he didn't leave Castillo Estate alone.'

'Wow.'

He rubbed his free hand over his growing stubble. '*Sí*. Wow.'

She frowned. 'You don't wear victory well,' she commented.

'I'm dealing with a slippery bastard. I won't celebrate until the ink is dry on our new agreement.' His hand reached her hip and circled sensuously before continuing its path of destruction. The unique scent of sandalwood and alpha male invaded her senses.

She forced herself not to lean in, not to abandon cheerfully all her caution for this man. But the sensation of being on a slippery slope escalated. So she covered deep disquiet with more conversation. 'Nevertheless, you should allow yourself a moment of satisfaction for progressing this far, this quickly.'

His mouth pursed. 'The prospect of spending time with my parents kills my celebratory spirit.'

'Spending time…?'

'I went to deliver the news of their…impending freedom…and to discuss Matias. They refused to talk about it tonight.'

'Have you considered that they're scared?'

'Being scared is acceptable. Burying their heads in the sand and refusing to even discuss it is not,' he stated. 'They wish to sleep on it before making their decision. They will give me an answer when they come to dinner tomorrow.'

Her eyes widened. 'They're coming here?'

He nodded grimly.

'If you're this unhappy about it, why did you agree to it?'

The corners of his mouth turned down. 'My happiness doesn't matter in this. I agreed for Matias.'

'Why a meal, though?'

He eyed her for a long second. 'Matias isn't the only reason for their request. They also want to meet you.'

Her mouth dropped open. 'Me? Why?' she blurted.

His gaze swept down for a handful of seconds. 'To satisfy whatever curiosity keeps them from facing reality, I guess.'

'Do they…do they know about the baby and my accident?'

His lip pursed. 'They know you're recovering from a trauma, but I didn't see the need to tell them about the baby. They were never interested in their son. I don't wish for them to have any interest in a grandchild.'

His tone was firm. Bitter. Punctuated with definitive finality as he dragged her lower and climbed on top of her.

Lowering his head, he brushed his mouth over hers in a whisper-thin caress. 'Since you seem rested and were considerate enough to wait up for me, *belleza*, I think we shouldn't let this opportunity go to waste, hmm?'

Every single pre-emptive she'd mentally erected crumbled to dust the moment he slid his tongue across her lower lip. As her hands found their way to his shoulders, she told herself she would take up arms to safeguard her feelings again tomorrow.

Tonight, she needed to experience her husband's lovemaking one more time.

CHAPTER ELEVEN

'YOU'RE MAKING A LIST?'

She heard the trace of amusement in Emiliano's voice a second before he dropped a kiss on her head.

'If you were given less than a day's notice to host your first ever in-laws' dinner, you would make a list, too. Don't scoff.'

His amusement disappeared. 'They are not your in-laws, except in name only. And don't fret about it. Alfie and Blanca will take care of everything.'

She looked out through the open doors of the kitchen to the courtyard where Alfie was hosing down the tiles. 'He has his hands full. Besides, keeping *my* hands full will stop me fretting.'

Emiliano's eyes glittered with the beginning of displeasure. 'Sienna…'

'It's done, Emiliano. The driver's taking Blanca and me into town in half an hour. She does the grocery shopping and I get to practise my Spanish. It's a win-win.'

'I disagree. You can stay at home instead, go for a swim, practise your Spanish on me. Win-win-win.'

She'd woken up this morning with a sense of dread hanging over her. She couldn't deny that a large part of it stemmed from last night and how fast she'd succumbed to the magic of being in Emiliano's arms. And, whichever way she tried to dress it up, she wasn't looking forward to meeting Emiliano's parents, knowing they had deliberately rejected one son while being cavalier with the other's health. Before she'd sat down to start a fresh list, she knew she needed some distance. And she was going to take it, regardless of the fumes of ire vibrating off the sleekly built man standing before her.

'It's a tempting offer, but I'm still going, Emiliano,' she stated firmly.

His jaw flexed with irritation. 'I'm beginning to think I should've booked a restaurant for tonight and been done with it.'

She hopped from the island counter, quickly dancing out of his reach when his hands started to move towards her.

Yes. Distance. Definitely.

Steady footsteps approached the kitchen and she looked up, relief spiking through her as the housekeeper entered. 'Well, it's too late now.' She started to walk out.

'Wait.' The bite in his tone was definitely growing.

She stopped, her nerves jangling as he strolled towards her. He hadn't yet shaved his stubble from last night and, with the predatory gleam in his eyes, he resembled a dark overlord intent on one thing only: establishing claim.

'Bésame adiós,' he ordered in a near growl.

There was no getting away from the demand. Not if she wanted to escape. Inhaling deeply, she rose on tiptoe and pressed her mouth against his. Hard. Quick.

She started to turn away.

One hand captured her nape, the other cupping her jaw, totally halting her retreat. Incisive eyes narrowed, he bared his teeth. 'Once again, with feeling.'

Sienna was at once elated and terrified by how high her senses leaped. So much so, she stood immobile as he slanted his mouth over hers and kissed her in a way that left little room for doubt that she was well and truly owned, her heart unmistakably on the line.

When he raised his head, she was panting. And his eyes gleamed with arrogant satisfaction. She stared dumbly when he held a granite-black credit card in front of her face between two fingers, before reaching behind her to tuck it into the pocket of her white capri trousers.

'Enjoy your shopping,' he rasped. 'And Alfie comes with you. Non-negotiable.'

Sienna stumbled away, barely noting the drive out of the villa or the expansive *pampas* that whizzed by her window.

Time passed. She wasn't sure how long. Alfie, in the passenger seat, glanced back at her, his gaze concerned. 'Everything all right, Sienna?'

She attempted a reassuring smile that failed completely. Because she wasn't all right. With one kiss, one final blow against her poorly erected defences, the truth had been laid bare.

She was in love with Emiliano. Irrevocably. Completely.

Her senses flared wide, utterly vulnerable at that silent, devastating admission.

Had it been heading there since that first admission of her deeper feelings on that forgotten trip to Hong Kong? Had it grown even more during the months now buried in the darkness of her memories?

Did he know how she felt?

Recalling the look she'd caught on his face on the plane yesterday, her heart dropped in further alarm. Was that why he wanted to talk?

'Sienna?'

Pushing the tsunami of questions away to be dealt with later, she summoned a smile. 'I'm fine.'

You hope.

Refusing to grant victory to the inner voice that mocked, she raised her chin. Yes. She hoped. When she'd bravely stepped up to the altar and said her vows, it'd been because she wanted this union to work. For her baby and for herself.

If the father of her child didn't want the love that blossomed in her heart for him, then...then...

Her breath shortened, actual physical pain lancing

through her head, as if the thought was dead against being formed. She gasped.

Over the buzzing in her ears she heard Alfie instructing the driver to pull over. 'No, it's okay. I'm okay.'

She would be. For her baby's sake, she had to be.

Letting that vow strengthen her, she resolutely shut off her thoughts, focusing on her first glimpse of the more urban parts of Cordoba. Like every other cosmopolitan metropolis, it contained flashy new buildings. But it was the more traditional architecture that she watched out for. Beside her, Blanca proudly pointed out pale gold stone churches, piazzas teeming with tourists splashing through fountains and Manzana Jesuitica, a UNESCO World Heritage site.

She smiled and nodded, aware of Alfie's frequent sidelong glances. It was almost a relief to arrive at the bustling square that was Cordoba's main produce market and lose herself in the sights and smells of Argentina.

Cured meats and Wagyu beef were chosen and expertly sliced... Wild pink salmon was carefully packaged and added to the ever-growing pile. Plump fruit and fresh vegetables were placed in cool boxes to protect them from the growing heat and, all too soon, they were piling back into the SUV.

But they only went a few streets before the driver was pulling to a stop once more.

'Why are stopping? Did we forget something?' she asked.

Alfie grinned. 'Yes, proper retail therapy for you. Boss's orders.'

She took a closer look at the street and shops in front of which they were parked: expensive cars and chic boutiques which reeked of exclusivity. Alfie got out and held her door open. Blanca smiled and waved her out with expressive hands.

A little relieved at the reprieve she'd been given before facing Emiliano again with the new knowledge burning in her heart, Sienna alighted and entered the nearest shop.

The staff was busy bustling around two women holding court at one end of the shop. One harried server offered her champagne, a look of relief crossing her face when Sienna refused. A second later, she darted off.

Not minding the peace, she took her time to browse. Her pregnancy wasn't overly visible yet, but she'd noticed a definite thickening of her waistline and a general tightness in her clothes. The chance to outfit herself with a confidence-boosting dress was suddenly welcome.

The drop-sleeve gown she found was a floaty, gossamer-light affair. In dark, layered purple, it was elegant enough to wear to dinner and loose enough to disguise her slight bump. The price tag however was staggering enough to give her pause.

'The dressing room is that way,' Alfie said. 'Here, I'll help you.' He took the dress from her and firmly led the way, as if he could sense her hesitation.

The harassed server approached them again and showed them to the large changing room before hurrying off once more. Alfie rolled his eyes, but grinned as he nudged her towards the wide cubicle.

The dress fitted like a dream, but she was still biting her lip about the price as she changed into her clothes and emerged from the changing room to hear raised voices.

'*Si*, Señora Castillo. *Immediatamente!*'

Sienna frowned. She didn't know how common the Castillo name was in this part of Argentina but what were the chances of coming across another one in Cordoba?

The older woman was still on a diva tirade. Alfie rolled his eyes when his gaze met hers. Deciding to buy the dress and leave as quickly as possible, she took the credit card out of her back pocket.

About to dismiss the scene, she froze when a younger voice joined in the haranguing.

'*Lo siento*, Señorita Cabrera,' one of the assistants offered.

The rest of the rapid-fire words were lost to Sienna as the fine hairs on her nape jerked upright. It would be a coincidence that the two names behind the reason for her being in Argentina belonged to random strangers.

Slowly, she emerged from the changing area, her attention on the two women seated behind the roped-off VIP area, each clutching a chilled glance of champagne in one hand and gesticulating to distraught assistants with the other.

The younger woman spotted Sienna first. Her dark brown gaze drifted over. Paused. Returned. Widened.

She turned, nudged the older woman and muttered under her breath. Then both glanced her way, eyes filled with curiosity.

The older woman rose first. Tall and willowy, she only needed to take a couple of steps towards her before Sienna became certain that she was looking at Emiliano's mother. They had the same eyes. The same curve of her lip. But, where Emiliano's regal posture and innate grace of movement was absorbingly effortless, everything about Señora Castillo seemed affected, right down to the tips of her manicured fake nails.

'Your name?'

Sienna blinked. 'Excuse me?'

She gave an uppity sniff as her gaze raked over Sienna. 'I am Valentina Castillo. My friend seems to think we might have a person of interest in common. I merely wish to ascertain if this is correct.' Her tone was clipped, the bites of heavily accented English supposed to give an impression of class. Sienna could only concentrate on the words that had just come out of her mouth.

Her friend? *'Person of interest?'*

The younger woman joined them, the swing in her shorter, voluptuous hips more natural. Up close, Sienna couldn't help but notice her stunning beauty. And the fact that something about her made her senses tweak in alarm even though, at closer scrutiny, her expression was more welcoming than Valentina's.

'You are Sienna Newman, *si*?' she asked in a soft, husky voice, her eyes now transmitting friendliness.

Sienna smiled. 'Sienna Castillo,' she corrected.

The women exchanged glances then stared back at her. From the corner of her eye, Sienna noted Alfie's concerned frown but she concentrated on Emiliano's mother, desperately probing for a sign of warmth or humanity. Coming up empty, she took a breath and attempted a smile regardless. 'If by *person of interest* you mean Emiliano, then, yes, we do. It's lovely to make your acquaintance, Señora Castillo.'

'That remains to be seen, my dear.' Her gaze dropped to the dress in Sienna's hand, then to the credit card. She couldn't have failed to see Emiliano's name embossed in gold letters. A look lanced through her eyes, even as one carefully plucked eyebrow rose.

Sienna wanted to shove the card back in her pocket, but she forced herself to remain still. She had nothing to be ashamed of. All the same, she made a mental note to find out where her own bank cards were when she got back.

Valentina dismissed her but, just before she turned away, Sienna also spotted something in the woman's gaze.

Fear.

'We will see you this evening. I hope you don't feel too out of your depth catering for our particular tastes.'

'Your son prides himself in having the best of everything. Don't worry, we have you covered.'

Sienna witnessed the tiniest grimace tweak her mother-in-law's features before a stiff smile slid into place. 'In that case, we look forward to making your better acquaintance, as you say. *Vamanos*, Graciela.' Her gentle tone as she addressed the younger woman spoke of a fondness.

Graciela Cabrera trailed behind the older woman, then at the last moment before they reached the door she darted back.

'I hope we meet again, but if we don't you should know that Emiliano is a wonderful man. One you should treasure.'

Sienna's mouth dropped open. 'I… Thank you.'

Graciela nodded, her eyes staying on Sienna's a moment longer before she turned and quickly walked out.

'Um… What was that all about?' Alfie enquired.

'I have no idea,' she murmured a split second before she experienced that twinge again, sharper this time. But the pain of her burgeoning headache was nowhere near the ache she felt in her heart for Emiliano. She hadn't wanted to believe that a mother could be so unfeeling. Having met Valentina Castillo, Sienna was willing to bet the woman's demeanour was a front. She might have taken a wrong path in the past where her second child was concerned, but the need she'd glimpsed ever so briefly in her eyes gave Sienna a little hope for her husband.

As for Graciela…

She frowned, touching a hand to her temple when the jumbled thoughts made her head pound harder.

'What do you say we get out of here?' Alfie suggested.

'Yes, good idea,' she replied.

The assistants, chattering quietly and looking relieved now that the drama queens had exited, came forward and rang up the dress.

Sienna got back into the SUV, feeling as if her life had changed but unable to put her finger on how.

Like the outbound journey, the return trip went by in a blur. The first thing she knew about being back at the estate was Emiliano bearing down on her, his face a mask of displeasure.

'I understand you met my mother,' he growled, taking her hands in his and peering down at her with dark, searching eyes.

'I had the pleasure, yes. Graciela Cabrera was there, too.'

He stiffened, his body taking on a grim alertness that twanged her already jangled nerves. 'What did she say?' he bit out.

'Graciela? She was nice. Your mother...' She paused, unwilling to pass negative judgement on the woman, especially when her beliefs about Valentina had grown stronger. Somewhere deep in her heart, she still harboured hope that his parents would wake up to the incredible, arrogant man who so easily held the world in his hand. The stunningly charismatic man she'd fallen in love with.

The reality of her ever-growing feelings rammed home just then. So powerfully that she couldn't stare into his eyes for fear he would decipher her emotions. Drawing her hands from his, she waved the question away. 'It's fine. She was probably as surprised as I was to meet me this way.'

He huffed with annoyance. 'I am one hundred per cent certain it is not fine, and you do not need to make excuses for her, but in the spirit of peace I will leave the subject alone.'

'Thank you,' she murmured. Then, eager to escape, because the temptation to stay was mounting by the second, she turned towards the kitchen. 'Blanca probably needs help—'

'No.' Emiliano's mouth thinned, despite the proffered peace. 'Blanca has assistants who have minions. You're officially barred from the kitchen until further notice.'

'But—'

'Let's not argue a pointless issue, *querida*. Come.' Without waiting for her consent, he caught her elbow, steered her into the living room and pressed her onto the wide sofa. Encouraging her to lie back, he eased her shoes off and propped her feet in his lap.

Sienna gave up attempting to find fortitude in the storm of domineering attitude. Just as she couldn't help greedily drinking him in, or stop the heat dredging through her pelvis at his dark, devastating looks. When his thumbs dug into her soles with pinpoint accuracy, she closed her eyes and moaned, surrendering to his touch.

'Cancelling tonight seems like a better prospect by the second,' he rasped.

Her eyes popped open. 'No, don't cancel. Your mother will think it's my fault.'

'I don't care what she thinks. Neither should you.'

She shook her head, hope still burning in her chest. 'But you do care how it might affect Matias. Once they satisfy their curiosity, they won't have a leg to stand on.'

He sighed, his jaw flexing for a second before he jerked out a nod. They stayed like that, Emiliano massaging her feet, Sienna desperately biting her tongue to stop the thick, emotive words that surged forth.

Because, really, what was the worst that could happen? *He could reject you. Reject your love.*

Chains tightened around her heart, which in turn robbed her of breath and silenced the words.

When he rose an hour later and held out his hand to her, she went with him upstairs to their bedroom. The impending dinner ominously had taken up room in their minds, which left very little room for banter as they undressed and got into the shower. Emiliano made no move to make love to her, much to her soul's mournful surprise. Telling herself it was for the best, and hearing the silent words ring hollow, she busied herself with getting ready.

Still in silence, they came downstairs and walked

through the house with the sound of last-minute preparations signalling his parents' imminent arrival.

He stood tall and proud next to her but she nevertheless felt him tense when headlights travelled slowly up the long drive. Even after the Mercedes stopped, his parents didn't alight for a full minute. Anger slowly building inside her on his behalf, Sienna linked her fingers with Emiliano's. His jaw tightened, but he didn't look at her, his focus unmoving on the idling vehicle.

When it opened and a man stepped out, her eyes widened.

She'd imagined she would be meeting a male version of Valentina. But the man who slowly walked up the steps and shook her hand appeared less…rigid. She even dared to consider that there was a malleable side to Benito Castillo as his eyes lingered on his son during their handshake.

Nevertheless, as he stepped back formally to introduce his wife, it was clear the two presented a united front.

It was also clear Valentina hadn't shared the fact that she and Sienna had already met with her husband. The knowledge wasn't worth puzzling over. The objective tonight was to wine, dine and somehow persuade Valentina and Benito Castillo to do the right thing by their older son sooner rather than later.

So she followed Emiliano into the living room where Alfie was waiting to prepare drinks.

While the men opted for scotch and Valentina a glass of white wine, she chose a lemon spritzer. They indulged in stilted conversation for interminable minutes before her mother-in-law's gaze settled on her. 'That dress suits you. You look…radiant.'

Beside her, she felt Emiliano's tension mount but she kept the smile pinned on her face. 'Thank you. Allow me to return the compliment.'

Valentina looked startled for a moment at being called

radiant, then her gaze skittered to her son. And, just like her husband's had, it lingered.

Sienna breathed easier, not sure how they would navigate themselves out of the quagmire but choosing to believe they would.

After a minute, Benito cleared his throat. 'About this business with Cabrera...'

'It's been taken care of. As of this afternoon, he will no longer be a problem. Castillo Estate is back under full Castillo care.'

A wave of relief washed over his parents' faces, although Valentina's mouth pursed. 'You have our undying gratitude, of course, but I can't help but think all this... unpleasantness could've been avoided if you'd honoured your word at the start.'

Emiliano inhaled sharply, his eyes darting to Sienna's before narrowing with vicious intent on his mother. 'I understand that gratitude is an alien concept to you, but we will *not* discuss subjects that are in the past.'

Valentina drank more wine and waved a compliant hand. 'Of course, I understand. Now that you're married, it would be distasteful of me to bring it up.'

Sienna's heart lurched. The glass in her hand shook wildly, spilling several drops of liquid on her dress. Thin-lipped and a little paler than he'd been a moment ago, Emiliano reached into his pocket and passed her a handkerchief.

She took it, but she was nowhere near interested in the stains on her dress. 'What...what does that mean?' she asked, the dread that had been haunting her growing exponentially.

'It means that whatever insane ideas they entertained to extricate themselves from their situation is no longer worth discussing, since Cabrera is no long an issue. *Está claro?*' The warning in his tone was deadly.

Enough to convince her there was more going on beneath the surface. Enough to tell her he'd just given her a non-answer.

Eyes a shade darker than her son's snapped. 'We are your parents, Emiliano. Show some respect!'

Emiliano surged to his feet. 'I will not be dictated to under my own roof. Perhaps you misunderstood what I meant when I said Castillo Estate was back in Castillo care. What I meant is it's back in *my* care. Part of my agreement with Cabrera was that he sells me all his shares. As of this afternoon, I own seventy-five per cent of the business. I will oversee the business from now until Matias is back at the helm. Then I will transfer control to him.'

Both Benito and Valentina wore equal expressions of astonishment. Valentina recovered first, a touch of anguish mingled with her shock. 'You would do that to us?'

'It's already done.' His merciless gaze flitted to the door leading to the dining room, where Alfie hovered. 'I believe dinner is served. While we eat, you will tell me when you will be instructing the doctors in Switzerland to bring my brother out of his coma,' he spat at his mother. 'But, make no mistake, by the time dessert is served I will have your agreement. Or you can kiss your precious estate goodbye.'

Dinner was a disaster. Fraught silence was followed by sniping between Valentina and Benito, followed by an increasingly circumspect Benito. Every now and then, his gaze landed on his son, his expression slowly changing from brooding to acceptance and eventually to grudging respect.

Emiliano finally laid down his fork. 'Is there something on your mind?'

Benito shrugged and picked up his replenished glass of red wine. '*Sí.* We wouldn't be in this mess if it weren't for your mother's obsession with the Cabreras. A habit I indulged unfortunately. We're lucky enough to have salvaged our family name. So we will do everything you want. And when Matias is back he will manage the Castillo business, with no interference from us.'

Valentina's gasp was followed by hot Spanish words exchanged with her husband, who shrugged some more and drank even harder. When she realised her tirade had lost its legs, she shifted her gaze to her son. 'I… We will do as your father says. And, for what it's worth, you should know we talked to Matias's doctors this morning. They are…hopeful.'

'Good, then everything is resolved.'

Valentina's expression dropped, her eyes displaying a greater depth of anguish than before.

Sienna glanced at Emiliano, curious as to how he was taking this turn of events. He wasn't looking at his parents. His eyes rested on her, their expression intently watchful. Almost dreading.

A shiver went over her as terror crept closer to her heart.

Throwing down her napkin, she stood. 'I'll go and see about dessert.' The ungracious voice that said she was up for anything that hurried this overwrought meal to its conclusion was ruthlessly silenced as she entered the kitchen.

Blanca had everything under control, of course.

Feeling superfluous and unwilling to return to the warped atmosphere of the dining room, Sienna carried on walking through the kitchen, stepping out into the outer courtyard. Inhaling the fresh, clean air did nothing for her raging thoughts and the almost fatalistic, dreadful premonition haunting her.

Footsteps sounded behind her, a click of heels bringing certain doom.

Sienna turned.

Valentina stood six feet away, her gaze resting on Sienna's stomach. 'Is that how you got him to go back on his word? By getting yourself pregnant? And don't bother denying it. Your abstention from drink and Emiliano watching you like a hawk tells me what I need to know.'

'I don't know what you mean. Go back on his word on what?' she asked through lips turning numb with fear.

'Ah, of course, you don't remember.'

'Don't remember what?' she probed again.

Valentina turned, as if she was about to walk away. 'It doesn't matter now that he's married, I suspect.'

'You do care for him. So why do you treat him like that? Why are you so afraid to show it?' Sienna blurted before she thought better of it.

Valentina's eyes widened. 'You don't know what you're talking about. I don't treat Emiliano in any particular way.'

'When was the last time you told him you loved him, or that you were proud of him?'

'He doesn't need that from me. The bond we share is enough.'

'Really? Well, I wouldn't know about that. I grew up without a mother, you see.'

'Is that supposed to make me feel sorry for you?'

Sienna stared at the older woman for a moment before she shook her head. 'No, but take it from me—your son needs to hear it from you.'

'Don't presume to think you know me enough to lecture me.'

'Very well. Please tell me what you meant by what you said before. "Now that he's married"?'

She spread her hands in a gesture so reminiscent of Emiliano's it was unsettling. 'I've been forbidden from talking about it.'

Her fists balled. 'Not by me.'

Her eyebrows rose. 'You have a backbone. You will need it to deal with my son. But are you sure it's strong enough to handle the truth?'

'What truth? Tell me,' she insisted, her voice rising with a touch of hysteria.

'Very well. A couple of months ago Emiliano was engaged to Graciela Cabrera. Their wedding had been planned for next month, on Valentine's Day. Benito thinks I'm obsessed but I only want what's best for both my sons. Graciela would've made him a good wife.'

'That's…that's a lie.' Her voice was bled of all substance.

Valentina's eyes, so similar to those of the man Sienna loved, narrowed. 'If you don't believe me, *ask him*.'

She didn't need to. Because she knew. Even before Graciela's words to her in the shop that had spoken of something else… Even before Emiliano's proposal that hadn't quite sat right… Deep in her heart, she *knew*.

Sienna opened her mouth to speak. Then quickly shut it, her hands flying to her head as every single twinge, tweak, dread and fear coalesced at the same time into a bolt of lightning that forked through her brain.

She stumbled forward, her hand flailing out in search of something, anything, to hold on to. Another arrow of pain cracked through her head. She cried out as the edges of her vision blurred.

Her baby. *Oh, God, her baby!*

Powerful feet thundered towards her, hands catching her as she lost feeling in her legs.

'*Madre de Dios*, what did you do to her?' was the last thing she heard.

She woke on the sofa to find Emiliano on his knees beside her, his face a grey mask as he gripped her hand. His breathing was hopelessly ragged, his eyes black, haunted pools.

'Sienna.' His voice was a hoarse, desperate plea.

She couldn't look at him. It simply hurt too much. So she directed her gaze over his shoulder to the heated argument going on between Valentina and Benito.

'*Basta!*' Emiliano snarled. 'My wife is like this because of you. Alfie will show you out. You're no longer welcome here.'

The bubble of pain bloomed as she shook her head.

'You're wrong. They had nothing to do with it. I remember, Emiliano. I remember everything. And this… *this was all because of you.*'

CHAPTER TWELVE

'WE NEED TO talk about this, Sienna.'

Three days had passed since her memory had returned. Since the sheer depths of Emiliano's cunning betrayal had shredded her heart to a million pieces.

Concern for her baby had made her agree to see the doctor Emiliano had summoned, the same concern keeping her confined to rest for three days when every screaming atom of her being wished she was elsewhere. Far away from here. From Emiliano.

God, just thinking about him hurt more than she would ever have thought possible. And having him here in her bedroom, speaking to her...

She took a deep breath and turned from the window to face him. Better to get this over with then she could go back to staring at the devastation that was her life.

Her face must have reflected the true depths of her wretchedness because he inhaled sharply. 'You need to be in bed.'

'I need to be several thousand miles from here. Away from you.'

His jaw clenched hard, as did the hands by his side. But he didn't leave as she wanted him to. He stayed put. Immovable. She found it overwhelmingly brutal just taking every breath.

'This isn't productive.'

'Productive? I'm sorry that regaining my memories to discover the man who dumped me for another woman has lied and manipulated me into marriage because he got me pregnant isn't *productive* for you.'

The doctor from Haven North with whom they'd videoconferenced had mentioned that more of her memories would return with each passing day. Sienna desperately prayed they didn't. With each new memory revealed, her heart broke all over again.

'I didn't lie to you. I just couldn't tell you the whole truth because it might have caused irreparable damage.'

'You twisted the situation to suit your own needs!'

'What needs? The need to ensure my brother didn't remain on a breathing tube for the rest of his life? Or the need to provide for my child's future?'

Her hand flew to her stomach, the thought that she would want less for her child ramping up her anger and misery. 'This child will want for nothing and I resent your implication otherwise. As for Matias, I get that you made a promise to him that you had to keep. What I can't live with is that you didn't see fit to tell me about it. You went ahead and made plans *for your life* that didn't take our relationship into account. Plans that involved another woman. Plans that were splashed all over the tabloids for the world to see and salivate over.'

'I never intended to marry her. But she asked for my help in dealing with her father—'

'I don't care! You knowingly put yourself in a position that would hurt me. And, when I tried to talk to you about it, you walked away.'

'Because you weren't in a state to listen to what I had to say.'

'Which was what? That, when it came right down to it, I featured very low on your list of priorities?'

His hand slashed through the air. 'I don't want to hear about lists!'

'I'm sorry if what's important to me doesn't coincide with what matters to you!' she snapped.

'*Dios mío*, I was hit with an unexpected situation on

what was supposed to be a turnaround visit. I had very little time to act.'

'You've made tougher decisions in a boardroom full of intransigent negotiators in a matter of hours. You were in Argentina for *six days*. And not once during that time did you call to tell me what was going on.'

'How would you have reacted if I'd called and told you that my brother had left me a message on what he thought was his possible deathbed to tell me to honour a ludicrous promise he'd made to get my parents out of their mess? That I was expected to hand myself over like a prized stud in some deal I wasn't aware of until I walked into my parents' house?'

She floundered for a second before she firmed her spine. 'I guess we'll never know, because you didn't.'

'I didn't because it was an absurd situation. One that I couldn't find an immediate solution to that didn't involve letting Matias down.'

'So you chose to let *me* down instead?'

'No. I chose to wait until we were together to tell you but…'

'But what?'

'I put myself in your shoes, considered how I would feel if you informed me you were engaged to another man.'

She stared at him, perverse curiosity eating at her. 'And?'

The feral growl that erupted from his throat startled her. She watched him spike a hand through his hair and pace for a minute before facing her. 'It was your birthday. I wanted you to enjoy your evening so I decided to wait till the next day to explain the situation. But the tabloid spread put a wrench in that.'

'So you thought the best solution then was to break up with me?'

'I thought I'd give us both a little space to regroup and for me to find an alternative solution.'

'And that involved trying to buy me with the penthouse and a car?'

He shrugged and she noted absently that his face was creased in lines that resembled anxiety. 'It was wrong, perhaps, but I wanted to keep you sweet while dealing with Rodrigo Cabrera. And I knew you loved the penthouse.'

'Not enough to live in it after it was clear we were over.'

'We weren't over. We're not over,' he denied through clenched teeth. 'We will *never* be over.'

She shook her head. 'You know what all of this tells me? That you were more concerned with everyone else's feelings than mine. And right now you're only here out of guilt and because I'm carrying your baby.'

'*Dios mío*, be reasonable.'

'No! You had weeks to fight for me. You didn't bother. I've seen you go after deals with more aggression simply because you were bored. How do you think it makes me feel to know I didn't even warrant a *bored* chase?'

His teeth bared. 'Because a large part of that time, you'd disappeared off the face of the earth. Then you had the audacity to turn up with another man whose presence in your life you rubbed in my face.'

She flushed, then felt a snap of irritation for feeling guilty. 'Don't turn this back on me. We are where we are today because of you. I don't hate you for trying to do right by your brother, but you didn't need to cast me aside to do so. Rejection like that isn't easy for me to forgive, Emiliano.' She stopped then regrouped when her voice broke. 'You know what it feels like to come second, to be discarded like an unwanted object. I may be strong enough to withstand it, but that doesn't mean I wish it to happen to me. I...I just can't come second in anyone's life. Ever again.'

He froze, the only movement in his whole formidable frame the eyes that narrowed with laser-like intent on her. 'What are you saying?' he asked in a clipped tone.

'I'm saying that I can never be sure that you're not here in this marriage just because of our child.'

'I'm here for you both!'

'But would you have asked me to marry you if I wasn't pregnant? Or was this whole thing staged to protect your position in your child's life?'

His mouth thinned and his nostrils flared. 'Nothing was staged. We're having a baby together. It's the most natural thing in the world for couples to take the next step.'

'Even when one of the couple has previously made it perfectly clear that marriage doesn't feature anywhere on his life's to-do list?'

He stalked in a tight circle before facing her again. 'I'm trying to do right by you, Sienna. Will you condemn me for that?'

Her heart lurched then broke. 'No, but I won't let you sacrifice yourself for me.'

'*Por el amor de Dios!* It is *not* a sacrifice.'

She took one step back. Then another. To stay here was to weaken and she would hate herself for it one day. The thought of what that would do to her child firmed her resolve.

'Call it what you will. But I don't want it.'

He stared at her with something akin to shock. Which turned to disbelief then cold determination. 'You don't want it. Explain to me in clear terms what you *do* want, then,' he demanded hoarsely.

Before she gave birth to the words, they burned like acid in her chest. But she had to speak them. Continuing to perpetuate a lie would kill what remained of her heart. Staying, knowing Emiliano wasn't in it for love, for *her*, would annihilate her soul. 'It means I want a divorce.'

Tawny eyes turned an eerie dark gold, the lines around his mouth deepening as his face hardened into a terrifying mask. 'I'm not prepared to dissolve our marriage over a simple disagreement.'

'It's not simple to me. I married you without the benefit of remembering that you hurt me deeply, Emiliano. And I can't trust that you won't do it again.' Not with what was most important to her besides her baby. Not with the feelings that were screaming under the weight of her hurt.

His face had lost a healthy dose of colour but the eyes that were locked onto her were dark pools of grim purpose. 'Be that as it may, my responsibility is to our child. We will not break up because you feel aggrieved. We once were in agreement that we would give this child the best of ourselves. That hasn't changed.'

'How can we do that when we're locked in battle?'

He spread his hands out in a gesture she would've been foolish to believe was harmless. 'You're the only one armed to the teeth here, *querida*. I'm just telling you where my hard boundaries are. We can work together to find common ground or you can attempt to take shots at me. Before you do, I should warn you that you will lose.'

'You can't force me to stay. Just as you can't keep what you never truly had.'

He looked stricken, as though he'd been gut-punched. His nostrils flared as he took rough, deep breaths.

Then, without another word, he walked out.

She'd come full circle. Her hand crept over her stomach. Fuller circle.

Sienna stared despondently around the flat she'd rented and tried to decorate but felt alien. Despite being back for almost two weeks and barely having left the flat, it still felt as if she was living in a stranger's property. A stranger who moved listlessly through the three rooms, eating for her child's sake and doing very little else.

In a way it was good that she hadn't grown attached to this flat. Having a baby who would quickly grow into an active toddler meant she would need a house with a garden. Somewhere more child-friendly where she could establish roots.

Her bump was definitely more rounded. Time was marching on whether she chose to acknowledge it or not. She only wished she could breathe, eat and sleep without the raw pain that dogged her whenever she thought of Emiliano.

Which was constantly.

How could she fall in love with the same man twice in one lifetime—and both times have her heart torn to pieces?

After their row in the bedroom, Emiliano had given her a wide berth for the rest of the day. When she'd requested dinner in her room, Alfie had delivered it.

The next morning, deciding it was a good time to start reclaiming her life, she'd come down to breakfast and been confronted with a grim-faced Emiliano. He'd stated with point-blank finality that he wouldn't discuss a divorce.

They'd compromised on a separation. And once again he'd walked away from her, but this time with a look that closely resembled fierce anguish.

That look had crossed her mind more times than she cared to recall.

As did the riddle of why he was so against regaining his freedom.

He hadn't needed to marry her. This wasn't the Middle Ages, where marriage was paramount in ensuring one's child's legitimacy. He didn't love her, granted. But he hadn't had to marry her. *But he had.*

The Emiliano she knew wasn't that selfless when it came to his freedom. Hadn't she, in the months before their relationship had started, predicted when his liaisons would end with almost clockwork precision? And hadn't that end been triggered by the first signs of clinginess?

'I'm here for you both,' he'd said. At the time, pain had been the dominant force riding her. Now, with time and distance, she thought, might she have dismissed those words too hastily? When they'd *both* agreed that their marriage primarily benefitted their child?

On the day she'd left Argentina, she'd breached the cold silence between them to let him know she wouldn't stand in the way of maintaining equal custody of their child. He'd coldly replied that they wouldn't need to discuss custody if they stayed married.

She shook her head now, feeling a little pathetic for desperately trying to find a salve for the constant wildfire that was her pain. A fire she feared she would never be able to put out.

Grabbing her laptop, she settled on the sofa and brought up the list of properties she'd put together for a possible viewing. Having made a shortlist, she was about to make an appointment when her phone rang.

David Hunter.

She'd sent him an email thanking him for his concern after having come home to dozens of messages from him. She'd declined his further calls about finding her a job. She was financially sound enough for now not to need a job right away. Although that would soon need to change.

She eyed the ringing phone then picked it up at the last moment.

'David, hello.'

'Sienna! Good to hear your voice,' he responded eagerly then checked himself. 'Um, I mean, I thought I would be talking to your voicemail again,' he semijoked.

'What can I do for you?' Her gaze landed on the sidebar of the property website and took note of the giddy advertisement for love and happiness, and her heart lurched.

Today was Valentine's Day. Hopelessly commercialised, but a day for lovers the world over nonetheless.

The day Emiliano would've married someone else…

But he hadn't.

Because he married you!

She pushed the insistent voice away as David cleared his throat. 'Uh, I know you aren't looking for anything right now, but I think I have something that might interest you.'

'Why?'

'It's a start-up, but the CEO thinks you might be able to put your own stamp on the job. And it's completely flexible. Hell, you can work from home if you want.'

She frowned. 'It sounds a little too good to be true. No start-up hedge fund can offer terms like that unless they're prepared to make a huge initial loss.'

'Well, this guy is pretty confident he can make things work. But he insists he wants you. And the meeting has to be today. He's flying out of the country tomorrow.'

Sienna looked down at herself and grimaced. She'd taken a shower this morning but she'd slipped back into her comfy onesie, preparing for a day of mindless TV to drown her pain.

She opened her mouth to say no then reconsidered. Her funds wouldn't last for ever, and if this offer was real she owed it to herself to consider it.

'Okay, where do I need to go?'

'It's just out of the city. He'll send a car for you. In, say, half an hour?'

'Uh…okay.'

'Great. Good luck, Sienna.' The wish was deep and heartfelt.

Frowning a little, she said goodbye and hung up.

Rising, she went to her small bedroom and critically

examined her wardrobe. She hadn't been in the mood for clothes shopping since her return, and with her expanding waistline most of her clothes no longer fit. Her gaze lit on a cashmere batwing-style jumper dress Emiliano had bought for her on a visit to Milan. The memories they evoked threatened to clog her throat but she had no time for painful trips down memory lane.

Briskly she tugged it off the hanger and slipped it on. The grey-and-black colourblock design was professional enough to pass muster. Adding tights and a pair of soft grey heeled boots, she caught her hair up in a loose but stylish bun. She was shrugging into her coat when her doorbell sounded.

Grabbing her handbag, she shut her front door. The February wind threatened to chill her to the bone as she hurried. The sight of the idling limo gave her momentary pause, but she wasn't unaccustomed to CEOs in her field of work wooing fund managers this way. Nodding to the driver, she settled into the back seat. An hour later, they turned into a long driveway.

The country house in Surrey was a stunning Georgian masterpiece. Sienna fell in love with it long before the limo pulled up to the imposing double front doors.

Stepping out, she walked up the shallow steps and pressed the bell.

For a moment, when he opened the door, she couldn't believe her eyes. Didn't want to. And then she didn't want to blink in case he was a figment of her imagination.

When he exhaled and swung the door wider, she took a short, desperate breath.

'Is this some sort of joke, Emiliano?'

'No, *amante*. This is far from a joke.' His voice was deep. Solemn. His eyes pleading.

She swung her head towards the limo. The *departing* limo.

'Come in, Sienna. *Por favor.*'

It was either stand out in the freezing cold or step into the warmth. Her feet moved forward before she'd given them complete control.

When the door shut behind her, she turned. For a moment, she couldn't find her voice. Emiliano dressed all in black had always had that power over her. This time wasn't any different. She didn't want to acknowledge the way the black sweater moulded his muscular chest or the tailored trousers clung to his powerful thighs.

So she dragged her gaze up to his.

'What is the meaning of this?'

'Give me ten minutes of your time. After that, if you want to leave I will send for the driver.'

Ten minutes. Not much time, considering the wasteland of pain that stretched before her. And this unexpected chance to be in his electrifying presence again, breathe him in, felt too hard to refuse.

Again her body reacted without total consent from her mind, her nod triggering a similar nod from him.

He led the way down a light oak-panelled hallway into a study. To one side, floor-to-ceiling bookshelves held hundreds of books. On the other side, a teak desk held pride of place. It was there that Emiliano headed. But he didn't take a seat. Instead, he reached across the desk and picked up a single sheet of paper.

'My next venture is one I intend to pour my heart and soul into, so I have taken a leaf out of your book and made a list.'

She gasped, her breath clogging in her chest. 'Emiliano…'

Turbulent eyes stopped her. 'Hear me out, Sienna. Please.'

She gestured for him to continue.

'For this venture, I need a partner who will steer me true. Who will forgive me when I misstep—and I will occasionally, because I'm not perfect. I need a partner whose trust I hope to gain and who knows she can rely on me day or night. I need a queen who will bear my children, love them and me without reserve, even when we mess up. I need a partner who will hold my heart in her hands the way I hope she will let me hold hers. I need a partner who will believe me when I say I will *always*, without exception, put her first.'

He lowered his hand, holding her captive with his mesmerising gaze.

'*Por favor, querida*, I need *you*.'

'Oh… Emiliano.'

He shuddered hard, emotion exploding from his eyes as the paper dropped from his fingers and floated to the floor, forgotten. In one desperate lunge, he arrived in front of her. 'I need you, Sienna. I *love* you. You think I married you because of our child. I married you because I couldn't see a day in my future that you weren't a part of. And, yes, I was terrified that if you knew *how* your accident happened you would leave me. If I hadn't dragged you out into that alley that night, you wouldn't have fallen. But, believe me, I would've come for you, fought tooth and nail for you. I only found out the day before you returned from South America where you'd gone. My pilots were on standby to fly out to Peru the next morning.' He shook his head. 'Seeing you in that restaurant with Hunter made me lose my mind.'

'Seeing you on that magazine cover with Graciela made me lose mine,' she confessed huskily.

'*Lo siento.* If it's any consolation, know that I've never messed up anything in my life the way I messed up then. And I will move mountains to make sure I don't cause you pain like that ever again.'

The solid promise in his words made her heart stutter, then beat wildly against her ribs. 'I love you. I was going to tell you that night…on my birthday. I was going to be brave and put my feelings out there,' she confessed brokenly. 'Tell you about my past, tell you I didn't care who knew about us, ask if you would be mine the way I was yours.'

He squeezed his eyes shut and his chest heaved in an audible inhale. '*Dios mío.* Forgive me, *mi corazón.* I beg you.'

'Tell me you love me again. Please. I would feel so much better.'

'I love you. *Te amo.* I love your bravery, your spirit, your kind heart. I love your body. I love your soul.' His hand dropped to her gently swollen belly. 'I love that our baby is nestled warm and safe inside your body. I love—'

She flung herself at him, shameless, happy tears spilling from her eyes as she pressed her mouth against his.

With a helpless groan, he caught her up against him, deepening the kiss almost immediately. Claiming her.

An eternity later, he lifted his head, brushed away her tears. 'The past few weeks have been hell, *querida*,' he muttered. 'Enough for me to confess I don't even mind these tears this time, because seeing them means you're here in front of me, not a figment of my desperate imagination.'

She laughed. Kissed him again just because she could. Of course that led to heat being generated at an alarming rate. Which led to her being scooped up in strong arms, carried to the living room, undressed and laid on a sheepskin rug before the roaring fire.

It led to exquisite lovemaking that had her crying out in ecstasy and wonder. And, afterwards, softly murmured admissions of love in dual tongues.

'I can't believe you used David,' she mused many hours later.

Her husband shrugged arrogantly. Oh, how she'd missed that shrug.

'He needed to be made aware that you were off limits

to him in this lifetime and the next. I merely utilised his expertise, and he earned a fat commission in the bargain. Win-win.'

She laughed. He joined in. Then they both sobered and stared deep into each other's eyes, letting their feelings speak for a moment.

'I asked myself how I could fall in love with you twice in one lifetime,' she whispered, her thumb tracing his full lower lip.

His fingers traced reverentially along her jaw. 'And?' he demanded gruffly.

'It was because my heart knew you were the one. My heart will always know you and love you, *mi amor*.'

'As will mine.'

EPILOGUE

'OKAY, *MI ÁNGEL*. Time for our big moment in the spotlight. I'll try and keep it together if you will. Deal?'

Emiliano smiled as he entered the nursery to the sight of his brother cradling his eight-week-old daughter. The size disparity was ridiculous, as was the extracautious way Matias was cradling Angelina, but his heart flipped over all the same.

He was getting used to that feeling. Getting used to it knocking him for six several dozen times a day. It started from the moment he woke up next to the woman of his heart, the woman who made him glad to be alive every day. Then it went on, a relentless insanity he never wanted to be cured of.

'You know she can't high-five you just yet, right, *mi hermano*? Or even understand a word you're saying?'

Matias spun carefully on his heel, his gaze touching briefly on Emiliano before returning to the treasure in his arms. 'Of course she can. I'm her godfather, which means we share a special bond. She smiled and pumped her fist just before you interrupted us.'

Shaking his head, Emiliano strolled closer, the magic of his daughter impossible to resist. He caressed her soft cheek with the back of his finger, his heart expanding when she leaned into him.

Angelina's eyes, a soft turquoise at birth, were slowly changing, taking on her mother's green eyes. Her hair was also soot-black like Sienna's, and Emiliano secretly hoped his daughter would take every single one of her mother's attributes, both inside and out. Every element of his wife's character and spirit deserved celebration.

'You look like a sap, you know that?' Matias mocked. But Emiliano noted the gruffness in his voice.

'What can I say? I'm a lucky man and I'm not ashamed to show it.'

'*Sí*, you are indeed lucky. As I am, after what you did.' The gaze that met his was solemn and fiercely sincere. It also held a brotherhood that Emiliano had severely missed and almost lost. 'I know what you risked for me. You have my undying gratitude.'

'You would've done the same for me.' He knew that in his soul and was only beginning to appreciate what that truly meant. He clasped his brother on the shoulder and deep understanding passed between them.

His daughter gurgled and his attention was immediately absorbed by her once more. Leaning down, he inhaled her sweet baby scent before kissing her gently on the forehead.

'Yeah, I still think you need to dial down the mush, though. It's unbecoming in a grown man,' Matias chided.

'Says the man who wept when I asked him to be god-father.'

Matias snorted. 'You shouted the question at me when I was in the middle of training a temperamental filly and I got kicked for my troubles. I invite you to experience that and tell me whether you wouldn't shed a tear, too.'

Emiliano laughed. After a few seconds Matias joined in. They were still laughing when his wife, the reason for his heartbeat, walked in.

'There you are. I was beginning to think you three had hopped on a plane and hightailed it for Tahiti.'

Sienna tried not stumble as two sets of tawny eyes looked up from her daughter and met hers across the nursery. One set held an everlasting love she still pinched herself over each time she felt that visceral connection. The other held warmth, acceptance and love.

Matias had made a full recovery since waking up from

his coma eight months ago. After having been released from the private Swiss hospital, he'd moved into the Cordoba mansion with them, Emiliano having decided to split his work life between Argentina and London.

Once Matias had completely recovered, he'd resumed the reins of Castillo Estate on the proviso that Benito and Valentina retired and relinquished all say in the running of the estate to him. They'd agreed and had since embarked on a world cruise, courtesy of Emiliano's yacht. Emiliano had deemed it a small price to pay to be rid of them for a while.

The relationship between Benito and Emiliano had altered for the better since the night Sienna had regained her memory. She held out hope for a further thawing in Valentina's character, as well. But, for now, she had all the family she needed.

A family she worshipped with every fibre of her being.

Emiliano held out his arm and she swayed to his side, accepting his kiss before smiling down at her precious daughter.

'The guests are waiting. This little angel needs to make her christening debut.'

The christening attendees included new friends they'd made here in Argentina and old acquaintances turned friends from London. The intimate affair was just what they'd both wanted.

'Let them wait a while longer. She is a female and it's her day. I believe it's her divine right to be fashionably late,' Emiliano said.

When Angelina gurgled her agreement, they all laughed. While Matias smiled with complete infatuation at his niece, Sienna's eyes met her husband's.

'*Te amo, mi corazón,*' he whispered against her lips. '*Para siempre.*'

* * * * *

A TANGLED AFFAIR

FIONA BRAND

For the Lord. Thank you.

The kingdom of heaven is like a merchant in search of fine pearls.

— Matthew 13:45

One

The vibration of Lucas Atraeus's cell phone disrupted the measured bunch and slide of muscle as he smoothly bench-pressed his own weight.

Gray sweatpants clinging low on narrow hips, broad shoulders bronzed by the early morning light that flooded his private gym, he flowed up from the weight bench and checked the screen of his cell. Few people had his private number; of those only two dared interrupt his early morning workout.

"*Si.*" His voice was curt as he picked up the call.

The conversation with his older brother, Constantine, the CEO of The Atraeus Group, a family-owned multibillion-dollar network of companies, was brief. When he terminated the call, Lucas was grimly aware that within the space of a few seconds a great many things had changed.

Constantine intended to marry in less than a fortnight's

time and, in so doing, he had irretrievably complicated Lucas's life.

The bride, Sienna Ambrosi, was the head of a Sydney-based company, Ambrosi Pearls. She also happened to be the sister of the woman with whom Lucas was currently involved. Although *involved* was an inadequate word to describe the passionate, addictive attraction that had held him in reluctant thrall for the past two years.

The phone vibrated again. Lucas didn't need to see the number to know who the second caller was; his gut reaction was enough. Carla Ambrosi. Long, luscious dark hair, honey-tanned skin, light blue eyes and the kind of taut, curvy body that regularly disrupted traffic and stopped him in his tracks.

Desire kicked, raw and powerful, almost overturning the rigid discipline he had instilled in himself after his girl-friend had plunged to her death in a car accident almost five years ago. Ever since Sophie's death he had pledged not to be ruled by passion or fall into such a destructive relationship ever again.

Lately, a whole two years lately, he had been breaking that rule on a regular basis.

But not anymore.

With an effort of will he resisted the almost overwhelming urge to pick up the call. Seconds later, to his intense relief, the phone fell silent.

Shoving damp, jet-black hair back from his face, he strolled across the pale marble floor to the shower with the loose-limbed power of a natural athlete. In centuries past, his build and physical prowess would have made him a formidable warrior. These days, however, Medinian battle was fought across boardroom tables with extensive share port-folios and gold mined from the arid backbone of the main island.

In the corporate arena, Lucas was undefeated. Relationships, however, had proved somewhat less straightforward.

All benefit from the workout burned away by tension and the fierce, unwanted jolt of desire, he stripped off his clothes, flicked the shower controls and stepped beneath a stream of icy water.

If he did nothing and continued an affair that had become increasingly irresistible and risky, he would find himself engaged to a woman who was the exact opposite of the kind of wife he needed.

A second fatal attraction. A second Sophie.

His only honorable course now was to step away from the emotion and the desire and use the ruthless streak he had hammered into himself when dealing with business acquisitions. He had to form a strategy to end a relationship that had always been destined for disaster, for both of their sakes.

He had tried to finish with Carla once before and failed. This time he would make sure of it.

It was over.

Lucas was finally going to propose.

The glow of a full moon flooded the Mediterranean island of Medinos as Carla Ambrosi brought her rented sports car to a halt outside the forbidding gates of Castello Atraeus.

Giddy delight coupled with nervous tension zinged through her as the paparazzi, on Medinos for her sister's wedding to Constantine Atraeus tomorrow, converged on the tiny sky-blue car. So much for arriving deliberately late and under cover of darkness.

A security guard tapped on her window. She wound the glass down a bare two inches and handed him the cream-colored, embossed invitation to the prewedding dinner.

With a curt nod, he slid the card back through the narrow gap and waved her on.

A flash temporarily blinded her as she inched the tiny rental through the crush, making her wish she had ignored the impulse that had seized her and chosen a sensible, solid four-door sedan instead of opting for a low-slung fun and flimsy sports car. But she had wanted to look breezy and casual, as if she didn't have a care in the world—

A sharp rap on her passenger-side window jerked her head around.

"Ms. Ambrosi, are you aware that Lucas Atraeus arrived in Medinos this morning?"

A heady jolt of anticipation momentarily turned her bones to liquid. She had seen Lucas's arrival on the breakfast news. Minutes later, she had glimpsed what she was sure must be his car as she had strolled along the waterfront to buy coffee and rolls for breakfast.

Flanked by security, the limousine had been hard to miss but, frustratingly, the darkly tinted windows had hidden the occupants from sight. Breakfast forgotten, she had both called and texted Lucas. They had arranged to meet but, frustratingly, a late interview request from a popular American TV talk-show host had taken that time slot. With Ambrosi's new collection due for release in under a week, the opportunity to use the publicity surrounding Sienna's wedding to showcase their range and mainstream Ambrosi's brand had been pure gold. Carla had hated canceling but she had known that Lucas, with his clinical approach to business, would understand. Besides, she was seeing him tonight.

Another camera flash made the tension headache she had been fighting since midafternoon spike out of control. The headache was a sharp reminder that she needed to slow down, chill out, de-stress. Difficult to do with the type A personality her doctor had diagnosed just over two years ago, along with a stomach ulcer.

The doctor, who also happened to be a girlfriend, had

advised her to lose her controlling, perfectionist streak, to stop micromanaging every detail of her life including her slavish need to color coordinate her wardrobe and plan her outfits a week in advance. Her approach to relationships was a case in point. Her current system of spreadsheet appraisal was hopelessly punitive. How could she find Mr. Right if no one ever qualified for a second date? Stress was a killer. She needed to loosen up, have some fun, maybe even consider actually sleeping with someone, before she ended up with even worse medical complications.

Carla had taken Jennifer at her word. A week later she had met Lucas Atraeus.

"Ms. Ambrosi, now that your sister is marrying Constantine, is there any chance of resurrecting your relationship with Lucas?"

Jaw tight, Carla continued to inch forward, her heart pounding at the reporter's intrusive question, which had been fired at her like a hot bullet.

And which had been eating at her ever since Sienna had broken the news two weeks ago that she had agreed to marry Constantine.

Tonight, though, she was determined not to resent the questions or the attention. After two years of avoiding being publicly linked with Lucas after the one night the press claimed they had spent together, she was now finally free to come clean about the relationship.

The financial feud that had torn the Atraeus and Ambrosi families apart, and the grief of her sister's first broken engagement to Constantine, were now in the past. Sienna and Constantine had their happy ending. Now, tonight, she and Lucas could finally have theirs.

A throaty rumble presaged the glare of headlights as a gleaming, muscular black car glided in behind her.

Lucas.

Her heart slammed against the wall of her chest. He was staying at the *castello,* which meant he had probably been at a meeting in town and was just returning. Or he could have driven to the small town house she and Sienna and their mother were renting in order to collect her. The possibility of the second option filled her with relieved pleasure.

A split second later the way ahead was clear as the media deserted her in favor of clustering around Lucas's Maserati. Automatically, Carla's foot depressed the accelerator, sending her small sports car rocketing up the steep, winding slope. Scant minutes later, she rounded a sweeping bend and the spare lines of the *castello* she had only ever seen in magazine articles jumped into full view.

The headlights of the Maserati pinned her as she parked on the smooth sweep of gravel fronting the colonnaded entrance. Feeling suddenly, absurdly vulnerable, she retrieved the flame-red silk clutch that matched her dress and got out of the car.

The Maserati's lights winked out, plunging her into comparative darkness as she closed her door and locked the car.

She started toward the Maserati, still battling the aftereffects of the bright halogen lights. The sensitivity of her eyes was uncomfortably close to a symptom she had experienced two months ago when she had contracted a virus while holidaying with Lucas in Thailand.

Instead of the romantic interlude she had so carefully planned and which would have generated the proposal she wanted, Lucas had been forced into the role of nursemaid. On her return home, when she had continued to feel offcolor, further tests had revealed that the stomach ulcer she thought she had beaten had flared up again.

The driver's side door of the car swung open. Her pulse rate rocketed off the charts. Finally, after a day of anxious waiting, they would meet.

Meet.

Her mouth went dry at a euphemism that couldn't begin to describe the explosive encounters that, over the past year, had become increasingly intense.

The reporter at the gate had put his finger on an increasingly tender and painful pulse. Resurrect her relationship with Lucas?

Technically, she was not certain they had ever had anything as balanced as a relationship. Her attempt to create a relaxed, fun atmosphere with no stressful strings had not succeeded. Lucas had seemed content with brief, crazily passionate interludes, but she was not. As hard as she had tried to suppress her type A tendencies and play the glamorous, carefree lover, she had failed. Passion was wonderful, but she *liked* to be in control, to personally dot every *i* and cross every *t*. For Carla, leaving things "open" had created even more stress.

Heart pounding, she started toward the car. The gown she had bought with Lucas in mind was unashamedly spectacular and clung where it touched. Split down one side, it revealed the long, tanned length of her legs. The draped neckline added a sensual Grecian touch to the swell of her breasts and also hid the fact that she had lost weight over the past few weeks.

Her chest squeezed tight as Lucas climbed out of the car with a fluid muscularity she would always recognize.

She drank in midnight eyes veiled by inky lashes, taut cheekbones, the faintly battered nose, courtesy of two seasons playing professional rugby; his strong jaw and firm, well-cut mouth. Despite the sleek designer suit and the ebony seal ring that gleamed on one finger, Lucas looked somewhat less than civilized. A graphic image of him naked and in her bed, his shoulders muscled and broad, his skin dark against crisp white sheets, made her stomach clench.

His gaze captured hers and the idea that they could keep
the chemistry that exploded between them a secret until
after the wedding died a fiery death. She wanted him. She
had waited two years, hamstrung by Sienna's grief at losing Constantine. She loved her sister and was fiercely loyal.
Dating the younger and spectacularly better looking Atraeus
brother when Sienna had been publicly dumped by Constantine would have been an unconscionable betrayal.

Tonight, she and Lucas could publicly acknowledge their
desire to be together. Not in a heavy-handed, possessive way
that would hint at the secretive liaison that had disrupted
both of their lives for the past two years, but with a low-key
assurance that would hint at the future.

As Ambrosi's public relations "face," she understood exactly how this would be handled. There would be no return
to the turgid headlines that had followed their first passionate night together. There would be no announcements, no
fanfare…at least, not until after tomorrow's wedding.

Despite the fact that her strappy high heels, a perfect color
match for the dress, made her more than a little unstable on
the gravel, she jogged the last few yards and flung herself
into Lucas's arms.

The clean scent that was definitively Lucas, mingled with
the masculine, faintly exotic undertone of sandalwood, filled
her nostrils, making her head spin. Or maybe it was the delight of simply touching him again after a separation that
had run into two long months.

The cool sea breeze whipped long silky coils of hair
across her face as she lifted up on her toes. Her arms looped
around his neck, her body slid against his, instantly responding to his heat, the utter familiarity of broad shoulders and
sleek, hard-packed muscle. His sudden intake of breath, the
unmistakable feel of him hardening against the soft contours
of her belly filled her with mindless relief.

Ridiculous tears blurred her vision. This was so *not* playing it cool, but it had been two months since she had touched, kissed, made love to her man. Endless days while she had waited for the annoying, debilitating ulcer—clear evidence that she had not coped with her unresolved emotional situation—to heal. Long weeks while she had battled the niggling anxiety that had its roots in the disastrous bout of illness in Thailand, as if she was waiting for the next shoe to drop.

She realized that one of the reasons she had not told Lucas about the complications following the virus was that she had been afraid of the outcome. Over the years he had dated a string of gorgeous, glamorous women so she usually took great care that he only ever saw her at her very best. There had been nothing pretty or romantic about the fever that had gripped her in Thailand. There had been even less glamour surrounding her hospital stay in Sydney.

Lucas's arms closed around her, his jaw brushed her cheek sending a sensual shiver the length of her spine. Automatically, she leaned into him and lifted her mouth to his, but instead of kissing her, he straightened and unlooped her arms from his neck. Cold air filled the space between them.

When she moved to close the frustrating distance he gripped her upper arms.

"Carla." His voice was clipped, the Medinian accent smoothed out by the more cosmopolitan overtones of the States, but still dark and sexy enough to send another shiver down her spine. "I tried to ring you. Why didn't you pick up the call?"

The mundane question, the edged tone pulled her back to earth with a thump. "I switched my phone off while I was being interviewed then I put it on charge."

But it had only been that way for about an hour. When she had left the private villa she was sharing with her mother and Sienna, she had grabbed the phone and dropped it in her purse. His hands fell away from her arms, leaving a palpable chill in place of the warm imprint of his palms. Extracting the phone from her clutch, she checked the screen and saw that, in her hurry, she had forgotten to turn it on.

She activated the phone, and instantly the missed calls registered on the screen. "Sorry," she said coolly. "Looks like I forgot to turn it back on."

She frowned at his lack of response. With an effort of will, she controlled the unruly emotions that had had the temerity to explode out of their carefully contained box and dropped the phone back in her clutch. So, okay, this was subtext for "let's play it cool."

Fine. Cool she could do, but not doormat. "I'm sorry I missed meeting you earlier but you've been here most of the day. If you'd wanted we could have met for lunch."

A discreet thunk snapped Carla's head around. Automatically, she tracked the unexpected sound and movement as the passenger door of the Maserati swing open.

Not male. Which ruled out her first thought, that the second occupant of the Maserati, hidden from her view by darkly tinted windows, was one of the security personnel who sometimes accompanied Lucas.

Not male. Female.

Out of nowhere her heart started to hammer. A series of freeze frames flickered: silky dark hair caught in a perfect chignon; a smooth, elegant body encased in shimmering, pale pearlized silk.

She went hot then cold, then hot again. She had the abrupt sensation that she was caught in a dream. A *bad* dream.

She and Lucas had an agreement whereby they could date others in order to distract the press and preserve the privacy she had insisted upon. But not here, not now.

Jerkily, Carla completed the movement she realized Lucas wanted from her: she stepped back.

She focused on his face, for the first time fully absorbing the remoteness of his dark gaze. It was the same cool neutrality she had seen on the odd occasion when they had been together and he'd had to take a work call.

The throbbing in her head increased, intensified by a shivery sensitivity that swept her spine. Her fingers tightened on her clutch as she resisted the sudden, childish urge to hug away the chill.

She drew an impeded breath. Another woman? She had not seen that coming.

Her mind worked frantically. No. It couldn't be.

But, if she hadn't felt that moment of heated response she *could* almost think that Lucas—

Emotion flickered in his gaze, gone almost before she registered it. "I believe you've met Lilah."

Recognition followed as Lilah turned and the light from the portico illuminated delicate cheekbones and exotic eyes. "Of course." She acknowledged Ambrosi's spectacularly talented head designer with a stiff nod.

Of course she knew Lilah, and Lilah knew her.

And all about her situation with Lucas, if she correctly interpreted the sympathy in Lilah's eyes.

Confusion rocked her again. How dare Lucas confide their secret to anyone without her permission? And Lilah Cole wasn't just anyone. The Coles had worked for Ambrosi's for as long as Carla could remember. Carla's grandfather, Sebastien, had employed Lilah's mother in Broome. Lilah, herself, had worked for Ambrosi for the past five years, the last two as their head designer, creating some of their most exquisite jewelry.

Lilah's smile and polite greeting were more than a little wary as she closed the door of the Maserati and strolled around the front of the car to join them.

The sudden uncomfortable silence was broken as the front

door of the *castello* was pushed wide. Light flared across
the smooth expanse of gravel, the soft strains of classical
music filtered through the haze of shock that still held Carla
immobile.

A narrow, well-dressed man Carla recognized as Tomas,
Constantine's personal assistant, spoke briefly in Medinian
and motioned them all inside.

With a curt nod, Lucas indicated that both Carla and Lilah
precede him. Feeling like an automaton, Carla walked toward the broad steps, no longer caring that the gravel was
ruining her shoes. Exquisite confections she had chosen with
Lucas in mind—along with every other item of jewelry and
clothing she was wearing tonight, including her lingerie.

With each step she could feel the distance between them,
a mystifying cold impersonality, growing by the second.
When his hand landed in the small of Lilah's back, steadying her as she hitched up her gown with a poised, unutter-
ably graceful movement, Carla's heart squeezed on a pang
of misery. In those few seconds she finally acknowledged
the insidious fear that had coexisted with her need to be with
Lucas for almost two years.

She knew how dangerous Lucas was in business. As Constantine's right hand, by necessity he had to be coldly ruthless.

The other shoe had finally dropped. She had just been
smoothly, ruthlessly dumped.

Two

Tucking a glossy strand of dark hair behind her ear—hair that suddenly seemed too lush and unruly for a formal family occasion—Carla stepped into the disorienting center of what felt like a crowd.

In reality there were only a handful of people present in the elegant reception room: Tomas and members of the Atraeus family including Constantine, his younger brother, Zane, and Lucas's mother, Maria Therese. To one side, Sienna was chatting with their mother, Margaret Ambrosi.

Sienna, wearing a sleek ivory dress and already looking distinctly bridal, was the first to greet her. The quick hug, the moment of warmth, despite the fact that they had spent most of the morning going over the details of the wedding together, made Carla's throat lock.

Sienna gripped her hands, frowning. "Are you okay? You look a little pale."

"I'm fine, just a little rushed and I didn't expect the media ambush at the gates." Carla forced a bright smile. "You know me. I do thrive on publicity, but the reporters were like a pack of wolves."

Constantine, tall and imposing, greeted her with a brief hug, the gesture conveying her new status as a soon-to-be member of Medinos's most wealthy, powerful family. He frowned as he released her. "Security should have kept them at bay."

His expression was remote, his light gray gaze controlled, belying the primitive fact that he had used financial coercion and had even gone so far as kidnapping Sienna to get his former fiancée back.

"The security was good." Carla hugged her mother, fighting the ridiculous urge to cling like a child. If she did that she would cry, and she refused to cry in front of Lucas.

A waiter offered champagne. As she lifted the flute from the tray her gaze clashed with Lucas's. Her fingers tightened reflexively on the delicate stem. The message in his dark eyes was clear.

Don't talk. Don't make trouble.

She took a long swallow of the champagne. "Unfortunately, the line of questioning the press took was disconcerting. Although I'm sure that when Lucas arrived with Lilah any misconceptions were cleared up."

Sienna's expression clouded. "Don't tell me they're trying to resurrect that old story about you and Lucas?"

Carla controlled her wince reflex at the use of the word *resurrect*. "I guess it's predictable that now that you and Constantine have your happy ending, the media are looking to generate something out of nothing."

Sienna lifted a brow. "So, do they need a medic down at the gates?"

"Not this time." Lucas frowned as Carla took another

long swallow of champagne. "Don't forget I was the original target two years ago, not the media."

And suddenly the past was alive between them, vibrating with hurtful accusations and misunderstandings she thought they had dealt with long ago. The first night of unplanned and irresistible passion they'd shared, followed by the revelation of the financial deal her father had leveraged on the basis of Sienna's engagement to Constantine. Lucas's accusation that Carla was more interested in publicity and her career than she had been in him.

Carla forced herself to loosen her grip on the stem of her glass. "But then the media are so very fascinated by your private life, aren't they?"

A muscle pulsed along the side of his jaw. "Only when someone decides to feed them information."

The flat statement, correct as it was, stung. Two years ago, hurt by his comments, she had reacted by publicly stating that she had absolutely no interest in being pursued by Lucas. The story had sparked weeks of uncomfortable conjecture for them both.

Sienna left them to greet more arrivals. Her anger under control, Carla examined the elegant proportions of the reception room, the exquisite marble floors and rich, Italianate decor. "And does that thought keep you awake at night?"

Lucas's gaze flared at her deliberate reference to the restless passion for her that he had once claimed kept him awake at nights. "I'm well used to dealing with the media."

"A shame there isn't a story. It could have benefited Ambrosi's upcoming product launch." She forced a brilliant smile. "You know what they say, any publicity is good publicity. Although in this case, I'm sure the story wouldn't be worth the effort, especially when it would involve dragging *my* private life through the mud."

Lucas's expression shuttered, the fire abruptly gone. "Then I suggest you sleep easy. *I* don't kiss and tell."

The sense of disorientation she had felt the past few minutes evaporated in a rush of anger. "Or commit to relationships."

"You were the one who set the ground rules."

Suddenly Lucas seemed a lot closer. "You know I had no other option."

His expression was grim. "The truth is always an option."

Her chin jerked up. "I was protecting Sienna and my family. What was I supposed to do? Turn up with you at Mom and Dad's house for Sunday dinner and admit that I was—"

"Sleeping with me?"

The soft register of his voice made her heart pound. Every nerve in her body jangled at his closeness, the knowledge that he was just as aware of her as she was of him. "I was about to say dating an Atraeus."

Sienna returned from her hostess duties to step neatly between them. "Time out, children."

Lucas lifted a brow, his mouth quirking in the wry half smile that regularly made women go weak at the knees. "My apologies."

As Constantine joined them, Lucas drew Lilah into the circle. "I know I don't need to introduce Lilah."

There was a moment of polite acknowledgment and brief handshakes as Lilah was accepted unconditionally into the Atraeus fold. The process of meeting Maria Therese was more formal and underlined a salient and well-publicized fact. Atraeus men didn't take their women home to meet their families on a casual basis. To her best knowledge, until now, Lucas had never taken a girlfriend home to meet his mother.

Lucas's *girlfriend*.

Lilah was smiling, her expression contained but lit with an unmistakable glow.

A second salient fact made Carla stiffen. A few months ago, while stuck overnight together at a sales expo in Europe, she and Lilah had discussed the subject of relationships. At age twenty-nine, despite possessing the kind of sensual dark-haired, white-skinned beauty that riveted male attention, Lilah was determinedly single.

She had told Carla a little of her background, which included a single mother, a solo grandmother and ongoing financial hardship. Born illegitimate, Lilah had early on given herself a rule. No sex before marriage. There was no way she was going to be left holding a baby.

While Carla had stressed about finding Mr. Right, Lilah was calmly focused on marrying him, her approach methodical and systematic. She had moved on a step from Carla's idea of a spreadsheet and had developed a list of qualifying attributes as precise and unwavering as an employment contract. Also, unlike Carla, Lilah had *saved* herself for marriage. She was that twenty-first century paragon: a virgin.

The simple fact that she was on Medinos with Lucas, thousands of miles from her Sydney apartment and rigorous work schedule, spoke volumes.

Lilah did not date. Carla knew that she occasionally accompanied a gay neighbor to his professional dinners and had him escort her to charity functions she supported. But their relationship was purely friendship, which suited them both. That was all.

Carla took another gulp of champagne. Her stomach clenched because the situation was suddenly blindingly obvious.

Lilah was dating Lucas because she had chosen him. He was her intended husband.

Anger churned in Carla's stomach and stiffened her spine. She and Lucas had conducted their relationship based on a set of rules that was the complete opposite of everything that

Lilah was holding out for: no strings, strictly casual and, because of the family feud, in secrecy.

An enticing, convenient arrangement for a man who clearly had never had any intention of offering *her* marriage.

Waiters served more chilled champagne and trays of tiny, exquisite canapés. Carla forced herself to eat a tiny pastry case filled with a delicate seafood mousse. She continued to sip her way through the champagne, which loosened the tightness of her throat but couldn't wash away the deepening sense of hurt.

Lilah Cole was beautiful, elegant and likable, but nothing could change the fact that Lilah's easy acceptance into the Atraeus fold should have been *her* moment.

The party swelled as more family and friends arrived. Abandoning her champagne flute on a nearby sideboard, Carla joined the movement out onto a large stone balcony overlooking the sea.

Feeling awkward and isolated amidst the crowd, she threaded her way through the revelers to the parapet and stared out at the expansive view. The breeze gusted, laced with the scent of the sea, sending coils of hair across her cheeks and teasing at the flimsy silk of her dress, briefly exposing more leg than she had planned.

Lucas's gaze burned over her, filled with censure, not the desire that had sizzled between them for the past two years.

Cheeks burning, she snapped her dress back into place, her mood plummeting further as Lilah joined Lucas. Despite the breeze, Lilah's hair was neat and perfect, her dress subtly sensual with a classic pureness of line that suddenly made Carla feel cheap and brassy, all sex and dazzle against Lilah's demure elegance. Her cheeks grew hotter as she considered what she was wearing under the red silk. Again, nothing with any degree of subtlety. Every flimsy stitch was designed to entice.

She had taken a crazy risk in dressing so flamboyantly, practically begging for the continuation of their relationship. After the distance of the past two months she should have had more sense than to wear her heart on her sleeve. Jerking her gaze away, she tried to concentrate on the moon sliding up over the horizon, the churning floodlit water below the *castello*.

A cool gust of wind sent more hair whipping around her cheeks. Temporarily blinded, she snatched at her billowing hemline. Strong fingers gripped her elbow, steadying her. Heart-stoppingly familiar dark eyes clashed with hers. Not Lucas, Zane Atraeus.

"Steady. I've got you. Come over here, out of the wind before we lose you over the side."

Zane's voice was deep, mild and low-key, more American than Medinian, thanks to his Californian mother and upbringing. With his checkered, illegitimate past and lady-killer reputation, Zane was, of the three brothers, definitely the most approachable and she wondered a little desperately why she hadn't been able to fall for him instead of Lucas. "Thanks for the rescue."

He sent her an enigmatic look. "Damsels in distress are always my business."

The warmth in her cheeks flared a little brighter. The suspicion that Zane wasn't just talking about the wind, that he knew about her affair with Lucas, coalesced into certainty.

He positioned her in the lee of a stone wall festooned with ivy. "Can I get you a drink?"

A reckless impulse seized Carla as she glanced across at Lucas. "Why not?"

With his arm draped casually across the stone parapet behind Lilah, his stance was male and protective, openly claiming Lilah as his, although he wasn't touching her in any way.

Unbidden, a small kernel of hope flared to life at that

small, polite distance. Ten minutes ago, Carla had been certain they were an established couple; that to be here, at a family wedding, Lucas would have had to have slept with Lilah. Now she was abruptly certain they had not yet progressed to the bedroom. There was a definite air of restraint underpinning the glow on Lilah's face, and despite his possessive stance, Lucas was preserving a definite distance.

A waiter swung by. Zane handed her a flute of champagne. "Do you think they've slept together?"

Carla's hand jerked at the question. Champagne splashed over her fingers. She dragged her gaze from the clean line of Lucas's profile and glanced at Zane. His expression was oddly grim, his jaw set. "I don't know why you're asking me that question."

Zane, who hadn't bothered with champagne, gave her a steady look, and humiliation curled through her. He knew.

Carla wondered a little wildly how he had found out and if everyone on the balcony knew that she was Lucas's ditched ex.

Zane's expression was dismissive. "Don't worry, it was a lucky guess."

Relief flooded her as she swallowed a mouthful of champagne. A few seconds later her head began to spin and she resolved not to drink any more.

Zane's attention was no longer on her; it was riveted on Lilah and realization hit. She wasn't the only one struggling here. "You want Lilah."

The grim anger she had glimpsed winked out of existence. "If I was in the market for marriage, maybe."

"Which, I take it, you're not."

Zane's dark gaze zeroed in on hers, but Carla realized he still barely logged her presence. "No. Are you interested in art?"

Carla blinked at the sudden change of subject. "Yes."

"If you want out of this wind, I'll be happy to show you the rogue's gallery."

She had glimpsed the broad gallery that housed the Atraeus family portraits, some painted by acknowledged masters, but hadn't had time to view them. "I would love to take a closer look at the family portraits."

Anything to get her off the balcony. "Just do me one favor. Put your arm around my waist."

"And make it look good?"

Carla's chin jerked up a fraction. "If you don't mind."

The unflattering lack of reaction to her suggestion should have rubbed salt into the wound, but Carla was beyond caring. She was dying by inches but she was determined not to be any more tragic than she had to be.

Lucas's gaze burned over her as she handed her drink to a waiter then allowed Zane's arm to settle around her waist. As they strolled past Lucas, she was forcibly struck by the notion that he was jealous.

Confusion rocked her. She hadn't consciously set out to make Lucas jealous; her main concern from the moment she had realized that Lucas and Lilah were together had been self-preservation. Lucas being jealous made no sense unless he still wanted her, and how could that be when he had already chosen another woman?

Carla was relieved when Zane dropped his arm the second they were out of sight of the balcony. After a short walk through flagged corridors, they entered the gallery. Along one wall, arched windows provided spectacular views of the moonlit sea. The opposite wall was softly lit and lined with exquisite paintings.

The tingling sense of alarm, as if at some level she was aware of Lucas's displeasure, continued as they strolled past rank after rank of gorgeous rich oils. Most had been painted pre-1900s, before the once wealthy and noble Atraeus family had fallen on hard times. Lucas's grandfather, after discovering an obscenely rich gold mine, had since purchased most of the paintings back from private collections and museums.

The men were clearly of the Atraeus bloodline, with strong jaws and aquiline profiles. The women, almost without exception, looked like Botticelli angels: beautiful, demure, virginal.

Zane paused beside a vibrant painting of an Atraeus ancestor who looked more like a pirate than a noble lord. His lady was a serene, quiet dove with a steely glint in her eye. With her long, slanting eyes and delicate bones, the woman bore an uncanny resemblance to Lilah. "As you can see it's a mixture of sinners and saints. It seemed that the more dissolute and marauding the Atraeus male, the more powerful his desire for a saint."

Carla heard the measured tread of footsteps. Her heart sped up because she was almost sure it was Lucas. "And is that what Atraeus men are searching for today?"

Zane shrugged. "I can't speak for my brothers. I'm not your typical Atraeus male."

Her jaw tightened. "But the idea of a pure, untouched bride still has a certain appeal."

"Maybe." He sent her a flashing grin that made him look startlingly like the Atraeus pirate in the painting. "Although, I'm always willing to be convinced that a sinner is the way to go."

"Because that generally means no commitment, right?"

Zane's dark brows jerked together. "How did we get on to commitment?"

Carla registered the abrupt silence as if whoever had just entered the gallery had seen them and stopped.

Her heart slammed in her chest as she caught Lucas's reflection in one of the windows. On impulse, she stepped close to Zane and tilted her head back, the move flirtatious and openly provocative. She was playing with fire, because Zane had a reputation that scorched.

Lucas would be furious with her. If he *was* jealous, her behavior would probably kill any feelings he had left for her, but she was beyond caring. He had hurt her too badly for her to pull back now. "If that's an invitation, the answer is yes."

Zane's gaze registered unflattering surprise.

Minor detail, because Lucas was now walking toward them. Gritting her teeth, she wound her finger in Zane's tie, applying just enough pressure that his head lowered until his mouth was mere inches from hers.

His gaze was disarmingly neutral. "I know what you're up to."

"You could at least be tempted."

"I'm trying."

"Try harder."

"Damn, you're type A. No wonder he went for Lilah."

Carla's fingers tightened on his tie. "Is it that obvious?"

"Only to me. And that's because I'm a control freak myself."

"I am *not* a control freak."

He unwound her fingers from his tie. "Whatever you say."

Cut adrift by Zane's calm patience, Carla had no choice but to step back and in so doing almost caromed into Lucas.

She flinched at the fiery trail of his gaze over the shadow of her cleavage, her mouth, the impression of heat and desire. If Zane hadn't been there she was almost certain he would have pulled her close and kissed her.

Lucas's expression was shuttered. "What are you up to?"

Carla didn't try to keep the bitterness out of her voice. "*I'm* not up to anything. Zane was showing me the paintings."

"Careful," Zane intervened, his gaze on Lucas. "Or I

might think you have a personal interest in Carla, and that couldn't possibly be, since you're dating the lovely Lilah."

A sharp pang went through Carla at the tension vibrating between the brothers, shifting undercurrents she didn't understand.

Spine rigid, she kept her gaze firmly on Zane's jaw. She hadn't liked behaving like that, but at least she had proved that Lucas did still want her. Although the knowledge was a bitter pill, because his reaction repeated a pattern that was depressingly familiar. In establishing a stress-free liaison with him based on her rules, she had somehow negotiated herself out of the very things she needed most: love, companionship and commitment.

Lucas had wanted her for two years, but that was all. The relationship had struggled to progress out of the bedroom. Even when she had finally gotten him to Thailand for a whole four-day minibreak, the longest period of time they had ever spent together, the plan had crashed and burned because she had gotten sick.

She wondered in what way she was lacking that Lucas didn't want a full relationship with her? That instead of allowing them to grow closer, he had kept her at an emotional arm's length and gone to Lilah for the very things that Carla needed from him.

She glanced apologetically at Zane in an effort to defuse the tension. "It's okay, Lucas and I are old news. If there was anything more we would be together now."

"Whereas marriage *is* Lilah's focus," Zane said softly.

Lucas frowned. "Back off, Zane."

Confusion gripped Carla along with another renegade glimmer of hope at Lucas's reaction. She was tired of thinking about everything that had gone wrong, but despite that, her mind grabbed on to the notion that maybe all he was doing *was* dating Lilah on a casual basis. Just because Lilah wanted marriage didn't necessarily mean she would get what she wanted.

Grimly, she forced herself to study the Atraeus bride in the painting again. It was the perfect reality check.

Her pale, demure gown was the epitome of all things virginal and pure. Nothing like Carla's flaming red silk dress, with its enticing glimpse of cleavage and leg. The serene eighteenth-century bride was no doubt every man's secret dream. A perfect wife, without a flirty bone in her body. Or a stress condition.

Lucas's gaze sliced back to Carla. "I'll take you back to the party. Dinner will be served in about fifteen minutes."

He *was* jealous.

The thought reverberated through her, but for the first time in two years what Lucas wanted wasn't a priority. *Her* rules had just changed. From now on it was commitment or nothing.

Her chin firmed. "No. I have an escort. Zane will take me back to the party."

For a long, tension-filled moment Carla thought Lucas would argue, but then the demanding, possessive gleam was replaced by a familiar control. He nodded curtly then sent Zane a long, cold look that conveyed a hands-off message that left Carla feeling doubly confused. Lucas didn't want her, but neither did he want Zane anywhere near her.

And if Lucas no longer wanted her, if they really were finished, why had he bothered to search her out?

Three

Lucas Atraeus strode into his private quarters and snapped the door closed behind him. Opening a set of French doors, he stepped out onto his balcony. The wind buffeted the weathered stone parapet and whipped night-dark hair around the obdurate line of his jaw. He tried to focus on the steady roar of the waves pounding the cliff face beneath and the stream of damp, salty air, while he waited for the self-destructive desire to reclaim Carla to dissolve.

The vibration of his cell phone drew him back inside. Sliding the phone out of his pocket, he checked the screen. Lilah. No doubt wondering where he was.

Jaw clenched, he allowed the call to go through to his voice mail. He couldn't stomach talking to Lilah right at that moment with his emotions still raw and his thoughts on another woman. Besides, with a relationship based on a few phone calls and a couple of conversations, most of

them purely work based, they literally had nothing to say
to each other.

The call terminated. Lucas found himself staring at a
newspaper he had tossed down on the coffee table, the one
he had read on the night flight from New York to Medinos.
The paper was open at the society pages and a grainy shot
of Carla in her capacity as the "face" of Ambrosi Pearls,
twined intimately close with a rival millionaire businessman.

Picking up the newspaper, he reread the caption that
hinted at a hot affair.

He had been away for two months but by all accounts she
had not missed him.

Tossing the newspaper down on the coffee table, he strode
back out onto the balcony. Before he could stop himself, he
had punched in her number on his phone.

Calling her now made no kind of sense.

He held the sleek phone pressed to his ear and forced himself to remember the one overriding reason he should never
have touched Carla Ambrosi.

Grimly, he noted that the hit of old grief and sharp-
enough-to-taste guilt still wasn't powerful enough to bury
the impulse to involve himself even more deeply in yet another fatal attraction.

When he had met Carla, somehow he had stepped away
from the rigid discipline he had instilled in himself after
Sophie's death.

The car accident hadn't been his fault, but he was still
haunted by the argument that had instigated Sophie's headlong dash in her sports car after he had found out that she
had aborted his child.

Sophie had been beautiful, headstrong and adept at winding him around her little finger. He should have stopped her,
taken the car keys. He should have controlled the situation. It
had been his responsibility to protect her, and he had failed.

They should never have been together in the first place.

They had been all wrong for each other. He had been disciplined, work focused and family orientated. Sophie had skimmed along the surface of life, thriving on bright lights, parties and media attention. Even the manner in which Sophie had died had garnered publicity and had been perceived in certain quarters as glamorous.

The ring tone continued. His fingers tightened on the cell. Carla had her phone with her; she should have picked up by now.

Unless she was otherwise occupied. *With Zane.*

His stomach clenched at the image of Carla, mouthwateringly gorgeous in red, her fingers twined in Zane's tie, poised for a kiss he had interrupted.

He didn't trust Zane. His younger brother had a reputation with women that literally burned.

The call went through to voice mail. Carla's voice filled his ear.

Despite the annoyance that gripped him that Carla had decided to ignore his call, Lucas was riveted by the velvet-cool sound of the recorded message. The brisk, businesslike tone so at odds with Carla's ultrasexy, ultrafeminine appearance and which never failed to fascinate.

During the two months he had been in the States he had refrained from contacting Carla. He had needed to distance himself from a relationship that during an intense few days in Thailand had suddenly stepped over an invisible boundary and become too gut-wrenchingly intimate. Too like his relationship with Sophie.

Carla, who was surprisingly businesslike and controlled when it came to communication, had left only one text and a single phone message to which he had replied. A few weeks ago he had seen her briefly, from a distance, at her father's funeral, but they hadn't spoken.

That was reason number two not to become involved with Carla.

The ground rules for their relationship had been based on what she had wanted: a no-strings fun fling, carried out in secret because of the financial scandal that had erupted between their two families.

Secrecy was not Lucas's thing, but since he had never planned on permanency he hadn't seen any harm in going along with Carla's plan. He had been based in the States, Carla was in Sydney. A relationship wasn't possible even if he had wanted one.

The line hummed expectantly.

Irritated with himself for not having done it sooner, Lucas terminated the call.

Grimly, he stared at the endless expanse of sea, the faint curve of the horizon. Carla not picking up the call was the best-case scenario. If she had, he was by no means certain he could have maintained his ruthless facade.

The problem was that, as tough and successful as he was in business, when it came to women his track record was patchy.

As an Atraeus he was expected to be coolly dominant. Despite the years he had spent trying to mold himself into the strong silent type who routinely got his way, he had not achieved Constantine's effortless self-possession. Little kids and fluffy dogs still targeted him; women of all ages gravitated to him as if they had no clue about his reputation as The Atraeus Group's key hatchet man.

Despite the long list of companies he had streamlined or clinically dismantled, he couldn't forget that he had not been able to establish any degree of control over his relationship with Sophie.

Jaw taut, Lucas padded inside. He barely noticed the

warm glow of lamplight, the richness of exquisite antiques and jewel-bright carpets.

His gaze zeroed in on the newspaper article again. A hot pulse of jealously burned through him as he studied the Greek millionaire who had his arm around Carla's waist.

Alex Panopoulos, an archrival across the boardroom table and a well-known playboy.

Given the limited basis of Lucas's relationship with Carla, they had agreed it had to be open; they were both free to date others. Like Lucas, Carla regularly dated as part of her career, although so far Lucas had not been able to bring himself to include another woman in his life on more than a strictly platonic basis.

Panopoulos was a guest at the wedding tomorrow.

Walking through to the kitchen, he tossed the paper into the trash. His jaw tightened at the thought that he would have fend off the Greek, as well.

He guessed he should be glad that it was Zane Carla seemed to be attracted to and not Panopoulos.

Zane had been controllable, so far. And if he stepped over the line, there was always the option that they could settle the issue in the old-fashioned way, down on the beach and without an audience.

Dinner passed in a polite, superficial haze. Carla made conversation, smiled on cue, and avoided looking at Lucas. Unfortunately, because he was seated almost directly opposite her, she was burningly aware of him through each course.

Dessert was served. Still caught between the raw misery that threatened to drag her under, and the need to maintain the appearance of normality, Carla ate. She had reached the dessert course when she registered how much wine she had drunk.

A small sharp shock went through her. She wasn't drunk, but alcohol and some of the foods she was eating did not mix happily with an ulcer. Strictly speaking, after the episode with the virus and the ulcer, she wasn't supposed to drink at all.

Setting her spoon down, she picked up her clutch and excused herself from the table. She asked one of the waitstaff to direct her to the nearest bathroom. Unfortunately, since her grasp of Medinian was far from perfect, she somehow managed to take a wrong turn.

After traversing a long corridor and opening a number of doors, one of which seemed to be the entrance to a private set of rooms, complete with a kitchenette, she opened a door and found herself on a terrace overlooking the sea. Shrugging, because the terrace would do as well as a bathroom since all she required was privacy to take the small cocktail of pills her doctor had prescribed, she walked to the stone parapet and studied the view.

The stiff sea breeze that had been blowing earlier had dropped away, leaving the night still, the air balmy and heavily scented with the pine and rosemary that grew wild on the hills. A huge full moon glowed a rich, buttery gold on the horizon.

Setting her handbag down on the stone pavers, she extracted the MediPACK of pills she had brought with her, tore open the plastic seal and swallowed them dry.

Dropping the plastic waste into her handbag, she straightened just as the door onto the terrace popped open. Her chest tightened when she recognized Lucas.

"I hope you weren't expecting Zane?"

"If I was, it wouldn't be any of your business."

"Zane won't give you what you want."

Carla swallowed to try and clear the dry bitterness in her

mouth. "A loving relationship? The kind of relationship I thought we could have had?"

He ignored the questions. "You should return to the dining room."

The flatness of Lucas's voice startled her. Lucas had always been exciting and difficult to pin down, but he had also been funny and unexpectedly tender. This was the first time she had ever seen this side of him. "Not yet. I have a…headache, I need some air." Which was no lie, because the headache was there, throbbing steadily at her temples.

She pretended to be absorbed by the spectacular view of the crystal-clear night and the vast expanse of sea gleaming like polished bronze beneath the moon. Just off the coast of Medinos, the island of Ambrus loomed, tonight seemingly almost close enough to touch. One of the more substantial islands in the Medinos group, Ambrus was intimately familiar to her because her family had once owned a chunk of it.

"How did you know these are my rooms?"

She spun, shocked at Lucas's closeness and what he'd just said. "I didn't. I was looking for a bathroom. I must have taken a wrong turn."

The coolness of his glance informed her that he didn't quite believe her. Any idea that Lucas would tell her that he had made a mistake and that he desperately wanted her back died a quick death.

A throb of grief hit her at the animosity that seemed to be growing by the second and she pulled herself up sharply. She had run the gamut of shock and anger. She was not going to wallow in self-pity.

It was clear Lucas wasn't going to leave until she did, so she picked up her bag and started toward the door.

Instead of moving aside, Lucas moved to block her path. "I'm sorry you found out this way. I did try to meet with you before dinner."

Her heart suddenly pounding off the register, she stared rigidly at his shoulder. "You could have told me when I called to cancel and given me some time. Even a text would have helped."

His dark brows jerked together. "I'm not in the habit of breaking off relationships over the phone or by text. I wanted to tell you face-to-face."

Her jaw tightened. It didn't help that his gaze was direct, that he was clearly intent on softening the blow. The last thing she wanted from Lucas was pity. "Did Lilah fly in with you?"

"She arrived this afternoon."

Relief made her feel faintly unsteady. So, Lilah hadn't been with Lucas in the limousine.

As insignificant as that detail was, it mattered, because when she had seen the limousine she had been crazily, sappily fantasizing about Lucas and the life they could now share. Although she should have known he hadn't arrived with Lilah, because there hadn't been any media reports that he had arrived at the airport with a female companion.

Lucas's gaze connected with hers. "Before you go back inside, I need to know if you intend to go to the press with a story about our affair."

Affair.

Her chin jerked up. For two years she had considered they had been involved in a relationship. "I'm here for Sienna's wedding. It's her day, and I don't intend to spoil it."

"Good. Because if you try to force my hand by going public with this, take it from me, I'm not playing."

Comprehension hit. She had been so absorbed with the publicity for Ambrosi's latest collection and the crazy rush to organize Sienna's wedding that she had barely had time to sleep, let alone think. When Sienna married Constantine, Carla would be inextricably bound to the Atraeus family.

The Atraeus family were traditionalists. If it were discovered that she and Lucas had been seeing each other secretly for two years, he would come under intense pressure from his family to marry her.

Now the comment about her looking for his rooms made sense.

What better way to force a commitment than to arrange for them both to be found together in his rooms at the *castello?* Anger and a burning sense of shame that he should think she would stoop that low sliced through her. "I hadn't considered that angle."

Why would she when she had assumed Lucas wanted her?

He ignored her statement. "If it's marriage you want, you won't get it by pressuring me."

Which meant he really had thought about the different ways she could force him to the altar. She took a deep breath against a sharp spasm of hurt. "At what point did I ever say I was after marriage?"

His gaze bored into hers, as fierce and obdurate as the dark stone from which the fortress was built. "Then we have an understanding?"

"Oh, I think so." She forced a bright smile. "I wouldn't marry you if you tied me up and dragged me down the aisle. Tell me," she said before she could gag her mouth and instruct her brain to never utter anything that would inform Lucas just how weak and vulnerable she really was. "Did you ever come close to loving me?"

He went still. "What we had wasn't exactly about love."

No. Silly her.

"There's something else we need to talk about."

"In that case, it'll have to wait. Now I really do have a headache." She fumbled in her clutch, searching for the painkillers she'd slipped in before she'd left the villa, just in case. In her haste the foil pack slipped out of her fingers and dropped to the terrace.

Lucas retrieved the pills before she could. "What are these?"

He held the foil pack out of her reach while he read the label. "Since when have you suffered from headaches?"

She snatched the pills from his grasp. "They're a left-over from the virus I caught in Thailand. I don't get them very often."

She ripped the foil open and swallowed two pills dry, grimacing at the extra wave of bitterness in her mouth when one of the pills lodged in her throat. She badly needed a glass of water.

Lucas frowned. "I didn't know you were still having problems."

She shoved the foil pack back in her clutch. "But then you never bothered to ask."

And the last thing she had wanted to do was let him know that she had been so stressed by the unresolved nature of their relationship that she had given herself an even worse stomach ulcer than she had started with two years ago.

After the growing distance between them in Thailand, she hadn't wanted to further undermine their relationship or give him an excuse to break up with her. Keeping silent had been a constant strain because she had wanted the comfort of his presence, had *needed* him near, but now she was glad she hadn't revealed how sick she really had been. It was one small corner of her life that he hadn't invaded, one small batch of memories that didn't contain him.

She felt like kicking herself for being so stupid over the past couple of months. If Lucas had wanted to be with her he would have arranged time together. Once, he had flown into Sydney with only a four-hour window before he'd had to fly out again. They had spent every available second of those four hours locked together in bed.

Cold settled in her stomach. In retrospect, their relationship had foundered in Thailand. Lucas hadn't liked crossing the line into caring; he had simply wanted a pretty, adoring lover and uncomplicated sex.

Lucas was still blocking her path. "You're pale and your eyes are dilated. I'll take you home."

"No." She stepped neatly around him and made a beeline for the open door. Her heart sped up when she realized he was close behind her. "I can drive myself. The last thing I want is to spend any more time with you."

"Too bad." His hand curled around her upper arm, sending a hot, tingling shock straight to the pit of her stomach as he propelled her into the hall. "You've had a couple of glasses of wine, and now a strong painkiller. The last thing you should do is get behind the wheel of that little sports car."

She shot him a coolly assessing look. "Or talk to the paparazzi at the gate."

"Right now it's the hairpin bends on the road back to the villa that worry me."

Something snapped inside her at the calm, matter-of-fact tone of his voice, as if he was conducting damage control in one of his business takeovers. "What do you think I'm going to do, Lucas? Drive off one of your cliffs into the sea?"

Unexpectedly his grip loosened. Twisting free, she grasped the handle of the door to the suite she had briefly checked out before, thinking it could be a bathroom. It was Lucas's suite, apparently. Forbidden territory.

Flinging the door wide, she stepped inside. She was about to prove that at least one of Lucas's fears was justified.

She was going to be her control-freak, ticked-off, stressed-out self for just a few minutes.

She was going to behave badly.

Four

The paralyzing fear that had gripped Lucas at the thought of Carla driving her sports car on Medinos's narrow roads turned to frustration as she stepped inside his suite.

Grimly, he wondered what had happened to the dominance and control with which he had started the evening.

Across boardroom tables, he was aware that his very presence often inspired actual fear. His own people jumped to do his bidding.

Unfortunately, when it came to Carla Ambrosi, concepts like power, control and discipline crashed and burned.

He closed the door behind him. "What do you think you're doing?"

Carla halted by an ebony cabinet that held a selection of bottles, a jug of ice water and a tray of glasses. "I need a drink."

Glass clinked on glass, liquid splashed. His frustration deepened. Carla seldom drank and when she did it had always been in moderation. Tonight he knew she'd had champagne, then wine with dinner. He had kept a watch on her intake, specifically so he could intervene if he thought she was in danger of drinking too much then making a scene. He had been looking for an opportunity to speak to her alone when she had walked out halfway through dessert. Until now he had been certain she wasn't drunk.

He reached her in two long strides and gripped her wrist. "How much have you had?"

Liquid splashed the front of her dress. He jerked his gaze away from the way the wet silk clung to the curve of her breasts.

Her gaze narrowed. A split second later cold liquid cascaded down his chest, soaking through to the skin.

Water, not alcohol.

Time seemed to slow, stop as he stared at her narrowed gaze, delicately molded cheekbones and firm jaw, the rapid pulse at her throat.

The thud of the glass hitting the thick kilim barely registered as she curled her fingers in the lapel of his jacket.

"What do you think you're doing?" His voice was husky, the question automatic as he stared at her face.

"Conducting an experiment."

Her arms slid around his neck; she lifted up onto her toes. Automatically, his head bent. The second his mouth touched hers he knew it was a mistake. Relief shuddered through him as her breasts flattened against his chest and the soft curve of her abdomen cradled his instant arousal.

His hands settled at her waist as he deepened the kiss. The soft, exotic perfume she wore rose up, beguiling him, and the fierce clamp of desire intensified. Two months. As intent as he had been on finishing with Carla, he didn't know how he had stayed away.

No one else did this to him; no one came close. To say he

made love with Carla didn't cover the fierceness of his need or the undisciplined emotion that grabbed at him every time he weakened and allowed himself the "fix" of a small window of time in her bed.

Following the tragedy with Sophie, he had kept his liaisons clear-cut and controlled, as disciplined as his heavy work schedule and workout routines. He had been too shell-shocked to do anything else. Carla was the antithesis of the sophisticated, emotionally secure women he usually chose. Women who didn't demand or do anything flamboyant or off-the-wall.

He dragged his mouth free, shrugged out of his jacket then sank back into the softness of her mouth. He felt her fingers dragging at the buttons of his shirt, the tactile pleasure of her palms sliding over his skin.

Long, drugging minutes passed as he simply kissed her, relearning her touch, her taste. When she moved restlessly against him, he smoothed his hands up over her back, knowing instinctively that if she was going to withdraw, this would be the moment.

Her gaze clashed with his and he logged her assent. It occurred to Lucas that if he had been a true gentleman, he would have eased away, slowed things down. Instead he gave into temptation, cupped her breasts through the flimsy silk of bodice and bra. She arched against him with a small cry. Heat jerked through him when he realized she had climaxed.

Every muscle taut, he swept her into his arms and carried her to the couch. Her arms wound around his neck as she pulled him down with her. At some point his shirt disappeared and Carla shimmied against him, lifting up the few centimeters he needed so he could peel away the flimsy scrap of silk and lace that served as underwear.

He felt her fingers tearing at the fastening of his trousers. In some distant part of his mind the fact that he didn't have a condom registered. A split second later her hands closed around him and he ceased to think.

Desire shivered and burned through Carla as Lucas's hands framed her hips. Still dazed by the unexpected power of her climax, she automatically tilted her hips, allowing him access. Shock reverberated through her when she registered that there was no condom.

She hadn't thought; he hadn't asked. In retrospect she hadn't wanted to ask. She had been drowning in sensation, caught and held by the sudden powerful conviction that if she walked away from Lucas now, everything they had shared, everything they had been to each other would be lost. She would never touch him, kiss him, make love with him again, and that thought was acutely painful.

It was wrong, crazily wrong, on a whole lot of levels. Lucas had broken up with her. He had chosen someone else.

His gaze locked with hers and the steady, focused heat, so utterly familiar—as if she really was the only woman in the world for him—steadied her.

Emotion squeezed her chest as the shattering intensity gripped her again, linking her more intensely with Lucas. She should pull back, disengage. Making love did not compute, and especially not without a condom, but the concept of stopping now was growing progressively more blurred and distant.

She didn't want distance. She loved making love with Lucas. She loved his scent, the satiny texture of skin, the masculine beauty of sleek, hard muscle. The tender way he touched her, kissed her, made love to her was indescribably singular and intimate. She had never made love with another man, and when they were together, for those moments, he was *hers*.

Sharp awareness flickered in his gaze. He muttered something in rapid, husky Medinian, an apology for his loss of control, and a wild sliver of hope made her tense. If Lucas had wanted her badly enough that he hadn't been able to stop long enough to take care of protection, then there had to be a future for them.

With a raw groan he tangled his fingers in her hair, a glint of rueful humor charming her as he bent and softly kissed her. Something small and hurt inside her relaxed. She wound her arms around his neck, holding him tight against her and the hot night shivered and dissolved around them.

For long minutes Carla lay locked beneath Lucas on the couch. She registered the warm internal tingle of lovemaking. It had been two months since they had last been together, and she took a moment to wallow in the sheer pleasure of his heat and scent, the uncomplicated sensuality of his weight pressing her down.

She rubbed her palms down his back and felt his instant response.

Lucas's head lifted up from its resting place on her shoulder. The abrupt wariness in his gaze reflected her own thoughts. They'd had unprotected sex once. Were they really going to repeat the mistake?

A sharp rap at the door completed the moment of separation.

"Wait," Lucas said softly.

She felt the cool flutter as he draped her dress over her thighs. Feeling dazed and guilty, Carla clambered to her feet, snatched up her panties and her bag and found her shoes.

"The bathroom is the second on the left."

Her head jerked up at the husky note in his voice, but Lucas's expression was back to closed, his gaze neutral.

He was already dressed. With his shirt buttoned, his jacket on, he looked smoothly powerful and unruffled, exactly as he had before they had made love. Somewhere in-

side her the sliver of hope that had flared to life when they
had been making love died a sudden death.

Nothing had changed. How many times had she seen him
distance himself from her in just that way when he had left
her apartment, as if he had already separated himself from
her emotionally?

As if what they had shared was already filed firmly in
the past and she had no place in his everyday life.

The moment was chilling, a reality check that was long
overdue. "Don't worry, I'll find it. I don't want anyone to
know I was here, either." Her own voice was husky but
steady. Despite the hurt she felt oddly distant and remote.

She stepped into the cool, tiled sanctuary of the bathroom and locked the door. After freshening up she set about
fixing her makeup. A sharp rap on the door made her jerk,
smearing her mascara.

"When you're ready, I'll take you home."

"Five minutes. And I'll take myself home."

She stared at her reflection, her too pale skin, the curious blankness in her eyes as if, like a turtle retreating into
its shell, the hurt inner part of her had already withdrawn.
With automatic movements, she cleaned away the smear and
reapplied the mascara.

When she stepped out of the bathroom the sitting room
was empty. For the first time she noticed the fine antiques
and jewel-bright rugs, the art that decorated the walls and
which was lit by glowing pools of light.

Lucas stepped in from the terrace, through an elegant set
of French doors.

She met his gaze squarely. "Who was at the door?"

"Lilah."

Oh, good. Her life had just officially gone to hell in a
handbasket. "Did she see me?"

"Unfortunately."

Lucas's choice of word finally succeeded in dissolving the curious blankness and suddenly she was fiercely angry. "What if I'm pregnant?"

A pulse worked in his jaw. "If you're pregnant, that changes things—we'll talk. Until you have confirmation, we forget this happened."

When Carla woke in the morning, the headache was still nagging, and she was definitely off-color. She stepped into the shower and washed her hair. When she'd soaped herself, she stood beneath the stream of hot water and waited to feel better.

She spread her palm over her flat abdomen, a sense of disorientation gripping her when she considered that she could be pregnant.

A baby.

The thought was as shocking as the fact that she had been weak enough to allow Lucas to make love to her.

If she was pregnant, she decided, there was no way she could terminate. She loved babies, the way they smelled, their downy softness and vulnerability, the gummy smiles—and she would adore her own.

Decision made. If—and it was a big *if*—she was pregnant she would have the child and manage as a single parent. Lucas wouldn't have to be involved. There was no way she would marry him without love, or exist in some kind of twilight state in his life that would allow him discreet access while he married someone else.

Turning off the water, she toweled herself dry, belted on a robe and padded down to breakfast. Her stomach felt vaguely nauseous and she wasn't hungry, but she forced herself to chew one of the sweet Medinian rolls she had enjoyed so much yesterday.

Half an hour later, she checked on Sienna, who was

smothered by attendants, then dressed for the wedding in an exquisite lilac-silk sheath. She sat for the hairdresser, who turned her hair into a glossy confection of curls piled on top of her head, then moved to another room where a cosmetician chatted cheerfully while she did her makeup.

Several hours later, with the wedding formalities finally completed and the dancing under way, she was finally free to leave her seat at the bridal table. Technically, as the maid of honor, her partner for the celebration was Lucas, who was the best man. Mercifully, he was seated to one side of the bride and groom, and she the other, so she had barely seen him all evening.

As she rose from the table and found the strap of her purse, which was looped over the back of her seat, lean brown fingers closed over hers, preventing her from lifting up the bag.

A short, sharp shock ran through her at the pressure. Lucas released his hold on her fingers almost immediately.

He indicated Constantine and Sienna drifting around the dance floor. "I know you probably don't want to dance, but tradition demands that we take the floor next."

She glanced away from the taut planes of his cheekbones and his chiseled jaw, the inky crescents of his lashes. In a morning suit, with its tight waistcoat, he looked even more devastatingly handsome than usual. "And is that what you do?" she said a little bitterly. "Follow tradition?"

Lucas waited patiently for her to acquiesce to the dance. "You know me better than that."

Yes, she did, unfortunately. As wealthy and privileged as Lucas was, he had done a number of unconventional things. One of them was to play professional rugby. Her gaze rested on the faintly battered line of his nose. An automatic tingle of awareness shot through her at the dangerous, sexy edge it added to features that would otherwise have been *GQ* perfect.

His gaze locked on hers and, as suddenly as if a switch had been thrown, the sizzling hum of attraction was intimately, crazily shared.

Her breath came in sharply. Not good.

Aware that they were now under intense scrutiny from guests at a nearby table, including Lilah, Carla placed her hand on Lucas's arm and allowed him to lead her to the dance floor.

Lucas's breath feathered her cheek as he pulled her close. "How likely is it that you are pregnant?"

She stiffened at the sudden hot flood of memory. On cue the music changed, slowing to a sultry waltz. Lucas pulled her into a closer hold. Heat shivered through her as her body automatically responded to his touch. "Not likely."

Since the virus she had caught in Thailand she hadn't had a regular cycle, mostly because, initially, she had lost so much weight. She had regained some of the weight but she hadn't yet had a period. Although she wasn't about to inform Lucas of that fact.

"How soon will you know?"

"I'm not sure. Two weeks, give or take."

"When you find out, one way or the other, I want to be informed, but that shouldn't be a problem. As of next week, I'm Ambrosi's new CEO."

She stumbled, missing a step. Lucas's arm tightened and she found herself briefly pressed against his muscular frame. Jerkily, she straightened, her cheeks burning at the intimate brush of his hips, a stark reminder of their lovemaking last night. "I thought Ben Vitalis was stepping in as CEO."

Lucas's specialty was managing hostile acquisitions. Since her family, embattled by long-term debt, had voluntarily offered The Atraeus Group a majority shareholding of Ambrosi Pearls, the situation was cut-and-dried. Lucas shouldn't have come within a mile of Ambrosi.

Unless he viewed *her* as a problem.

Her chin jerked up as another thought occurred to her. "You told Constantine about us."

His brows jerked together. "No."

Relief flooded her. The thought that Lucas could have revealed their relationship now, when it was over, would have finally succeeded in making her feel cheap and disposable.

She drew in a steadying breath. "When was the decision made?"

"A few weeks ago, when we knew Ambrosi was in trouble."

"It's not necessary for you to come to Sydney. In the unlikely event that there is a baby, I will contact you."

His glance was impatient. "The decision is made."

She drew an impeded breath at the sudden graphic image of herself round and heavy with his child. She didn't think a pregnancy was possible, but clearly Lucas did.

The music wound to a sweeping, romantic halt. There was a smattering of applause. Carla allowed Lucas to complete the formalities by leading her off the dance floor.

The rest of the evening passed in a haze. Carla danced with several men she didn't know, and twice with Alex Panopoulos, an Ambrosi client she'd had extensive dealings with in Sydney. The wealthy owner of a successful chain of high-end retail stores, Alex was a reptile when it came to women. He was also in need of a public relations officer for a new venture and spent the first dance fishing to see if she was available. Halfway through the second dance, Lucas cut in.

His gaze clashed with hers as he spun her into a sweeping turn. "Damn. What are you doing with Panopoulos?"

"Nothing that's any of your business. Why? Do you think

I'm in danger of meeting a man who might actually propose?"

"Alex Panopoulos is a shrewd operator. When he marries, there will be a business connection."

She stared at the clean line of his jaw. "Are you suggesting that all he wants is an affair?"

His grip on her fingers tightened. "I have no idea what Panopoulos wants. All I know is that when it comes to women he doesn't have a very savory reputation."

"I'm surprised you think I need protection."

"Trust me, you don't want to get involved with Panopoulos."

Dragging free of his gaze, she stared at the muscular column of his throat. "Maybe he wanted something from me that has nothing to do with sex? Besides, you're wasting your breath trying to protect me. From now on, who I choose to be with is none of your business."

"It is if you're pregnant."

The flash of possessive heat in his gaze and the tightening of his hold finally succeeded in making her lose her temper. "I might have some say in that."

Five

Lucas leaned against the wall in a dim alcove, arms folded over his chest as he observed the final formality of the wedding, the throwing of the bouquet.

Zane joined him, shifting through the shadows with the fluid ease that was more a by-product of his time spent on the streets of L.A. than of the strict, conventional upbringing he'd received on Medinos. He nodded at Carla, who was part of a cluster of young women gathered on the dance floor. "Not your finest hour. But, if you hadn't rescued her, I was thinking of doing it myself."

"Touch Carla," Lucas said softly, "and you lose your hand."

Zane took a swallow of beer. "Thought so."

Lucas eyed his younger brother with irritation. Four years difference and he felt like Methuselah. "How long have you known?"

"About a year, give or take."

The bouquet arced through the air straight into Carla's hands. Lucas's jaw tightened as she briskly handed it to one of the pretty young flower girls and detached herself from the noisy group. She made a beeline for her table, picked up the lilac clutch that went with her dress, and made her way out of the *castello's* ballroom.

Lucas glanced at Zane. "Do me a favor and look after Lilah for me for the rest of the evening."

Zane's expression registered rare startlement. "Let me get this right, you won't let me near Carla, but with Lilah it's okay?"

Lucas frowned at his turn of phrase, but his attention was focused on the elegant line of Carla's back. "The party's almost over. An hour, max."

"That long."

Impatiently, he studied the now empty hallway. "She'll need a ride back to the villa."

"Not a problem. Aunts at six o'clock." With a jerk of his chin, indicating direction, Zane snagged his beer and made a swift exit.

Pushing away from the wall, Lucas started after Carla, and found himself the recipient of a shrewd glance from his mother and steely speculation from a gaggle of silver-haired great-aunts.

He groaned inwardly, annoyed that he had dropped his guard enough that not only Zane but his mother had become aware of his interest in Carla. The last thing he needed was his mother interfering in his love life.

Seconds later, he traversed the vaulted hallway and stepped outside onto the graveled driveway just as the sound of Constantine and Sienna's departing helicopter cut the air.

The sun was gone, the night thick with stars, but heat still flowed out of the sunbaked soil as he strode toward Carla.

The ambient temperature was still hot enough that he felt uncomfortable in his suit jacket.

A stiff sea breeze was blowing, tugging strands loose from the rich, dark coils piled on top of Carla's head, making her look sexily disheveled. The breeze also plastered her dress against her body, emphasizing just how much weight she had lost.

His frown deepened. A regular gym bunny, Carla had always been fit and toned, with firm but definite curves. The curves were still there but if he didn't miss his guess she had dropped at least a dress size. After the virus she had picked up in Thailand, weight loss was understandable, but she should have regained it by now.

She spun when she heard the crunch of gravel beneath his shoes. A small jolt went through him when he registered the blankness of her gaze.

Carla didn't do sad. She had always been confident, sassy and adept at using her feminine power to the max. For Carla, masculine conquest was as natural as breathing. He had assumed that when their relationship was at an end she would have a lineup of prospective boyfriends eager to fill the gap.

In that moment it hit him forcibly that as similar as Carla was to Sophie with her job and her lifestyle, there were some differences. Sophie had been immature and self-centered, while Carla was fiercely loyal to her sister and her family, to the point of putting her own needs aside so as not to hurt Sienna. Even though that loyalty had clashed with what he had wanted, he had respected it. It also occurred to him that in her own way, Carla had been fiercely loyal to him. She had dated other men, but only ever in a business context for Ambrosi Pearls.

Broodingly, he considered the fact that Carla had been a virgin the first time they had made love, that she had never slept with anyone but him. He realized he had conveniently pushed the knowledge aside because it hadn't fitted the picture of Carla he had wanted to see.

He had been the one who had held back and played it safe, not Carla, and now the sheer intimacy of their situation kept hitting him like a kick to the chest.

He should let her go, but the shattering fact that he could have made her pregnant had changed something vital in his hard drive.

They were linked, at least until he had ascertained whether or not she was carrying his child. Despite his need to end the relationship, he couldn't help but feel relieved about that fact. "The limousines are gone. If you want a lift, I'll drive you."

"That won't be necessary." Carla extracted a cell phone from her clutch. "I'll get a taxi."

"Unless you've prebooked, with all the guests on Medinos for the wedding, you'll have difficulty getting one tonight."

She frowned as she flipped the phone closed and slipped it back in her clutch. "Then I'll ask Constantine."

He jerked his head in the direction of the helicopter, which was rapidly turning into a small dot on the horizon. "Constantine is on honeymoon. I'll take you."

Her glare was pointed. "I don't understand what you're doing out here. Shouldn't you be looking after your new girlfriend?"

"Zane's taking care of Lilah." Before she could argue, he cupped her elbow and steered her in the direction of the *castello's* stable of garages.

She jerked free of his hold. "Why doesn't Zane take me home and you go and take care of Lilah?"

His jaw clamped. "Do you want the lift or not?"

She stared at a point somewhere just left of his shoulder. Enough time passed that his temper began to spiral out of control.

Carla shrugged. "I'll accept a lift because I need one, but please don't touch me again."

"I wasn't trying to 'touch' you."

Her gaze connected with his, shooting blue fire. "I know what you were doing. The same thing you tried to do on the dance floor. Save it for Lilah."

He suppressed the cavemanlike urge to simply pick her up and carry her to the car. "You don't look well. What's wrong with you?"

"Nothing that a good night's sleep won't fix." Her gaze narrowed. "Why don't you say what's really bothering you? That, with all the paparazzi still on the loose, you can't take the risk that I might give them a story? And I think we both know that I could give them quite a story, an exposé of the *real* Lucas—"

Lucas gave in to the caveman urge and picked her up. "Did I mention the paparazzi?"

She thumped his shoulder with her beaded purse. "Let me down!"

Obligingly, he set her down by the passenger door of the Maserati. He jerked the door open. "Get in. If you try to run I'll come after you."

"There has to be a law against this." But she climbed into the sleek leather bucket seat.

"On Medinos?" Despite his temper, Lucas's mouth twitched as he slid behind the wheel and turned the key in the ignition. For the first time in two months he felt oddly content. "Not for an Atraeus."

Carla's tension skyrocketed when, instead of responding to her request and parking out on the street, Lucas drove into the cobbled driveway of the villa. At that point, he insisted on taking the house key from her and unlocked the door. When she attempted to close the door on him, he simply stepped past her and walked into the small, elegant house, switching on lights.

A narky little tension headache throbbing at her temples, Carla made a beeline for the bathroom, filled the glass on the counter with water and took her pills. Refilling the glass, she sat down on the edge of the bath and sipped, waiting to feel better.

A sharp rap on the bathroom door made her temper soar. She had hoped Lucas would take the hint and leave, but apparently he was still in the house. Replacing the glass on the counter, she checked her appearance then unlocked the door and stepped out into the hall.

He was leaning against the wall, arms crossed over his chest. She tried not to notice that, though he was still wearing his jacket, his tie and waistcoat were gone and several buttons of his shirt were undone revealing a mouthwatering slice of bronzed skin. "I'm fine now. You can leave."

She stepped past him and headed for the front door. Her spine tightened as Lucas followed too close behind, and she remembered what had happened the last time they had been alone together.

Note to self, she thought grimly as he peeled off into the sitting room and picked up his tie and waistcoat, *do not allow yourself to be alone with Lucas again.*

Opening the front door, she stood to one side, allowing him plenty of space. "Thank you for the lift."

He paused at the open door, making her aware of his height, the width of his shoulders, the power and vitality that seemed to burn from him. "Maybe you should see a doctor."

"If I need medical help, I'll get it for myself." She glanced pointedly at her wristwatch, resisting the urge to squint because one of the annoying symptoms of the headache now seemed to be that her eyes were ultrasensitive to light.

Not good. Her doctor had warned her that stress could

cause a viral relapse. With her father's funeral, Sienna's wedding and the breakup with Lucas, she was most definitely under stress.

His hand landed on the wall beside her head. Suddenly he was close enough that his heat engulfed her, and his clean, faintly exotic scent filled her nostrils.

Grimly, she resisted the impulse to take the half step needed, wrap her arms around his neck and melt into a goodnight kiss that would very likely turn into something else. "Um, shouldn't you be getting back to Lilah?"

For the briefest of moments he hesitated. His gaze dropped to her mouth and despite the tiredness that pulled at her, she found herself holding her breath, awareness humming through every cell of her being.

He let out a breath. "We can't do this again."

"No." But it had been an effort to say that one little word, and humiliation burned through her that, despite everything, she was still weak enough to want him.

His hand closed into a fist beside her head, then he was gone, the door closing gently behind him.

Carla leaned her forehead against the cool cedar of the door, her face burning.

Darn, darn, darn. Why had she almost given in to him? Like a mindless, trained automaton responding to the merest suggestion that he might kiss her.

After the stern talking-to she had given herself following the episode on the dance floor, she had succeeded in making herself look needy, like a woman who would do anything to get him back into her bed.

The pressure at her temples sharpened. Feeling more unsteady by the second, as if she was coming down with the flu, Carla walked to her bedroom. The acute sensitivity of her eyes was making it difficult to stand being in a lit room. No doubt about it, the virus had taken hold.

Removing her jewelry, she changed into cool cotton drawstring pants and a tank. She pulled on a cotton sweatshirt and cozy slippers against the chill and walked through to the bathroom. After washing and moisturizing her face, she pulled the pins out of her hair, which was an instant relief.

A discreet vibration made her frown. Her cell phone had a musical ring tone, and so did Sienna's. Margaret Ambrosi didn't own a cell, which meant the phone must belong to Lucas.

She padded barefoot into the sitting room in time to see the phone vibrate itself off the coffee table and drop to the carpet. A small pinging sound followed.

Carla picked up the phone. Lucas had missed a call from Lilah; now he had a text message, also from Lilah.

Fingers shaking slightly, she attempted to read the text but was locked out. A message popped up requesting she unlock the phone.

Not a problem, unless Lucas had changed his PIN since the last time they had dated.

Not dated, she corrected, her mood taking another dive. *Slept together.*

The last time he had stayed over at her apartment, before the holiday in Thailand, Lucas had needed to buy a new phone. The PIN he had used had been her birth date. At the time she had been ridiculously happy at his sentimental streak. She had taken it as a definite, positive *sign* that their relationship was progressing in the right direction.

She held her breath as she keyed in the number. The mail menu opened up.

The message was simple and to the point. Lilah was waiting for Lucas to call and would stay up until she heard from him.

The sick feeling in her stomach, the prickling chill she'd felt when he had broken up with her the previous night, came back at her full force. If she'd needed reinforcement of her decision to stay clear of Lucas Atraeus, this was it.

He was involved with someone else. He had *chosen* someone else, and the new woman in his life was waiting for him.

Closing the message, she replaced the phone on the coffee table and walked back to the bathroom. She switched off lights as she went, leaving one lamp burning in the sitting room for her mother when she came home. The relief of semidarkness was immense.

In the space of the past few minutes, she realized, the throbbing in her head had intensified and her skin hurt to touch. She swallowed another headache tablet, washing it down with sips of water. The sound of the doorbell jerked her head up. The sharp movement sent a stab of hot pain through her skull.

Lucas, back for his phone.

Setting the glass down, she walked back out to the hall, which was lit by the glow from the porch light streaming through two frosted sidelight windows. The buzzer sounded again.

"Open up, Carla. All I want is my phone."

That particular request, she decided, was the equivalent of waving a red rag at a bull. "You can have the phone tomorrow."

"I still have the key to this door," he said quietly. "If you don't unlock it, I'll let myself in."

Over her dead body.

"Just a minute." Annoyed with herself for forgetting to reclaim the key, she reached for the chain and tried to engage it. In her haste it slipped from her fingers.

She heard Lucas say something short and sharp. Adrenaline pumped. He knew she was trying to chain the door against him. The metallic scrape of a key being inserted into the lock was preternaturally loud as she grabbed the chain again.

Before she could slot it into place the door swung open, pushing her back a half step. Normally, the half step back wouldn't have fazed her, but with the weird shakiness of the virus she was definitely not her normal, athletic self and had to clutch at the hall table to help with her balance. Something crashed to the floor; glass shattered. She registered that when she had grabbed at the table her shoulder must have brushed against a framed watercolor mounted on the wall.

Lucas frowned. "Don't move."

Ignoring him, she bent down and grasped the edge of the frame.

Lean fingers curled around her upper arms, hauling her upright. "Leave that. You'll cut yourself."

Too late. Curling her thumb in against her palm, she made a fist, hiding a tiny, stinging jab that as far as she was concerned was so small it didn't count as a cut. She blinked at the bright porch light. "I didn't give you permission to come in, and you don't have the right to give me orders."

"You *did* cut yourself." He muttered something in Medinian. She was pretty sure it was a curse word. "Give me the watercolor before you do any more damage."

Her grip on the watercolor firmed, even though his request made sense. If she got blood on the painting it would be ruined. "I don't need your help. Get your phone and go."

"You look terrible."

"Thanks!"

"You're as white as a sheet."

He released her so suddenly she swayed off balance. By the time she recovered he had laid claim to her sore thumb and was probing at the small cut. But she still had the painting. "Neat trick."

His gaze was oddly intent. "There doesn't seem to be any glass in it."

He wrapped a handkerchief around her thumb and closed her fingers around it to apply pressure. "How long have you been sick?"

Her jaw tightened. She was being childish, she knew, but she hated being sick. It literally brought out the worst in her. "I'm not sick. Like I said before, all I need is a good night's sleep, so if you don't mind—"

The brush of his fingers against her temple as he pushed hair away from her face distracted her.

"Does that hurt? Don't answer. I can see that it does."

He leaned close. Arrested by his nearness, she studied the taut line of his jaw, suddenly assaulted by a myriad of sensations—the heat from Lucas's body, the clean scent of his skin, the rasp of his indrawn breath. That was one of the weird things about the virus: it seemed to amplify everything, hearing, scent, emotions, as if protective layers had been peeled away, leaving her senses bare and open.

In a slick move, he took the watercolor while her attention was occupied by the intriguing shape of his cheekbones, which were meltdown material.

A small sound informed her that he had placed the painting on the hall table. Out of nowhere her stomach turned an uncomfortable somersault. "I think I'm going to be sick."

His hand closed around her upper arm, and the heat from his palm burned through the cotton sweatshirt. Then they were moving, glass crunching under the soles of her slippers as he guided her out of the entrance hall into the sitting room. Another turn and they were in the bathroom.

Long minutes later, she rinsed her mouth and washed her face. She had hoped that Lucas would have left, but he was leaning against the hallway wall looking patient and composed and drop-dead gorgeous. In contrast she felt bedraggled and washed-out and as limp as a noodle.

Disgust and a taut, burning humiliation filled her. It was a rerun of Thailand, everything she had never wanted to happen again.

He folded his arms across his chest. "I'm guessing this is a relapse of the virus."

Keeping one hand on the wall for steadiness, she made a beeline for her bedroom. "Apparently. This is the first recurrence I've had." Her head spun and for a split second she thought she might be sick again, although she was fairly certain there was nothing left in her stomach. Two more wavering steps then the blissful darkness of her bedroom enfolded her. "Don't turn on the light. And don't come in here. This is *my* room." And as such it was off-limits to men who didn't love her.

"You should have told me you were still ill."

Her temper flashed, but if it was measured on a color spectrum it would have been a washed-out pink, not the angry red it had been earlier in the evening. She didn't have the energy for anything more and she was fading fast. "I didn't *know* I was still ill."

"That's some temper you've got."

Her teeth would have gritted if she'd had the strength. "Inherited it from my mother." She dragged her coverlet back. "She'll be home soon." The thought filled her with extreme satisfaction. She hadn't been able to kick Lucas's butt out, but Margaret Ambrosi would. Especially if she found him in her little girl's room.

Gingerly she sat on the side of the bed. Now that the stomach issue was over her attention was back on her head, which was pounding. What she needed was another pain-killer, because the last one had just been flushed.

Dimly, she registered that despite her express order, Lucas *was* in her room. "I told you not to be here."

He crouched down and eased her slippers off her feet. "Or what? You'll lose that famous temper?"

"That's right." A shiver went through her at the burning heat of his hands on her feet. The chill on her skin made her realize that the next stage of the virus was kicking in. Oh, goody, she thought wearily, Antarctic-cold shivers followed by sweats that rivaled burning desert sands. Exactly how she always wanted to spend a Saturday night.

"I'll take the risk. I survived Thailand, I can survive this."

He pulled her to her feet. Her nose bumped against his shoulder. Automatically, she clutched his lean waist and leaned into his comforting strength. She inhaled, breathing in his scent, and for a crazy moment all she wanted to do was rest there.

A split second later, the sheet peeled back, Lucas eased her into bed and pulled the sheets and coverlet over her.

With a sigh, she allowed her head to sink into the feather pillow. "All I need is another one of the painkillers on the bathroom vanity and some water and I'll be fine." It was surrender, she knew it, but she really did need the pill.

She registered his near silent footfalls as he walked to the bathroom, the hiss of water as he filled the glass, then he was back. His arm came around her shoulders as he propped her up so she could take the pill and drink the water. When she was finished he set the glass down on her bedside table.

She settled back on the pillows. "You know what? You're good at this."

"I had lots of practice in Thailand. Do you need anything else?" His voice was closer now, the timbre low and deliciously gruff.

It was the kind of velvety masculine rumble that, if they had been in bed together, would have invited a snuggling session. Then suddenly she remembered. Lucas was with Lilah now; he no longer wanted her. If he felt anything for her, it had to be pity. A weak, watered-down version of fury roared through her.

She peeled her lids open and peered at Lucas, ready to read him the riot act, then forgot what she was about to say because there was a strange, intent expression on his face. "Nothing. You can leave. Phone's on the coffee table. That was what you came for, wasn't it?"

He was so close she could feel the heat blasting off his body, see his gaze sliding over her features, cataloging her white face and messy hair. For shallow, utterly female reasons she wished that her face was glowing instead of chalky-white and that she had taken the time to brush her hair. Mercifully, the strong painkiller finally kicked in, taking the heat out of the ache in her head and dragging her down into sleep. "I don't want you here."

It was a lie. The virus had made her so weak that she was fast losing the strength to keep up the charade, even to herself.

"I'm staying until I know you'll be all right."

"I would like you to leave. Now." The crisp delivery she intended was spoiled by the fact that the words ran together in a drunken, blurred jumble.

She was certain the soft exhalation she heard had something to do with amusement, which made her even more furious. The mattress shifted as he planted a hand on either side of her head and leaned close. "What are you going to do if I don't? Make me leave?"

For a crazy moment she thought he was actually flirting with her, but that couldn't be. "Don't have to," she mumbled, settling the argument. Her eyelids slid closed. "You've already gone."

Silence settled around her, thick, heavy, as the sedative effect of the pills dragged her down.

"Do you want me back?"

The words jerked her awake, but they had been uttered so quietly she wasn't sure if she had imagined them or if Lucas had actually spoken.

She could see him standing in her bedroom doorway. Maybe she had been dreaming, or worse, hallucinating. "I took codeine, not truth serum."

"It was worth a try."

So he *had* asked the question.

She pushed up on one elbow. The suspicion that he was sneakily trying to interrogate her while she was drowsy from the pills solidified. Although she couldn't fathom why he would be interested in what she really thought and felt now. "I don't know why you're bothering. Thank you for helping me, but please leave now."

He shook his head. "You're...different tonight."

Different? She had been dumped. She had committed the cardinal sin of making love with her ex and could quite possibly be pregnant.

"Not different." Turning over, she punched the pillow and willed herself to go to sleep. "Real."

Six

Ten days later, Carla strolled into the Ambrosi building in Sydney.

When she reached her office, her assistant, Elise, a chirpy blonde with a marketing degree and a formidable memory for names and statistics, was in the process of hanging up the phone. "Lucas wants you in his office. *Now*."

A jolt of fiery irritation instantly evaporated the peace and calm of four days spent recuperating at her mother's house, the other five in the blissful solitude of the Blue Mountains at a friend's holiday home. "Did he say why?"

Elise looked dreamily reflective. "He's male, hot *and* single. Does it matter?"

Nerves taut, Carla continued on to her desk and deliberately took time out to examine the list of messages and calls Elise had compiled in her absence. Keeping her bag hooked over her shoulder, she checked her calendar and noted she had two meetings scheduled.

When she couldn't stall any longer, she strolled to Sienna's old office, frowning at the changes Atraeus money had already made to her family's faltering business. Worn blue carpet had been replaced with a sleek, dove-gray weave. Fresh paint and strategically placed art now graced walls that had once been decorated solely with monochrome prints of Ambrosi jewelry designs.

Feeling oddly out of place in what, from childhood, had been a cozily familiar setting, she greeted work colleagues.

Directing a brittle smile at Sienna's personal assistant, Nina—Lucas's PA now—she stepped into the elegant corner office.

Lucas, broad shouldered and sleekly powerful in a dark suit with a crisp white shirt and red tie, dominated a room that was still manifestly feminine as he stood at the windows, a phone held to one ear.

His gaze locked with hers, he terminated the call. "Close the door behind you and take a seat."

Suddenly glad she had made an extra effort with her appearance, she closed the door. The sharp little red suit, with its short skirt and fitted V-necked jacket, always made her feel attractive and energized. It probably wasn't the best idea for dealing with Lucas, but she hadn't worn it for him. She had a job interview at five with Alex Panopoulos, and she needed to look confident and professional. His upmarket Pan department stores were branching into jewelry manufacture and he had been chasing her all week to come in for an interview.

She hated the idea of leaving Ambrosi Pearls, but she had to be pragmatic about her position. When Constantine had offered the company back to Sienna on her wedding day they had held a family meeting. In essence, they had agreed to honour their debts, so the transfer of the company to The Atraeus Group had gone through as planned. With Sienna's marriage to Constantine binding both families together, combined with Constantine's assurance that he would keep the company intact, it had seemed the most sensible solution.

As a consequence, Carla now owned a block of voting shares. They would assure her of an income for the rest of her life, but they gave her no effective power. Her current personal contract as Ambrosi Pearls's public relations executive was up for renewal directly after Ambrosi's new product launch in a week's time. She didn't anticipate that Lucas would renew it. Her tenure as "The Face of Ambrosi" was just as shaky, but as she provided that service for free to help the company save money, it was no skin off her nose if Lucas no longer wanted her face on the posters.

Annoyance flickered in Lucas's gaze when she didn't immediately sit. He replaced the phone on its base. "I didn't expect you back in so soon."

She lifted a brow. "I felt okay, so there was no point in staying at home."

"I've been trying to reach you all week. Why didn't you return my calls?"

She shrugged. "I was staying with friends and didn't take my phone." She had left the phone at her apartment on purpose. The last thing she had needed was to have a desperately low moment and make the fatal mistake of trying to call or text Lucas.

There was a small charged silence. "How are you?"

"Fine. A couple of days in bed and the symptoms disappeared." She smiled brightly. "If that's all…"

"Not exactly." His gaze rested on her waist, where the jacket cinched in tight. "Are you pregnant?"

Despite her effort at control, heat flooded her cheeks. "I don't know yet. I have a test kit, but it's early to get an accurate reading."

"When will you know?"

She frowned, feeling distinctly uncomfortable with the subject and the way he was regarding her, as if she was a concubine who had somehow escaped the harem and he had ownership rights. "I should know in another couple of days. But whether I'm pregnant or not, it needn't concern you."

Actually, she could find out right that minute if she wanted. The test kit had said a result could be obtained in as early as seven days. She had studied the instructions then chucked the box in the back of one of her drawers. She still felt too raw and hurt to face using the kit and discovering that not only had she lost Lucas, her life was about to take a huge, unplanned turn. In a few days, when she felt ready, she would do the test.

Anger flickered in his gaze. "You would abort the child?"

"*No.*" She felt shocked that he had even jumped to that conclusion. If there was a child, there was no way she would do anything other than keep the baby and smother it with love for the rest of its life. "What I meant is that *if* there is a child, I've decided that you don't have to worry, because you don't need to be involved, or even acknowledge—"

"Any child of mine would be acknowledged."

The whiplash flatness of his voice, as if she had scraped a raw nerve, was even more shocking. Carla sucked in a breath and forced herself to loosen off the soaring tension. She was clearly missing something here. "This is crazy. I don't know why we're discussing something that might never happen. Is that all you wanted to know?"

"No." He propped himself on the edge of the desk. "Have a seat. There's something else we need to discuss."

There were three comfortable client seats; she chose the one farthest away from Lucas. The second she lowered herself into the chair she regretted the decision. Even though he wasn't standing, Lucas still towered over her. "Let me

guess—I'm fired in a week's time? I'm surprised it took you
so long to get around to—"

"I'm not firing you."

Carla blinked. Constantine had fired Sienna almost immediately, although his reasons had been understandable.
Continuing on as CEO of a company in Sydney while he
was based in Medinos had not been viable.

His gaze flicked broodingly over the crisp little suit. "Do
you always dress like that for work?"

His sudden change of tack threw her even more off balance. She realized that from his vantage point he could see
more than the shadowy hint of cleavage that was normally
visible in the vee of the jacket. She squashed the urge to drag
the lapels together. "Yes. Is there a problem?"

He crossed his arms over his chest. "Nothing that an extra
button or a blouse wouldn't fix."

She shot to her feet. "There is nothing wrong with what
I'm wearing. Sienna was perfectly happy with my wardrobe."

He straightened, making her even more aware of his
height, the breadth of his shoulders, the incomprehensible
anger simmering behind midnight-dark eyes.

"Sienna was female."

"What has that got to do with anything?"

"From where I'm standing, quite a lot.

She didn't know what was bothering him. Maybe a major
deal had fallen through, or even better, Lilah had dumped
him. Whatever it was she would swear that he was behaving proprietorially, but that couldn't be. He had dumped her
without ceremony; he had made it clear he didn't want her.
To add insult to injury, the tabloids were having a field day
reporting his relationship with Lilah.

His gaze dropped once again to the vee of her jacket.
"Who are you meeting today?"

Temper soaring at the lightning perusal, the even more pointed innuendo, she reeled off two names.

"Both male," he said curtly.

"Chandler and Howarth are contemporaries of my father! And I resent the implication that I would resort to using sex to make sales for Ambrosi, but if you prefer I could turn up for work in beige. Or, since this conversation is taking a medieval turn, maybe you'd prefer sackcloth and ashes."

His mouth twitched at the corners and despite her spiraling anger she found herself briefly mesmerized by the sudden jolt of charm. Lucas was handsome when he was cool and ruthless, but when he smiled he was drop-dead gorgeous in a completely masculine way that made her go weak at the knees and melt.

"You don't own anything beige."

"How would you know?" she pointed out, glad to get her teeth into something that could generate some self-righteous anger.

She wasn't vengeful, nor did she have a desire to hurt Lucas. It was simply that she was black-and-white in her thinking. They were either together or they weren't, and she couldn't bear the underlying invitation in his eyes, his voice, to be friends now that he had decreed their relationship was over. "As I recall, you were more interested in taking my clothes off than noticing what I was wearing. You had no more interest in my wardrobe than you had in any other aspect of my life."

His brows jerked together. "That's not true. You were the one who decreed we had to live separate lives."

Her hands curled into fists. "Don't say it didn't suit you."

"It did, at the time."

"Ha!" But the moment of triumph was hollow. She just wished she had realized she wasn't built for such a shallow, restricted relationship.

Pointedly, she checked her wristwatch. "I have a meeting in ten minutes. If there's nothing else, I need to go. With the product launch in two days' time, there's a lot to do."

"That's what I wanted to talk to you about. We've made some changes to the arrangements for the launch party. Nina will be heading up the team running the promotion."

Not fired, Carla thought blankly. Sidelined.

She took a deep breath and let it out slowly, but when she spoke her voice was still unacceptably husky. "Some product launch without the most high-profile component, or have you forgotten that I'm 'The Face of Ambrosi'?"

Broodingly, Lucas surveyed Carla's perfect face, exquisite in every detail from exotic eyes to delicate cheekbones and enticing mouth. Add in the outrageously sexy tousle of dark hair trailing down her back and she was spectacularly irresistible.

Ambrosi had cut costs and cashed in on Carla's appeal, but he found himself grimly annoyed every time he noticed one of the posters. "It's hard to miss when your face is plastered all over the front of the building."

And in every one of the perfumed women's magazines he had been forced to flick through since he'd stepped into Sienna Ambrosi's front office.

Triumph glowed briefly in her gaze. "You can't sideline me. I have to be there." She began ticking off all the reasons he couldn't surgically remove her from the campaign.

His frustration levels increased exponentially with every valid reason, from interviews with women's magazines to a promotional stunt she had organized.

"I have to be there—it's a no-brainer. Besides, the costuming has all been completed to my measurements."

He cut her off in midstream. "No."

Carla's eyes narrowed. "Why not?"

Not a subject he was prepared to go live on, he thought, gaze fixed on the sleek fit of her red suit.

Every time he saw one of the posters, he had to fight the irrational urge to rip it down. The idea that Carla would do a promotional show in the transparent, pearl-encrusted creation he had viewed in front of an audience filled with voyeuristic men was the only no-brainer in the equation.

Over his dead body.

He felt as proprietary as he imagined a father would feel keeping his daughter from hormonal teenage boys. Not that his feelings were remotely fatherly. She could threaten and argue all day; it wasn't going to happen.

"You haven't been well, and you could be pregnant," he said flatly. "I'll do the interviews, and I've arranged for a model to take your place for the promotion. Nina is hosting the promotional show. Elise will take care of the styling."

Styling. He gripped the taut muscles at his nape. A week ago he didn't even know what that meant.

"I'm so well I'm jumping out of my skin. I'm here to work. The launch is *my* project."

"Not anymore."

Silence hung heavy in the air. Somewhere in the office a clock ticked; out on the street someone leaned on a car horn. Carla groped for the fire-engine-red bag that matched her suit.

Lucas's stomach clenched when he saw tears glittering on her lashes. Ah, damn… He resisted the sudden off-the-wall urge to coax her close and offer comfort. He had expected opposition—a fight—but he hadn't been prepared for this level of emotion. Somewhere in the raft of detail involved with taking over Ambrosi and figuring out how to handle Carla, he had forgotten how passionately intense and protective she was about her family and the business. Although how he could forget a detail that had seen *him* sidelined in Carla's life, he didn't know. "Carla—"

"Don't." She turned on her heel.

Jaw clenched against the need to comfort her and soothe away the hurt, he reached the door first. His hand landed on the cream-and–gilt-detailed panel of the door, preventing her from opening it. "Just one more thing. My mother and Zane fly in tomorrow. I've organized a press conference to promote The Atraeus Group's takeover of Ambrosi and the product launch, then a private lunch. As a family member and PR executive your presence is required at both."

She stared blankly ahead. "Will Lilah be there?"

"Yes."

Lucas had to restrain himself from going after Carla as she strode out of his office. His jaw tightened as he noted the outrageously sexy red heels and the enticing sway of her hips as she walked. The fact that he had lost his temper was disturbing, but ten days kicking his heels while she had disappeared off the radar had set him on edge. The second he had seen her in the red suit he had lost it. He had been certain she wasn't wearing anything but a bra under the tight little jacket, and he had been right.

Closing the door, he prowled back to the window and held aside the silky curtains that draped the window, feeling like a voyeur himself as he watched Carla stroll out onto the street and climb into the sports car that was waiting for her.

He had questioned her assistant extensively about her meetings, then, dissatisfied with her answers, had looked both Chandler and Howarth up on the internet.

Elise had been correct in her summation. Both men were old enough to be her father. Unfortunately, that didn't seem to cut any ice with him. They were men, period.

At a point in time when he should have been reinforcing

the end of their relationship by keeping his distance, he had never felt more possessive or jealous.

Instead of moving to Sydney, he should have stepped back and simply kept in touch with Carla. If she was pregnant, whether she told him or not, he would soon have known. Instead he had grabbed at the excuse to be close to her.

The fact that he had lost control to the extent that he had made love to Carla after they had broken up, *without protection,* still had the power to stun him.

Worse, he found the idea that they could have made a baby together unbearably sexy and appealing.

Maybe it was a kickback to his grief and loss over Sophie, but a part of him actually hoped Carla was pregnant.

He dropped the curtain as the taxi merged into traffic. Broodingly, he reflected that when it came to Carla Ambrosi, he found himself thinking in medieval absolutes.

For two years one absolute had dominated: regardless of how risky or illogical the liaison was, he had wanted Carla Ambrosi.

Despite breaking up and replacing her with a new girlfriend—a woman he had not been able to bring himself to either touch or kiss—nothing had changed.

Seven

Carla checked the time on the digital clock in her small sports car. She had ten minutes to reach Alex Panopoulos's office and rush hour was in full swing, the traffic already jammed.

On edge and impatient, Carla used every shortcut she knew, but even so she was running late when she reached the dim underground garage.

Late for an interview that was becoming increasingly important, she grabbed her handbag and portfolio and exited the car.

Her heels tapped on concrete as she strode to the elevator, just as a sleek dark car cruised into a nearby space. The tinted driver's side window was down, giving her a shadowy glimpse of the driver. The car reminded her of the vehicle Lucas's security detail used when he was in town.

Frowning, she stepped into the elevator and keyed in the PIN she had been given. She punched the floor number, then

wished she hadn't as the doors slid shut, nixing her view of
the driver before he could climb out of the car. Maybe she
was paranoid, or simply too focused on Lucas, but for a split
second she had entertained the crazy thought that the driver
could be Lucas.

She kept an eye on the floor numbers as they lit up. She
caught her reflection in the polished steel doors. The scene
with Lucas accusing her of dressing to entice replayed in
her mind.

Hurt spiraled through her that he clearly had such a bad
opinion of her and was so keen to get rid of her that he had
replaced her both personally and professionally. She wondered if he intended to escort Lilah to the event, then grimly
decided that of course he would.

As a publicity stunt, the move couldn't be faulted. The
media would love Lilah fronting for Ambrosi and the further evidence of her close relationship with Lucas. Ambrosi
couldn't ask for a better launch gimmick…except maybe an
engagement announcement at the launch party.

Her chest squeezed tight on a pang of misery. Suddenly,
that didn't seem as ludicrous or far-fetched as it should, given
that Lucas and Lilah had only been publicly dating for a
couple of weeks. Lucas was legendary for his ruthless effi-
ciency, his unequivocal decisions. If he had decided Lilah
was the one, why wait?

The elevator doors opened onto a broad carpeted corridor. Discreetly suited executives, briefcases in hand, obviously leaving for the day, stepped into the elevator as she
stepped out.

The receptionist showed her into Alex's office.

Twenty minutes later, the interview over, Carla stepped
out of the lift and strode to her car. She had been offered the
job of PR executive for Pan Jewelry, but she had turned it
down. Five minutes into the interview she had realized that

Alex hadn't wanted her expertise; he had wanted to utilize her connection with the Atraeus family. Apparently, he could double his profit base in two years if they allowed Pan to trade in the luxury Atraeus Resorts.

She had been prepared to withstand his smooth charm, possibly even reject an attempt at seduction. She had done that before, on more than one occasion. Alex had made it clear he was prepared to deal generously with her in terms of position and salary, including a free apartment, if she came to him.

Stomach churning at the sexual strings that were clearly attached to his offer, and because she had missed lunch, Carla tossed her portfolio and purse on the backseat of her car. Flipping the glove box open, she found the box of cookies she kept there for just such an emergency. Part of the reason she had ended up with an ulcer was that she had a high-acid system. She had to be careful of what she ate, and of not eating at all. Stress coupled with an empty stomach was a definite no-no. Popping a chunk of the cookie in her mouth, she drove out of the parking garage.

The car she had thought could possibly belong to Lucas's security guy was no longer in its space, but, as she took the ramp up onto the sunlit street, the distinctive dark sedan nosed in behind her.

Spine tingling with a combination of renewed anger and the flighty, unreasoning panic of knowing someone was following her—no matter how benign the reason—she sped up. The car stayed with her, confirming in her mind that it *was* one of Lucas's men snooping on her.

Still fuming at his high-handed behavior, she pulled into her apartment building. When the sedan slid past the entrance and kept on going, she reversed out and made a beeline for Lucas's inner-city apartment.

Twenty minutes later, after running the gauntlet of a concierge and one of Lucas's security detail, she pressed the buzzer on Lucas's penthouse door.

It swung open almost immediately. Lucas was still dressed in the dark pants and white shirt he had worn to the office that morning, although minus the tie and with the shirt hanging open to reveal a mouthwatering slice of taut and tanned torso. He leaned one shoulder against the door-jamb, unsubtly blocking her from barging into his apartment.

"Tell me that wasn't you following me."

"It wasn't me following you. It was Tiberio."

"In that case, do you really want to have this discussion in the hallway, where anyone can overhear?"

Cool amusement tugged at his mouth. "I rent the entire floor. The other three apartments are all occupied by my people."

"Let me rephrase that, then. Do you really want to have this discussion where your employees can overhear what I'm about to say?"

His jaw tightened, but he stepped back, leaving her just enough room to march past him. She was in the hallway, strolling across rug-strewn wooden floors into an expansive, airy sitting room before she had time to consider the unsettling fact that Lucas might not be alone. With his shirt hanging open and his sleeves unbuttoned it was highly likely he had company.

Her stomach churned at the thought. She'd had plenty of time on the drive over to consider that Lilah could be here.

She breathed a sigh of relief when she registered that the sitting room, at least, was unoccupied, although that didn't rule out the bedrooms. Until that moment she hadn't known just how much she dreaded seeing Lilah in Lucas's home, occupying the position in his life that until a few days ago she had foolishly assumed was hers.

Fingers tightening on her purse, she surveyed the sitting room with its eclectic mix of artwork and sculpture. Some she knew well; at least two she had never seen. "Nice paintings."

But then that had been one of the things that had attracted her to Lucas. He wasn't stuffy with either his thinking or his enjoyment of art.

As her gaze was drawn from one new painting to the next, absorbing the nuances of line, form and color, her stomach tensed. "A new artist?"

"You know me." His gaze was faintly mocking as he walked through an open-plan dining area to a modern kitchen and opened the fridge. "I'm always on the lookout for new talent."

It occurred to her that the artist could be Lilah, who painted in her spare time, and jealousy gripped her. Before she could stop herself she had stepped closer to the nearest of the new paintings, so she could study the signature. S. H. Crew, not L. Cole.

Her knees felt a little shaky as she moved on to the next painting, also by S. H. Crew. For some odd reason, the thought that Lilah might appeal to Lucas on a creative, spiritual level was suddenly more sharply hurtful than her physical presence would have been.

Lucas loomed over her, the warm scent of his skin, the faint undernote of sandalwood, making her pulse race. "Is it safe to give you this?"

"Not really." Jaw clenching against an instant flashback of the scene on Medinos when she had dashed water over Lucas, and the lovemaking that had followed, she took the glass of ice water. She strolled the length of the sitting room and drifted into a broad hall that served as a gallery. She sipped water and pretended to be interested in the paintings that flowed along a curving cream wall that just happened to lead to the master bedroom. "So why did you have me followed?"

He strolled past her and stood, arms folded over his chest, blocking her view of his bedroom. "I wanted to see what you were up to. Tell me," he said grimly, "what did Panopoulos offer you?"

She blinked at the mention of Panopoulos's name, but it went in one ear and out the other. She was consumed with suspicion because Lucas clearly did not want her to see into his bedroom, and the notion that Lilah was there, maybe even in his bed, was suddenly overwhelming.

Setting the water down on a narrow hall table she marched past him. Lucas's hand curled around her arm as she stepped through the door, swinging her around to face him, but not before she had ascertained that his bedroom was empty. And something else that made her heart slam hard against the wall of her chest.

What he hadn't wanted her to see. A silk robe she had left at his apartment by mistake the last time she had been here almost three months ago, and which was exactly where she had left it, draped over the back of a chair. The aquamarine silk was wildly exotic, sexy and utterly feminine. No woman would have missed its presence or significance and allowed it to remain. The robe was absolute proof that Lilah had never been in Lucas's bedroom.

Her heart beat a queer, rapid tattoo in her chest. "You haven't slept with her yet."

Lucas let her go, his gaze glittering with displeasure. "Maybe I was in the process of getting rid of your things before I invited her over."

Anger flaring, she backed up a half step. The cool solidity of the door frame stopped her dead. "I'm here now, you can hand it to me personally."

"Is that a command, or are you going to ask me nicely?"

Wary of the banked heat in Lucas's gaze, which was clearly at odds with the coolness of his tone, she controlled her temper with difficulty. "I just did ask you nicely."

"I'm willing to bet you were nicer to Alex Panopoulos when you walked into his office in that suit. Did you finally agree to sleep with him?"

"*Sleep* with him?" The words came out as an incredulous yelp. She couldn't help it, she was so utterly distracted by the fact that Lucas thought she could be even remotely interested in Alex Panopoulos, a man she barely tolerated for the sake of business. "Well, I haven't jumped into his bed, yet. Does that make you feel better about me?"

Hot anger simmered through her, doubly compounded by the humiliating fact that Panopoulos *had* wanted to sleep with her.

With a suddenness that shocked her, Lucas leaned forward and kissed her. The sensual shock of the kiss, even though she had half expected it and had goaded him into it, sent a wave of heat through Carla. Until that moment, she hadn't understood how much she had wanted to provoke him, how angry she was at his defection. She was also hurt that he still didn't know who she was after more than two years, and evidently didn't have any interest in knowing, when she was deeply, painfully in love with him.

She blinked, dazed. At some point, she realized, probably that first time they had met, something had happened. After years of dating men and knowing they weren't right, she had taken one look at Lucas and chosen him.

That was why she had broken almost every personal rule she'd had and slept with Lucas in the first place, then continued with the relationship when she knew any association with him would hurt her family. If she had been sensible and controlled she would have stepped back and waited. After all, if a relationship had legs it should stand the test of a little time. But she hadn't been able to wait. She had wanted him, needed him, right then, the same way she needed him now.

Two years. She blinked at the immensity of her self-deception. She had buried the in-love thing behind the pretense that theirs was a modern relationship between two overcommitted people with the added burden of some crazy family pressures. Anything to bury the fact that the sporadic interludes with Lucas in no way satisfied her need to be loved.

Her arms closed convulsively around his neck. She shouldn't be kissing him now, not when she wanted so much more, but in that moment she ceased to care.

"What's wrong?" Lucas pulled back, his gaze suddenly heart-stoppingly soft. "Am I hurting you?"

"No." *Yes.* Her hands tangled in the thick black silk of his hair and dragged his mouth back to hers. "Just kiss me."

Long minutes later they made it to the bed. She dragged his shirt off his shoulders and tossed it aside. Her palms slid across his sleek, heavy shoulders and muscled chest. Giddy pleasure spun through her as he removed her clothing, piece by piece, and she, in turn, removed his.

Time seemed to slow, then stop as she fitted herself against him and clasped his head, pulling his mouth to hers, needing him closer, needing him with her. Late-afternoon sun slanted through the shutters, tiger striping his shoulders as his gaze linked with hers and she suddenly knew why making love with Lucas had always been so special, so important. For those few minutes when they were truly joined it was as if he unlocked a part of himself that normally she could never quite reach, and he was wholly hers. In those few moments she could believe that he did love her.

Cool air swirled around naked skin as he sheathed himself. Relief shivered through her as they flowed together. She was utterly absorbed by the feel of him inside her, his touch and taste, the slow, thorough way he made love to her, as if he knew her intimately, as if they did belong together.

Aside from those few minutes on Medinos it had been long months since they had last made love, and she had missed him, missed this. As crazy as it seemed, despite everything that had gone wrong, everything that was still wrong, this part was right.

His head dipped, she felt the softness of his lips against her neck. Her stomach clenched, the slowly building tension suddenly unbearable as she tightened around him. She felt his raw shudder. In that moment her own climax shimmered through her with an intense pleasure that made tears burn behind her lids, and the room spun away.

Long minutes later the buzzer at the front door jerked her out of the sleepy doze she had fallen into. With smooth, fluid movements, Lucas rolled out of bed, snagged his clothes off the floor and walked through to the adjoining bathroom. Seconds later, he reappeared, fastening dark trousers around narrow hips as he strolled to the door.

Carla didn't wait to see who it was. Snatching up her clothes, including her bra, which had ended up hooked over a bedside lamp, she hurried into the bathroom to freshen up and change. Her clothes were crumpled and her hair was a tumbled mass, but she couldn't worry about that. Her priority was to leave as quickly as possible.

Slipping into her shoes, she searched and found her bag on the floor just outside the bedroom door. She must have dropped it when Lucas had kissed her there. Her cheeks burned with embarrassment as she marched through the sitting room where Lucas was talking in low, rapid Medinian to two of his security personnel.

Lucas said her name. She ignored him and the curious looks of the men, in favor of sliding through the open door and making a dash for the elevator.

Relief eased some of her tension when she saw that the doors were open. Jogging inside, she jabbed the ground floor button as Lucas appeared in the corridor.

"Wait," he said curtly.

The doors closed an instant before he reached the elevator. Heart pounding, Carla examined her reflection in the mirrored rear wall and spent the few seconds repairing her smudged mascara. She winced at her swollen lips and the pink mark on her neck where Lucas's stubble must have grazed her. She looked as if she had just rolled out of bed.

The elevator stopped with a faint jolt. Shoving her mascara back in her bag, Carla strolled quickly through the foyer, ignoring the concierge, who stared at her with a fascinated expression.

She almost stopped dead when she saw Lilah sitting in a chair, flipping through a magazine, obviously waiting. Pretending she hadn't noticed her, Carla quickened her step. Now the two security staff talking with Lucas in hushed, rapid Medinian made sense. Lilah had wanted to go up to Lucas's apartment, but they had known Carla was there.

Mortified, she dimly registered Lilah's white face, the shock in her eyes, as she pushed the foyer doors wide. The sound of traffic hit her like a blow. The sun, now low on the horizon, shone directly in her eyes, dazzling her, a good excuse for the tears stinging her eyes. Her throat tightened as she started down the front steps.

As she stepped onto the sidewalk a hand curved around her arm, stopping her in her tracks.

Her heart did a queer leap in her chest as she spun. "Lucas."

Eight

Carla wrenched free. Lucas was still minus his shirt, his hair sexily tangled. If she looked rumpled, he definitely looked like he had just rolled out of the love nest. "How did you get down so fast?"

"There's a second, private lift."

Her fingers tightened on the strap of her bag. "More to the point, why did you bother?"

His gaze narrowed. "I won't glorify that with an answer. What did you think you were doing running out like that?"

Now that the initial shock of Lucas chasing after her was over, she was desperate to be gone. She needed to be alone so she could stamp out the crazy notion that kept sliding into her mind that there was still a chance for them. She had to get it through her skull that there was no hope. She was the one who got lost in useless emotion, while Lucas remained coolly elusive.

Her gaze flashed. "We were finished, weren't we?" *In*

more ways than one. "Or was there something else you wanted?"

Heat burned along his cheekbones. "You know I never viewed you that way."

"How, then?"

He said something low and taut in Medinian that she was pretty sure was a swear word or phrase of some kind. Not for the first time it occurred to her that for her own peace of mind she really should learn some of that language.

His palm curved around the base of her neck, his fingers tangling in her hair. A split second later his mouth closed over hers.

A series of flashes, the slick, motorized clicking of a high-speed camera jerked them apart. A reporter with an expensive-looking camera had just emerged from a parked car.

A shudder of horror swept Carla. When the press recognized her they would put one and one together and make seven. Before she arrived back at her apartment they would have her entangled in a second-time-around affair with Lucas. By morning they would have her cast off and pregnant or, more probably, since Lucas was involved with Lilah, caught up in some trashy love triangle.

Most of it, unfortunately, was embarrassingly true.

A strangled sound jerked her head around. Bare meters away, directly behind Lucas, Lilah was caught in an awkward freeze-frame.

Carla's stomach lurched as if she'd just stepped into a high-speed elevator on its way down. That was a definite "go" on the love triangle.

Lilah spun on her heel and walked quickly away.

With a final, manic series of clicks the reporter slid back into the car from which he had emerged. With a high-pitched whine reminiscent of a kitchen appliance the tiny hatchback sped away.

Lucas swore softly, this time in English, and released his grip on her nape. His gaze was weary. "Did you know he was out here?"

Her temper soared at what she could only view as an accusation. She gestured at her crumpled clothing and hair, the smeared makeup. "Do I look like I'm ready to be photographed by some sleazy tabloid reporter?"

Lucas's brows jerked together. "You did it once before."

A tide of heat swept her at his reference to her admittedly outrageous behavior in making their first breakup public and the resulting scandal that had followed. "You deserved that for the way you treated me."

"I apologized."

He had apologized. And she had forgiven him, then continued to sleep with him. There was a pattern there, somewhere.

His head jerked around as he spotted Lilah climbing into a small sedan. Slipping a cell phone out of his pants pocket, he punched in a number.

Carla blinked at his sudden change of focus. Feeling oddly deflated and emptied of emotion, she rummaged in her purse to find her car keys. "Before you ask the question, the reporter didn't follow me. Why would he? I'm not your girlfriend."

Lucas frowned and gave up on the call, which clearly wasn't being picked up.

He was no doubt calling Lilah, trying to soothe her hurt and explain away his mistake. Despite the fact that Carla knew she was the one in the wrong for sleeping with Lucas, she found she couldn't bear the thought of Lucas trivializing what they had just shared.

He had the nerve to try the phone number again.

A red mist swam before her eyes. Before she even registered what she was about to do, her hand shot out, closed around the phone and she flung it as hard as she could onto the road. It bounced and flew into several pieces. A split second later a truck ran over the main body of the phone, smashing it flat.

There was a moment of silence.

Lucas's expression was curiously devoid of emotion. "That was an expensive phone."

"So sue me, but I find it insulting and objectionable that the man I've just slept with should phone another woman in my presence. You could have at least waited until I had left."

His gaze narrowed. "My apologies for accusing you of calling the press in. I forgot about Lilah."

"Something you seem to be doing a lot lately. I don't know what you're doing out here with me when you should be concentrating on getting back with her."

A swirling breeze started up, making her feel chilled. She rubbed at the gooseflesh on her arms, suddenly in urgent need of a hot bath and an early night. Technically, she was still recovering from the viral relapse and under doctor's orders to take it easy, not that she would tell Lucas that. She was supposed to take an afternoon nap if she could fit it in. Ha!

She started toward her car. Lucas stepped in front of her, blocking her path.

She stared at his sleek, bare shoulders and muscled chest, the dark line of hair that arrowed down to the waistband of his pants. She was tired, and her body still ached and throbbed in places from what they had done in his penthouse apartment. What they had done was *wrong,* but that didn't stop the automatic hum of desire.

"I have no plans on 'getting back' with Lilah. Do you intend to sleep with Panopoulos?"

She went still inside at the first part of that sentence, although she felt no sense of surprise that Lucas was breaking up with Lilah. If he could gravitate back to her so easily then clearly there wasn't much holding them together. Then a second thunderbolt hit her.

Lucas was jealous.

Make that *very* jealous. She didn't know why she hadn't seen it before, but the knowledge demystified his overbearing reaction to her job interview with Alex Panopoulos. It also cast a new light on the dictatorial way he had decided that she would no longer be "The Face" or act in the promotional play she had planned to stage as part of Ambrosi's product launch. She had thought he was downgrading her both personally and professionally because he didn't want her, but the opposite was true.

A glow of purely feminine pleasure soothed over the hurt he had inflicted by demoting her. The launch was *her* baby. She had meticulously planned every detail, always shooting for perfection, and she needed to be there to make sure everything went smoothly. She still didn't like what he had done, but she understood his reasoning now and, because it involved his emotions for her, she would allow him to get away with being so high-handed.

Her chin came up at the question about Alex Panopoulos, although it no longer had any sting. "You're not my boyfriend," she said flatly. "You have no right to ask that question."

Maybe not. But that situation was about to change.

Lucas's jaw locked as he controlled the surge of cold fury at the thought of Carla and Panopoulos together. When he had asked her before she had said she hadn't slept with him, and he believed her, but he knew Alex Panopoulos. He was wealthy and spoiled and used to having what he wanted. If he wanted Carla, he wouldn't give up.

His hands curled into fists at the almost overwhelming urge to simply pick Carla up and carry her back up to his apartment and his bed. Instead, he forced himself to stillness as Carla climbed behind the wheel of her sports car and shot away from the curb.

He was finished with caveman tactics. Finesse was now required.

He examined his options as he took the stairs into his apartment building and strode through the foyer. They were not black-and-white, exactly, but close.

He stepped into the elevator, which Tiberio was holding for him. It was a fact that ever since he had first seen Carla he hadn't been able to keep his hands off her. His attempt to create distance and sever their relationship had backfired. Instead of killing his desire, distance had only served to increase it to the point that the very thing he had been trying to avoid happened: he lost control.

He could deny the story the tabloids would print and which would no doubt hit the stands by morning, or he could allow the story to stand. If he took the second option, Carla's name would be dragged through the mud. He would not allow that to happen.

Until that afternoon, he had been certain about the one thing he didn't want: a forced marriage to Carla Ambrosi.

But that had been before she had waved Alex Panopoulos in his face.

The elevator door slid open. Jaw tight, Lucas strode to his apartment and waited for Tiberio to swipe the key card.

He walked through to his bedroom, every muscle locking tight as he studied the rumpled bed. He picked up the sexy, exotic silk wrap, his fingers closing on the silk. Her delicate feminine scent still clung to the silk, the same scent that currently permeated the very air of his room and would now be in his bed.

If she had wanted to force his hand, he reflected, she could have done it at the beginning, when the media had published the story about the first night they had spent together. Instead, she had walked away from him. He was the one who'd had to do the running.

He had gotten her back, but only after weeks of effort. His fingers tightened on the silk. It was an uncomfortable fact that he wanted Carla more now than he had in the beginning. With each encounter, instead of weakening, his need had intensified.

Now Panopoulos had entered the picture.

Alex was a clever man who had leveraged a modest fortune into an impressive retail empire. Lucas was aware that he wouldn't miss the opportunity to enhance his bid to place his stores in Atraeus resorts by marrying close to his family.

Lucas reached for his cell phone, and remembered that Carla had destroyed it. He shook his head at the irrational urge to grin. The destruction of personal property, especially his, shouldn't be viewed as sexy.

He found the landline then, irritated because his directory had been on his dead cell and he had to ring his PA on Medinos to find the unlisted number. Frustrating minutes later, he made the call. Panopoulos picked up almost immediately.

Lucas's message was succinct and direct.

If Panopoulos offered Carla any kind of position within his company, or laid so much as a finger on her, he would lose any chance at a business alliance with The Atraeus Group. Lucas would also see to it personally that a lucrative business deal Panopoulos was currently negotiating with a European firm The Atraeus Group had a stake in, deVries, would be withdrawn.

Panopoulos's voice was clipped. "Are you warning me off because Constantine is now married to Carla's sister?"

"No." Lucas made no effort to temper the cold flatness of his reply. "Because Carla Ambrosi is mine."

The instant he said the words satisfaction curled through him. Decision made.

Carla was his. Exclusively his.

He was over making excuses to be with her. He wanted her. And he would do what he had to to make sure that not Panopoulos or any other man went near her again.

Terminating the call, Lucas propped the phone back on its rest.

Panopoulos was smart; he would back off. Now all Lucas had to do was talk to Lilah, then deal with the press and Carla.

Carla wouldn't like his ultimatum, but she would accept it. The damage had been done in the instant the reporter had snapped them on the street.

The following morning, after a mostly sleepless night, Carla dressed for the scheduled press conference and luncheon with care. Bearing in mind the elegance of the restaurant Lucas had booked, she chose a pale blue dress that looked spectacular against her skin and hair. It was also subtly sexy in the way it skimmed her curves and revealed a hint of cleavage. High, strappy blue heels made her legs look great, and a classy little jacket in powder-blue finished off the outfit.

Normally she would dress in a more low-key way for a press conference, but any kind of meeting with Lucas today called for a special effort. The heels were a tad high, but that wasn't a problem; she had learned to balance on four-inch stilettos from an early age. She figured that by now that particular ability was imprinted in her DNA.

She decided to leave her hair loose, but took extra care with her makeup in an effort to hide the faint shadows under her eyes.

Minutes later, after sipping her way through a cup of coffee, she stepped out of her apartment. As she locked the door, she noticed a familiar sleek sedan parked across the entrance to her driveway, blocking her in. Her tiredness evaporated on a surge of displeasure.

As she marched toward the car she could make out the shadowy outline of a man behind darkly tinted windows. It would be one of Lucas's security team, probably the guy who had tailed her to her interview with Alex Panopoulos.

Temper escalating, she bent down and tapped on the passenger-side window. Tinted glass slid down with an expensive hum. Glittering dark eyes locked with hers and a short, sharp jab of adrenaline shot through her. Lucas.

Dressed in a gray suit with a metallic sheen and a black T-shirt, his hair still damp from his shower, Lucas looked broodingly attractive. His hair was rumpled as if he'd run his fingers through it. He looked edgy and irritable, the shadow on his jaw signaling that he hadn't had time to shave.

The irritating awareness that still dogged her despite her repeated efforts to reprogram her mind kicked in, making her belly clench and her jaw set even tighter. "What are you doing here?"

"Keeping the press off." Lucas jerked his head in the direction of a blue hatchback parked on the opposite side of the street.

With an unpleasant start, Carla recognized the reporter who had snapped them outside Lucas's apartment the previous evening. "He wouldn't be here if he wasn't following you."

"He arrived before I did."

Her stomach sank. That meant the press would be going

all out with whatever story they could leverage out of that kiss. "Even more reason for you not to be here."

He leaned over and opened the passenger door. "Get in."

Carla gauged the time it would take to dash to her small garage, open the door and back her convertible out. With the reporter just a few fast steps away it would be no contest.

The flash and whir of the camera sent a second shot of adrenaline zinging through her veins as she slid into the passenger seat and slammed the door. The thunk of the locks engaging coincided with the throaty roar of the engine as the vehicle shot away from the curb. Seconds later, they were on the motorway heading into town and forced to an agonizing crawl by rush-hour traffic.

Carla relaxed her death grip on her purse, strapped on her seat belt and checked the rearview mirror. Anything but acknowledge the fact that she was once more within touching distance of Lucas Atraeus.

And riding in his car.

Although this wasn't his personal car. His taste usually ran to something a little more muscular and a lot faster, like the Maserati, but the intimacy still set her on edge and recalled one too many memories she would rather forget.

The first time they had made love had been in a car.

Two years ago he had given her a lift home from a dinner at a restaurant, a family meet-and-greet following Constantine and Sienna's first engagement.

Accepting a lift with Lucas, when she had expected to be delivered home the same way she had arrived, via hired limousine service, had seemed safe despite his bad-boy reputation with the tabloids. Plus there was the fact that recently he had been photographed on two separate occasions, each time with a different gorgeous girl.

Despite telling herself that he was clearly not on the hunt, when she slid into his car, she had felt a deliciously edgy

kind of thrill. Lucas was gorgeous in a dangerous, mascu
line way, so she was more than a little flattered to be singled
out for his attention.

It had taken a good half hour to reach her apartment during which time Lucas had played cruising music and asked
her about her family and whether or not she was dating.

When they'd reached her place it was pitch-dark. Instead
of parking out on the street, Lucas had driven right up to
her garage door and parked beneath the shelter of a large
shade tree. An oak overhung the driveway and blocked the
neighbor's view on one side. Her security lights had flicked
on as Lucas turned off the engine, although they remained
encapsulated in darkness since the garage blocked the light
from reaching the car.

With the music gone, the silence took on a heavy intensity,
and her stomach had tightened on a kick of nerves because
she knew in that moment that despite her frantic reasoning to
the contrary, he *did* want to kiss her. If Lucas was just dropping her home, he wouldn't have driven right into her driveway, and so far up it that the car was partially concealed.

He had barely touched her all night, although she had
been aware that he had been watching her and, admittedly,
she had played to her audience.

But all of the time she had flirted and played she had been
on edge in a feminine way, her nerves tingling. She was used
to being pursued, that went with the fashion industry and the
PR job. But Lucas was in a whole different league and she
hadn't made up her mind that she wanted him to catch her.

She had turned her head, bracing herself for the jolt of
eye contact, and his mouth caught hers, his tongue siding
right in. A burning shaft of heat shot straight to her loins
and she went limp.

Long seconds later, he had released her mouth. She gulped
in air and then his mouth closed on hers again and she was

sinking, drowning. Her arms closed convulsively around his neck, her fingers tangling in his hair, which was thick and silky and just long enough to play with. Not a good idea, since playing with Lucas Atraeus was the dating equivalent of stroking a big hunting cat, but the second he had touched her, her normal rules had evaporated.

She'd felt the zipper of her silk sheath being eased down her spine, the hot shock of his fingers against the bare skin of her back.

He'd muttered something in Medinian, too thick and rapid for her to catch, and lifted his head, jaw taut. "Do you want this?"

She realized he was holding on to control by a thread. The realization of his vulnerability was subtly shocking.

From the first her connection with Lucas had been powerful. Cliché or not, she had literally glanced across the restaurant and been instantly riveted.

Head and shoulders above most of the occupants of the room, all three Atraeus brothers had been compelling, but it had been Lucas's faintly battered profile that had drawn her.

She had let out a shuddering breath, abruptly aware of what he was asking. Not just a kiss. Somehow they had already stepped way beyond a kiss.

He'd bent his head as if he couldn't bear not to touch her. His lips feathered her throat, sending hot rills of sensation chasing across her skin, and abruptly something slotted into place in her mind.

She had been twenty-four, and a virgin, not because she had been consciously celibate but for the simple reason that she had never met anyone with whom she wanted to be that intimate. No matter how much she liked a date, if they couldn't knock her sideways emotionally, she refused to allow anything more than a good-night kiss.

Making love with Lucas Atraeus hadn't made sense for

a whole list of logical reasons. She barely knew him, and so there was no way she could be in love, but instead of recoiling, she'd found herself irresistibly compelled to throw away her rule book. On an instinctive level, with every touch, every kiss, Lucas Atraeus felt utterly right. "Yes."

A car horn blasted, shattering the recall, jerking Carla's gaze back to the road.

"What's wrong?"

Lucas's deep, raspy voice sent a nervy shock wave through her. His gaze caught hers, dispatching another electrical jolt. "Nothing."

His phone vibrated. He answered the call, his voice low. A couple of times his gaze intercepted hers and that weird electrical hum of awareness zapped her again, so she switched back to watching the wing mirror. Once she thought she spotted the blue hatchback and she stiffened, but she couldn't be certain.

"He's not behind us. I've been checking."

Which raised a question. "You said he got to my place before you did, so how did you know he was there?"

Constantine inched forward in traffic, braked, then reached behind to the backseat and handed her a newspaper, which had been folded open.

The headline, Lightning Strikes Twice for Atraeus Hatchet Man, sent her into mild shock, although she had been expecting something like it.

They hadn't made the front page, but close. A color photo, which had been taken just as Lucas had kissed her, was slotted directly below the story title.

Her outrage built as she skimmed the piece. According to the reporter, the romantic fires had been reignited during a secret tryst while she'd been on Medinos. An "insider" had supplied the tidbit that the wedding had literally thrown them together and they were now a hot romantic item. Again.

Although the speculation that Lucas would pop the question was strictly lighthearted. According to the "source," if Carla Ambrosi hadn't had what it took to keep Atraeus interested the first time around, the "reheat" would be about as exciting as day-old pasta.

Carla dropped the newspaper as if it had scorched her fingers. The instant she had seen her name coupled with Lucas's she should have known better than to read on.

Two years ago when Lucas had finished with her after that one night, she had been angry enough to go to the press. They'd had a field day with speculation and innuendo. Her skin was a lot thicker now, but the careless digging into her personal life, and the outright lies, still stung.

Reheat.

Her jaw tightened. If she ever found out who the cowardly "insider" was, the next installment of that particular story could be printed in the crime pages.

Folding the newspaper, she tossed it on the backseat. "You should have called me. You didn't have to show up on my doorstep."

Making it look like there really was substance to the story.

"If I'd called, you would have hung up on me."

She couldn't argue with that, because it was absolutely true.

Lucas signaled and made a turn into the underground parking garage beneath the Ambrosi building.

Carla was halfway out of the car, dragging her bag, which had snagged on a tiny lever at the base of the seat, when movement jerked her head up. A man with a camera loomed out of the shadows, walking swiftly toward them. Not the guy in the blue hatchback, someone else. The pale gleam of a van with its garish news logo registered in the background.

Lucas, who had walked around to open her door, said

something curt beneath his breath as she yanked at the strap. The bag came free and she surged upright.

"Smile, Mr. Atraeus, Ms. Ambrosi. Gotcha!"

The camera flashed as she lurched into Lucas.

The touching was minimal—her shoulder bumped his, he reached out to steady her—but the damage was done. In addition to the kiss outside Lucas's apartment the tabloids now had photos of Lucas picking her up from her apartment then delivering her to work.

The day-old pasta had just gotten hotter.

Nine

When Carla stepped out of her office to attend the press conference later on that morning, one of Lucas's bodyguards, Tiberio, was waiting for her in the corridor.

Lucas wasn't in the office. He had left after dropping her off that morning, so there was no one to interpret. After a short, labored struggle with Tiberio's fractured English, Carla finally agreed that, yes, they would both follow Lucas's orders and Tiberio could drive her to the press conference and see her safely inside.

On the way down to the parking garage, she decided that she was secretly glad Lucas had delegated Tiberio to mind her. She had been dreading dealing with the paparazzi when she arrived at the five-star hotel where the press conference was being held.

To her surprise, Tiberio opened the door on a glossy black limousine, not the dark sedan Lucas's security usually drove. When she slid into the leather interior, she was startled to discover that Lucas was already ensconced there, a briefcase open on the floor, a sheaf of papers in his hand.

The door closed, sealing her in. Lucas said something rapid to Tiberio as he slid behind the wheel. There was a discreet thunk, followed by the low hum of the engine.

She depressed the door handle, when it wouldn't budge, her gaze clashed with Lucas's. "You locked it."

His expression was suspiciously bland. "Standard security precaution."

Daylight replaced the gloom of the parking garage as they glided up onto the street. Her uneasiness at finding Lucas in the car coalesced into suspicion; she was beginning to feel manipulated. "Tiberio said you had ordered him to mind me, that he was supposed to drop me at the press conference. He didn't say we would be traveling together."

Lucas, still dressed in the silver-gray suit and black T-shirt he had been wearing that morning, but now freshly shaved, retrieved a cell phone from his briefcase. "Is there a problem with going together?"

She frowned. "After what happened, wouldn't it be the smart thing to arrive separately?"

Lucas's attention was centered on what was, apparently, a swanky new phone. "No."

Her frustration spiked as he punched in a number and lifted the phone to his ear then subsided just as quickly as she listened to his deep voice, the liquid cadences of his rapid Medinian. Reluctantly fascinated, she hung on every word. He could be reciting a grocery list and she could still listen all day.

Minutes later, the limousine pulled into a space outside the hotel entrance. When she saw the media crush, she experienced a rare moment of panic. Publicity was her thing; she had a natural bent for it. But not today. "Isn't there a back entrance we can use?"

Lucas, seemingly unconcerned, snapped his phone closed and slipped it into his pocket.

She flashed him an irritated look. "The last thing we need right now is to be seen arriving together, looking like we *are* a couple."

"Don't worry, the media will be taken care of. It's all arranged."

Something about his manner brought her head up, sharpened all her senses. "What do you mean, 'arranged'? If the media doesn't see me for a few days, the story will die a death."

"No, it won't," Lucas said flatly. "Not this time."

The door to the limousine popped open. Lucas exited first. Reluctantly Carla followed, stepping into the dusty, steamy heat of midtown Sydney.

The media surged forward. To Carla's relief they were instantly held at bay by a wall of burly men in dark suits.

Lucas's hand landed in the small of her back, the heat of his palm burning through her dress, then they were moving. Carla kept her spine stiff, informing Lucas that she wasn't happy with either the situation or his touch, which seemed entirely too intimate.

The glass doors of the hotel threw a reflection back at her. Lucas stood tall and muscled by her side, his gaze with that grim, icy quality that always sent shivers down her spine. With the other men flanking them in a protective curve, she couldn't help thinking they looked like a trailer for a gangster flick.

The doors slid open, and the air-conditioned coolness of the hotel foyer flowed around her as they walked briskly to a bank of elevators. A security guard was holding an empty elevator car. Relief eased some of her tension as they stepped inside.

Before the doors could slide closed a well-dressed female reporter, microphone in hand, cameraman in tow, side-stepped security and grabbed the door, preventing it from closing.

"Mr. Atraeus, Ms. Ambrosi, can you confirm the rumor that Sienna Atraeus is pregnant?"

There was a moment of confusion as security reacted, forcing the woman and her cameraman to step back.

Lucas issued a sharp order. The doors snapped closed and she found herself alone with Lucas as the elevator lurched into motion.

Carla's stomach clenched at the sudden acceleration.

Sienna pregnant.

"Constantine phoned me earlier to let me know that Sienna was pregnant and that it was possible the story had been leaked."

A hurt she had stubbornly avoided dealing with hit her like a kick in the chest.

She didn't begrudge Sienna one moment of her happiness, but it was a fact that she possessed all the things that Carla realized *she* wanted. Not necessarily right now, but sometime in the future, in their natural order, and with Lucas.

But Lucas was showing no real signs of commitment.

Blankly, she watched floor numbers flash by. If she were pregnant she had to assume there would be no marriage, no happy ending, no husband to love and cherish her and the child.

She became aware the elevator had stopped. She sucked in a deep breath, but the oxygen didn't seem to be getting through. Her head felt heavy and pressurized, her knees wobbly. Not illness, just good old-fashioned panic.

Lucas took her arm, holding her steady. The top of her head bumped his chin, the scrape of his stubbled jaw on the sensitive skin of her forehead sending a reflexive shiver through her. She inhaled, gasping air like a swimmer surfacing, and his warm male scent, laced with the subtle edge of cologne, filled her nostrils.

Lucas said something curt in Medinian. "Damn, you *are* pregnant."

A split second later the elevator doors slid open.

Fingers automatically tightening around the strap of her handbag, which was in danger of sliding off her shoulder, she stepped out into a broad, carpeted corridor. Lucas's security, who must have taken another elevator, were waiting.

Lucas's hand closed around her arm. "Slow down. I've got you."

"That's part of the problem."

"Then deal with it. I'm not going away."

She shot him an icy glare. "I thought leaving was the whole point?"

He traded a cool glance but didn't reply because they had reached the designated suite. A murmur rippled through the room as they were recognized, but this time, courtesy of the heavy presence of security, there was no undisciplined rush.

Tomas, Constantine's PA, and Lucas's mother, Maria Therese, were already seated. Carla took a seat next to Lucas. Seconds later, Zane escorted Lilah into the room.

Her stomach contracted as the questions began. The presence of a mediator limited the topics to the Atraeus takeover of Ambrosi, Ambrosi's new collection and the re-creation of the historic Ambrosi pearl facility on the Medinian island of Ambrus. However, when Lucas rose to his feet, indicating that the press conference was over, a barrage of personal questions ensued.

Lucas's fingers laced with hers, the contact intimate and unsettling as he pulled her to her feet. When she discreetly tried to pull free, wary of creating even more unpleasant speculation, he sent her a warning glance, his hold firming.

As they stepped off the podium the media, no longer quietly seated, swirled around them. The clear, husky voice of a well-known television reporter cut through the shouted questions. A microphone was thrust at Lucas's face.

The reporter flashed him a cool smile. "Can you confirm or deny the reports that you've resumed your affair with Carla?"

Lucas pulled her in close against his side as they continued to move at a steady pace. His gaze intersected with hers, filled with cool warning. "No official statement has been issued yet, however I can confirm that Carla Ambrosi and I have been secretly engaged for the past two years."

The room erupted. Lucas bit out a grim order. The security team, already working to push the press back, closed in, forcing a bubble of privacy and shoving Carla up hard against Lucas. His arm tightened and she found herself lifted off her feet as he literally propelled her from the room.

Shock and a wave of edgy heat zapped through her as she clung to his narrow waist and scrambled to keep her balance. Seconds later they were sealed into the claustrophobic confines of what looked like a service elevator, still surrounded by burly security.

Carla twisted, trying to peel loose from his hold. Lucas easily resisted the attempt, tightening his arms around her. In the process she ended up plastered against his chest. The top button of her dress came unfastened and his hand, which was spread across her rib cage, shifted up so that his thumb and index finger sank into the swell of one breast.

As if a switch had been thrown, she was swamped by memories, some hot and sensuous enough that her breasts tightened and her belly contracted, some hurtful enough that her temper roared to life.

Lucas's gaze burned over the lush display of cleavage where the bodice of her dress gaped. "Keep still," he growled.

But she noticed he didn't move his hand.

She was *not* enjoying it. After the humiliation of the previous evening the last thing she needed was to be clamped against all that hot, hard muscle, making her feel small and wimpy and tragically easy. Unfortunately, her body wasn't in sync with her mind. She couldn't control the heat flushing her skin or the automatic tightening of her nipples, and Lucas knew it.

The doors slid open. Before she could protest, they were moving again, this time through the lower bowels of the hotel. A door off a loading bay was shoved wide and they spilled out onto a walled parking area where several vehicles, including a limousine, were parked.

Her fury increased. Here was the back entrance she had needed an hour ago.

Hot, clammy air flowed around her as she clambered into the limousine, clutching her purse. Lucas slid in beside her, his muscled thigh brushing hers. She flinched as if scalded and scooted over another few inches.

His gaze flashed to hers as they accelerated away from the curb. "All right?"

His calm control pushed her over the edge. She reached for her seat belt and jammed the fastenings together. "Secretly *engaged?*"

A week ago an engagement was what she had longed for, what she would have *loved.* "Correct me if I'm wrong, maybe I blacked out at some stage, but I don't ever remember a proposal of marriage."

She caught Tiberio's surprised glance in the rearview mirror.

Lucas's expression was grim. A faint hum filled the air as a privacy screen slid smoothly into place, locking them into a bubble of silence.

She stared at Lucas, incensed. Thanks to the mad dash

through the hotel, her hair had unwound and was now cascading untidily down her back, and she was perspiring. In contrast, Lucas looked cool and completely in control, his suit *GQ* perfect. "An engagement is the logical solution."

"It's damage control, and it's completely unnecessary." She remembered her gaping bodice and hurriedly refastened the button. "I may not be pregnant."

Her voice sounded husky and tight, even to herself, and she wondered, a little wildly, if he could tell how much she suddenly wanted to be pregnant.

"Whether you're pregnant or not is a consideration, but it isn't an issue, yet."

Something seized in her chest, her heart. For a crazy moment she considered that he was about to admit that he was in love with her, that he didn't care if she was pregnant or not, he couldn't live without her. Then reality dissolved that fantasy. "But what the newspapers are printing is. Do you know how humiliating it is to be offered a forced marriage?"

Irritation tinged with outrage registered in his expression. "No one's *forcing* you to do anything. Marriage as an option can't be such a shock. Not after what happened on Medinos. And last night."

"Well, I guess that puts things in perspective. It's a *practical* option."

Her mood was definitely spiraling down. Practicality spelled death for all romance. Cancel the white wedding with champagne and rose petals. Bring on the registry office and matching gray suits.

"I wouldn't propose marriage if I didn't *want* to marry you."

Her gaze narrowed. "Is that the proposal?"

His expression was back to remote. "It isn't what I had planned, but, yes."

"Uh-huh." She drew a deep breath and counted to ten.

"The biggest mistake I made was in agreeing to sleep with you."

Suddenly he was close, one arm draped behind her, his warm male scent laced with the enticing cologne stopping the breath in her throat. "On which occasion?"

She stared rigidly ahead, trying to ignore the heated gleam in his eyes, the subtle cajoling that shouldn't succeed in getting her on side, but which was slowly undermining her will to resist.

That was the other thing about Lucas, besides the power and influence he wielded in the business world. When he wanted he could be stunningly seducingly attentive. But this time she refused to be swayed by his killer charm. "All of them."

He wound a strand of her hair around one finger and lightly tugged. She felt his breath fanning her nape. "That's a lot of mistakes."

And she had enjoyed every one of them.

She resisted the urge to turn her head, putting her mouth bare inches from his and letting the conversation take them to the destination he was so blatantly angling for—a bone-melting kiss. "I should never have slept with you, period."

He dropped the strand of hair and sat back, slightly, signaling that he had changed tack. "Meaning that if you had played your cards right," he said softly, "you could have had marriage in the beginning?"

Ten

Like quicksilver the irresistible pull of attraction was gone, replaced by wrenching hurt. "Just because I didn't talk about marriage, that didn't mean I thought it would never be on the agenda for us. And what is so wrong with that?"

Silence vibrated through the limousine. She saw Tiberio glance nervously in the rearview mirror. She turned her head to watch city traffic zip by and registered that her stomach felt distinctly hollow.

Glancing at her watch, she noted the time. She'd only had coffee for breakfast and it was after one. She would be eating lunch soon, which would fix the acid in her stomach, but she couldn't wait that long. Fumbling in her purse, she took out the small plastic bag that contained a few antacid tablets and a couple of individually packaged biscuits. After unwrapping a slightly battered biscuit, she took a bite.

"Marriage is on the agenda now," Lucas reminded her. "I need an answer."

She hastily finished the biscuit and stuffed the plastic bag back in her purse.

Lucas watched her movements with an annoyed fascination. "Do you usually eat when marriage is being proposed?"

"I was hungry. I needed to eat."

"I'll have to remember that should I ever have occasion to propose again."

She closed the flap on her purse. Maybe it was childish not to tell him that she had ended up with an ulcer, but it was no big deal and she was still hurt that he hadn't ever bothered to check up on her after he had deposited her on the plane home from Thailand. The memory of his treatment of her, which had been uncharacteristically callous, stiffened her spine. "I don't know why you want marriage now when clearly you broke up with me because you didn't view me as 'wife' material."

His gaze was unwavering, making her feel suddenly uncomfortable about giving him such a hard time.

"As it happens, you've always fulfilled the most important requirement."

She was suddenly, intensely conscious of the warmth of his arm behind her. "Which is?"

Her breath seized in her throat as Lucas cupped her chin with his free hand. She had a split second to either pull back or turn her head so his mouth would miss hers. Instead, hope turned crazy cartwheels in her stomach, and she allowed the kiss.

Long, breathless minutes later he lifted his head. "You wanted to know why marriage is acceptable to me. This is why."

His thumb traced the line of her cheekbone, sending tingling heat shivering across the delicate skin and igniting a familiar, heated tension. His mouth brushed hers again, the kiss lingering. The stirring tension wound tighter. Reflexively, she leaned closer, angling her jaw to deepen the kiss. Her hand slid around to grip his nape and pull him closer still.

When he finally lifted his head, his gaze was bleak. "Two months without you was two months too long. What happened on Medinos and in my apartment is a case in point. I want you back."

Carla released her hold on his nape and drew back. Her mouth, her whole body, was tingling.

It wasn't what she wanted to hear, but the hope fizzing inside refused to die a complete death.

Lucas had tried to end their relationship; it hadn't happened. She hadn't chased him. If he had truly wanted an end, she was in no doubt that he would have icily and clinically cut her out of his life.

He hadn't been able to because he couldn't resist her.

He might label what held them together as sex; she preferred to call it chemistry. There was a reason they were attracted to each other that went way beyond the physical into the area of personality and emotional needs. Despite their difficulties and clashes, at a deep, bedrock level she knew they were perfect for each other.

That they had continued their relationship for two years was further proof that whatever he either claimed or denied, for Lucas she was different in some way. She knew, because she had made it her business to check. Lucas was only ever recorded by the tabloids as having one serious relationship before her, a model called Sophie, and that had been something like five years ago. The fact that he wanted the marriage now, when a pregnancy was by no means certain, underlined just how powerfully he did want her.

It wasn't love, but everything in her shouted that it had to be possible for the potent chemistry that had bound Lucas to her for the past two years to turn to love.

She was clutching at straws. Her heart was pounding and her stomach kept lurching. There was a possibility that Lucas might never truly love her, never fully commit himself to the relationship. There was a chance she was making the biggest mistake of her life.

But, risky or not, if she was honest, her mind had been made up the second she'd heard his announcement to the press.

She loved Lucas.

If there was a chance that he could love her, then she was taking it.

Lucas activated the privacy screen. When it opened, he leaned forward and spoke in rapid Medinian to Tiberio. He caught the skeptical flash of his chief bodyguard's gaze in the rearview mirror as he confirmed that they would be making the scheduled stop at the jewelers.

However, the wry amusement that would normally have kicked up the corners of his mouth in answer to Tiberio's pessimism was absent. When it came to Carla, he was beginning to share Tiberio's doubts. She hadn't said yes, and he was by no means certain that she would.

Carla, who was once again rummaging in her handbag, stiffened as the limousine pulled into the cramped loading bay of a downtown building. "This isn't the restaurant."

Lucas climbed out as Tiberio opened the door then leaned in and took Carla's hand. "We have one stop to make before lunch."

As Carla climbed out he noted the moment she spotted the elegant sign that indicated this was the rear entrance to the premises of Moore's, a famous jeweler. A business that just happened to be owned by The Atraeus Group.

Her expression was accusing. "You had this all planned."

"Last night you knew as well as I that the story would go to press."

Her light blue gaze flashed. Before she could formulate an argument and decide to answer his proposal with a no, Lucas propelled her toward the back entrance.

Frustration welled that he hadn't been able to extract an answer from her *and* that he couldn't gauge her mood, but he kept a firm clamp on his temper. An edgy, hair-trigger temper that, until these past two weeks, he hadn't known existed.

He offered her his arm and forced himself to patience when she didn't immediately take it.

Clear, glacial-blue eyes clashed with his. "What makes you think I'm actually going to go through with this?"

Lucas noted that she stopped short of using the word *charade.* "I apologize for trying to bulldoze you," he said grimly. "I realize I've mishandled the situation."

He had used business tactics to try to maneuver Carla into an engagement. He had assumed that when he proposed marriage she would be, if not ecstatic, then, at least, happy.

Instead, she was decidedly *unhappy,* and now he was being left to sweat.

He acknowledged that he deserved it. If patience was now required to achieve a result, then he would be patient. "The ring is important. I need you to come inside and choose one."

"I suppose we need one because we've been *secretly engaged* for two years, so of course you would have loved me enough to buy a ring."

Ignoring Tiberio's scandalized expression, he unclenched his jaw. *"Esattamente,"* he muttered, momentarily forgetting his English. "If you don't have a ring, questions will be asked."

"So the ring is a prop, a detail that adds credence to the story."

The door popped open. A dapper gray-haired man, elegant in a dark suit and striped tie, appeared along with a security guard. "Mr. Atraeus," he murmured. "Ms. Ambrosi. My name is Carstairs, the store manager. Would you like to come this way?"

Keeping his temper firmly in check, Lucas concentrated on Carla. If she refused the ring, he would arrange for a selection to be sent to his apartment and she could choose one there. What was important was that she accept his proposal, and that hadn't happened yet. "Are you ready?"

Her eyes clashed with his again, but she took his arm.

Jaw clenched, Lucas controlled his emotions with a forcible effort. Fleetingly, he registered Tiberio's relief, an exaggerated expression of his own, as he walked up the steps and allowed Carla to precede him into the building.

She would say yes. She had to.

The turnaround was huge, but now that he had made the decision that he wanted her in his life permanently, he felt oddly settled.

Like it or not he was involved, his feelings raw, possessive. Sexually, he had lost control with Carla from the beginning, something that had never come close to happening with any other woman.

It was also a blunt fact that the thought of Carla with Panopoulos, or any man, was unacceptable. When he had walked into that particular wall, his reaction had cleared his mind. Despite everything that could go wrong with this relationship, Carla was his.

If he had to be patient and wait for her, then he would be patient.

Carla stepped into the room Carstairs indicated, glad for a respite from the odd intensity of Lucas's gaze and her own inner turmoil. For a fractured moment, she had been an inch away from giving up on the need to pressure some kind of admission out of Lucas and blurting out "yes." She would marry him, she would do whatever he wanted, if only he would keep on looking at her that way. But then the emotional shutters she had never been able to fathom had come crashing down and they had ended up stalemated again.

The room was an elegant private sitting room with sleek leather couches offset by an antique sideboard and coffee tables. Classical music played softly. The largest coffee table held a selection of rings nestled in black velvet trays.

Carstairs, who seemed to be staring at her oddly, indicated that she take a seat and view the rings, then asked if she would like coffee or champagne. Refusing either drink with a tight smile, she sat and tried to concentrate on the rings. Lucas, who had also refused a drink, paced the small room like an overlarge caged panther, then came to stand over her, distracting her further.

His breath stirred her hair as he leaned forward for a closer look. Utterly distracted by his closeness, she stared blindly at the rings, dazzled by the glitter but unable to concentrate, which was criminal because she loved pretty jewelry. "I didn't think you were interested in jewelry."

"I'm interested in you," he said flatly. "This one."

He picked out a pale blue pear-shaped stone, which she had noticed but bypassed because it occupied a tray that contained a very small number of exquisite rings, all with astronomical price tags.

He handed it to her then conferred briefly with Carstairs. "It's a blue diamond, from Brazil. Very rare, and the same color as your eyes. Do you like it?"

She studied the soft, mesmerizing glow of the diamond, but was more interested in the fact that he had picked the ring because it matched her eyes. She slipped the ring on her finger. Wouldn't you know, it was a perfect fit and it looked even better on. "I love it."

His gaze caught hers, held it, and for a moment she felt absurdly giddy.

"Then we'll take it." He passed Carstairs his credit card.

Yanking the ring off, she replaced it on its plush velvet tray and pushed to her feet, panic gripping her. "I haven't said yes yet."

Lucas said something in rapid Medinian to Carstairs. With a curt bow, the store manager, who could evidently speak the language, left the room, still with Lucas's card, which meant Lucas was buying the ring, regardless. Simultaneously, an elegant older woman in a simple black dress collected the remaining trays and made a swift exit along with Tiberio, leaving them alone. The blue ring, she noticed, was left on the coffee table.

In the background the classical music ended. Suddenly the silence was thick enough to cut.

Carla shoved to her feet and walked to the large bay window. She stared out into the tiny yard presently dominated by the limousine, and the issue she'd been desperate to ignore, which had hurt more than anything because it had cut into the most tender part of her, surfaced. As hard as she had tried for two years to be everything Lucas could want or need, it hadn't been enough. When the pressure had come on to commit, he hadn't wanted *her*. He had wanted Lilah, who in many ways was her complete opposite: calm, controlled and content to keep a low profile.

In retrospect, maybe she had tried too hard and he hadn't ever really seen her, just the glossy, upbeat side that was always "on." The one time he had truly seen her had been in Thailand. She had been too sick to try to be anything but herself, and he had run a mile. "What about Lilah?"

"I spoke to Lilah last night. Zane is taking care of her."

She met his gaze in the window. "I thought you were in love with her."

He came to stand behind her. "She was my date at the wedding, that was all. And, no, we didn't sleep together. We didn't kiss. I didn't so much as hold her hand."

Relief made Carla's legs feel as limp as noodles. He pulled her back against him in a loose hold, as the palm of one hand slid around to cup her abdomen.

"Marriage wasn't on my agenda, with anyone, but the situation has…changed. Don't forget it's entirely possible you're pregnant."

Lucas's hold tightened, making her intensely aware of his hard, muscled body so close behind her. Their reflection bounced back at her, Lucas large and powerfully male, herself paler and decidedly feminine. "I can't marry solely for a baby that might not exist! There has to be something more. Sienna is married to a man she loves. A man who loved her enough that he kidnapped her—"

"Are you saying you want to be *kidnapped?*"

She stared at the dark, irritable glitter of Lucas's eyes, the tough line of his jaw. Her own jaw set. "All I'm saying is that Constantine loves Sienna. It matters."

There was an arresting look in his eyes. "You love me."

Eleven

Carla inhaled sharply at the certainty in Lucas's voice, feeling absurdly vulnerable that, after two years of careful camouflage, she was so transparent now. She was also hurt by his matter-of-fact tone, as if her emotional attachment was simply a convenience that smoothed his path now. "What did you expect, that I was empty-headed enough that I was just having sex with you?"

"Meaning that was how I was with you?" His grip on her arms gentled. "Calm down. I didn't know until that moment. I'm…pleased."

"Because it makes things easier?"

"We're getting married," he said flatly. "This is not some business deal."

He didn't make the mistake of trying to kiss her. Instead he released her, walked over to the coffee table and picked the ring up.

The diamond shimmered in the light, impossibly beautiful, but it was the determined set to Lucas's jaw, the rock-solid patience in his gaze, that riveted her. "What if I'm not pregnant?"

"We'll deal with that possibility when we get to it."

Her jaw tightened. She didn't want to create difficulties, but neither could she let him put that ring on her finger without saying everything that needed to be said. "I'm not sure I want marriage under these conditions."

"That's your choice," he said flatly, his patience finally slipping. "But don't hold out for Alex Panopoulos to intervene. As of yesterday he has reviewed his options."

The sudden mention of Panopoulos was faintly shocking. "You warned him off."

"That's right." Lucas's voice was even, but his expression spoke volumes, coolly set with a primitive gleam in his eyes that sent a faint quiver zapping down her spine.

Just when she thought Lucas was cold and detached he proved her wrong by turning distinctly male and predatory.

It wasn't much, it wasn't enough, but it told her what she needed to know: Lucas was jealous. Given his cool, measured approach to every other aspect of his life, if he was jealous then he had to feel something powerful, something special, for her.

It was a leap in the dark. Marriage would be an incredible risk, but the past two years had been all about risk and she had already lost her heart. It came down to a simple choice. She could either walk away and hope to fall out of love with Lucas or she could stay and hold out for his love.

Her chin came up. When it came down to it she wasn't a coward. She would rather try and fail than not try at all.

"Okay," she said huskily, and extended her hand so he could slide the ring on her finger.

The fit was perfect. She stared at the fiery blue stone, her chest suddenly tight.

Lucas lifted her fingers to his lips. "It looks good."

The rough note in his voice, the unexpected caress, sent a shimmering wave of emotion through her. "It's beautiful."

He bent his head. Before she could react, he kissed her on the mouth. "I have good taste."

Despite her effort to stay calm and composed and not let Lucas see how much this meant to her, a wave of heat suffused her cheeks. "In rings or wives?"

He grinned quick and hard and dropped another quick kiss on her mouth. "Both."

Lucas shepherded Carla into the backseat of the limousine, satisfaction filling him at the sight of the ring glowing on her finger.

She loved him.

He had suspected it, but he hadn't known for sure until she had said the words. Her emotional involvement was an element he hadn't factored in when he had decided on marriage. He had simply formulated a strategy and kept to it until she had capitulated.

Now that he knew she loved him and had agreed to marry him, there would be no reason to delay moving her in with him. No reason to delay the wedding.

Marriage.

Since Sophie's death, marriage had not been an option, because he had never gotten past the fact that he still felt responsible for the accident.

It had taken a good year for the flashbacks of the accident to fade from his mind, another six months before he could sleep without waking up and reliving that night.

Sometimes, even now, he still woke up at night, reliving their last argument and trying to reinvent the past. He had avoided commitment for the simple reason that he knew his own nature: once he did commit he did so one hundred percent and he was fiercely protective. The night Sophie had died, he had been blindsided by the fact that she had aborted his child. He'd allowed her to throw her tantrum and leave. Maybe he was overcompensating now, but he would never allow himself, or any woman he was with, to be put in that situation again.

Until Carla, he had avoided becoming deeply involved with anyone. The week in Thailand had been a tipping point. Caring for Carla in that intimate situation had pushed him over an invisible boundary he had carefully skirted for five years. He hadn't liked the intense flood of emotion, or the implications for the future. He knew the way he was hard-wired. For as long as he could remember he had been the same: when it came to emotion it was all or nothing.

Now that Carla had agreed to marry him and it was possible that he would be a father, if not in the near future, then sometime over the next few years, he was faced with a double responsibility. He could feel the possessiveness, the desire to cushion and protect already settling in.

With Sophie he hadn't had time to absorb the impact of her pregnancy because it had been over before he had known about it. She hadn't given him a chance. With Carla the situation was entirely different. He knew that she would never abort their child. She would extend the same fiercely protective, single-minded love she gave her family to their baby.

Any child Carla had would be loved and pampered. Unlike Sophie, she would embrace the responsibility, the chills and the spills.

It was an odd moment to realize that one of the reasons he wanted to marry Carla was that he trusted her.

During the drive to the restaurant Lucas had booked, Carla wavered between staring with stunned amazement at the engagement ring and frantically wondering what Lucas's mother was going to think.

Like every other member of the Atraeus family, Maria Therese would know that Carla and Lucas had more than a hint of scandal in their past. Plus, the first and only time they had met, Lucas had been dating Lilah.

Lucas, who had been preoccupied with phone calls for the duration of the short trip to the restaurant, took her arm as she exited the limousine. "Now that we're engaged, there is one rule you will follow—don't talk to the press unless you've cleared it with me."

Carla stiffened. "PR is my job. I think I can handle the press."

Lucas nodded at Tomas, who was evidently waiting for them at the portico of the restaurant. "PR for Ambrosi is one thing. For the Atraeus family the situation is entirely different."

"I think I can be trusted."

His glance was impatient. "I know you can handle publicity. It's the security aspect that worries me. Every member of my family has to take care, and situations with the press provide prime opportunities for security breaches. If you're going to be talking to the press, a security detail needs to be organized. And by the way, I've booked you into the hotel for the launch party. We leave first thing in the morning."

Carla stopped dead in her tracks, a small fuzzy glow of happiness expanding in her chest. Lucas had obviously taken care of that detail before he had asked her to marry him, righting a wrong that had badly needed fixing. She knew she wouldn't be in charge of running the show, but that was a mere detail. She would still be able to make sure everything came off perfectly and that was what mattered. She was finally starting to believe that this marriage could work. "My contract as Ambrosi's public relations executive is up for renewal next week."

"It's as good as signed."

"That was almost too easy."

His arm slid around her waist, pulling her in against his side as they walked into the restaurant. "I was going to renew it anyway. You're damn good at the job, and besides, I want you to be happy."

Her happiness expanded another notch. It wasn't perfection yet—she still had to deal with that emotional distance thing that Lucas constantly pulled—but it was inching closer.

Maria Therese, Zane and Lilah were already seated at the table. Carla's stomach plunged as Lucas's mother gave her a measuring glance. With her smooth, ageless face and impeccable fashion sense, the matriarch of the Atraeus family had a reputation for being calm and composed under pressure. And with her late husband's affairs, there had been constant media pressure. "Does your mother know how long we've been involved?"

"You're an Ambrosi and my future wife. She'll be more than happy to accept you into the family."

Carla's stomach plunged. "Oh, good. She knows."

The resort chosen for the product launch was Balinese in style. Situated in its own private bay with heavy tropical gardens, it was also stunningly beautiful.

The hotel foyer was just as Carla remembered it when she had originally investigated the resort for the launch party. Constructed with all the grandeur of a movie set, it was both exotic and restful with a soaring atrium and tinkling fountains.

When Carla checked in at the front desk, however, she found that the guest room that had originally been booked for her had been canceled and there were no vacancies. Every room had been booked for the launch.

Lucas, casual in light-colored pants and a loose gauzy white shirt that accentuated his olive skin and made his shoulders look even broader, slipped his platinum card across the counter. "You're sharing with me. The suite's in my name."

So nice to be told. Even though she understood that Lucas was behaving this way because he was still unsure of her and he wanted to keep her close, there was no ignoring that it was controlling behavior. Pointedly ignoring the interruption, she addressed the receptionist. "Are you sure there are no rooms left? How about the room that was originally booked for Lilah Cole?"

Lilah had originally been slated to attend the launch. As the head designer she had a right to be there, but she had pulled out at the last minute.

The receptionist dragged her dazzled gaze off Lucas. "I'm sorry, ma'am, there was a waiting list. The room has already been allocated."

Carla waited until they were in the elevator. The feel-good mood of the two-hour drive from Sydney in Lucas's Ferrari was rapidly dissolving. Maybe it was a small point since they were engaged, but she would like to have been asked before Lucas decided she would be sharing his room. Lucas's controlling streak seemed to be growing by leaps and bounds and she was at a loss to understand why. She had agreed to marry him; life should be smoothing out, but it wasn't. Lucas was oddly silent, tense and brooding. Something was wrong and she couldn't figure out what it was.

Lucas leaned against the wall, arms folded over his chest, his gaze wary. "It's just a hotel room. I assumed you would want to share."

"I do."

Lucas frowned. The relaxed cast to his face, courtesy of an admittedly sublime night spent together in his bed, gone. "Then what's wrong? You already know that Lilah and I were not involved."

"It's not Lilah—"

The doors slid open. A young couple with three young children were waiting for the elevator.

Lucas propelled her out into the corridor. "We'll continue this discussion in our room."

Their luggage had already been delivered and was stacked to one side, but Carla barely registered that detail. The large airy room with its dark polished floors, teak furniture and soaring ceilings was filled with lush bouquets of roses in a range of hues from soft pinks to rich reds. Long stemmed and glorious, they overflowed dozens of vases, their scent filling the suite.

Dazed, she walked through to the bedroom, which was also smothered with flowers. An ice bucket of champagne and a basket crammed with fresh fruit and exquisitely presented chocolates resided on a small coffee table positioned between two chairs.

Lucas carried their bags into the bedroom. The second he set them down she flung her arms around him. "I'm sorry. You organized all this—it's beautiful, gorgeous—and all I could do was complain."

His arms closed around her, tucking her in snugly against him. The comfort of his muscled body against hers, the enticement of his clean scent, increased her dizzy pleasure.

The second she had seen what Lucas had done, how focused he was on pleasing her, the notion that there was something wrong had evaporated. Now she felt embarrassed and contrite for giving him such a hard time.

Carla spent a happy hour rearranging the flowers and unpacking. By the time she had finished laying out her dress for the evening function, Lucas had showered, changed into a suit and disappeared, called away to do a series of interviews.

A knock on the door made her frown. When she opened it a young woman in a hotel uniform was standing outside with a hotel porter. After a brief conversation she discovered that Lucas had arranged for the items to be delivered for her perusal. Anything she didn't want would be returned to the stores.

Feeling a bit like Alice falling down the rabbit hole, Carla opened the door wider so the porter could wheel in a clotheshorse that was hung with a number of plastic-shrouded gowns. At the base of the clotheshorse were boxes of shoes from the prominent design stores downstairs. She signed a docket and closed the door behind the hotel employees.

A quick survey of the gowns revealed that while they were all her size and by highly desirable designers, they were definitely not her style. Two had significantly high necklines, one a soft pink, the other an oyster lace. Both were elegant and gorgeously detailed, but neither conformed to her taste. The pink was too ruffled, like a flapper dress from the 1920s, and the oyster lace was stiffly formal and too much like a wedding gown.

The other boxes contained matching shoes and wraps and matching sets of silk underwear. She couldn't help noticing that none of the shoes had heels higher than two inches.

As dazzled as she was by the lavish gifts, nothing about any of them fitted her personality or style. Each item was decidedly conventional and, for want of a better word, boring, like something her mother would have worn.

Her pleasure in unwrapping the beautiful things was dissolving by the second. Aside from the underwear, which was sexy and beautiful, it was clear that Lucas had had one thought in mind when he had had the things sent up: he was trying to tone her down. That brought them back to the original problem. Despite the engagement, Lucas still didn't accept her for who she was. If he couldn't accept her, she didn't see how he could ever love her.

She found her phone and jabbed in the number of Lucas's new phone. He picked up on the second ring, his voice impatient.

She cut him off. "I'm not wearing any of these dresses you've just had sent up."

"Can we discuss this later?" The register of his voice was low, his tone guarded, indicating that he wasn't alone.

Carla was beyond caring. "I'm discussing it now. I resent the implication that I dress immodest—"

"When did I say—"

"I'm female and, newsflash, I have a *figure*. I do not buy clothes to emphasise sex appeal—"

"Wait there. I'm coming up."

A click sounded in her ear. Heart pounding, she snapped her phone closed, slipped it back in her bag and surveyed the expensive pile of items. Hurt squeezed her chest tight.

She had repacked the shoes and started on the underwear when the door opened.

Lucas snapped the door closed behind him and jerked at his tie. "What's the problem?"

Carla glanced away from the heated irritation in his gaze, his ruffled hair as if he'd dragged his fingers through it, and the sexy dishevelment of the loose tie.

She picked up the pink ruffled number. "This, for starters."

He frowned. "What's wrong with it?"

She draped the gown against her body. "Crimes against humanity. The fashion police will have me in cuffs before I get out of the elevator."

He pinched the bridge of his nose as if he was under intense pressure. "Do you realize that on Medinos, as your future husband I have the right to dictate what you wear?"

For a moment she thought he was joking. "That's *medieval*—"

"Maybe I'm a medieval kind of guy."

She blinked. She had been wanting to breach his inner barriers, but now she was no longer sure she was going to like what she'd find. The old Lucas had been a pussycat compared to what she was now uncovering. "I buy clothes because they make me look and feel good, not to showcase my breasts or any other part of my anatomy. If that means I occasionally flash a bit of cleavage, then you, and the rest of Medinos, are just going to have to adjust."

She snatched up the pink silk underwear, which in stark contrast to the dress was so skimpy it wouldn't keep a grasshopper warm. "Are these regulation?"

He hooked the delicate thong over one long brown finger. "Absolutely."

Carla snatched the thong back and tossed the pink underwear back in its box. Retrieving the list of items she had signed for, she did what she had been longing to do—ripped it into shreds and tossed the pieces at Lucas. The issue of clothing, as superficial as it seemed, ignited the deep hurt that Lucas still viewed her as his sexy, private mistress and not his future wife. "You can have your master plan back."

Lucas ignored the fluttering pieces of paper. "What master plan?"

"The one where you turn me into some kind of perfect stuffed mannequin and put me in a room on Medinos with one of those wooden embroidery frames in my hand."

Lucas rubbed the side of his jaw, his gaze back to wary. "Okay, I am now officially lost."

"I resent being treated as if I'm too dumb to know how I

should dress. This is not digging gold out of rocks or sweaty men building a hotel, this is a *fashion* industry event."

His jaw took on an inflexible look she was beginning to recognize. "We're engaged. Damned if I'm going to let other men ogle you."

She threw up her hands. "You're laying down the law, but you don't even know what I plan to wear tonight."

Marching to the bed, she held up a hanger that held a sleek gold sheath with a softly draped boat-shaped neckline. "It's simple, elegant, shows no cleavage—and, more to the point, I like it."

"In that case, I apologize."

Feeling oddly deflated, she replaced the dress on the bed. When she turned, Lucas pulled her into his arms.

Her palms automatically spread on his chest. She could feel the steady pound of his heart beneath the snowy linen of his shirt, the taut, sculpted muscle beneath. Her heart rate, already fast, sped up, but he didn't try to pull her closer or kiss her.

"It wasn't my intention to upset you, but there is one thing about me that you're going to have to understand—I don't share. When it comes down to it, I don't care what you wear. I just don't want other men thinking you're available. And from now on the press will watch you like a hawk."

"I'm not irresponsible, or a tease." She released herself from his hold. The problem was that she had never understood Lucas's mood swings; she didn't understand him. One minute he was with her, the next he was cut off and distant and she needed to know why, because that distance frightened her. Ultimately it meant it was entirely possible that one day he could close himself off completely and leave her.

She began carefully rehanging the dresses, needing something to do. "Why did you never want any kind of long-term relationship with me? You planned to finish with me all along."

He gripped his nape. "We met and went to bed on the same night. At that point marriage was not on my mind."

"And after Thailand it definitely wasn't."

"I compressed my schedule to be with you in Thailand. Taking further time off wasn't possible."

"What if I'd been *really* ill?"

His gaze flashed with impatience. "If you had been ill, you would have contacted me, but you didn't."

"No."

"Are you telling me you *were* ill and didn't contact me?" he asked quietly.

"Even if I was," she said, folding the oyster silk lingerie into the cloud of tissue paper that filled the box, "you didn't want to know because looking after me in Thailand was just a little too much reality for you, wasn't it?"

"Tell me more about how I was thinking," he muttered. "I'm interested to know just how callous you think I am."

Frustration pulling at her, she jammed the lid on the box. Lucas had cleverly turned the tables on her, but she refused to let up. It suddenly occurred to her that Lucas's behavior was reminiscent of her father's. Roberto Ambrosi had hated discussing personal issues. Every time anyone had probed him about anything remotely personal he had turned grouchy and changed the subject. Attack was generally seen as the most effective form of defense.

She realized now that every time she got close to what was bothering Lucas, he reacted like a bear with a sore head. If he was snapping now, she had to be close. "If I wasn't what you wanted before," she said steadily, "how can I be that person now?"

There was a small, vibrating silence. "Because I realized you weren't Sophie."

Carla froze. "Sophie Warrington?"

"That's right. We lived together for almost a year. She died in a car accident."

Carla blinked. She remembered the story. Sophie Warrington had been gorgeous and successful. She had also had a reputation for being incredibly spoiled and high maintenance. She had lost a couple of big contracts with cosmetic companies because she had thrown tantrums. She had also been famous for her affairs.

Suddenly, Carla's lack of control in the relationship made sense. She was dealing with a ghost—a gorgeous, irresponsible ghost who had messed Lucas around to the point that he had trouble trusting any woman.

Let alone one who not only looked like Sophie but who was caught up in the same glitzy world.

Twelve

Half an hour later, after taking her medication with a big glass of water, she nibbled on a small snack then decided to go for a walk along the beach and maybe have a swim before she changed for the evening function. It wouldn't exorcise the ghost of Sophie Warrington or her fear that Lucas might never trust enough to fall in love with her, but at least it would fill in time.

Winding her hair into a loose topknot, she changed into an electric blue bikini and knotted a turquoise sarong just above her breasts. After transferring her wallet to a matching turquoise beach bag, she slipped dark glasses on the bridge of her nose and she was good to go.

Half an hour later, she stopped at a small beach café, ordered a cool drink and glimpsed Tiberio loitering behind some palms. She had since found out that Tiberio wasn't just a bodyguard, he was Lucas's head of security. That being the case, the only logical reason for him to be here was that Lucas had sent him to keep an eye on her.

Annoyed that her few minutes of privacy had been invaded by security that Lucas hadn't had the courtesy to advise her about, she finished the drink and started back to the resort.

The quickest way was along the long, curving ocean beach, which was dotted with groups of bathers lying beneath bright beach umbrellas. As she walked, she stopped, ostensibly to pick up a shell, and glanced behind. Tiberio was a short distance back, making no attempt to conceal himself, a cell phone held to his ear.

No doubt he was talking to Lucas, reporting on her activities. Annoyed, she quickened her pace. She reached the resort gardens in record time but the fast walk in the humidity of late afternoon had made her uncomfortably hot and sticky. She strode past the cool temptation of a large gleaming pool. Making an abrupt turn off the wide path, she strode along a narrow winding bush walk with the intention of losing herself amongst the shady plantings.

Beneath the shadowy overhanging plants, paradoxically it was even hotter. Slowing down, she unwound her sarong and tied it around her waist for coolness and propped her dark glasses on top of her head.

Footsteps sounded behind her, coming fast. Annoyed, she spun, and came face-to-face with Alex Panopoulos.

Dressed in a pristine business suit, complete with briefcase, his smooth features were flushed and shiny with perspiration.

She frowned, perversely wondering what had happened to Tiberio, and suddenly uncomfortably aware of the brevity of her bikini top. "What are you doing here?"

Alex set his briefcase down and jerked at his edgily patterned tie. "I just arrived and was walking to my chalet when I saw you."

She frowned, disconcerted by the intensity of his expression and the fact that he had clearly run after her. "There was no need. I'll see you tonight at the presentation."

"No you won't. My invitation was rescinded."

"Lucas—"

"Yes," he muttered curtly, "which is why I wanted to talk with you privately."

His gaze drifted to her chest, making her fingers itch with the need to yank the sarong back up. "If it's about the job—"

"Not the job." He stepped forward with surprising speed and gripped her bare arms. This close the sharp scent of fresh sweat and cologne hit her full force.

His gaze centered on her mouth. "You must know how I feel about you."

"Uh, not really. Let me go." She tried to pull free. "I'm engaged to Lucas."

"Engagements can be ended."

A creepy sense of alarm feathered her spine. He wasn't letting go. She jerked back more strongly, but his grip tightened, drawing her closer.

The thought that he might try to kiss her made her stomach flip queasily. Alex had frequently made it clear that he was attracted to her, but she had dismissed his come-ons, aware that he also regularly targeted other women, including her sister, Sienna.

Deciding on strong action, she planted her palms on his chest but, before she could shove, Panopoulos flew backward, seemingly of his own accord. A split second later Lucas was towering over her like an avenging angel.

Alex straightened, his hands curling into fists.

Lucas said something low and flat in Medinian.

Alex flinched and staggered back another step, although Lucas hadn't either stepped toward him or touched him.

Flushing a deep red, Panopoulos lunged for his briefcase and stumbled back the way he'd come.

With fingers that shook slightly with reaction, Carla untied the sarong, dragged it back over her breasts and knotted it. "What did you say to him?"

Lucas's gaze glittered over her, coming to rest on the newly tied knot. "Nothing too complicated. He won't be bothering you again."

"Thank you. I was beginning to think he wasn't going to let go." Automatically, she rubbed at the red marks on her arms where Panopoulos had gripped her just a little too hard.

With gentle movements, Lucas pushed her hands aside so he could examine the marks. They probably wouldn't turn into bruises, but that didn't change the cold remoteness of his expression.

"Did he hurt you?"

"No." From the flat look in his dark eyes, the grim set to his jaw, Carla gained the distinct impression that if Panopoulos had stepped any further over the line than he had, Lucas wouldn't have been so lenient. A small tingling shiver rippled the length of her spine as she realized that Lucas was fiercely protective of her.

It was primitive, but she couldn't help the warm glow that formed because the man she had chosen as her mate was prepared to fight for her. In an odd way, Lucas springing to her defense balanced out the hurt of discovering how affected he'd been by Sophie Warrington. To the extent that his issues with her had permeated every aspect of his relationship with Carla.

His hand landed in the small of her back, the touch blatantly dominant and possessive, but she didn't protest. She was too busy wallowing in the happy knowledge that Lucas hadn't left it to Tiberio to save her. Instead, he had interrupted what she knew was a tight schedule of interviews and come after her himself. Despite the unpleasant shock of the encounter, she was suddenly glad that it had happened.

When they reached the room, Lucas kicked the door shut and leaned back against the gleaming mahogany and drew her close.

Carla, still on edge after the encounter, went gladly. Coiling her arms around his neck, she fitted her body against the familiar planes and angles of his, soaking in the calm reassurance of his no-holds-barred protection.

Tangling the fingers of one hand in her hair, Lucas tilted her head back and kissed her until she was breathless.

When he lifted his head, his expression was grim. "If you hadn't tried to get away from Tiberio, Panopoulos wouldn't have had the opportunity to corner you."

She felt her cheeks grow hot. "I needed some time alone."

"From now on, while we're at the hotel you either have security accompany you, or I do, and that's nonnegotiable."

"Yes."

He cupped her face, his expression bemused. "That was too easy. Why aren't you arguing?"

She smiled. "Because I'm happy."

A faint flush rimmed his taut cheekbones and suddenly she felt as giddy as a teenager.

"Damn, I wish I didn't have interviews." His mouth captured hers again.

She rose up into the kiss, angling her jaw to deepen it. This time the sensuality was blast-furnace hot, but she didn't mind. For the first time in over two years Lucas's kiss, his touch, felt absolutely and completely right.

He wanted her, but not just because he desired her. He wanted her because he *cared*.

* * *

Carla showered and dressed for the launch party. Lucas walked into the suite just as she was putting the finishing touches to her makeup.

"You're late." Pleasurable anticipation spiraled through her as he appeared behind her in the mirror, leaned down and kissed the side of her neck.

His gaze connected with hers in the mirror. "I had an urgent business matter to attend to."

And she had thrown his busy schedule off even further because he'd had to interrupt his meetings to rescue her.

The happy glow that had infused her when he'd read Panopoulos the riot act reignited, along with the aching knowledge that she loved him. It was on the tip of her tongue to tell him just how much when he turned and walked into the bathroom. Instead she called out, "I'll see you downstairs."

Minutes later, with Tiberio in conspicuous attendance, she strolled into the ballroom, which was already filled with elegantly gowned and suited clients, the party well under way.

She threaded her way through the crowd, accepting congratulations and fielding curious looks. When she walked backstage to check on the arrangements for the promotional show, Nina's expression was taut.

She threw Carla a harassed look. "A minor glitch. The model we hired is down with a virus, so the agency did the best they could at short notice and sent along a new girl." She jerked her head in the direction of the curtained-off area that was being used as dressing rooms.

Dragging the curtain back far enough so she could walk through, Carla stared in disbelief at the ultrathin model. She was the right height for the dress, but that was all. Obviously groomed for the runway, she was so thin that the gown, which had originally been custom-made for Carla, hung off her shoulders and sagged around her chest and hips.

Carla's assistant, Elise, was working frantically with pins. The only problem was, the dress—an aquamarine creation studded with hundreds of pearls in a swirling pattern that was supposed to represent the sea—could only be taken in at certain points.

To add insult to injury, the model was a redhead and nothing about the promotion was red. Everything was done in Ambrosi's signature aquamarine and pearl hues. The color mix was subtle, clean and classy, reflecting Ambrosi's focus on the luxury market.

"No," Carla said, snapping instantly into work mode, irritated by the imperfections of the model and the utter destruction of the promotion that had taken her long hours of painstaking time to formulate. "Take the pins out of the dress."

She smiled with professional warmth at the model and instructed her to change, informing her that she would be paid for the job and was welcome to stay the weekend at Ambrosi's expense, but that she wouldn't be part of the promotion that evening.

Clearly unhappy, the model shimmied out of the gown on the spot and walked, half-naked and stiff backed, into a changing cubicle. At that point, another curtain was swished wide, revealing the gaggle of young ballet girls, who were also part of the promotion, in various states of undress.

Tiberio made a strangled sound. Clearly unhappy that he had intruded into a woman's domain, he indicated he would wait in the ballroom.

Elise carefully shook out the gown, examined it for signs of damage and began pulling out the pins she'd inserted. "Now what?" She indicated her well-rounded figure. "If you think I'm getting into that dress, forget it."

"Not you. Me."

Nina looked horrified. "I thought the whole point of this was that you weren't to take part."

Carla picked up the elegant mask that went with the outfit and pressed it against her face. The mask left only her mouth and chin visible.

Her stomach tightened at the risk she was taking. "He won't know."

Thirteen

Carla stepped into the gown and eased the zipper up, with difficulty. The dress felt a little smaller and tighter than it had, because it had been taken in to fit the model who was off sick.

She fastened the exquisite trailing pearl choker, which, thankfully, filled most of her décolletage and dangled a single pearl drop in the swell of her cleavage.

Cleavage that seemed much more abundant now that the dress had been tightened.

She surveyed her appearance in the mirror, dismayed and a little embarrassed by the sensual effect of the too-tight dress.

Careful not to breathe too deeply and rip a seam, she fastened the webbed bracelet that matched the choker and put sexy dangling earrings in her lobes. She fitted the pearl-studded mask and surveyed the result in the mirror.

With any luck she would get through this without being

recognized. A few minutes on stage then she would make her exit and quickly change back into her gold dress and circulate.

Elise swished the curtain aside. "It's time to go. You're on."

Lucas checked his watch as he strolled through the ballroom, his gaze moving restlessly from face to face.

Tiberio had informed him that Carla was assisting the girls backstage with the small production they had planned. He had expected no less. When it came to detail, Carla was a stickler, but now he was starting to get worried. She should have been back in the ballroom, with him, by now.

He checked his watch again. At least Panopoulos was out of the picture. He had made certain of that.

Every muscle in his body locked tight as he remembered the frightened look on Carla's face as she'd tried to shove free of him. When he'd seen the marks on Carla's arms, he had regretted not hitting Panopoulos.

Instead, he had satisfied his need to drive home his message by personally delivering the older man to the airport and escorting him onto a privately chartered flight out.

Panopoulos had threatened court action. Lucas had invited him to try.

Frowning, he checked the room again. He thought he had seen Carla circulating when he had first entered the room, but the gold dress and dark hair had belonged to a young French woman. He was beginning to think that something else had gone wrong since the heart-stopping passion of those moments in their room and she had found something else to fret about.

The radiant glow on her face when he'd left her had hit him like a kick in the chest, transfixing him. He could remember her looking that way when they had first met, but gradually, over time, the glow had gone. He decided it was a grim testament to how badly he had mismanaged their relationship that Carla had ceased to be happy. From now on he was determined to do whatever it took to keep that glow in her eyes.

A waiter offered him a flute of champagne. He refused. At that moment there was a stir at one end of the room as Nina, who was the hostess for the evening, came out onto the small stage.

Lucas leaned against the bar and continued to survey the room as music swelled and the promotional show began. The room fell silent as the model, who was far more mouth-wateringly sexy than he remembered, moved with smooth grace across the stage. *Floor show* wasn't the correct terminology for the presentation but he was inescapably driven to relabel the event.

Every man in the room was mesmerized, as the masked model, playing an ancient Medinian high priestess, moved through the simple routine, paying homage to God with the produce of the sea, a basket of Ambrosi pearls. With her long, elegant legs and tempting cleavage, she reminded him more of a Vegas dancer than any depiction of a Medinian priestess he had ever seen.

His loins warmed and his jaw tightened at his uncharacteristic loss of control. He had seen that dress on the model who was supposed to be doing the presentation. At that point the gown, which was largely transparent and designed so that pearl-encrusted waves concealed strategic parts and little else, had looked narrow and ascetically beautiful rather than sexy. He hadn't been even remotely turned-on.

The model turned, her hips swaying with a sudden sinuous familiarity as she walked, surrounded by a gaggle of young ballet dancers, all carrying baskets overflowing with free samples of Ambrosi products to distribute to clients.

Suspicion coalesced into certainty as his gaze dropped to the third finger of her left hand.

He swallowed a mouthful of champagne and calmly set the flute down. The mystery of his future wife's whereabouts had just been solved.

He had thought she was safely attired in the gold gown, minus any cleavage. Instead she had gone against his instructions and was busy putting on an X-rated display for an audience that contained at least seventy men.

Keeping a tight rein on his temper, he strode through the spellbound crowd and up onto the stage. Carla's startled gaze clashed with his. Avoiding a line of flimsy white pillars that were in danger of toppling, he took the basket of pearls she held, handed them to one of the young girls and swung her into his arms.

She clutched at his shoulders. "What do you think you're doing?"

Grimly, Lucas ignored the clapping and cheering as he strode off the stage and cut through the crowd to the nearest exit. "Removing you before you're recognized. Don't worry," he said grimly, "they'll think it's part of the floor show. The Atraeus Group's conquering CEO carrying off the glittering prize of Ambrosi Pearls."

"I can't believe you're romanticizing a business takeover, and it is *not* a floor show!"

He reached the elevator and hit the call button with his elbow, his gaze skimmed the enticing display of cleavage. "What happened to the model I employed?"

"She came down with a virus. The replacement they sent didn't fit the dress. If I hadn't stepped in, the only option would have been to cancel the promotion."

A virus. That word was beginning to haunt him. "And canceling would have been such a bad idea?"

"Our events drive a lot of sales. Besides, I'm wearing a mask. No one knew."

"*I* knew."

She ripped off the mask, her blue gaze shooting fire. "I don't see how."

He took in the sultry display of honey-tanned skin. Cancel the Vegas dancer. She looked like an extremely expensive courtesan, festooned with pearls. *His* courtesan.

It didn't seem to matter what she wore, he reflected. The clothing could look like a sack on any other woman, but on Carla it became enticingly, distractingly sexy. "Next time remember to take off the engagement ring."

The elevator doors opened. Seconds later they had reached their floor. Less than a minute later Lucas kicked the door to their suite closed.

"You realize I need to go back to the party."

He set her down. "Just not in that dress."

"Not a problem, it's not my color." Carla tugged at the snug fit of the dress. Fake pearls pinged on the floor. A seam had given way while Lucas was carrying her, but on the positive side, at least she could breathe now. She eyed Lucas warily. "What do you think you're doing?"

He had draped his suit jacket over the back of a couch, loosened his tie and strolled over to the small business desk in the corner of the sitting room. She watched as he flipped his laptop open. "Checking email."

The abrupt switch from scorching possessiveness to cool neutrality made her go still inside. She had seen him do this often. In the past, usually, just before he would leave her apartment he would begin immersing himself in work—phone calls, emails, reading documents. She guessed that on some level she had recognized the process for what it was; she just hadn't ever bothered to label it. Work was his coping mechanism, an instant emotional off button. She should know. She had used it herself often enough.

She watched as he scrolled through an email, annoyed at the way he had switched from blazing hot to icy cool. Lucas had removed her from the launch party with all the finesse of a caveman dragging his prize back to the fire. He had gotten his way; now he was ignoring her.

The sensible option would be to get out of the goddess outfit, put on another dress and go downstairs and circulate before finding her gold dress and handbag, which she had left backstage. But that was before her good old type A personality decided to make a late comeback.

Ever since she had been five years old on her first day at school and her teacher, Mrs. Hislop, had put daddy's little girl in the back row of the classroom, she had understood one defining fact about herself: she did not like being ignored.

Walking to the kitchenette, she opened cupboards until she found a bowl. She needed to eat. Cereal wasn't her snack of choice this late, but it was here, and the whole point was that she stayed in the suite with Lucas until he realized that she was not prepared to be ignored.

She found a minipacket of cereal, emptied it into the bowl then tossed the packaging into the trash can, which was tucked into a little alcove under the bench.

Lucas sent her a frowning glance, as if she was messing with his concentration. "I thought you were going to change and get back to the party."

She opened the fridge and extracted a carton of milk. "Why?"

"The room is full of press and clients."

She gave him a faintly bewildered look, as if she didn't understand what he was talking about, but inwardly she was taking notes. He clearly thought she was a second Sophie, a party girl who loved to be the center of attention. "Nina and Elise are taking care of business. I don't need to be there."

"It didn't look that way ten minutes ago."

She shrugged. "That was an emergency."

Aware that she now had Lucas's attention, she opened the carton with painstaking precision and poured milk over the cereal. Grabbing a spoon, she strolled out into the lounge, sat on the sofa and turned the TV on. She flicked through the channels till she found a talk show she usually enjoyed.

Lucas took the remote and turned the TV off. "What are you up to?"

Carla munched on a spoonful of cereal and stared at the now blank screen. Before the party she had found reasons to adore Lucas's dictatorial behavior. Now she was back to loathing it, but she refused to allow her annoyance to show. She had wanted Lucas's attention and now she had gotten it. "Considering my future employment. I'm not good with overbearing men."

"You are not going to work for Panopoulos."

She ate another mouthful of cereal. He was jealous; she was getting somewhere. "I guess not, since I have an iron-clad contract I signed only yesterday."

Lucas tossed the remote down on the couch and dispensed with his tie. "Damn. You must be sleeping with the boss."

"Plus, I have shares."

"It's not a pleasing feminine trait to parade your victories." He took the cereal bowl from her and set it down on the coffee table. Threading her fingers with his, he pulled her to her feet.

More pearls pinged off the dress as she straightened. A tiny tearing sound signaled that another seam had given. "You shouldn't take food from a woman who could be pregnant."

His gaze was arrested. "Do you think you are?"

"I don't know yet." She had left the test kit behind. With everything that had happened, taking time out to read the instructions and do the test hadn't been a priority.

"I could get used to the idea." Cupping her face, he dipped his head and touched his mouth to hers.

The soft, seducing intimacy of the kiss made Carla forget the next move in her strategy. Before she could edit her response, her arms coiled around his neck. He made a low sound of satisfaction, then deepened the kiss.

Hands loosely cupping her hips, he walked her backward, kiss by drugging kiss, until they reached the bedroom. She felt a tug as the zipper on the dress peeled down, then a loosening at the bodice. More pearls scattered as he pulled the dress up and over her head and tossed it on the floor.

"The dress is ruined." Not that she really cared. It had only been a prop and it had served its purpose, in more ways than one.

"Good. That means you can't wear it again."

Stepping out of her heels, she climbed into bed and pulled the silk coverlet over her as she watched him undress. With his jet-black hair and broad, tanned shoulders he looked sleek and muscular.

The bed depressed as he came back down beside her. The clean scent of his skin made her stomach clench.

He surveyed the silk coverlet with dissatisfaction. "This needs to go." He dragged it aside as he came down on the bed. One long finger stroked over the pearl choker at her throat down to the single dangling pearl nestled in the shadowy hollow between her breasts. "But you can keep this on."

She had forgotten about the jewelry. Annoyed by the suggestion, which seemed more suited to a mistress than a future wife, she scooted over on the bed, wrapping the coverlet around her as she went. "You just destroyed an expensive gown. If you think I'm going to let you make love to me while I'm wearing an Ambrosi designer orig—"

His arm curled around her waist, easily anchoring her to the bed. "I'll approve the write-off for it."

Despite her reservations, unwilling excitement quivered through her as he loomed over her, but he made no effort to do anything more than keep her loosely caged beneath him.

"Whether we make love or not," he said quietly, "is your decision, but before you storm off, you need to know that I've organized a special license on Medinos. We're going to be married before the week is out."

"You might need my permission for that."

Something flared in his gaze and she realized she had pushed him a little too hard. "Not on Medinos."

"As I recall from Sienna's wedding, I still have to say yes."

Frustration flickered in his gaze and then she finally got him. For two years she had been focused on organizing their time together, taking care of every detail so that everything was as perfect as she could make it, given their imperfect circumstances. Lucas had fallen in with her plans, but she had overlooked a glaring, basic fact. Lucas was male; he needed to be in control. He now wanted her to follow the plan he had formulated, and she was frustrating him.

He cupped her face. "I have the special license. I don't care where we get married, just as long as it happens. Damned if I want Panopoulos, or any man, thinking you're available."

Unwilling delight filtered through the outrage that had driven her ever since she had realized that Lucas had developed a coping mechanism for shutting her out. The incident with Alex seemed a lifetime away, but it had only been hours.

She understood that in Lucas's mind he had rescued her for a second time that day, this time from a room full of men. As domineering and abrasive as his behavior was, in an odd way, it was the assurance she so badly needed that he cared. After watching him detach and walk away from her for more than two years, she wasn't going to freeze him out just when she finally had proof that he was falling for her.

"Yes."

His gaze reflected the same startled bemusement she had glimpsed that afternoon. "That's settled, then."

Warmth flared to life inside her. The happy glow expanded when he touched his lips to hers, the soft kiss soothing away the stress of dealing with Lucas's dictatorial manner. Sliding her fingers into the black silk of his hair, she pulled him back for a second kiss, then a third, breathing in his heat and scent. The kiss deepened, lingered. The silk coverlet slid away and she went into his arms gladly.

Sometime later, she woke when Lucas left the bed and walked to the bathroom, blinking at the golden glow that still flooded the room from the bedside lamp. Chilled without his body heat, she curled on her side and dragged the coverlet up high around her chin.

The bed depressed as Lucas rejoined her. One arm curled around her hips, he pulled her back snug against him. His palm cupped her abdomen, as if he was unconsciously cradling their baby.

Wistfully, her hand slipped over his, her fingers intertwining as she relaxed back into the blissful heat of his body. She took a moment to fantasize about the possibility that right at that very moment there could be an embryo growing inside her, that in a few months they would no longer be a couple, they would be a family. "Do you think we'll make good parents?"

"We've got every chance."

She twisted around in his grip, curious about the bitter note in his voice. "What's wrong?"

He propped himself on one elbow. "I had a girlfriend who was pregnant once. She had an abortion."

"Sophie Warrington?"

"That's right."

"You told me about her. She died in a car accident."

There was silence for a long, drawn-out moment. "Sophie had an abortion the day before she died. When she finally got around to telling me that she'd aborted our child before even telling me she was pregnant, we had a blazing argument. We broke up and she drove away in her sports car. An hour later she was dead."

Carla blinked. She hadn't realized that Lucas had split with Sophie before she had died. She smoothed her palm over his chest. "I'm sorry. You must have loved her."

"It was an addiction more than love."

Something clicked into place in her mind. Lucas had once used that term with regard to her. She hadn't liked it at the time, because it implied an unwilling attraction. "You don't see me as another Sophie?"

His hand trapped hers, holding it pressed against his chest so she could feel the steady thud of his heart. "You are similar in some ways, but maybe that's how the basic chemistry works. Both you and Sophie are my type."

Her stomach plunged a little. There it was again, the unwilling element to the attraction.

She knew he hadn't considered her marriageable in the beginning, because in his mind marriage hadn't fitted with the addictive sexual passion she had inspired in him. Admittedly, she hadn't helped matters. She had been busy trying to de-stress in line with her doctor's orders and keep their relationship casual but organized until the problems between both families had been rectified. In the process she had given him a false impression of her values. He had gotten to know who she really was a little better in the past few days, but that was cold comfort when she needed him to love her.

Fear spiked though her at the niggling thought that, if he

categorized her as being like Sophie, it was entirely possible that he wouldn't fall in love with her, that he would always see her as a fatal attraction and not his ideal marriage partner.

If she carried that thought through to its logical conclusion, it was highly likely that once the desire faded, he would fall for the kind of woman that in his heart he really wanted. "What happens when I get old, or put on weight, or…get sick?"

Physical attraction would fade fast and then where would they be?

She cupped his jaw. "I think I need to know *why* you can't resist me, because if what you feel is only based on physical attraction, it won't last."

He stoked a finger down the delicate line of her throat to her collarbone. "It's chemistry. A mixture of personality and the physical."

She frowned, her dissatisfaction increasing. "If you feel this way about me then how could you have been attracted to Lilah?"

As soon as she said Lilah's name, she wished she hadn't. Despite having Lucas's ring on her finger, she couldn't forget the weeks of stress when Lucas had avoided her then the sudden, hurtful way he had replaced her with Lilah.

"If you're jealous of Lilah, you don't need to be."

"Why?" But the question was suddenly unnecessary, because the final piece of the puzzle had just dropped into place. Lucas hadn't wanted Lilah for the simple reason that he had barely had time to get to know her. She had been part of a coldly logical strategy. An instant girlfriend selected for the purpose of spelling out in no uncertain terms that his relationship with Carla was over.

Fourteen

Carla stiffened. All the comments he'd made about her not needing to worry about Lilah and the quick way he had ended his relationship with her suddenly made perfect sense. "I have no reason to be jealous of Lilah, because you were never attracted to her."

His abrupt stillness and his lack of protest were damning.

"You manufactured a girlfriend." Her throat was tight, her voice husky. "You picked out someone safe to take to the wedding to make it easy to break up with me. You knew that if I thought you had fallen for another woman I would keep my distance and not make a fuss."

He loomed over her, his shoulders blocking out the dim glow from the lamp. "Carla—"

"No." Pushing free of his arms, she stumbled out of bed and struggled into her robe.

She yanked the sash tight as another thought occurred, giving her fresh insight into just how ruthless and serpentine

Lucas had been. "And you didn't pick just anyone to play your girlfriend. You were clever enough to select someone from Ambrosi Pearls, so the relationship covered all bases and would be in my face at work. That made it doubly clear to me that you were off-limits. It also made it look like you wanted her close, that you couldn't bear to have her out of your sight."

The complete opposite of his treatment of her.

Through the course of their relationship she had been separated and isolated from almost every aspect of his personal and business life.

Suddenly the room, with its romantic flowers, her clothes and jewelry draped over furniture and on the floor, emphasized how stupid she had been. Lucas's silence wasn't making her feel any better. "You probably even wanted to push me into leaving Ambrosi, which would get me completely out of your hair."

He shoved off the bed, found his pants and pulled them on. "I had no intention of depriving you of your job."

She stared at him bleakly, uncaring about that minor detail, when his major sin had been his complete and utter disregard for her feelings and her love. "What incentive did you offer Lilah to pose as your girlfriend?"

"I didn't pay Lilah. She knew nothing about this beyond the fact that I asked her to be my date at Constantine's wedding. That was our first, and last, date."

He caught her around the waist and pulled her close. "Do you believe me?"

She blinked. "Do you love me?"

There was the briefest of hesitations. "You know I do."

She searched his expression. It was a definite breakthrough, but it wasn't what she needed, not after the stinging hurt of finding out that he had used Lilah to facilitate getting rid of her.

His gaze seared into hers. "I'm sorry."

He bent and kissed her and the plunging disappointment receded a little. He was sorry and he very definitely wanted her. Maybe he even did love her. It wasn't the fairy tale she had dreamed about, but it was a start.

A few days ago she had been desperate for just this kind of chance with Lucas. Now too she was possibly pregnant. She owed it to herself and to Lucas to give him one more chance.

After an early breakfast, Carla strolled into the conference room Ambrosi had booked for its sales display. Lucas had phone calls to make in their suite, then meetings with buyers. Carla had decided to make herself useful and help Elise put together the jewelry display and set out the sales materials and press kits.

The fact that, if Lilah had been here, setting up the jewelry would have been her job was a reminder she didn't need, but she had to be pragmatic. Lilah was likely to be a part of the landscape for the foreseeable future, and she probably wasn't any happier about the situation than Carla. They would both have to adjust.

Security was already in place and lavish floral displays filled the room with the rich scent of roses. Elise had arranged for Ambrosi's special display cases to be positioned around the room. All that remained was for the jewelry, which was stored in locked cases, to be set out and labeled.

Elise, already looking nervous and ruffled, handed her a clipboard. "Just to make things more complicated, last night Lilah won a prestigious design award in Milan for some Ambrosi pieces. The buzz is *huge*." She snapped a rubber band off a large laminated poster. "Lucas had this expressed from the office late last night." She unrolled the poster, which was a blown-up publicity shot of Lilah, looking ultrasleek and gorgeous in a slim-fitting white suit, Ambrosi pearls at her lobes and her throat With the pose she had struck and her calm gaze square on to the camera, Carla couldn't help thinking she looked eerily like the Atraeus bride in the portrait both she and Zane had studied at the prewedding dinner.

Elise glanced around the room. "I think I'll put it there, so people will see it as soon as they walk into the room. What do you think?"

Carla stared at the background of the poster. If she wasn't mistaken Lilah's image was superimposed over a scenic shot of Medinos—probably taken from one of the balconies of the *castello*. It was a small point, but it mattered. "Lucas ordered that to be done *late* last night?"

If that was the case, the only window of time he'd had was the few minutes after he had abducted her from the party when he had suddenly lost all interest in her because he had been so absorbed with what he was doing online.

Ordering a poster of the gorgeous, perfect Lilah.

Elise suddenly looked uncertain. "Uh, I think so. That's what he said."

Carla smiled and held out her hand. "Cool. Give the poster to me."

Elise went a little pale, but she handed the poster over.

Carla studied the larger-than-life photo. Her first impulse was to fling it into the ocean so she didn't have to deal with all that perfection. With her luck, the tide would keep tossing the poster back.

"I need scissors."

Elise found a pair and handed them over. Carla spent a happy few minutes systematically reducing the poster to an untidy pile of very small pieces.

Elise's eyes tracked the movement as Carla set the scissors down. She cleared her throat. "Do you want to sort through the jewelry, or would you prefer I did that?"

"I'm here to help. I'll do it."

"Great! I'll do the press kits." She dug in her briefcase. "Here's the plan for the display items. With all of the other publicity about, uh, Lilah, our sales have gone through the roof. We've already received orders from some of the attending clients so some of that jewelry is for clients and not for display. With any luck, they've kept the orders separate."

Carla slowly relaxed, determinedly thinking positive thoughts as she checked off the orders against the packing slip and set those packages to one side. Her mood improved by the second as she began putting the display together, anchoring the gorgeous, intricate pieces securely on black velvet beds then locking the glass cases. Lilah may have designed most of the jewelry, but they were Ambrosi pieces and she was proud of them. She refused to allow any unhappiness she felt about Lilah affect her pride in the family business.

A courier arrived with a package. Elise signed for it, shrugging. "This is weird. All the rest was delivered yesterday."

Carla took the package and frowned. The same courier firm had delivered it, but this one wasn't from the Ambrosi warehouse in Sydney. The package had been sent by another jeweler, the same Atraeus-owned company from which Lucas had purchased her engagement ring. That meant that whatever the package contained it couldn't be either an order for a customer or jewels for the launch.

Anticipation and a glow of happy warmth spread through her as she studied the package. She had her ring, which meant Lucas must have bought her something else, possibly a matching pendant or bracelet.

Her heart beat a little faster. Perhaps even matching wedding rings.

The temptation to open the package was almost overwhelming, but she managed to control herself. Lucas had bought her a gift, his first real gift of love, without pressure or prompting. She wasn't about to spoil his moment when he gave her the special piece he had selected.

She studied the ring on her finger, unable to contain her pleasure. She didn't care about the size of the diamond or the cost. What mattered was that Lucas had chosen it because it matched her eyes. Every time she looked at the ring she remembered that tiny, very personal, very important detail. It was a sign that he was one step closer to truly loving and appreciating her. After what had happened last night, how close they had come to splitting up again, she treasured every little thing that would help keep them together.

Elise finished shoving boxes and Bubble Wrap in the bin liner the hotel had provided. She waggled her brows at the package. "Not part of the display, huh? Looks interesting. Want me to take it to Lucas? I'm supposed to take the Japanese client he's meeting with to the airport in about ten minutes."

"Hands off." Carla's fingers tightened on the package. Despite knowing that Elise was teasing her, she felt ridiculously possessive of whatever Lucas had bought for her.

A split second later, Lucas strolled into the conference room. Immediately behind him, hotel attendants were setting up for morning tea, draping the long tables in white tablecloths and setting out pastries and finger food. Outside, in the lobby, she could hear the growing chatter. Any minute now, buyers and clients would start pouring into the conference room and there would be no privacy. The impulse to thrust the package at Lucas and get him to open it then and there died a death.

Lucas's gaze locked with hers then dropped to the glossy cut-up pieces of poster still strewn across the table. He lifted a brow. "What's that?"

"Your poster of Lilah."

There was a moment of assessing silence.

Lucas was oddly watchful, recognizing and logging the changes in her. As if he was finally getting that she was a whole lot more than the amenable, compartmentalized lover he had spent the past two years holding at a distance.

In that moment Carla knew Lilah had to go completely, no matter how crucial she was to Ambrosi Pearls. If she and Lucas were to have a chance at a successful marriage, they couldn't afford a third person in the equation.

Lucas lifted a brow. "What's in the package?"

"Nothing that won't keep." She pushed the package out of sight in her handbag then briskly swept all the poster fragments into the trash.

Whatever Lucas had bought her, she couldn't enjoy receiving it right at that minute, not with the larger-than-life specter of Lilah still hanging over them.

The weekend finished with a dinner cruise, by the end of which Lucas was fed up with designer anything. Give him steel girders and mining machinery any day. Anything but the shallow, too bright social whirl that was part and parcel of the world of luxury retailing.

He kept his arm around Carla's waist as they stood on the quay, bidding farewell to the final guests.

Carla was exhausted—he could feel it in the way she leaned into him—and her paleness worried him. The last thing she needed was another viral relapse.

He had insisted she fit in a nap after lunch. It had been a struggle to make her let go of the organizational reins, but in the end he had simply picked her up and carried her to their room. He had discovered that there was something about the masculine, take-charge act of picking Carla up that seemed to reach her in a way that words couldn't.

She had been oddly quiet all day, but he had expected that. He had made a mistake with the poster. The second he had walked into the conference room that morning and seen the look on Carla's face he had realized just how badly he had messed up. He had grimly resolved to take more care in future.

Her quietness had carried over into the evening. He had debated having her stay in their suite and rest, but in the end he had allowed her to come on the cruise for one simple reason. If he left her behind, she might not be there when he returned.

Lucas recognized Alan Harrison, a London buyer and the last straggling guest.

He paused to shake Lucas's hand. "Lilah Cole, the name on everyone's lips. You might have trouble holding on to her now, Atraeus. I know Catalano jewelry in Milan is impressed with her work. Wouldn't be surprised if they try and spirit her away from you."

Lucas clenched his jaw as Carla stiffened beside him. "That won't happen for at least two years. Lilah just signed a contract to take on the Medinos retail outlet as well as head up the design team."

"Medinos, huh? Smart move. Pretty girl, and focused. Got her in the nick of time. Another few days and you would have lost her."

Carla waited until Harrison had gone then gently detached herself from his hold. "You didn't tell me you had renewed Lilah's contract."

There was no accusation in her voice, just an empty neutrality, but Lucas had finally learned to read between the lines. When Carla went blank that was when she was feeling the most, and when *he* was being weighed in the balance.

Two years, and he hadn't understood that one crucially important fact. "I offered her the Medinos job a couple of days ago. If I'd realized how much it would hurt you I would have let her go. At the time removing her to Medinos for two years seemed workable, since I'll be running the Sydney office for the foreseeable future and we'll be based here."

"You did that for me." There was a small, vibrating silence and he was finally rewarded with a brilliant smile. "Thank you."

"You're welcome." Grinning, he pulled her into his arms.

Carla slipped out of her heels as she walked into their suite. Her feet were aching but she was so happy she hardly noticed the discomfort.

Lucas had finally crossed the invisible line she had needed him to cross; he had committed himself to her, and the blood was literally fizzing through her veins.

Maybe she should have felt this way when they had gotten engaged, but the reality was that all he'd had to do was say words and buy a ring. As badly as she had wanted to, she hadn't felt secure. Now, for the first time in over two years, she finally did.

The fact that he had arranged for Lilah to work in Medinos because they would be based in Sydney for two years had been the tipping point.

He had made an arrangement to ensure their happiness. He had used the word *they*. It was a little word, but it shouted commitment and togetherness.

Two years in Sydney. Together.

Taking Lucas by the hand, she pulled him into the bedroom, determinedly keeping her gaze away from the bedside bureau where she had concealed the package that had arrived that morning. "Sit down." She patted the bed. "I'll get the champagne."

He shrugged out of his jacket and tossed it over a chair before jerking at his tie. "Maybe you shouldn't drink champagne."

"Sparkling water for me, champagne for you."

"What are we celebrating, exactly?"

"You'll see in a minute."

He paused in the act of unbuttoning his shirt. "You're pregnant."

The hope in Lucas's voice sent a further shiver of excitement through her. Not only did he want her enough that he had bought her a wonderful surprise gift, he really did want their baby. Suddenly, after weeks, years, of uncertainty everything was taking on the happy-ever-after fairy tale sparkle she had always secretly wanted.

Humming to herself, she walked into the kitchen and opened a chilled bottle of vintage French champagne. The label was one of the best. The cost would be astronomical, but this was a special moment. She wanted every detail to be perfect. She put the champagne and two flutes on a tray and added a bottle of sparkling water for herself. On the way to the bedroom, she added a gorgeous pink tea rose from one of the displays.

She set the tray down on the bedside table as Lucas padded barefoot out of the bathroom. In the dim lamp-lit room with his torso bare, his dark dress trousers clinging low on narrow hips, his bronzed, muscular beauty struck her anew and she was suddenly overwhelmed by emotion and a little tearful.

Lucas cupped her shoulders and drew her close. "What's wrong?"

She snuggled against him, burying her face in the deliciously warm, comforting curve of his shoulder. "Nothing, except that I love you."

There was a brief hesitation, then he drew her close. "And I love you."

Carla stiffened at the neutral tone of his voice then made an effort to dismiss the twinge of disappointment that, even now, with this new intimacy between them, Lucas still couldn't relax into loving her.

She pushed away slightly, enough that she could see his face and read his expression, but she was too late to catch whatever truth had been in his eyes when he had said those three little words.

Forcing a bright smile, she released herself from Lucas's light hold, determined to recapture the soft, fuzzy fairy-tale glow. "Time for the champagne."

Lucas took the bottle from her and set it back down on the tray.

He reeled her in close. "I don't need a drink."

His head dipped, his lips brushed hers. She wound her arms around his neck, surrendering to the kiss as he pulled her onto the bed. Long seconds later he propped his head on one elbow and wound a finger in a coiling strand of her hair. "What's wrong? You're like a cat on hot bricks."

Rolling over, Carla opened the bureau drawer and took out the courier package. "This came today."

The heavy plastic rustled as she handed it to Lucas. Instead of the teasing grin she had expected, Lucas's gaze rested on the courier package and he went curiously still.

A sudden suspicion gripped her.

Clambering off the bed she took the package and ripped at the heavy plastic.

"Carla—"

"No. Don't talk." Tension banded her chest as she walked out to the kitchen, found a steak knife in the drawer and slit the plastic open. A heavy, midnight-blue box, tied with a black silk bow, the jeweler's signature packaging, tumbled out of layers of Bubble Wrap onto the kitchen counter.

Not an oblong case that might hold a necklace, or a bracelet. A ring box.

Lucas loomed over her as she tore the bow off. Maybe

it was a set of wedding rings. Lucas wanted an early wedding. It made sense to order the rings from the same place they had bought her engagement ring.

"Carla—"

She already knew. Not wedding rings. She flipped the jewelry case open.

A diamond solitaire glittered with a soft, pure fire against midnight-blue velvet.

Fingers shaking, she slid the ring onto the third finger of her right hand. It was a couple of sizes too small and failed to clear her knuckle. The bright, illusory world she had been living in dissolved.

The ring had never been meant for her. The elegant, classic engagement ring had been selected and sized with someone else in mind.

Lilah.

Fifteen

Carla replaced the ring in its box and met Lucas's somber gaze head-on. "You weren't just dating Lilah to facilitate making a clean break with me, were you? You intended to marry her."

Lucas's expression was calmly, coolly neutral. "I had planned to propose marriage, but that was before—"

"Why would you want to marry Lilah when you still wanted me?" She couldn't say *love,* because she now doubted that love had ever factored in. Lucas had wanted her, period. He had felt desire, passion: lust.

"It was a practical decision."

"Because otherwise you were worried that when Constantine and Sienna tied the knot you might be pressured into marrying me."

Impatience flashed in his gaze. "No one could pressure me into marriage. I wanted you. I would have married you in a New York second."

Realization dawned. "Then lived to regret it."

"I didn't think what we had would last."

"So you tied yourself into an arrangement with Lilah so you couldn't be tempted into making a bad decision."

His brows jerked together. "There was no 'arrangement.' All Lilah knew was that I wanted to date her."

"With a view to marriage."

"Yes."

Because she wouldn't have gone out with him otherwise. Certainly not halfway across the world to a very public family wedding.

Hurt spiraled through her that Lucas hadn't bothered to refute her statement that marrying her would have been a bad decision. And that he had so quickly offered Lilah what she had longed for and needed from him.

Throat tight, eyes stinging, Carla snapped the ring box closed and jammed it back into the courier bag. She suddenly remembered the odd behavior of the manager of Moore's. It hadn't been because their engagement was so sudden, or because of the scandal in the morning paper. The odd atmosphere had been because Lucas had bought *two* engagement rings in the same week for two separate women.

Blindly, she shoved the courier bag at Lucas. "You were going to propose to her *here,* at this product launch." Why else would he have requested the ring be couriered to the hotel?

Carla remembered the flashes of sympathy in Lilah's gaze on Medinos, her bone-white face outside of Lucas's apartment when the reporter had snapped Carla and Lucas kissing. Lilah had expected more than just a series of dates. She wouldn't have been with Lucas otherwise.

"You were never even remotely in love with Lilah."

"No."

Her head jerked up. "Then, why consider marriage?"

His expression was taut. "The absence of emotion worked for me. I wasn't after the highs and lows. I wanted the opposite."

"Because of Sophie Warrington."

"That's right," he said flatly. "Sophie liked bright lights, publicity. She loved notoriety. We clashed constantly. The night of the crash we argued and she stormed out. That was the last time I saw her alive. I shouldn't have let her go, should have stopped her—"

"If she wasn't your kind of girl, why were you with her?"

"Good question," he said grimly. "Because I was stupid enough to fall for her. We were a mismatch. We should never have been together in the first place."

Carla's jaw tightened. "You do still think I'm like her," she said quietly. "Another Sophie."

His expression was closed. "I...did."

The hesitation was the final nail in the proverbial coffin. Her stomach plummeted. "You still do."

"I've made mistakes, but I know what I want," Lucas said roughly.

"Me, or the baby I might possibly be having?" Because if Lucas still didn't know who she was as a person, the baby seemed the strongest reason for marriage. And she couldn't marry someone who saw his attraction to her as a weakness, a character flaw. She stared blankly around the flower-festooned room. "If you don't mind, I'd like to get some sleep."

Stepping past Lucas, she walked into the bedroom and grabbed a spare pillow and blanket from the closet.

"Where are you going?"

"To sleep on the couch."

"That's not necessary. I'll take the couch."

She flinched at the sheer masculine beauty of his broad shoulders and muscled chest. She had fallen in love with a mirage, she thought bleakly, a beautiful man who was prepared to care for her but who, ultimately, had never truly wanted to be in love with her. "No. Right now I really would prefer the couch."

His fingers curled around her upper arms. "We can work this through. I can explain—"

She went rigid in his grip. The pillow and blanket formed a buffer between them that right now she desperately needed because, despite everything, she was still vulnerable. "Let me go," she said quietly. "It's late. We both need sleep."

His dark gaze bored into hers, level and calm. "Come back to bed. We can talk this through."

She fought the familiar magnetic pull, the desire to drop the pillow and blanket and step back into his arms. "No. We can talk in the morning."

A familiar cramping pain low in her stomach pulled Carla out of sleep. A quick trip to the bathroom verified that she had her period and that she was absolutely, positively not pregnant.

Numbly, she walked back to the couch but didn't bother trying to sleep. Until that moment she hadn't realized how much she had desperately needed to be pregnant. If there was a child then there had been the possibility that she could have stayed with Lucas. Now there wasn't one and she had to face reality.

Lucas had broken up with Sophie when she had aborted his child. He had also proposed marriage when he had thought she could be pregnant. For a man who had gone to considerable lengths to cut her out of his life, that was a huge turnaround. She could try fooling herself that it was because he loved her, even if he didn't quite know it, but she couldn't allow herself to think that way. She deserved better.

Now she knew for sure she wasn't pregnant. There were no more excuses.

Her decision made, she opted not to shower, because that would wake Lucas. Instead, she found her gym bag, which was sitting by the kitchen counter and which contained fresh underwear, sweatpants, a tank and a light cotton hoodie. She quickly dressed and laced on sneakers. Her handbag with all her medications was in the bedroom. She couldn't risk getting that, but she had a cash card and some cash tucked in her gym bag. That would give her enough money and the ID she needed to book a flight back to Sydney. She had plenty of medication at home, so leaving the MediPACKs in her purse wasn't a problem. She would collect her hand-bag along with the rest of her luggage from Lucas when he got back to Sydney.

Working quickly, she jammed toiletries into the sports bag. She paused to listen, but there was no sound or move-ment from the bedroom. She wrote a brief note on hotel paper, explaining that she was not pregnant and was there-fore ending their engagement. She anchored the note to the kitchen counter with the engagement ring.

Picking up the sports bag and hooking her handbag over her shoulder, she quietly let herself out of the room.

Within a disorientingly short period of time the elevator shot her down to the lobby. The speed with which she had walked away from what had been the most important adult relationship of her life made her stomach lurch sickly, but she couldn't go back.

She couldn't afford to commit one more minute to a man who had put more creative effort into cutting her out of his life than he ever had to including her.

A small sound pulled Lucas out of a fitful sleep.

Kicking free of the tangled sheet, he pushed to his feet and pulled on the pair of pants he'd left tossed over the arm of a chair.

Moonlight slanted through shuttered windows as he walked swiftly through the suite. His suspicion that the sound that had woken him had been the closing of the front door turned to certainty when he found a note and Carla's engagement ring on the kitchen counter.

The note was brief. Carla wasn't pregnant. Rather than both of them being pushed into a marriage that clearly had no chance of working, she had decided to give him his out.

She had left him.

Lucas's hand closed on the note, crumpling it. His heart was pounding as if he'd run a race and his chest felt tight. Taking a deep breath, he controlled the burst of raw panic.

He would get her back. He had to.

She loved him, of that fact he was certain. All it would take was the right approach.

He had messed up one too many times. With the double emotional hit of discovering that he had intended to propose to Lilah then the shock of discovering that she wasn't pregnant, he guessed he shouldn't be surprised that she had reacted by running.

Like Sophie.

His stomach clenched at the thought that Carla could have an accident. Then logic reasserted itself. That wouldn't happen. Carla was so *not* like Sophie he didn't know how he could have imagined she was in the first place.

But this time he would not compound his mistake by failing to act. He would make sure that Carla was safe. He would not fail her again.

He loved her.

His stomach clenched as he examined that reality. He couldn't change the past; all he could do was try to change the future.

Sliding the note into his pocket along with the ring, he strode back to his room to finish dressing. He pulled on shoes and found his wallet and watch. The possibility that he could lose Carla struck him anew and for a split second he was almost paralyzed with fear. Until that moment he hadn't understood how necessary Carla was to him.

For more than two years she had occupied his thoughts and haunted his nights. He had thought the affair would run its course; instead his desire had strengthened. In order to control what he had deemed an obsession, he had minimized contact and compartmentalized the affair.

The strategy hadn't worked. The more restrictive he had become in spending time with Carla, the more uncontrollable his desire had become.

She wasn't pregnant.

Until that moment he hadn't known how much he had wanted Carla to be pregnant. Since the out-of-control lovemaking on Medinos, the possibility of a pregnancy had initiated a number of responses from him. The most powerful had been the cast-iron excuse it had provided him to bring her back into his life. But as the days had passed, the thought of Carla losing her taut hourglass shape and growing soft and round with his child had become increasingly appealing. Along with the need to keep Carla tied close, he had wanted to be a father.

Pocketing his keys, he strode out of the suite. Frustration gripped him when he jabbed the elevator call button then had to wait. His gaze locked on the glowing arrow above the doors, and he scraped at his jaw, which harbored a five-o'clock shadow.

Dragging rough fingers through his rumpled hair, he began to pace.

He couldn't lose her.

Whatever it took, he would do it. He would get her back.

He recalled the expression on Carla's face when she had found the engagement ring he had ordered for Lilah,

ıer stricken comment that Constantine had wanted Sienna
nough that he had kidnapped her.

Raw emotion gripped him.

Almost the exact opposite of his behaviour.

Carla walked quickly through the lobby, which was empty
xcept for a handful of guests checking out. She had wasted
antic minutes checking the backstage area. It had been
mpty of possessions, which meant either Elise or Nina had
ıer things.

Too fragile to bear the stirring of interest she would cause
y waiting inside, she avoided the concierge desk and made
beeline for the taxi stand.

Not having her medication wasn't ideal. She hadn't taken
any last night, and now she would go most of the day with-
ut them. Antacids would have to do. She could wait out the
hort flight to Sydney and the taxi ride home, where there
was a supply of pills in her bathroom cupboard.

A pale-faced group of guests, obviously catching an early
light out, were climbing into the only taxi waiting near the
ıotel entrance. Settling her gym bag down on the dusty pave-
nent, she settled herself to wait for the next taxi to turn into
he hotel pickup area.

Long seconds ticked by. She glanced in at the empty re-
:eption area, her tension growing, not because she was des-
erate to escape, she finally admitted to herself, but because
a weak part of her still wanted Lucas to stride out and stop
ıer from going.

Not that Lucas was likely to chase her.

Shivering in the faint chill of the air, she stared at the
oleak morning sky now graying in the east as a cab finally
oraked to a halt beside her.

She slipped into the rear seat with her bag, requested
he cab driver take her to the airport and gave the hotel en-

trance one last look before she stared resolutely at the road unfolding ahead.

Why would Lucas come after her, when she was giving him the thing he had always valued most in their relationship, his freedom?

Lucas caught the flash of the taxi's taillights as it turned out of the resort driveway and the panic that had gripped him while he'd endured the slow elevator ride turned to cold fear.

Sliding his phone out of his pocket, he made a series of calls then strode back into the hotel and took the elevator to the rooftop.

Seconds later, Tiberio phoned back. He had obtained Carla's destination from the taxi company. She was headed for Brisbane Airport. He had checked with the flight desk and she had already booked her flight out to Sydney.

The quiet, efficient way Carla had left him hit Lucas forcibly. No threats or manipulation, no smashed crockery or showy exit in a sports car, just a calm, orderly exit with her flight already arranged.

He felt like kicking himself that it had taken him this long to truly see who she was, and to understand why she was so irresistible to him. He hadn't fallen into lust with a second Sophie. He had fallen in love for the first time—with a woman who was smart and fascinating and perfect for him.

Then he had spent the past two years trying to crush what he felt for her.

Issuing a further set of instructions, Lucas settled down to wait.

Carla frowned as the taxi took the wrong exit and turned into a sleepy residential street opposite a sports field. "This isn't the way to the airport."

The driver gave her an odd look in the rearview mirror

and hooked his radio, which he'd been muttering into for the past few minutes, back on its rest. "I have to wait for someone."

Carla started to argue, then the rhythmic chop of rotor blades slicing the air caught her attention. A sleek black helicopter set down on the sports field. A tall, dark-haired man climbed out, ducking his head as he walked beneath the rotor blades.

Her heart slammed in her chest. She had wanted Lucas to come after her. Contrarily, now that he was here, all she wanted to do was run.

Depressing the door handle, she pushed the door wide and groped for the cash in the side pocket of her gym bag. She shoved some money at the driver, more than enough to cover his meter, and dragged the sports bag off the backseat. A split second later the world flipped sideways and she found herself cradled in Lucas's arms.

Her heart pounded a crazy tattoo. The strap of the sports bag slipped from her fingers as she grabbed at his shoulders. "What do you think you're doing?"

His gaze, masked by dark glasses, seared over her face. "Kidnapping you. That's the benchmark, isn't it?"

Her mouth went dry at his reference to the conversation they'd had when she had listed the things Constantine had done that proved his love for Sienna. Her pulse rate ratcheted up another notch.

She stared into the remote blankness of the dark glasses, suddenly terribly afraid to read too much into his words. "If you're afraid I'm going to do something silly or have an accident, I'm not. I'm just giving you the out you want."

"I know. I read the note." He placed her in the seat directly behind the pilot. "And by the way, here it is."

He took out a piece of the hotel notepaper, tore it into

pieces and tossed it into the downdraft of the blades. The scraps of paper whirled away.

"What are you doing now?" she asked as he started to walk away from the chopper.

The noise muffled his reply. "Getting your shoes and makeup and whatever else it is that makes you happy."

Seconds later, he tossed her sports bag on the floor at her feet and belted himself in beside her.

"Where are we going?" She had to yell now above the noise from the chopper.

Lucas fitted a set of earphones over her head then donned a set himself. "A cabin. In the mountains."

A short flight later the helicopter landed in a clearing. Within minutes the pilot had lifted off, leaving them with a box stamped with the resort's logo on the side. Lucas picked it up. She guessed it was food.

Carla stared at the rugged surrounding range of the Lamingtons, the towering gum trees and silvery gleam of a creek threading through the valley below. "I can't believe you kidnapped me."

"It worked for Constantine."

Her heart pounded at his answer. It wasn't quite a declaration of love, but it was close.

She followed Lucas into the cabin, which was huge. With its architectural angles, sterile planes of glass and comfortable leather couches it was more like an upscale executive palace than her idea of a rustic holiday cottage.

He placed the box on a kitchen counter then began unloading what looked like a picnic lunch. A kidnapping, Atraeus-style, with all the luxury trappings.

Frustrated by his odd mood and the dark glasses, she walked outside, grabbed her sports bag and brought it into the house. She could feel herself floundering, unable to ask the questions that mattered in case the hope that had flared to life when he had bodily picked her up and deposited her in the helicopter was extinguished. "It's not as if this is a real kidnapping."

He stopped, his face curiously still. "How 'real' did you want it to be?"

Sixteen

"We're alone. We're together." Lucas reached for calm when all he really wanted was to pull her close and kiss her.

But that approach hadn't worked so far. Carla had actually tried to run from him, which had altered his game plan somewhat. Plan B was open-ended, meaning he no longer knew what he was doing except that he wasn't going to blow this now by resorting to sex. "We can do what we should have done last night and talk this out. Have you eaten?"

"No." She stared absently at the rich, spicy foods and freshly squeezed juice he had set out then began rummaging through her gym bag just in case there was a stray pack of antacids in one of the pockets.

Lucas, intensely aware of every nuance of expression on Carla's face, tensed when she picked up the phone on the counter. "What's wrong? Who are you calling?"

She frowned when the call wasn't picked up. "Elise. She can get me some medication I need."

"What medication?" But suddenly he knew. The small bag of snacks she carried, her preoccupation with what she was eating and the weight loss. "You're either diabetic or you've got an ulcer."

"The second one."

He could feel his temper soaring. "Why didn't you tell me?"

"You weren't exactly over the moon when I got ill in Thailand."

"You had a virus in Thailand."

"And the viral bacteria just happened to attack an area of my stomach that was still healing from an ulcer I had two years ago. Although I didn't find that out until the ulcer perforated and I got to hospital."

He felt himself go ice-cold inside. "You had a perforated ulcer?" For a split second he thought he must have misheard. "You could have died. Why didn't you tell me?"

Her gaze was cool. "After what happened in Thailand I didn't want you to know I was sick again." She shrugged. "Mom and Sienna didn't know about you, so it was hardly likely they would call you. Why would they? You had no visible role in my life."

That was all going to change, he thought grimly. From now on he was going to be distinctly, in-your-face visible.

He felt like kicking himself. In Thailand he had distanced himself from Carla when she was sick because the enforced intimacy of looking after her had made him want a lot more than the clandestine meetings they'd had through the year. Pale and ill, sweating and shivering, Carla hadn't been either glamorous or sexually desirable. She had simply been *his*.

He had wanted to continue caring for her, wanted to keep her close. But the long hours he had spent sitting beside her bed, waiting for her fever to break, had catapulted him back to his time with Sophie.

He had not wanted her to be that important to him. He hadn't wanted to make himself vulnerable to the kind of guilt and betrayal his relationship with Sophie had resulted in. He could admit that now.

"When was the last time you had your medication?"

She punched in another number. "Lunch, yesterday. That's why I'm calling the resort. Either Nina or Elise can go to the suite and find my handbag, which is where I keep my Medi-PACKs. I'm hoping Tiberio or one of your other bodyguards could drive up with it."

"If you think I'm taking two hours to get you the medication you need, think again." Lucas's cell was already in his hand. He speed dialed and bit out commands in rapid Medinian, hung up and slipped the phone back in his pocket. "Our ride will be here in fifteen minutes."

She slipped her phone back in her handbag. "I could have waited. It's not that bad. I just have to manage my stomach for a few weeks."

"You might be able to wait, but *I* can't. What do you think it did to me to hear that you almost died in hospital?"

"I didn't *almost* die." She grimaced. "Although it wasn't pleasant, that's for sure. It wasn't as if I wasn't used to dealing with the ulcer. It just got out of hand."

He went still inside. "How long did you say you had the ulcer?"

"Two years or so."

Around the time they had met. His jaw tightened at this further evidence of how blind he had been with Carla. He knew ulcers could be caused by a number of factors, but number one was stress. In retrospect, the first time they had made love and he had found out she was a virgin he should have taken a mental step back and reappraised. He hadn't done it. He hadn't wanted to know what might hurt or upset

Carla, or literally eat away at her, because he had been so busy protecting himself.

"News flash," she said with an attempted grin. "I'm a worrier. Can't seem to ditch the habit."

He reached her in two steps and hauled her close. "The woman I love collapses because she has a perforated ulcer," he muttered, "and all you can say is that it *wasn't pleasant?*"

Carla froze in Lucas's arms and, like a switch flicking, she swung from depression and despair to deliriously happy. She stared, riveted by his fierce gaze, and decided she didn't need to pinch herself. "You really do love me?" He had said the words last night but they had felt neutral, empty.

"I love you. Why do you think I couldn't resist you?"

"But it did take you two years to figure that out."

"Don't remind me. Tell me how you ended up with the ulcer."

"Okay, here it goes, but now you might fall out of love with me. I'm a psycho-control-freak-perfectionist. I worked myself into the ground trying to lift Ambrosi's profile and micromanage all of our advertising layouts and pamphlets. When I started color coordinating the computer mouses and mouse pads, Sienna sent me to the family doctor. Jennifer gave me Losec and told me to stop taking everything so seriously, to lighten up and change my life. A week later, I met you."

"And turned my life upside down."

"I wish, but it didn't seem that way." She snuggled in close, unable to stop grinning, loving the way he was staring at her so fiercely. "All I knew was that I was running the relationship in the exact opposite way I wanted, supposedly to avoid stress. If you'd arrived in my life a couple of weeks early, you would have met a different woman."

"I fell in love with you. Instantly."

She closed her eyes and basked for just a few seconds. "Tell me again."

"I love you," he said calmly and, finally, he kissed her.

During the short helicopter ride, Lucas insisted on being given a crash course on her condition. When they reached the doctor's office, which was in a nearby town, Carla took Losec and an antibiotic under the eagle eye of both the doctor and Lucas.

At Lucas's insistence, the doctor also gave her a thorough checkup. Twenty minutes later she was given a clean bill of health.

They exited the office and strolled around to the parking lot to wait for the rental vehicle that Tiberio, apparently, had arranged to have delivered.

Lucas had kept his arm around her waist, keeping her close. "How are you feeling?"

"Fine." She leaned on him slightly. Not that she needed the support, but she loved the way he was treating her, as if she was a piece of precious, delicate porcelain. She could get used to it.

Lucas cupped her face, his fingers tangling in her hair. "I need to explain. To apologize."

Carla listened while Lucas explained about how her illness in Thailand had forced him to confront the guilt and betrayal of the past and had pushed him into a decision to break off with her.

His expression was remote. "But as you know, I couldn't break it off completely. When Constantine told me he was marrying Sienna, I knew I had to act once and for all."

"So you asked Lilah to accompany you to the wedding."

"She was surprised. Before that we had only ever spoken on a business level."

"But she guessed what was going on the night before the wedding."

"Only because she saw us together." He pulled her close, burying his face in her hair. "I'm not proud of what I did but I was desperate. I didn't realize I was in love with you until I read the note you left in the hotel room and discovered that you had left me. It was almost too late."

He hugged her close for long minutes, as if he truly did not want to let her go. "I've wasted a lot of time. Two years."

"There were good reasons we couldn't be together in the beginning. Some of those reasons were mine."

He frowned. "Reasons that suited me."

Gripping her hands gently in his, he went down on one knee. "Carla Ambrosi, will you marry me and be the love of my life for the rest of my life?"

He reached into his pocket and produced the sky-blue diamond ring, which he must have been carrying with him all along, and gently slipped it on the third finger of her left hand.

Tears blurred Carla's eyes at the soft gleam in Lucas's gaze, the intensity of purpose that informed her that if she said no he would keep on asking until she was his.

Emotion shimmered through her, settled in her heart, because she *had* been his all along.

"Yes," she said, the answer as simple as the kiss that followed, the long minutes spent holding each other and the promise of a lifetime together.

* * * * *

REUNION WITH BENEFITS

HELENKAY DIMON

One

Spencer Jameson wasn't accustomed to being ignored.

He'd been back in Washington, DC, for three weeks. The plan was to buzz into town for just enough time to help out his oldest brother, Derrick, and then leave again.

That's what Spence did. He moved on. Too many days back in the office meant he might run into his father. Eldrick Jameson was the family patriarch, a recently retired businessman on his fourth wife...and the main reason Spence wanted to be anywhere but the DC metro area most of the time.

But dear old Dad was not the problem this trip. The new wife had convinced him to move to Tortola, an island over fifteen hundred miles away. That was almost enough distance, though Spence would have been fine with more.

No, Spence had a different target in mind today. Abigail Rowe, the woman currently pretending he didn't exist.

He used the keys he borrowed from the office manager to open the door to the abandoned elementary school in northeast DC. The building had been empty for two years, caught in a ball of red tape over government regulations and environmental concerns. Derrick wanted the company to buy it and do a complete internal rebuild to turn the massive property into something usable. Spence was on-site meeting the head of the team assigned to make it happen…the head being *her*, and she actually didn't know he was attending.

He followed the sound of voices, a man's deep laughter and the steady rumble of a lighter female one. Careful not to give away his presence, Spence leaned against the outer hall wall and peeked into what he guessed used to be the student dining hall. Paint peeled off the stucco walls. Old posters were half ripped down and half hanging by old tape. Rows of luncheon tables and benches had been replaced with one folding table and a couple of chairs that didn't look sturdy enough to hold an adult.

A woman stood there—*the* woman. She wore a sleek navy suit with a skirt that stopped just above the knee. She embodied the perfect mix of professionalism and sexiness. The flash of bare long legs brought back memories. He could see her only from behind right now but that angle looked really good to him.

Just as he remembered.

Her brown hair reached past her shoulders and ended in a gentle curl. Where it used to be darker, it now had light brown highlights. Strands shifted over her shoulder as she bent down to show the man standing next to her—almost on top of her—something in a file.

Not that the other man was paying attention to whatever she said. His gaze traveled over her. As she talked and pointed, he leaned back slightly and stared at her legs then up higher.

Spence couldn't exactly blame him, but nothing about that look was professional or appropriate. The lack of respect was not okay. The guy's joking charm gave way to something much more territorial and heated. As far as Spence was concerned, the other man was begging for a punch in the face.

As if he sensed his behavior was under a microscope, the man glanced up and turned. Spence got a full-on view of him. He looked like every blond-haired, blue-eyed guy in his midthirties who hung out in bars around the city looking for young Capitol Hill interns to date. Good-looking in a still-brags-about-his-college-days kind of way. That sort of thing was big in this town, as if where you went to school defined you a decade or so later.

Point was, Spence knew the type. Charming, resourceful and looking for an easy lay. He knew because he'd been that guy. He just grew out of it well before he hit thirty.

The other man's eyebrows rose and he hesitated for a second before hitting Spence with a big flashy smile. "Good afternoon."

At the intrusion, Abby spun around. Her expression switched from surprised to flat-mouthed anger in the span of two seconds. "Spencer."

It was not exactly a loving welcome, but for a second he couldn't breathe. The air stammered in his lungs. Seeing her now hit him like a body blow. He had to fight off the urge to rub a hand over his stomach.

They'd worked together for months, every day with him wanting to break the office conduct rules and ask her out. He got close but backed off, sensing he was crossing a line. Then she made a move. A stolen touch here. A kiss there. He'd battled with his control and waited because he needed to be careful. But he'd wanted her from the first moment he saw her. Now, months later, the attraction still lingered...which ticked him off.

Her ultimate betrayal hadn't killed his interest in her, no matter how much he wanted it to.

"Spencer Jameson?" The guy walked toward Spence with his arm extended. "Excellent to meet you."

"Is it?" Spencer shook the guy's hand as he stared at Abby. He wasn't sure what was going on. Abby was supposed to be here with her team. Working. This felt like something else.

"I didn't realize you'd be joining us." Her deep voice stayed even, almost monotone.

If she was happy to see him, she sure hid it well. Frustration pounded off her and filled the room. The tension ratcheted up to a suffocating degree even though none of them moved.

Spence tried not to let his gaze linger on her. Tried not to show how seeing her again affected him. "Where are the others?"

The man did a quick look around the empty room. "Excuse me?"

"Derrick told me—"

"Rylan Stamford is the environmental engineer who is performing the site assessment." She even managed to make that sentence sound angry and clipped.

The job title didn't really explain why Rylan looked ready to jump on Abby a second ago. Spence sensed Rylan's mind wasn't only on the job. "Our assessment?"

"The city's," Abby said. "Rylan isn't employed by us."

Rylan's smile grew wider. "But I've been working very closely with Abby."

Yeah, Spence kind of hated this guy. "I'm sure."

Abby exhaled loud enough to bring the conversation to a halt. She turned back to the table and started piling the paperwork in a neat stack. "Did you need something, Spence?"

She clearly wanted to be in control of the conversation and them seeing each other again. Unfortunately for her, so did he. And that started now. "We have a meeting."

She slowly turned around again. "We do?"

"Just the two of us." The idea was risky and maybe a little stupid, but he needed to stay in town until his soon-to-be sister-in-law gave birth. Derrick's fiancée's pregnancy was high-risk and Spence promised to help, to take some of the pressure off Derrick.

"Oh, I see."

That tone… Abby may as well have threatened to hit him with her car. She definitely was not happy to see him. Spence got that. "No, you don't."

She sighed. "Oh, really?"

If words had the force of a knife, he'd be sliced to pieces. She'd treated him to a prickly, unwelcome greeting and, if anything, the coolness had turned even icier since then.

The reaction struck him as interesting, infuriating even, since *he* was the injured party here. She cheated on him. Well, not technically, since they weren't officially going out back then, but she'd done the one thing he could not stand—she used him to climb the ladder to get to a stronger, more powerful Jameson: his father.

Spence glanced at Rylan. He stood there in his perfectly pressed gray suit and purple tie. He had the right watch. The right haircut. He'd shined his shoes and combed his hair. Nothing—not one damn thing—was out of place on this guy.

Clearly Rylan hoped this was a date or the prelude to a date and not an informal afternoon business meeting.

Well, that was enough of that.

"Are you done here?" Spence asked Rylan, making sure his tone suggested the answer should be yes.

"Absolutely." Rylan's sunny disposition didn't dim one bit. He put a hand on Abby's arm and gave it a squeeze. "I'll call you tomorrow so we can go over the list of concerns." His hand dropped as he faced Spence again and nodded. "Mr. Jameson."

Yeah, whatever. "Rylan."

Spence watched the engineer leave. He'd never had such a sudden negative reaction to a person in his life. Rylan could have said anything and Spence would have disliked him.

Abby leaned back with her hands resting on the table on either side of her hips. "Heavy-handed as always, I see."

Facing her head-on, without a buffer, tested the defenses he'd thrown up against her. He shouldn't care. It shouldn't mean anything. If only his brain and his body would listen to that order.

Despite standing ten feet apart, Spence felt a familiar sensation spark inside him. Desire mixed with lust and a bit of confusion. The intensity hit him full force.

"Did I interrupt your date?"

She rolled her eyes. "Right. Because I'm incapable of meeting with a man without crawling all over him."

"You said it, not me."

She exhaled loud enough to let him know she had better things to do. "What do you want?"

She didn't back down. He'd always loved that about

her. The boss-employee boundaries didn't mean much to her. If she had a thought, she said it. If she disagreed, she let him know. She'd been tactful in not making angry announcements in the office lunchroom, but she wasn't the type to coddle a man's ego, either.

He'd found that sexy. So sexy even as his life crumbled around him and his relationship with his father, which had never been good, disintegrated.

"Is that how you talk to your boss?" He figured he may as well try to reestablish the lines between them. Like it or not, they had to figure out a way to tolerate each other.

For him, it meant ignoring the way she walked and the sound of her voice. Forgetting that he once was willing to go against his father to be with her. But he had to smash all of those feelings, all that vulnerability, now.

"Is that what you are? Last I checked, you ran out of the office and never looked back. If this were a cartoon, you would have left a man-size hole in the wall." She smiled for the first time.

"I'd had a surprise." As if that was the right word for seeing the woman you wanted locked in the arms of a father who turned out to be a constant disappointment.

She pushed away from the table. Without looking at him, she finished straightening the stacks of files. Made each edge line up. "You still think you're the victim then?"

"You were kissing my father."

She glanced over at him again. "Why are you here, Spence?"

No denial, but just like the last time they'd talked—yelled and argued with each other—and a hint of sadness settled in her big brown eyes. Her shoulders fell a bit and for just a second, she didn't look like the confident, in-charge woman he knew her to be.

He had no idea what that meant. But he did have a job to do. "This is an important project and—"

"I mean in DC." She picked up the stack of files and hugged them tight to her chest. "Are you back permanently?"

He hated that question. Derrick had asked it. People at the company had asked. The guy at the rental car company wanted to know. Spence gave her the same answer he'd given to everyone for three weeks. "Derrick needs some help."

"Huh." She frowned at him as her gaze wandered over his face. "I don't really think of you as the type to drop everything and come running to assist someone else."

Charming. "It's not as if we know each other all that well, do we?"

"I guess not." She bent down and picked up her bag. She looked cleaned up and ready to bolt.

"Derrick's fiancée has a health issue," he said.

The anger drained from Abby's face. So did some of the color. She took a step forward with her hand out, but dropped her arm right before she touched him. "Did something new go wrong with the pregnancy?"

"You know about that?" Sure, the pregnancy had been on the gossip sites. One of the playboy Jameson heirs settling down was big news. Their lives had been followed and dissected for years. Every mistake highlighted. Every girlfriend photographed. The rumors, the lies. But the family hadn't confirmed the pregnancy because it was too soon and too personal. "Are you two friends?"

Abby's expression went blank. "You sound horrified by the idea."

Admittedly, he was acting like a jerk, as if every-thing was about him. Ellie, Derrick's fiancée, needed support. Spence got that. But still… "Well, it will be a bit uncomfortable, don't you think?"

"As uncomfortable as this conversation?"

For some reason, the response knocked the wind right out of him. He almost smiled, but managed to beat it back at the last minute. "Look, we're going to need to get along."

She shrugged. "Why?"

Man, she had not changed one bit. *"Why?"*

"You've been back for three weeks and we've suc-cessfully avoided each other. I say we keep doing that."

She sounded aloof and unaffected, but he could see her white-knuckle grip on the files. Much tighter and she'd cut off circulation to her fingers. In fact, this close he saw everything. The flecks of gold around the out-side of her eyes. The slight tremor in her hands.

He could smell her, that heady mix of ginger and something sweet. It was her shampoo and it floated to him now.

He inhaled, trying to calm the heartbeat pounding in his ears. "Now who's running?"

"Do you really want to have this conversation? Be-cause we can." She took one more step. The move left little more than a whisper of air between them. "I'm not the one who saw something, misinterpreted it and then threw the mother of all hissy fits."

The air in the room closed in around him. He could actually feel it press against his back. "Misinterpreted?"

"You're offended by my word choice?"

"You were kissing my father!" He shouted the accu-sation loud enough to make the walls shake.

A sharp silence descended on them right after. In

the quiet, she retreated both physically and emotionally. The air seemed to seep right out of her.

"That's what you think you saw." Not a question. Not really even a statement. She said the words and let them sit there.

The adrenaline shooting through him refused to ease off. "Hell, yes!"

"You can let yourself out." She walked around him and headed for the door.

"Hey." His hand brushed against her arm. He dropped it again when she glared at him. "Fine. No touching."

"None." Which sounded like *not ever*.

Regret plowed into him. He came here for them to talk this out. He'd gone into the computer and looked up her schedule. Came here unannounced, thinking he'd have the upper hand.

"I want us to be civil toward each other," he said as he struggled to bring his voice back under control.

She shook her head. "No."

"What?" He'd been the one to offer the olive branch. He hadn't insisted on an apology or that she take responsibility. But she still came out swinging and didn't stop.

"You lied to me," she said in a voice growing stronger with each word.

For a second, his brain misfired. He couldn't think of a response. "When?"

"You let me believe you weren't *that guy*, but you are. Rich, entitled, ready to bolt, tied to his daddy and desperate for approval." She counted out his perceived sins on her fingers.

That fast his temper skyrocketed again. Heat flushed through him "That's enough."

"The suggestion still stands. We ignore each other."

"Does that mean you're going to leave every room I enter? Get off projects I'm overseeing?"

She shrugged. "That all works for me."

No, he was not going to be pushed into a corner. He was the boss. He wasn't the one who screwed everything up.

He pointed at her. "You did this to us."

Her mouth dropped open. For a second, she didn't say anything, and then she clenched her teeth together. "You're unbelievable."

She slipped by him a second time. Got the whole way to the doorway.

"Stop trying to storm off, and talk to me." He didn't try to grab her but he did want to.

She was absolutely infuriating. Every word she said pushed him until the frustration mixed with the attraction and it all pounded in his head.

"Okay." She whipped around and faced him again. "You want me to talk, try this. You're no better than your father."

The words sliced through him. Ripped right through the layers of clothing and skin.

"I guess you should be the one to compare us since you kissed both of us." When she just stood there, staring at him, he wanted to lash out even harder. "What, no comeback?"

"Stay out of my way."

"Or?"

"Don't push me, Spence. Other people might be afraid of you or want to impress you, but I know better." She shook her head. "What you need is for someone to kick your butt. Keep talking and I will."

Two

Everything was weird now. For the last few weeks, Abby didn't think twice about heading over to Ellie's house on the tree-lined street in Georgetown for a visit. She lived with and was engaged to Derrick Jameson and their high-risk pregnancy had people at work, their friends—everyone—on edge.

Derrick was Spence's older brother, and Spence was the nightmare that just wouldn't go away, so Abby was torn. Being friends with someone tied that closely to the man who broke her heart promised more pain. That was the last thing Abby needed.

Ellie and Abby met by accident, really. Someone wrongly suggested Abby and Derrick were having a "thing" and Ellie stopped by Abby's office to apologize for getting her dragged into their personal business and someone else's vendetta. Abby still didn't understand what happened, but she was grateful for the warning and the show of trust from Ellie, a woman who didn't know her at all at that point. That was three weeks ago and they'd been friends since.

Trust was more than she ever got from Spence, the man she'd planned to date, sleep with, before he stormed off refusing to listen to her months ago. The awful day played out so clearly on a loop in her head.

Panic and frustration whirled together in her mind. "It's not what you think."

"I have eyes, Abby." And that furious gaze switched back and forth between her and his father...and his hand on her waist. The noise rumbling out of Spence almost sounded like a snarl. "You want the top of the Jameson food chain? He's all yours. Good luck."

She tried to follow him but Eldrick held on. "Spence, wait—"

"I told you." Eldrick smiled down at her as she yanked her arm out of his grip. "You're going after the wrong Jameson."

"I'm so happy you came..." Ellie's smile fell as she talked. "What happened?"

The memory blinked out at the sound of Ellie's voice. Abby snapped back into reality as she stood in the doorway to Ellie and Derrick's bedroom, holding a box of brownies from that place in Foggy Bottom that Ellie had raved about a few days before.

Abby had no idea what conversation she missed as her mind wandered, but both Derrick and Ellie stared at her. Ellie was cuddled up in a blanket in the center of the gigantic never-seen-a-king-size-bed-that-big bed with pillows tucked around her body and the television remote control in her hand. Derrick, still wearing his dress pants and button-down shirt, sat next to her. Not on top of her, but close enough for the intimacy, the closeness, to flow around them. His only nod to being home and not at work came in the removal of his tie. It lay over the armrest of the overstuffed chair by the bed.

"Nothing." That seemed like a reasonable response to most things, so Abby went with that as her answer.

"Huh." Ellie made a face. "You look furious."

Derrick let out a long breath. "So, Spence."

"Definitely Spence," Ellie said with a nod.

Well, they weren't wrong. Derrick and Spence were brothers and her bosses. But still. "I don't know how you two are related."

"We're actually a lot alike." Derrick smiled at first but when Abby stood there, not moving, Derrick bit his bottom lip. "But I can see that's the wrong answer."

"Did something happen?" Ellie patted an empty space on the bed, inviting Abby farther into the room to take a seat.

Seeing the two of them, with Derrick's arm resting on the pillows behind Ellie and his fingers slipping into her hair and massaging her neck, struck Abby with the force of a slap. A pang of something…jealousy, regret, longing…moved through her. She couldn't identify the feeling or grab on to it long enough to assess it. But the idea that she was interrupting did crash on top of her.

She was about to drop the brownies and run when she saw both of their faces. The concern. Derrick was the big boss and he deserved to know Spence hadn't really done anything wrong. This time.

She shook her head. "Nothing, really. He walked onto my job site unannounced."

Derrick winced. "Yeah, about that."

Ellie's head slowly turned and she pinned Derrick with a you're-in-trouble glare. "What did you do?"

"With you being on bed rest—"

"Don't blame me," Ellie warned.

"Let me try again." Derrick, the tough, no-nonsense boss who sent employees scurrying, cleared his throat. "Since I can't be in the office as much as usual right now—"

Ellie's sigh echoed around the room. "You're still blaming me."

They were so cute, so perfectly in sync, that Abby took pity on Derrick. "Let me guess. Spence is overseeing some of the projects now that he's back in town."

Derrick closed his eyes for a second before opening them again. Relief poured off him. "Thank you and yes."

She wasn't willing to let him *all* the way off the hook. "Like the one I'm in charge of."

"The key phrase there is that *you are in charge*. Spence watching over the project is in line with office procedure. It's purely a we-need-to-know-what's-happening check. You know that."

"That was a lot of words," Ellie said in a stunned voice.

"I wanted to be clear."

This time, she rolled her eyes at him. "Uh-huh. You're sure you're not doing something else?"

Derrick smiled. "I have no idea what you're talking about."

Abby got it. Derrick rarely explained himself. He'd gone into an office-manual description with his answer. That immediately put Abby on edge. The idea of Derrick playing matchmaker or trying to push people together to talk…forget it. That was ridiculous. He wasn't that great with people, which is why his assistant, Jackson Richards, worked nonstop and everyone ran to him for everything.

It also explained why the entire office celebrated when Derrick fell in love with Ellie. Everyone hoped love would soften him. It had, except for the palpable panic that now hovered around him due to the endangered pregnancy.

Still, shortly after Spence left town, Abby had been promoted. She'd seriously considered turning the offer down out of fear of it being perceived as a payoff to get her to keep quiet about the Jameson men shenanigans. Then she decided she qualified for the position and needed the money because there was no way she was staying at Jameson for long.

She went from assistant to project manager. Now she had a seat at the manager's table. She didn't need a full-time babysitter, and certainly not *that* full-time babysitter. "Spence showed up at a site meeting unannounced."

"He does have access to your calendar," Derrick said.

Ellie patted Derrick's knee where it lay curled on the bed beside her. "I love you but you're not very good at this."

Loyalty. Derrick and Spence had it. Abby got that.

"No, it's fine." She tried to keep her voice even but knew she failed when Derrick frowned and Ellie's eyes widened.

"Really?" Ellie snorted. "Because that tone did not sound fine."

Derrick had stopped massaging Ellie's neck but he started again. "I think she's afraid she'll upset you if she launches into her why-I-hate-Spence speech."

Ellie waved the concern away as she turned the television from muted to off. "Nope. Jameson family gossip is ridiculously delicious. I'm always happy to hear it."

Hate Spence. If only. Abby's life would be so much easier if she did hate Spence. She'd tried. Her mind spun with all the ways he'd failed her. How he hadn't believed her or let her explain. She could call up a ton of hate for the elder Mr. Jameson and heaps of anger and disappointment for Spence, but that was it. And seeing him again...her normal breathing still hadn't returned.

She'd heard his deep, rich voice in the hallway at work and ducked into the closest office to avoid him. Then there was his face. That gorgeous face. The straight black hair and striking light brown eyes. He'd been blessed with those extraordinary Jameson genes, including a hint of his Japanese grandmother around the nose and cheeks. Tall, almost six-two with impossibly long legs and a trim waist, Spence was a bit more muscled than Derrick. Spence's shoulders, and that pronounced collarbone, cried out for kisses.

Not that she noticed.

She was trying really hard not to notice.

With a shake, she forced her mind back to work and the best way to survive being in the same building as Spence. "Well, hopefully it was a one-time thing and I can submit reports or tell Jackson and make Jackson talk to Spence."

Derrick frowned. "That sounds like an efficient use of office resources."

"It might keep Spence alive." Ellie slipped her fingers through Derrick's as she spoke. "Just saying."

The gentle touch seemed to spark something in Derrick. He sat up a bit straighter as he looked at Abby. "If it's a problem to deal with Spence, I'll switch projects with him. I'll be the silent Jameson looming in the background on yours."

As if she could agree to that. Saying yes to the offer suggested she couldn't handle pressure, and that was not a message Abby wanted to send.

Ellie visibly squeezed his hand. "That's not really how you run the office, is it?"

"No," Derrick said.

Abby shrugged. "Sort of."

For a few seconds, no one spoke. They all looked at each other, back and forth, as the tension rose. Abby wasn't clear on what was happening. Maybe some sort of unspoken chat between Ellie and Derrick. But Abby did know that the cool room suddenly felt suffocating. Even the cream-colored duvet cover with the tiny blue roses—an addition she would bet money moved in with Ellie—didn't ease the mood.

"Everything okay in here?" Spence's firm voice boomed into the silence.

He hovered right behind her. Abby could almost feel the heat pulse off his body. When he exhaled, his warm breath blew across the back of her neck.

Time to go. That phrase repeated in her head until it took hold.

"Spence." Ellie smiled. "Look, it's Spence."

"I do live here. Temporarily, but still."

In the bedroom down the hall. Abby knew because she'd walked by it a few days ago and glanced in. Saw a bag and hoped it meant nothing. Then she recognized Spence's tie from the day before flung over the unmade bed.

"For now." Abby meant to think and not say it, but she managed to mumble it.

Of course Spence heard and placed a hand on her lower back. "Meaning?"

The touch, perfectly respectable and so small, hit her like a live wire. Energy arced through her. She had to fight the urge to lean into him. To balance her body against his. "I'm sure you'll be on your way again soon."

Spence's exhale was louder, more dramatic this time. "That's not—"

Derrick stood up. "As fun as it is to see you two work things out by lobbing verbal volleys at each other, Ellie does need her rest."

"I'm having fun." Ellie caught Derrick's hand.

Abby silently thanked Derrick for giving her the easy out. Once she maneuvered her way through the three-story brick mansion, she'd be gone.

She put the box of brownies on the bed and pointed to them. "I just wanted to drop them off. Don't eat them all at once."

"You're very sweet." Ellie went to work on the tape holding the sides of the box down. "I make no promises about how fast they'll be gone." She shot Derrick and Spence a serious look. "So we're clear, I'm not sharing."

"No one would dare defy that order." Abby could not escape fast enough. "I'll text you later."

She pivoted around Spence and practically raced down the hall. Moved as fast as her stupid spiky heels would let her without wiping out in an inglorious sprawl. The humming in her head blocked out all sounds. She didn't realize she'd been followed until she reached the bottom of the intricately carved wooden staircase and heard footsteps behind her.

She turned around just as she left the steps. Spence was there. Of course he was.

With his palm flattened against the wall and his other on the banister, he stopped. She couldn't help but stare. His body was an amazing mystery to her. A package she ached to unwrap. How long were his arms, anyway?

His expression stayed blank as his gaze searched her face. "What are you doing here?"

"Visiting Ellie." Not a lie. She'd brought a treat and everything.

Spence finished coming down the stairs. Slipped his body by hers until they stood side by side. "How do you even know her?"

He still towered over her. She stood a good five-eight and with the heels could talk to anyone without feeling as if someone was trying to intimidate her. But Spence still towered, though he did stand a few steps back, giving her space.

"I do work at the company," she pointed out, not knowing what else to say.

"A lot of people work there. None of them show up at the boss's house." Spence folded his arms across his middle and stared her down. "What's really going on?"

He had to be kidding with this. "Do you think I'm stalking you?"

"Are you?"

She was doing the exact opposite, whatever that was called. Hiding from him? Sort of. Trying to find breathing room to center her control and ease the disappointment that clawed at her every time she thought about him and what could have been. "Lately, when I come over I text first to make sure you're gone. Happy?"

His arms slid down until they hung at his sides again. "Isn't that a bit extreme?"

"No." It was self-preservation.

She refused to get snared in another Jameson trap. She trusted Derrick. He'd delivered on every promise he'd made to her back then, when he begged her to stay with the company after... Spence.

"Sooner or later, we're going to need to talk to each other," Spence said.

"I disagree." Not her most mature answer ever but probably the most honest one.

"Abby, come on."

The tone of his voice suggested he was done playing games. Well, that made two of them. "It's fascinating that you ran off without saying a word months ago, but now you want some big chatty moment with me. I guess us talking is fine so long as it's convenient to you."

"We're adults."

Lecturing. Great. Just what she wanted from him. "One of us is."

With that, she turned and walked out. She'd reached her maximum load on Jameson testosterone for one day. She needed her shoes off and her feet up. Some wine. No Spence.

A Spence-free zone. The idea made her smile as she walked down the hall then closed the front door behind her.

"She's not wrong," Derrick said as he slowly walked down the stairs.

"You want to clue me in here?" Because Spence felt deflated and empty. The gnawing sensation refused to leave him. He'd blown out of the office all those months ago. Traveled around. Helped out on random building sites across the east. Lived a life so different from the spectacle he'd grown up in. All that competition. How his father pitted the three of them against each other. How Derrick always tried to protect them from Dad's wrath, especially Carter, the youngest.

They lost their mom to cancer. Their father didn't even have the decency to let her live out her life in peace. No, he moved her to a facility then marched in there one day and demanded a divorce so he could marry his mistress. He thought she was pregnant but she wasn't, so he quickly dumped the mistress, too. Then he ran through others. He was on wife number four and insisted this one had changed him. Yeah, right. The man treated women as disposable and his sons as property.

All that playing, all that acting at being a Big Man, and he let the business slide. Derrick had stepped in and saved it years ago. They all had to work there from the time they were teens. It was a family requirement, but Derrick was the one who rescued them all—including their father—and restored the family checking account when he took over the day-to-day operations four years ago.

That incredible turnaround was one of the reasons Spence stood on Derrick's first floor now. He owed Derrick. He also loved Derrick and wanted to help. That meant sticking around. Worse, it meant facing his demons and dealing with Abby.

Spence wasn't good at standing still. He'd always been the brother to keep moving. Go away to school. Go farther to a different school. Try to work somewhere else. Delay full-time work with the family as long as possible.

The Jameson name choked him. He didn't find it freeing or respectable. Forcing his feet to stay planted was taking all of his strength. He didn't have much left over to do battle with Abby.

"Are you admitting you're clueless? That's a start." The amusement was right there in Derrick's voice.

At the sound, some of the churning in Spence's gut eased. He had no idea how to handle Abby, but he could do the fake fighting-with-his-brother thing all day. "Don't make me punch you while your fiancée is on bed rest. She shouldn't see you beg and cry right now."

"Are you quoting from a dream you once had? Because that's not reality."

They'd physically fought only once. It was years ago, over their mother. Spence had been desperate to keep her in the house with nurses. Derrick, barely in his twenties, had tried to make it happen but couldn't. Spence had needed an outlet for his rage and Derrick was right there. The perfect target.

There was an almost three-year age difference between them, but Spence still got his ass kicked. And he'd deserved it because his anger really should have been aimed at his father. Spence was thirty-three now. In theory, he knew better.

"Spence, she's one of the best we have." Derrick sat down on a step a few from the bottom and started counting out Abby's attributes on his fingers. "She can multitask and oversee projects, keep things moving. She's smart. She's a great negotiator."

It was an impressive list, but Spence already knew it by heart. Every time he tried to run through her sins in his mind, the image of her face would pop up and his thoughts would stumble. "I feel like you're reading her résumé to me."

"Don't scare her away."

There was no amusement in his tone now. Spence got the message. "You do understand she screwed me, right?"

"I don't know what happened back then because you bolted and when I tried to talk with her, in part to make sure we weren't going to get sued, she refused to say one single negative thing about you." Derrick threw up his hands before balancing them on his thighs again. "Hell, I can name twenty bad things just sitting here and without thinking very hard, but she protected you."

"She sure has no problem listing out my faults now."

"Do you hear what I'm saying?"

"That you're nosy as hell." Spence dropped down on the step two down from Derrick and stretched out sideways so he could look at Derrick. "What's your actual point?"

"Maybe you got it wrong back then."

Spence leaned his head back against the staircase railing and stared up at the ceiling. "I saw her kissing Dad."

"Right, because our father never set anyone up or did anything to mess with us."

That got Spence's attention. His head lowered and he looked at Derrick. "I don't—"

"When rumors were going around about me in an attempt to convince Ellie to dump me, Abby's name came up."

"What?"

"Some people think the two of us had a thing. There are whispers, none of them true, but they're out there." Derrick shrugged. "Ellie heard, wanted to apologize to Abby for dragging her into our personal mess, they met and, honestly, it's like they've known each other for years."

Derrick and Abby. Fake or not, there was an image Spence never wanted in his head. But Abby and Ellie? No one was safe if those two put their powers together. "That's just great."

"For you, no. Abby is going to be around here for Ellie. And she's a big part of the managerial team at work." Derrick dropped his arm and touched the step right by Spence's shoulder. "I want you here and I will do anything to keep you in the office and in town, but even I can't work miracles. You have to fix this because I can't."

"I've never heard you admit that before."

"You're going to run into her."

Derrick sounded so serious. Spence wanted to make a joke or ignore the whole conversation. He knew he couldn't do either. "I can handle it."

"I'm wondering if the rest of us will survive it."

Suddenly, so was Spence.

Three

Abby sat in a conference room on the fifteenth floor of the swanky office building where Jameson Industries was located. A glass wall with the glass door fronted the room, facing into the hall. The room was reserved for relatively few people in the company because it connected to Jackson Richards's office next door. He used it. Derrick used it. Today, she used it.

She looked at the stack of papers in front of her, then to her laptop, then across the small round table to Jackson. He was Derrick's right-hand man and the most accessible person on the management staff. He was also tall and lean with a runner's body and, if rumors were correct, the one every single woman in the office named as the most eligible and interesting man in the office. There hadn't been an actual poll, to her knowledge, but she got asked at least a few times a week if he was dating anyone. Not that Abby saw him in a romantic way. She didn't.

She considered Jackson one of her closest friends, if not *the* closest. After a relatively solitary existence growing up—just her and her mom and the apartment manager who watched her when her mom worked the night shift at the diner—dating here and there, keeping attachments light in case she needed to get up and go, Jackson acted as a lifeline for her. They even lived in condos next door to each other, which was more of an accident than anything else. But when you heard about a good deal on a downtown DC property with a doorman and reasonable monthly fees, you jumped on it. Jackson sure had.

But right now she was at work and out of patience. She beat back the urge to knock her head against the table. "If I have to read one more email from Rylan, my brain will explode."

The man sent her the most mundane emails. The status check today, which he sent a day earlier than he said he would, was to tell her nothing had changed. Yeah, she guessed that much. But with emails clogging her inbox and her mind on constant wandering mode these days, she needed something solid. Jackson was it.

"Good thing we have good health insurance here," Jackson said as he closed the file he was reading.

She snorted. "I'm pretty sure head explosion isn't covered."

"He is persistent." Jackson glanced at the conference room door as it opened. "Speaking of which…"

"Hello." Spence stepped inside. He didn't make a move to sit down. He stopped and rested his palms on the back of the chair nearest to him.

That fast, the oxygen sucked out of the room. The easy banter with Jackson gave way to suffocating ten-

sion. It pressed in on Abby, proving what she already
knew. Seeing Spence grew harder each time, not easier.

Jackson smiled as he moved some of the files and
papers around to make room in front of an open chair.
"Hey, Spence."

As far as Abby was concerned, all of that accommodating was unnecessary. She had no interest in sitting there, explaining her projects to Spence. She had a
file made up with the relevant information and emailed
him the rest. She'd done her part to keep the machine
running.

"Right." She shut her laptop, careful not to slam the
cover down, and stood up. "I'm going to head back to
my office."

"I need to talk to you for a second." Spence's gaze
moved from her to Jackson.

Jackson sighed. "Why are you looking at me? I'm
supposed to be in here. I'm not leaving."

"Help me out," Spence said.

Jackson shook his head as he stood up. "Did you not
hear my dramatic sigh?"

"It was tough to miss."

"That's because I spend half my life rescuing Jamesons from certain disaster." Jackson ended the back-and-
forth with a smack against Spence's shoulder.

Some of the tension drained away as Jackson and
Spence fell into their easy camaraderie. That sort of
thing always amazed Abby. Men could argue and go
at each other, but if they were friends or related, they
seemed to have this secret signal, heard only by them,
that triggered the end of the battle. Then all the anger
slipped away.

She wished she possessed that skill.

She glanced at Jackson. "You deserve a raise."

"Hell, yeah." Jackson winked at her as he walked out of the conference room through the connecting door to his office.

A second later, Spence slid into the seat Jackson abandoned. He flipped through a whole repertoire of nervous gestures, none of which she'd seen from him before. He rubbed the back of his neck. Shifted around in his seat. Put a hand on the table then took it off. But he didn't say a word.

After about a minute, the silence screamed in her head. "You're up, Spence. You're the one who wanted to talk."

Fight was probably more accurate. They couldn't seem to be civil to each other for more than a few minutes at a time since living in the same town again. They verbally sparred. Every conversation led them back to the same place—he believed she came on to his father. The idea made her want to heave.

He let out a heavy sigh that had his chest lifting and falling. "We got off on the wrong foot."

"When?"

He frowned. "What?"

"Now or back then?" She was having a hard time keeping up, so he was going to need to be more specific. "Maybe when we were starting to go out and had plans for our first official date that Friday. You left on Thursday without a word."

The memories flashed in her brain and she blinked them out. She refused to let the sharp pain in her chest derail her. This close, right across the table, she could see the intensity in his eyes, smell that scent she associated with him. A kind of peppery sharpness that reeled her in. In the past. Not now. She wouldn't let it happen now.

"You are determined to make this difficult." He had the nerve to look wounded.

She pushed down her anger and lifted her chin. "Do you blame me?"

"Actually, yes." He sat back in the chair. The metal creaked under his weight as he lifted the front two legs off the floor. "You kissed my father."

And there it was. The only point he could make, so he did it over and over until it lost its punch. "So you've pointed out. Repeatedly."

"Okay. Enough." A thud echoed through the small room as the front legs of his chair hit the floor again.

"I agree." She stood up. Her vision blurred. She struggled through a haze of anger and disappointment to see the stacks of documents and folders in front of her.

"Please, sit." His hand slipped over hers. "I know you think I'm an ass, but I'm here because I am worried about Ellie and the baby. The chance of my big brother running himself into the ground is really good. He may be acting cool, but he's a panicked mess."

Part of her wanted to throw his hand off hers. The other part wanted to grab hold. Her life would have been so much easier if she could have hated him. She begged the universe to let that happen.

Instead, she slipped her hand out from under his, stopped moving her things around and looked at him. "Of course he is. He loves Ellie."

Spence's gaze traveled over her face. "You like Derrick."

All the blood ran out of her head. "You're not accusing me—"

"No!" Spence held up both hands as if in mock surrender. "I mean, respect. Friendship. Deeper than a boss, but not romantic."

Her heartbeat stopped thundering in her ears. It was as if he opened his mouth and her body prepared for battle. The whole thing gave her a headache. "That's fair. Yes."

"Any chance we could get there? I'd like us to be friends." His hand rested on the table, so close to hers.

She stared at his long fingers. She'd always loved his hands. They showed strength. Seeing them made her wonder what they would feel like on her.

She pushed the thought away. "No."

"Abby, come on."

"I have that level of trust and understanding with Derrick because there is nothing else in the way. Nothing else between us because I don't have any other feelings for him." The words echoed in her head. She closed her eyes for a second before opening them again, hoping she'd only thought them. But no, there he was. Staring at her. Clear that he heard every syllable.

His eyebrow lifted. "But you do feel something for me?"

The look on his face. Was that satisfaction or hope? She couldn't tell. Didn't want to know. She never meant to open that door. Thinking it and saying it were two very different things, and she'd blown it. Now she rushed to try to fix the damage. "Did. That's over."

"Is it?"

He stood up then. Took one step toward her. Not too close, but enough to cut off her breathing. To make her fight not to gasp.

"I want to kiss you." He put his hands on her arms and turned her slightly until they faced each other. "Tell me no if you don't want me to."

They'd kissed before. Gone to dinner, stolen a few minutes in closed conference rooms now and then.

But this one was lined with windows on one side. She looked over his shoulder, thinking someone would be out there. That her brain would click on and common sense would come rushing back. For once, no one rushed up and down the hall.

She opened her mouth to say no, sensing he actually would stop. But she couldn't get the word out. Not that one. "Yes."

With the unexpected green light, he leaned in. His mouth covered hers and need shot through her. The press of his mouth, the sureness of his touch. His lips didn't dance over hers. They didn't test or linger. No, this was the kind of kiss where you dove in and held on.

His mouth slipped over hers and her knees buckled. She grabbed on to the sleeve of his shirt. Dug her fingers into the material as desire pounded her. Her brain shut down and her body took over. She wanted to wrap her legs around his and slip her fingers through that sexy dark hair.

Voices in the hallway floated through her. She heard laughter and the mumbling. The noise broke the spell.

"Stop." She pushed away from him. Still held on but lessened her grip and put a bit of air between them. "Don't."

Her gaze went back to the glass wall. She heard talking but didn't see anyone. Not unusual at this end of the hall since only Derrick and Jackson had offices there. But she took the sound of voices as a warning. Forcing her fingers to uncurl, she dropped her arms and stepped back another step, ignoring the way the corner of her chair jammed into the side of her thigh.

"Sorry." Spence visibly swallowed. "I know I'm your boss and it's weird."

She looked at him then. Really looked. Saw the flush

on his cheeks and his swollen lips. That haze clouding his eyes. He had been as spun up and knocked off balance as she was. It was tempting to shut it all down and let him believe this was about Human Resources and office rules, but it wasn't. Employees could date and this wasn't about that.

"We both know this isn't workplace harassment. You asked permission and I said yes. I know my job doesn't depend on kissing you. There's no big power play here." She laid a lot of sins at his feet, but not that one. His father? Yes. But not Spence.

"I guess that's something."

"You hated me and ran away but never threatened my job. You're not that guy." She waved a hand between them. "But this—us—we've proven it doesn't work. We're miserable around each other."

"I never hated you."

No way was she going to dissect that and examine it. "Okay."

"And are we? You make me feel a lot of things, Abby. Miserable isn't one of them."

And she was ignoring that, too. She had to. Believing, even for a second, that he might trust her, that he might get what he did when he sided with his father months ago, was too dangerous. He'd been clear about what he thought of her back then. They needed to stick with that and stay away from each other.

She grabbed her laptop. Almost dropped it. "I need to prep for another meeting with Rylan."

Spence watched the fumbling. Even tried to help when the laptop started its dive, but when she pulled it all together, he stepped back again. Slipped his hands in his pants pockets. "When is it? I'll come with you."

"To the meeting? Do you think I can't handle it?" He

really was determined to babysit her. Thinking about that killed off her need to unbutton his shirt and strip it off him. Mostly.

"That guy's interest in you is not entirely professional."

Her brain cells scrambled. She didn't understand what he was saying or why now. "And you're worried I'll kiss him, too?"

"I'm concerned he won't know where the line is. I don't want you to be put in an untenable position." Whatever he saw on her face had him frowning. "What?"

"Where was this Spence months ago?" She would have done anything to have him stick up for her then. To be on her side.

"What does that mean?"

She retreated back behind her safe wall. Her mother had taught her to be wary. She'd learned the hard way from the man who never stuck around to be a dad. Then her mom taught the ultimate lesson when she died in that diner shooting. Abby had to be stronger, smarter. Always be ready. Always be careful.

"I'll be fine." Somehow, she made her legs move. The shaking in her hands had her laptop bouncing against her chest from the death grip she had on it. She ignored all of it, and Spence, as she walked out.

But that kiss she would remember.

Spence couldn't forget the kiss or that look on Abby's face. It was as if she expected him not to believe her, not to stick up for her. Then his mind slipped back to another office. Another kiss. He'd walked in and his life had turned upside down. All that hatred for his father manifested itself in one horrible second, and he'd taken it out on Abby. She knew about his father's charm and his effect on women. He'd just hoped she would be different.

That realization brought him to Derrick's office. Spence didn't want to talk, but hanging out with Derrick generally calmed him. He was a reminder that the Jameson men could turn out to be decent. Their grandfather was a disgraced congressman. Dad was considered a big-time successful businessman who always had a beautiful woman on his arm. Spence and his brothers had spent too much time in the public eye as props for family photos and public relations schemes.

But Derrick was the real thing. He didn't see it, but Carter and Spence did.

As soon as Spence walked in, Derrick motioned for him to take the seat on the other side of his massive desk. Without saying a word, Derrick opened the top drawer and took out a large envelope. "Here."

Spence wasn't exactly looking for work talk but he sensed that's not what this was anyway. "Do I want to know what this is?"

"It's from Dad."

The damn agreement. Despite all of Derrick's hard work, Eldrick owned the majority of the company. He promised to turn it over, but not before he put his boys through another set of tests. It was his way of holding on to power and exerting control.

Derrick had been given a specific time to clean up his reputation. He was also supposed to lure Carter and Spence home, which proved easy enough once Derrick admitted it to them. But he did more than that. He managed to run a multimillion-dollar company, expand its holding, meet their father's conditions and land the best woman for him.

For Derrick—easy. For anyone else? Likely impossible. Spence hated to guess what his task was. "Lucky me."

Derrick dropped the envelope on the desk. "Rip it up without opening it."

The suggestion didn't make sense. "What?"

"Walk away from this."

"Isn't this my stipulation, the things I have to do? The way you explained it to me before, Dad only turns over the business if we all do his bidding. You had the biggest part and finished. Now it's my turn." Still, Spence couldn't bring himself to touch the envelope.

"Don't let him do this. It's manipulation."

It was. No one debated that. Not the lawyers who drew up the documents. Not Jackson, the only person outside of the family who knew other than Ellie. The requirements were personal and not likely to be legally enforceable, but with controlling interest, dear old Dad could sell the company and take the company that meant everything to Derrick away from him at any time. Spence refused to let that happen, even if it meant staying and working there.

"You deserve to run the company. You saved it." To Spence, it was that simple. He'd talked to Carter, their younger, California-living brother. He agreed with Spence. Whatever it took to beat the old man and get Derrick the business, they would do it.

Derrick shrugged. "I'll find another way."

"I'm thinking it's time I stepped up and took responsibility." Something even Spence had to admit he should have done before. Stopped running long enough to help.

"Are we only talking about the job?" Derrick smiled as he asked the question.

"This isn't about Abby." It was infuriating how she

was the first thing that popped into his mind—always Spence couldn't kick that habit.

"Right, Abby." Derrick made a humming sound. "Do you notice how you brought up her name, not me?"

Spence was not touching that. He knew he had a weakness for her. There was no need to pretend otherwise. "I was talking about being more engaged here, at work."

Derrick sat back in his chair. "I can't say I hate that idea."

"Yeah, well, don't get excited. I might suck at it."

This time, Derrick laughed. He'd so rarely done that in the past, but he did it now that he'd found Ellie. "I like the positive attitude."

Spence never had one of those before. Maybe it was time he tried. "I'm being realistic."

"I'll take whatever I can get."

Four

Abby kicked off her high heels and dropped down on her sectional sofa. Next, she propped her feet up on the round leather ottoman in front of her. If she had the energy, she'd change out of her work clothes. She picked dropping her head back against the cushions and closing her eyes instead.

The condo was on the seventh floor of a securebuilding that sat a block off of Logan Circle. The trendy area became trendy during the last decade. Now galleries and restaurants and fitness studios lined the streets. Several parks nearby provided great places to run and bike, but she tried never to do either. She preferred walking the city and turning her muscles to mush in kickboxing classes.

She picked the building because of the location. She was able to get in on the newly refurbished space before the prices skyrocketed and used a work bonus to do it. Now she laughed when she heard what people were willing to pay for studios on lower floors in the building. It was an odd feeling when the place you lived became a place you likely could no longer afford if you were trying to buy *right now*.

There were four condos per floor and those were serviced by a private elevator. A penthouse stretched the full length of the building on the floor above but there was never any noise up there except when the couple who lived there threw one of their lavish rooftop garden parties. She'd never been invited but she loved sitting out on her tiny balcony and listening to the music and laughter as it spun through the DC night.

The best part of the building was her neighbor— Jackson. His two-bedroom also had a den. She didn't need the extra space or the bigger price tag, but she loved having him close by. The man appreciated takeout. One of his many fine attributes.

The door opened after a quick knock. She didn't get up because she didn't have to. She'd texted Jackson as she walked in the door. She wanted Chinese food and could almost always convince him to share with her.

"You're drinking wine already?" He laughed as he relaxed into the corner seat of her sectional.

She opened her eyes and looked at him. He'd stripped off his tie and rolled up the sleeves of his shockingly white dress shirt. His hair showed signs that he'd run his fingers through it repeatedly during the day.

He really was attractive. Those big eyes and the athletic build. Decent and smart. Hardworking and compassionate. Funny. And she felt nothing but a big loving friendship for him.

Clearly there was something wrong with her. She knew what it was and didn't try to hide it. "Spence."

"Ah." Jackson reached behind him to the table that sat there. "Here's the bottle."

Abby watched Jackson fill a glass for himself then put the bottle on a wooden tray on the ottoman for easy reach. If they were going to talk about Spence, and they were because she needed to blow off some of the frustration pinging around inside of her, then she might need a second glass.

She skipped over the kissing part of the afternoon and how that rocked her so hard she'd spent the rest of the day brushing her fingertips over her lips. "He talks and I want to punch him in the face."

"That sounds like a healthy reaction."

She ran her fingers up and down the stem of her glass. "Doesn't it make you frustrated, having to deal with the Jamesons and their money and power and bullying behavior?"

His eyebrow lifted. "Are we still talking about work?"

"He makes me..." She couldn't even find the right word. Hot, angry, spun up, frustrated. They all fit.

"Want to punch him." Jackson toasted her with his glass. "Yeah, I got it."

"I love Ellie. She's funny and smart and charming and doesn't take their crap."

"Sounds like someone else I know." When she frowned, he kept talking. "It does. You don't get onto the managerial team at a family-owned company unless you're good. You're damn good."

"Like you?" She knew the truth. Jackson was a star at work. Derrick depended on him. Everyone did. Even she did. If you needed an answer, he likely had it.

He acted as if he were thinking something over. "Maybe I do deserve a raise."

"I'm tired of all of it."

"Wait." He put down his glass, took hers and did the same with it. "That sounds suspiciously like you're thinking about finding a new job and leaving."

She felt a little lost without the glass to grab on to and started talking with her hands. "Don't you toy with the idea? Leave, open your own place. Do some consulting."

"Sounds risky but potentially rewarding, except for the part where you'll work round the clock, be panicked about finances and eat peanut butter for every meal so you can stockpile cash." He shook his head. "I've already lived that life. I really don't want to go back."

They shared a similar background, having been raised by single moms who barely earned enough money to keep the lights on. But he hadn't been alone. He had a sister, a twin. But it had just been Abby. She depended on her mom until the day she lost her, and she'd mourned her every day since. Missed the vanilla-scented shampoo she used. Her smile. The way she laughed at bad horror movies. That loss, so deep and raw, never disappeared. Moving forward became easier but was never easy.

But this was about her, and her work life and figuring out the best choice for her, separate from the Spence piece of the puzzle. "Me, either, but I'm not afraid of putting in the hours."

"I don't doubt you at all." Jackson studied her for a second before picking up her wineglass and handing it to her again. "Not to bring up a rough subject, but you know Eldrick is coming to town, right?"

Spence's dad. Abby despised the man.

"What?" The glass slipped in her hands and wine splashed over the side and dribbled down her hand.

She caught it before it hit her light gray couch or her silk blouse.

"I had a feeling you didn't know."

"Are you sure it's happening?" Because that was her nightmare. Dealing with Spence was rough. Not smashing a computer over Eldrick's head might prove impossible.

He'd left shortly after he'd kissed her all those months ago, made it clear he did it to teach Spence a lesson. Since then, he'd married another wife and left the country. Abby seethed every day since. She'd hoped he'd stay on that beach in Tortola forever, but no such luck.

"Found out today." Jackson kept watching her, as if he were assessing if he should shut up or provide more details. "It's for Ellie and Derrick's engagement party. They postponed it when Ellie fainted and figured out she was pregnant. Derrick told his dad to stay away, but now the shindig is back on and father Jameson is flying in with the newest wife."

"Ever met her?"

"No, but Derrick had her investigated, so I learned too much." Jackson made a you-don't-want-to-know face.

Abby rolled her eyes. "Of course he did."

"The Jameson men are somewhat predictable."

"It's scary."

"Eldrick Jameson is…" Jackson made a humming sound. "I can't actually think of a decent thing to say about that man."

"Me, either. But go back a second. Ellie is still on bed rest." Abby didn't want her friend confined, but she didn't want a reason to see Eldrick, either.

"I don't think that means we tie her to the bed and keep her there. She's allowed to move."

"But a party? Isn't that stressful?" It would be for Abby.

"They're being extra careful." Jackson shrugged. "Getting the doctor's okay and all that. Trust me, Derrick isn't happy about it, either. I think after all the rumors in the paper about them, Ellie wants the party to stop any whispers."

That meant this was happening. It sounded like Derrick was throwing up roadblocks but none of them showed any promise in stopping the party. "Ugh."

Jackson laughed. "I can hear the excitement in your voice."

He might as well have said *funeral*. "I hate parties. Derrick hates parties."

"But he loves her."

That made Abby smile. "They really are too cute. I mean it. *Too* cute."

"Well, if it's any consolation, they were a mess at first. Derrick nearly blew it about a hundred times." Jackson shook his head. "It was kind of pathetic."

"Maybe there's some relationship malfunction in the Jameson gene pool."

Jackson drained his glass and poured another. "I've often thought that."

"I'm supposed to go over and see Ellie at lunch tomorrow." Abby wanted to cancel, or at least get some sort of promise that Spence would not show up. He seemed to be doing that a lot these days.

"Business?"

"Girl talk."

Jackson made a face. "Do I want to know what that means?"

"I don't know." It wasn't exactly Abby's strength, either. She'd grown up with few friends and kept that streak going most of her life. That's why when Ellie took her in and insisted they get to know each other, and then introduced her to her best friend, Vanessa, Abby didn't balk. She took the risk this one time and it had paid off. Spending time with Ellie made Abby smile. "She texted. I'm going."

"The things we do to make the pregnant woman happy."

Abby lifted her near-empty glass. "I'll toast to that."

The next afternoon, Abby arrived at Ellie's house, weighed down with bags of food. Derrick had to go into work for a few meetings, so Abby used the code and slipped through the layers of security to get inside. Then up the stairs. A few minutes later, she unloaded the salads and caprese-on-focaccia sandwiches onto the tray set up on the edge of Ellie's bed with drinks and what looked like a bowl of pretzels.

Ellie sat propped up in the chair next to the bed with her legs stretched out on the ottoman in front of her. Abby guessed she wasn't on the bed because it was covered with envelopes and papers.

"The sandwiches smelled so good on the walk over from the deli that I almost ate one." Abby pushed some of the paperwork to the side and sat on the edge of the bed. "What is all this?"

Ellie smiled as she grabbed a sandwich out of the bag. "It's party time. Two and a half weeks."

"Really?" Abby tried to keep the dread out of her voice but she was pretty sure it seeped in. "You know you're supposed to be in bed, right?"

"The doctor gave the okay. I have to sit for most of it, some of it with my feet up, which is really boring. The party has to be in the afternoon and not long." Ellie unwrapped the paper and ripped off a piece of focaccia. "I'm pretty sure Derrick will carry around a timer and make sure I don't stand for more than three minutes at a time."

"Because that sounds reasonable."

"He's ridiculous." But a huge grin formed on Ellie's lips as she shrugged. "It's kind of adorable."

"I'm surprised he didn't fire the doctor and find one who forbids parties." Abby felt bad that the idea sounded so good to her. "The man is not a great socializer."

"As opposed to you."

She had to cut this off. Spence was going to be Ellie's brother-in-law, which meant whining about him would put her in a terrible position. Abby didn't want to do that. "We're not talking about Spence."

Ellie's hands dropped to her lap and her smile grew even wider...if that was possible. "Look how you jumped right to him. Interesting."

"Don't make me grab the food and run." Abby took her time digging around in the bag, looking for a napkin.

"That's just mean." Ellie barely let the words sit there before she launched into her next point. "But I would say—"

"Oh, here we go." Abby gave up. She could only fake interest in the inside of a bag for so long before it seemed weird, and she feared she was nearing that line. "I'm listening."

She also twisted the paper napkin between her fingers. In, out and around. Tight enough that she heard the paper rip.

"The sparks between you two? Whoa."

Oh, man. That couldn't be true. She'd tried so hard to hide it, to fight it off.

Abby refolded the mangled napkin, then turned to the sandwich. Unwrapped each edge. But the grumbling in her stomach from before had vanished. This topic seemed to zap the hunger right out of her.

She dumped the uneaten sandwich on the tray next to her. "What you're sensing? That's anger."

"Babe, I know anger. That is not what I see." Ellie took a bite, then another.

"We may have some…unresolved issues."

"The queen of understatement."

Yeah, no kidding. But that led to a bigger issue, one Abby was not totally sure how to discuss. "I need you to know that I might not be at the engagement party."

"Wrong." Ellie smiled and reached for her bottle of water. "But why are you under that incorrect assumption?"

Abby tried to pick up anger, anything in Ellie's voice that suggested disappointment. She sounded more resigned to prove Abby wrong than anything else.

"Those unresolved issues relate to Papa Jameson and—"

"The kiss?" Ellie's eyebrow lifted. "Yeah, I don't blame you there. My father-in-law-to-be deserves a good kick."

Apparently there was an office memo no one bothered to tell her about. As far as Abby knew, Derrick had kept the kiss information limited to a very few in the office. The idea that someone other than a small circle and Ellie might know made Abby's stomach roll. She didn't want to be viewed as someone who lied and schemed her way to the top. She didn't care what choices other people made, but she'd earned this position by working her butt off.

Abby picked up the napkin then put it down again. "You know about that?"

"Of course. It's the kiss heard 'round the family." Ellie looked at Abby's face and her smile disappeared. She waved a hand and shook her head. "No, don't panic. Actually, I made Derrick tell me, but he wasn't all that forthcoming with juicy details. All I know is Spence thinks you were playing a power game and kissed his dad."

Abby's stomach refused to stop somersaulting. If this kept up, she could forget about lunch because she'd be seeing her breakfast again. "He's an idiot."

"Which one?"

And that's why she liked Ellie so much. "Good point. Both of them."

Ellie winced. "I haven't met father Jameson yet."

"Lucky you."

"How bad was it back then?"

Intolerable. All hands and creepy looks. Word was Spence's father liked to pick interns by their looks— young, pretty and blonde. A practice Derrick immediately stopped once he figured it out. But there was no reason to completely terrify Ellie during her shaky pregnancy. "Bad enough that I'm considering skipping a party and missing cake, which is sacred food in my book."

"If I let you punch him, will you come?" Ellie sounded excited by the idea.

So was Abby. "Which him?"

"Either. Both."

So tempting. "That might be a deal I can't pass up."

"Believe it or not, I really like Spence," Ellie said.

Some of Abby's amusement faded. "Let's not go there."

"Of course, I've only know him for a few weeks."

"I worked with him, was wildly attracted to him. Fought it off and lost. And then I *really* lost." That was more than Abby usually admitted. Jackson knew pieces of the story and a bit about her feelings, about how hurt and torn apart she'd been. Derrick had made it clear back then he'd collected some of the facts but not all of them. It didn't matter because Abby didn't want to relive any of it.

"Any chance Spence can redeem himself?" Ellie asked.

Abby had asked herself that a thousand times over the last few months. She dreamed about Spence showing up and apologizing. Ran through all these scenarios on what she would say. But Spence stole that opportunity away from her, too, because he never came back for her. He came back for Derrick and Ellie. Abby vowed not to forget that.

She cleared her throat, swallowing back the lump that had formed there. "I have to be smarter than that, more self-protective this time around."

The memory of the kiss flashed in her mind. Not the one that destroyed everything. The one from yesterday. The new one that carried a note of hope and a hint of desperation. The feelings had thrummed off Spence. And she'd been trying to forget them, talk herself out of the way her heart leaped and her body turned all mushy when his lips touched hers, ever since.

Ellie shook her head. "Men. They do ruin things sometimes."

Abby suddenly felt like eating again. "No kidding."

Five

She'd ignored him for three days. Spence wasn't great about being shut out of anything. He also didn't trust Rylan, and that's exactly who Abby was meeting with today. Right now.

The door stood open. Papers were strewn across the conference room table. Maps and documents with official government seals. A thick binder filled with information Spence knew would bore him.

Spence waited until the last minute to slip into the room she'd reserved for the meeting. Rylan stood by the window, looking down into the street. The only noise in the room came from the sound of the automatic room fan. That and the squeak of Abby's chair as she moved it back and forth while studying the paper in front of her.

She glanced up as soon as the door clicked shut. "You're sitting in on all of my meetings now?"

The refusal to back down… Spence found that so sexy. "I actually work here."

She treated him to the perfect eye roll. It almost shouted *you're a jerk*. "For now."

Spence kept walking until he got to her side. Then he slid into the seat next to her with his arm resting on the table. "This idea you have that I'm ready to bolt? Get it out of your head. It's not happening."

She slowly lowered her pen. "It did before."

Shot landed. Spence felt it vibrate through him. The truth really did suck sometimes.

"Derrick needs me here." That was also true. He'd come back for his brother and his growing family. Spence had repeated that to himself during the entire journey to DC. Now he wondered if something else pulled him there. An invisible thread that bound him to Abby. A need to come home and resolve the seemingly unresolvable.

She tapped her pen end over end against the table. The clicking sound turned to a steady thump when she started to hit it harder. "And no one needed you before?"

"Didn't feel like it." He'd felt betrayed, yet not. Almost as if he'd expected Abby to disappoint him back then.

Man, that was not something he wanted to examine too closely. At least not there, in an office conference room.

Rylan picked that moment to turn around and face the room. "Is everything okay between you two?"

Abby lifted her hand without looking in Rylan's direction. "You remember Rylan."

"Hard to forget." Rylan was the kind of guy who lingered. Maybe not dangerous but not honest, either. Spence knew the other man was stringing the approval process out. He was either receiving a payment from a competing company under the table, or he had a crush on Abby. Spence hated both options. "Do we have the final okay to proceed?"

Rylan stepped up to the table. "Soon."

A pounding started at the base of the back of Spence's neck. "What does that mean?"

Rylan's mouth opened and closed a few times before he actually stumbled and got a few words out. "There is still some work to be done."

Ah, work. Sure. "Then why are you here instead of off doing it?"

Rylan glanced at Abby but she just smiled at him. That told Spence that she was sick of the stalling, too.

"This is a status meeting," Rylan finally said.

"Didn't you two meet about a week ago?" Spence leaned back in his chair, enjoying the line of sweat that appeared on Rylan's forehead. "I'm asking but, see, I know that answer because I was there."

"I also needed to deliver some documents to Abby." Rylan picked his briefcase off the floor and took out a white envelope. He handed it to her without breaking eye contact with Spence.

She took it and tucked it into her file. "Thank you."

Since she wasn't balking at his heavy-handed behavior, Spence figured he had the green light to continue. Rylan stood frozen with his hand on the back of one of the chairs. He didn't make a move to sit down or do anything that looked like work.

"And now you can go." Spence made the words sound like an order.

It worked because Rylan took off on a frenzy of activity. He loaded up his briefcase and reached for his suit jacket. He nearly tripped over his own feet getting to the door. "I'll call you as soon as I have the answers you need."

The door slammed behind him. Then Spence was alone with Abby. He hoped this round would go better than the last few. Except for the kiss. He'd be happy to repeat that.

Abby flicked the pen back and forth between her fingers. She seemed calm, maybe even a little amused.

Spence was smart enough to know quiet sometimes meant dangerous. He seriously considered ducking.

She waited a few more minutes, drawing out the tension and letting it build before she talked. That pen kept twirling in the air. "Is your plan to walk into every meeting I have and bully people?"

The tone. So judging. "Have you always been this dramatic?"

She eyed him up. "Yesterday you sat in on a meeting at the office and never said a word."

He suddenly felt sorry for the people who worked under her. She knew how to use that voice, that look, to set the tone. No one had to guess her mood. "I'm confused. You want me to talk, then you don't."

"It made people uncomfortable."

He knew the feeling. "You mean you?"

The invisible hold pulling between them broke. She looked away as she shook her head. "Your ego is amazing."

"Thank you." He stretched his arm out along the table. Almost touched her but was smart enough not to try. "About Rylan."

She straightened up the stack of papers in front of her. "We need him to sign off on a variety of environmental issues. He's dragging his feet, but it will happen. You know that."

So professional. Every word was true. That's how the process worked, but Spence was talking about something very different. He sensed she knew that. "And you know he's interested in more than hazardous waste."

"He's still within a reasonable time frame for getting the work done."

An interesting answer. One he decided to hit head-on. "Are you ignoring his crush in order to smooth the way for our approvals?"

"You didn't actually accuse me of using my looks to get what I want, so I'll let that pass." She stood up.

"I'm not a total jerk, Abby. I'm concerned that he's making you uncomfortable or that he's harassing you. Neither is okay." Not liking the way it felt to sit while she loomed over him, he stood up, too. Kept his distance, or as much as being around the corner from each other at the table would allow. "I don't want him crossing a line."

Her eyes narrowed. It looked like she was studying him, trying to figure out if he was lying or not. "Women in the workplace have to maneuver through a labyrinth of ridiculous male behavior to get things done. But I have hard limits. I don't sleep around to get what I want."

The words struck right at the heart of their issues, but that's not where he was going, and digging into the past would only shut down the conversation. "I wasn't suggesting that."

"You did before."

He could not go back over that ground one more time. Part of him wanted to forgive and forget and move on. He didn't know if he could, but he was sure she was not up for the "forget" part. "Abby."

She went back to the papers. Stacked and restacked the same group twice before looking up at him again. "I'm just making my position clear since you think this has been an issue for me in the past. Don't want to be wrongly accused again."

"You'll tell me if you need me to—"

"That's the thing, Spence." She dropped the papers she was holding and they fell against the table with a whoosh. "You can't swoop in and fix this."

"First, I do not swoop."

She snorted. "If you say so."

"Second, I don't want any woman in this office to deal with nonsense." And he meant that. The last few generations of Jameson men had issues with women. He was determined to break the cycle and he knew Derrick and Carter wanted that, too.

"That last part is a responsible and appropriate thing for a boss to say, and maybe even a little sweet, but it's also impossible. There will always be some level of nonsense."

The words deflated him. "I'm sorry."

"For?"

The list was so damn long and went far beyond the topic they were discussing. "Everything? I'm really not sure, but I hate this feeling. The wall between us. The anger. The broken trust."

She blew out a long breath. "It's in the past. We should let it go."

He knew that made sense but it sounded wrong. They kept going at each other, but under all that anger, all the frustration and disappointment, something else lingered. Something he wasn't ready to let go of. "What if I don't want it to stay in the past? We could go over it now."

The color left her face. "Sometimes you need to move on."

"And sometimes you need to stick around and fix things." He stepped in closer and took her hands in his.

"You're saying   "

He wasn't even sure. "Finish the sentence."

His thumb rubbed over the backs of her hands. A light caress over her smooth skin. Then his hand slipped up. To her wrist, then a bit higher. Fingers on bare skin.

She jerked away, pulling back and putting space between them again. Her hands visibly shook as she grabbed for her files and her phone. "Thanks for the offer of help with Rylan, but I've got this."

He thought about stopping her, but now wasn't the time. When she walked out the door, leaving it hanging wide-open behind her, he wondered if the time would ever be right.

An hour later, Spence turned up in Derrick's office. He'd gotten back to his desk after the run-in with Abby and another half hour walking around the building, trying to make sense of the conflicting messages bombarding his brain, and saw the note. A summons of sorts.

Derrick started talking the minute Spence crossed the threshold to his plush corner office. "We have a problem."

"Our father plans on visiting, so we have more than one." Spence still hadn't figured out how he was going to handle seeing him. They hadn't spoken since the infamous kiss that ruined everything. Eldrick had tried in his usual smart-ass bragging way. Spence had ignored him and his envelope.

Derrick looked up as he settled back in his chair. "For once I'm not talking about him. I'm talking about you."

Spence stopped in midstep across the room. "Excuse me?"

"There's been a lot of talk in the office. Gossip."

There always was. That was the nature of an office.

People locked into a confined space all day. They were bound to get bored and start talking about nonwork things. Spence was sure Derrick hated that reality, but it was a fact. "Since when do you care about that?"

"People have noticed the tension between you and Abby. It's been weeks and it's not getting better."

Spence felt something twist inside him. He made it to the chair across from Derrick but didn't sit in in. He stood, gripping the back with a white-knuckled grip.

"What people?" Because Spence couldn't tolerate people whispering about Abby. No matter what had happened between them now or back then, she was great at her job. She deserved the office's respect. It was not as if the past was anyone else's business anyway.

"People who work in this building. People with eyes."

"Come on." Spence refused to believe it was that widespread. He hadn't even been home a month and except for the glass-walled office kiss, he'd been careful.

"You really don't have any idea, do you?" Derrick rocked back and forth in his chair. "Well, the people who work here need to think that management is at least somewhat competent."

Fair enough. "Isn't it your job to install that faith?"

"When I'm not here, it's yours." Derrick leaned forward with his elbows balanced on the edge of his desk. "Which brings me to my point."

Spence knew they'd get there eventually. "Feel free to skip any part of this lecture."

"You need to get yourself in line." Derrick dropped that bomb then stopped talking.

Figured, his brother picked now as the perfect time to get cryptic. Spence had that sort of luck. "That's it?"

"Yes."

"Your pep talks suck, Derrick."

Light streamed in the window. Before Ellie, Derrick kept the blinds closed. Not anymore. That realization made Spence smile when nothing else about this talk did.

"You have a thing for Abby. That's not new. It's not a great idea in an office environment either, but with consent, open communication and ground rules it's workable." Derrick exhaled. "That's direct from Human Resources, by the way. I needed to be able to sleep, so I checked."

"This is about you now?"

"The point is you're avoiding how you feel about her." When Spence started to respond, Derrick talked right over him. "Unfortunately, that's not new, either. But the mess is making people twitchy, so fix it."

Spence's fingers tightened on the back of the chair. "Is this some new Human Resources program I don't know about? A sort of tough love thing?"

"The engagement party is back on. Business associates will be there. People from the office will be there. And Abby will be there." Derrick looked less happy the longer he talked.

Spence heard about the party from Ellie, so this wasn't exactly news. "Okay."

"Inside and outside of the office, you need to either deal with the fact you have feelings for Abby or bury them deep enough that they're no longer an issue."

Burying them. He'd give anything to be able to do that. "We're trying."

Derrick shrugged. "I have no idea what that means."

That made two of them. "To get along. We're trying."

Derrick laughed then. "How's that going for you?"

"It's a work in progress."

* * *

Abby sat at her desk. She'd finally stopped shaking. Spence did that to her. Got her churned up then broke her down. She didn't know how much more she could take.

With her door closed for a bit of privacy, she leaned back in the leather chair. Spun it around until she faced the windows. She looked out over the traffic. Watched a car weave in and out, riding right up on the bumpers of the ones in front of it. Talk about anxiety. It was enough to make her happy she took the metro or walked to most places.

After a few minutes, she spun her chair again. Looking at the files and the light flashing on her desk phone signaling messages, she thought about those brownies she got for Ellie. Those sounded good right now. Always, actually.

Her gaze fell on the school project file and a memory tugged at her. It took a few seconds, and then she remembered the envelope from Rylan. She reached into the folder and grabbed it. Tore the closed tab. The whole time she hoped this was work-related and not some sort of weird date invitation.

She slipped her fingers inside and took out the white piece of paper. The stationery made her heart stop. Her involuntary gasp filled the room. Berger & Associates. She knew the name all too well. Jameson's direct competition on most prestigious commercial build-out jobs.

They'd once made her a job offer. Very lucrative. All she had to do was sell her soul and spill all the proprietary information she knew about Jameson's financial dealings. Things that would give Berger the edge in bidding on jobs. Never mind that telling those secrets would likely get her sued by Derrick and make her an outcast in the DC business community.

But the timing had been interesting. Berger swooped in right after the kiss with Eldrick happened. It was as if they'd sensed her rage and vulnerability and pounced. Still, she turned them down. Angry or not, she would always turn that kind of offer down.

They'd tried a few times since but never with much enthusiasm. A call here. A stray comment at this meeting over there. Now this.

She scanned the note. It was terse and unsigned. Basically just a date and time for a meeting and the name of a restaurant in Foggy Bottom. Then there was the last line: "You don't have a choice. Make this happen."

For the fifth time today, she got dizzy and the world flipped upside down on her. The game never ended... no matter how tired she was of playing it.

Six

The next two weeks passed in a blur. The office was on fire with work and party details. Derrick came in and out, looking and sounding grumpy and tired. The only thing that made him smile were the calls from Ellie. Spence seriously considered setting up a video system where Derrick could watch Ellie all day and maybe relax a little. Jackson told him no because he was pretty sure that crossed a line.

But Ellie had come through the weeks with little pain and no bleeding. The pregnancy was still considered high-risk and would be until the end, but Ellie had just moved into week ten and found some comfort in that, even though twelve seemed to be some sort of magic number for her.

Derrick hadn't found any peace. Spence was pretty sure Derrick would never be calm and not panic where Ellie was concerned.

At least the party had started. Spence looked over

the green lawn that stretched out behind the family's Virginia estate. Set in the country, it consisted of acres of rolling hills outlined by tall trees for privacy. A rectangular pool that no one had been in for years lay perpendicular to the house. The pristine water glistened, as did the intricate inlay of stone surrounding it.

He grew up here but hadn't been back for more than a year. Walking inside required that he exorcise more than one ghost, so he stayed outside.

His father hated anyone stepping on the lawn. The house rules were pretty strict. No one in his locked office. No one could eat dinner until he did. No noise in the house once he got home. Feet off the furniture. No running in the house. And those were the easy ones. He could go on for hours about how his property must be respected.

With that history, Spence couldn't help but smile when he saw how Derrick had set up tall tables in the grass and all along the brick pathways that led from the house to the pool, then branched off to the pool house and over to the guesthouse. People mingled and servers passed food and drinks. Soft music blasted from the outdoor speakers and lights that had been strewn above him twinkled even though the sun had not gone down.

The place had a festive air. For the first time, in what had to be more than a decade, laughter floated around the property. People smiled and looked at ease. Everyone seemed to be having fun, including the mother-and wife-to-be who sat in her light blue dress at a table closest to the back patio area with Derrick hovering over her shoulder. She wore her hair back and greeted guests. If an internet gossip site hadn't announced her pregnancy prematurely, people likely wouldn't guess.

Everything looked perfect. The party took place in

the backyard, which consisted of acres of rolling hills and a perfectly manicured green lawn. From where Spence stood in the rear of the soaring three-story red-brick main house, he could watch people bustle in and out of the four sets of French doors outlined by columns, leading into what his father always called the great room.

Ivy covered most of the first floor's exterior walls. And there, standing on the second-floor balcony overhang above the house's back entrance stood Abby. She wore a purple cocktail dress. Sort of a lacy material that slipped over her impressive curves, highlighting each one. Her brown hair down fell unbound and free. When she turned to point out something on the far lawn to Jameson Industries' head of sales, the sun caught the strands, turning them a lighter caramel color.

A second later, she leaned in and the older man on the other side of her said something that made her laugh. That open, genuine smile stole his breath. He put his hand against his stomach without thinking. Her body made him ache to settle the anger that lingered between them and move on to touching.

"Is it wrong that I want this over?" Jackson asked as he joined Spence at one of the high tables.

Spence forced his gaze off the woman who snagged every thought out of his head and onto the friend he'd missed as he traveled around, away from DC. "Not having fun?"

"Your father is coming. Carter is supposed to finally breeze into town. Derrick is a damn mess and there is no way Ellie is going to sit for her own engagement party." Jackson shrugged. "So, yeah. Everything is about normal around here."

"When you put it like that, I'm wondering why the

two of us didn't go on an impromptu vacation and skip this." Spence saw a flash of purple and looked up again. Abby was talking to a business associate now. Someone Spence considered forgettable. But her? No. She stood out in any crowd.

Her memory lingered. Seeing her here, out of the office, lighter and not bogged down by their arguments or a stack of work, eased some of the tightness in his chest. She put in almost as many hours as Derrick usually did, but now she looked relaxed. Or she did until she started talking to this new guy.

"Well, you're in love and fighting it. I'm guessing that's your excuse."

Spence barely heard what Jackson said but he could tell from Jackson's amused expression that he needed to. He shook his head and focused in on the conversation in front of him. "What?"

"Unless you're okay with the idea of Abby dating…" Jackson spun around and pointed at a random blond-haired guy Spence had never seen before "…that guy. He was sniffing around her earlier."

The words came together in Spence's head and his insides froze. Heat washed through him, a kind of fighting preparation where his body switched to high alert and his brain kicked into gear.

"You seem pretty protective. Are you interested in her?" Because Spence had no idea what he would do then. He'd walked away from her and she was a grown-up. Next to his brothers, Jackson was his closest friend. They all considered him family. But damn.

"Hold up." Jackson put up a hand and looked like he was trying to swallow a smile. "Don't start swinging. I care about Abby as a friend. Only a friend."

Spence felt the tension ease out of him. "Oh, right."

"A friend who will beat you to death if you hurt her again."

Spence fumbled with his drink, almost dropping it before setting it down. "I didn't see that coming."

Jackson moved the glass out of spilling range. "You know Abby and I hang out all the time, right?"

"Well...no. You...you do?" Spence stammered his way through the response but his mind went blank. He didn't even remember Jackson and Abby talking all that much before he left town.

"That will teach you to go away and not visit."

Another apology Spence needed to make. He just wasn't sure how to admit that he had to go away because seeing her chipped away at him until he couldn't think straight. That he stayed gone until Derrick called because that's how he'd learned to deal with personal conflict: he stepped away from it.

"Ellie's brother is here. He seems to be behaving," Jackson said as he gestured toward a nearby table.

Noah had a history of issues, just two of which centered on decision-making and controlling his anger. He had been a huge issue in Derrick and Ellie's relationship at the start. But the twenty-year-old was brilliant and Derrick had become a mentor to him. Things were smoothing out on that front. "He's doing better. Fitting in at work and is opening up a bit to Derrick, which is kind of funny to watch."

Jackson nodded. "I love sitting in on meetings between the two of them, even though I rarely understand what Noah is saying."

Spence cleared his throat as he searched for the right words. "About me leaving—"

"She's been nervous lately, and that's not her style. I'm not sure if it's because of you or—"

"Wait a second." The conversation kept rolling and Spence had yet to catch up, but he couldn't let this part pass. "I have no intention of hurting her."

Jackson lifted his glass and took another sip. "Because you love her."

The words skidded across Spence's brain. He wanted to deny but that's not what came out. "Stop saying that."

Jackson slowly lowered his glass again. "I notice you haven't told me I'm wrong about the love thing. Not even a 'get out of here.'"

"And I notice you waited to ambush me with this topic at a very public event."

Jackson took a sip of his beer. "I'm a pretty smart guy."

"You are." Carter stepped up to the table out of nowhere. "And trouble. Six-foot-something of pure trouble."

Seeing his baby brother, hearing that familiar amused voice, stunned Spence for a second. Carter looked the same except for the short scruff of a beard. He'd always possessed the clean-shaven baby face look. Not now. The straight black hair and black eyes were the same. He loomed tall and strong. None of that had changed.

"Carter," Spence greeted his brother then stepped back for Jackson to take a turn.

More than one head turned as the three men shook hands and hugged. Spence saw a few people point. He glanced up to the second-story deck and saw Abby watching rather than paying attention to the man talking to her.

"Who takes more than four weeks to drive across the country? How lazy are you?" Jackson asked as he flagged down a server and grabbed a glass of water for Carter.

He downed it in one sip. "I was hoping Dad would come and go before I got here."

Jackson shook his head. "You're not that lucky."

"None of us are," Spence said.

Carter reached for another glass of water from a passing tray and scanned the area. "There are a lot of people here. Do we even know this many people? I sure don't like this many people."

None of them were that great with crowds, but Carter had "it"—the charm that allowed him to talk to anyone about anything for a good twenty minutes. The sunny smile and ability to chime in at the right times. After all that interested listening, he could slip away without crushing feelings.

Most people who met him described him as the kind of guy who really listened. Spence doubted that was actually true. Carter had perfected the art of faking it. A good skill to have if you wanted to survive in the Jameson family.

"Ellie insisted if this was going to be a big party, it had to include friends, family and work people." Jackson shook his head as he spoke.

"She also demanded cupcakes," Spence said.

Carter's gaze traveled over the crowd, hesitating a few times before he spied Derrick and smiled. "Where exactly is my cupcake-eating future sister-in-law? I'm dying to meet the woman who managed to tame Derrick. She's like a miracle worker."

"You'll like her." Spence did. He couldn't imagine anyone not liking her.

"She's there." Jackson pointed at the same table Ellie had been sitting at for an hour. Derrick had moved back, but not far. "The pretty brunette talking with my sister. The other woman at the table is Ellie's best friend, Vanessa."

"Who Jackson finds very attractive." Spence had heard Jackson talk about Vanessa a few times, which was a few times more than he usually spoke about any woman in his life.

He shrugged. "I do have eyes."

"Wait a second." Carter's smile widened. "Your sister is here?"

"She's off-limits to you." Jackson grumbled something about the Jameson men being nothing but trouble.

"You've been saying that for years." Carter slapped Jackson on the back and took off. "I'll be back. Try not to burn down the house while I'm gone."

Spence watched as Carter stopped in front of Ellie and Zoe, Jackson's sister. He picked Zoe up and spun her around. After some whispering with Ellie, he pulled her to her feet and hugged her, too.

Spence shook his head. "The charmer."

"In case you were wondering, I saw Abby go into the house." Jackson peered over the top of his glass at Spence. "Just helping."

"She's free to move around."

"How very open-minded of you."

"I mean..." Yes, he wanted to talk with her. Spence could at least admit that to himself. Seeing Derrick happy and Carter at home had Spence longing for something he couldn't quite name or describe. The sensation hit him in waves and each time it crashed in, her name formed in his mind. "Fine."

"That's what I thought."

Spence reached over and polished off the rest of Jackson's drink. "You're not as smart as you think you are."

Jackson laughed. "Yes, I am."

* * *

Abby was now very clear on what the phrase "made my skin crawl" meant. Ten minutes ago, she'd turned to leave the balcony and go down and check on Ellie. Got two steps before Jeff Berger slipped in front of her. She hadn't known he was invited but she guessed she should have assumed. His company often went up against Jameson Industries on bids. Management from both companies joked about a friendly competition between the companies. She now knew that carried with it a seedy underbelly.

"It's been a long time. I've called and haven't heard back from you." Jeff swirled the liquor in his glass. "I'm beginning to think you're ignoring me."

"Weird, right?"

"Honestly, I'm not used to that type of response."

She guessed it would cause a scene if she tossed his sorry butt off the balcony of this sweet house, so she refrained. "From women?"

"From anyone."

Lovely. But she was not surprised to hear it. Jeff had *that* look. The typical DC dude-with-money-and-connections look. He was older than Derrick by about ten ears, maybe forty-five or so. He had twin boys in private school. They played lacrosse because Jeff had. They'd probably go to some Ivy League school because Jeff did. Grow up to take over Daddy's company like Jeff intended to do.

He walked around in a fog of privilege, once commenting that it was amazing how far the Jameson family had gotten, what with having a Japanese grandmother and all. As if their background should have discounted them from making money or fitting in with the oldmoncy boys who liked to drink their lunches on Capitol Hill restaurants.

Jeff wasn't old. There was nothing infirm about him. The receding hairline did nothing to dim what Abby supposed were his objective good looks. At least that's what other people said. He did nothing for her.

He played golf and belonged to a country club because he was supposed to, but he stayed fit. Every time there was a charity run in town, he was there with his sneakers on…making sure to get his photo taken for the newspaper. He put on a hell of a show. Abby had to give him that.

She sensed he also secretly despised Derrick and his success. "I'm surprised you're here."

Jeff's phony smile faltered a bit. "Derrick and I are business acquaintances."

"Not friends."

He made an annoying tsk-tsk sound. "What does that word even mean?"

No surprise he wouldn't be familiar with the definition. She decided to cut through the garbage and get straight to the only issue between them. "Despite the covert agent thing you did with the note—and I will be talking with Rylan about that, by the way—I won't be showing up to the meeting as ordered."

"Of course you will." Jeff took another swallow as he watched the activity on the grass below. "And do you know why, Abby? Because you are a very smart woman. You also have a lot to lose."

The anxiety churning in her stomach took off now. She'd gone from wanting to see Spence and hating how much she wanted to see him, to dreading this conversation. Life kept whizzing by her and she could not grab on and slow it down.

But she wasn't about to buy into whatever nonsense Jeff had planned. "Threats?"

"Think of this more as a conversation. One that will benefit you, if you play the game right." He leaned down with his elbows on the banister and surveyed the property as if he owned it. "After all, you wouldn't want Derrick or Spence to think you betrayed them."

The word twisted in her head. Now that he'd planted it, she doubted she'd think of anything else. "I didn't."

Jeff stood up straight again and stared down at her, letting his gaze wander all over her. "You will."

The look wasn't predatory. This was a power play. Another one she'd walked into the middle of thanks to her work. "Don't even try it, Jeff."

His eyebrow lifted. "Word is Spence is sniffing around you again. You wouldn't want to mess that up."

"Go to hell."

He winked at her. "We'll talk soon."

Spence started up the carved staircase running up the middle of the house. It rose then stopped at a landing and split with separate staircases going off to the right and left. As kids, he and his brothers would race cars down the steps, but only when his parents weren't home to yell about the game.

This time when he looked up at the landing, he saw strappy high-heel shoes and long legs. Amazing legs. Like, killer those-things-should-be-insured legs. The edge of a purple cocktail dress. A little higher as his gaze slipped over her hips then on up.

Abby.

His heart revved. He could feel his blood pressure spike. All that talk about her and love, and there she was.

She walked down the stairs, taking her time. Entic-

ing with a slight sway of her hips. Mentally slicing his
control to shreds as she took each step. She stopped on
the one above him but didn't say anything.

"There you are." His gaze met hers and the picture in
his head—the one of them together, him stripping that
dress off her shoulders—screeched to a halt in his head.

She smiled but it didn't reach her eyes. She scanned
the downstairs as if looking for someone and not wanting to see them. His dad, maybe? Whatever was happening inside her had her looking uncharacteristically
shaky and unsure.

He reached out for her hand and was surprised when
she grabbed on. "Hey, are you okay?"

He guided her down to the floor, hearing the click
of her heels against the polished hardwood. He slipped
her hand under his arm and touched her fingers. Ice-
cold.

With the fake smile in place, she cleared her voice
before answering. "Fine."

"That's not really believable."

She shook her head. "Spence, I can't discuss this
right now."

"Okay, wait. You're obviously upset." He guided her
around the banister and into a hall. It ran the length of
the right side of the house.

Leaning against the wall, he tried to block their view
from the people walking in and out of the house. Many
stopped and stared at the artwork trailing up the staircase and the massive chandelier hanging in the center
hall. Others smiled on the way to one of the house's
nine bathrooms a few doors down.

A thousand thoughts streamed through his head. He
blamed his father for putting her in this state. He also
played a part. So did too much work. There was a lot

of responsibility to go around, but he wanted to lessen the burden. "Talk to me."

"I'm on edge and…" She shook her hands in front of her, like she was trying to get the feeling back in them.

He had no idea what was going on in her head but the aching need he had for her turned into something else. "What is it? Tell me so I can help."

She looked at him then. Met his gaze straight on. "I have all of this energy bouncing around inside me. Add in alcohol and, well, it's a combination for bad decisions."

"Am I a bad decision?" He knew the answer but asked anyway.

Her gaze traveled over him. Hesitated on his mouth, then dipped lower. To the base of his throat. "The absolute worst."

That look. It was almost as if… What the hell was happening? He grabbed on to the last of his common sense. Something was wrong. She didn't seem like herself and there was no way he was going to take advantage of that. "Maybe you should go upstairs and rest and then we can—"

"Kiss me."

That fast the world flipped on him. Tension ratcheted up. Not the I'm-worried kind but the let's-get-naked type. "Excuse me?"

"Where does that door lead?" She pointed at the one over his shoulder and when he didn't answer, she reached across him and turned the knob. A quick flick of the wall switch and the oversize pantry was bathed in light. "This will work."

He was pretty sure he was having a stroke. His muscles refused to work. He couldn't form a sentence. It was a struggle just to get out her name. "Abby…"

She backed him up against the packed shelves lining the wall. Their bodies barely touched as they brushed over each other. It was enough to set off an explosion in his head. The good kind. The kind where he wanted to touch her and taste her and do everything he'd dreamed of doing with her but figured he would never get the chance.

"I'm tired of wanting you and fighting it." She grabbed the post behind his head with one hand. The other went to the top of his shirt to play with the buttons there. "I'm tired of trying to do the right thing."

Wanting you? He was half-sure he made that part up in his head. "Abby, what's going on?"

"I'm here in this beautiful place. Watching you. Seeing all these people. Thinking about my choices." She dropped her head down to rest on his chest.

Her scent wound around him. Soft hair slid over his skin. He was pretty certain she could hear his heartbeat because it hammered loud enough to fill his ears.

Knowing he could pull back if she asked him to, because that would always be the answer for him, he slipped his fingers through her soft hair. "Is this the alcohol talking?"

"I've only had one half-filled glass of Champagne."

Her voice vibrated against his chest. Warm breath skipped over his bare skin.

There was no way he was going to survive this.

His fingers continued to gently massage the back of her neck. "I don't want to take advantage of you."

Her head shot up. "You're not your father."

"What?"

"Kiss me."

Her eyes were clear and he didn't smell alcohol. But the stench of regret would be sickening and strong if he got this moment wrong. "I'm trying not to be a jerk here."

She undid his top shirt button. Then the next. "I'll sign a release if you want or go tell a witness I asked for this or—"

"Stop talking."

He left her for a second. Didn't go far. With his hands shaking, he turned the lock on the door, grateful there was one. The mumble of voices rose and fell outside the door as people walked down the hall. No one tried to come in, but there really wasn't a reason to. At least he hoped that was true.

He looked at her, studied that stunning face and saw the heat move into her eyes. Still, they had to be clear because this could go so wrong. "Be sure."

"Spence, you are never going to get a greener light."

She stood there in that sexy dress with her hands crossed over her chest. She wasn't hiding from him. No, he got the sense she was ready. Very ready.

"You'll tell me if—"

She reached out and hooked her finger through his belt loop. Pulled him close. "Green light."

Seven

Spence's mouth covered hers and the last of her doubts blinked out. Thoughts and unwanted feelings had been whirling in her head since he stepped back into town. They came together in one blinding certainty when his hands slid up her sides—she wanted this.

Those palms cupped her breasts through her dress and her skin caught fire. She waited for the material to melt away, for her knees to give out, but somehow she stayed upright and dressed.

Those amazing fingers massaged and caressed. It took all of her control not to reach behind herself for the zipper and strip the top down. Feel him skin to skin.

"Spence..." She didn't know exactly what she wanted, so she let the whispered plea sit there.

Backing her against the shelves, he trapped her between his arms. He grabbed on to the bars on either side of her head and leaned in. Rubbed his body against hers as his mouth treated her to a heart-stopping kiss. The kind that knocked common sense far into next month.

"You are so sexy." That hot mouth traveled down her neck.

A shiver raced through her. And when those lips slipped to her ear and his tongue licked along the top edge, the shiver turned to a full-body tremble. She held on to his waist to keep from falling down.

His muscles tensed under her fingers and his breathing came harder. It thudded under her fingertips as need flashed in his eyes. He didn't do anything to hide her effect on him…and she loved that.

They broke into a wild frenzy of touching and she was knocked harder into a shelf behind her. A can crashed to the floor. Then another. She kicked them out of the way and blocked every sound, including the whooshing of her heartbeat in her ears. Her focus centered on his mouth and the energy spinning around them.

Expert hands traveled over her and around to her back. The screech of her zipper rose above the other sounds a second before his palm brushed over her bare skin. Fingers slid under her bra. The cool air hit her as the front of her dress fell down. It heated again when he lifted his head and stared at her.

Fingertips skimmed over the rounded tops of her breasts. The touch was so reverent, so loving, her breath hiccuped in her throat.

"Touch me." She breathed the order against his neck. He already was but that didn't matter to her. She wanted the imprint of his fingers all over her.

That amazing mouth kissed a trail along the top lacy edge of her bra. Her head fell back as his lips went to work. His tongue licked over her nipple as one hand slipped down the front of her in a slow slide that ignited every cell.

Needing to get closer, to bring him in, she opened her legs as wide as her dress allowed. When that didn't bring her relief, she shimmied, tugging the material up to the top of her thighs.

It was all the invitation he needed. His hand tunneled under her dress to skim along the elastic band of her underwear. The tiny bikini briefs were no defense against his fingers. They pressed up and under. Then he was touching her. Swirling his finger over her.

Need walloped her. It pressed in on her from every direction. She lifted her leg and wrapped it around his thigh. The position gave him free access and he didn't hesitate. His finger slipped inside her. Pumped back and forth until her lower body matched its rhythm.

Relief at being touched gave way to a new tension. A pounding need to feel him everywhere. "Spence, now."

A warning flashed in her mind. She was on the Pill but they should take more precautions. But the minute the thought entered her mind it left again. All of those weeks of fighting amounted to foreplay. The talking, the kissing…she was wound up and burning for him.

Her throat felt scratchy and her skin hot. She couldn't move fast enough, rip the buttons on his shirt open with enough force. Once her fingers touched the firm muscles of his chest, she dragged them down.

The shelves rattled behind her as he picked her up and wrapped both legs around him, low on his hips. Her dress bunched around her waist. He tugged on her underwear. Pulled and yanked.

"Rip it." She almost yelled the order.

"I'll buy you ten pairs," he said through harsh breaths.

His hands shook as the material tore, shredded in his hand. She didn't know if he dropped it or stripped it away. Didn't really care. She was too busy craving the weight of his body. It anchored him but she wanted more.

She fumbled with his belt as tension thumped around her. She got the zipper down and shoved the material out of the way. When she wrapped her fingers around his length, he swore then took in a big gulping breath. His control seemed to snap. With jerky movements, he put a hand over hers and squeezed and the resulting groan vibrated through him.

Between his finger inside her and his mouth on her neck, her body flipped to ready. She arched her hips, trying to drag him inside her. When that failed, she slipped her thumb over his tip. His body actually fell forward. The shelves clanked behind her as they moved, but she didn't care.

They could have been screaming, drawing the attention of everyone at the party, but none of that mattered. Just the man wrapped around her and the feel of his mouth on her skin.

"Now, Spence." She was two seconds from begging.

She opened her mouth to do it when she felt him. Just the tip, rubbing over her. Back and forth, moving deeper with each pass. Then he pushed inside her. Slow, in a seduction that had her hips bucking. As he shifted, her internal muscles adjusted and clamped down on him, clinging to him.

"Damn, Abby." He was panting now as his arms supported her and his mouth traveled to that sensitive space right behind her ear.

When a noise rumbled up her chest, she put the back of her hand over her mouth and bit it. But her control faltered with each delicious thrust. The steady in and out had her body tightening. Every cell pulsed. After one last push inside her, she came apart. The orgasm screamed through her as her hips continued to move back and forth.

He kept plunging as the sweat broke out at the base of his neck. When her body started to wind down, she concentrated on him. Kissed that sexy collarbone and dragged her teeth along his neck.

That's all it took. He moaned as his hips tipped forward one last time. His fingers tightened on the back of her thighs. She held on as the orgasm hit him. His body rocked against her and she felt it all. Finally, his head dipped until his forehead rested against her chest. The pulses continued for a few more seconds before his body relaxed and his weight pressed heavier against her.

His labored breathing blew across her chest. The sleek muscles of his back tensed as she traced her fingers over them. She tried to soothe him with gentle kisses on the top of his head.

After a few seconds, he turned his head to the side and rested his cheek against her chest. "Well, that was amazing."

She had no idea where he found the energy to speak. She couldn't even manage to use that breathy voice like he did. Her muscles refused to listen as her body curled into his.

"Yeah." That took all she had but at least she managed to whisper something into his hair.

He lifted his head and stared down at her. Those sexy eyes, all intense and unreadable, watched her. "Any regrets?"

His voice sounded scratchy and oh-so-sexy. She

knew she could be coy or play games, but she couldn't muster up the energy for that, either. "None."

A second later, the doorknob rattled and they both jumped. Their bodies hadn't separated or cooled. They both held their breaths. After a second shake of the knob, the voices in the hall died down and whoever was out there seemed to move away.

"That was close," she said, even though she didn't care.

She knew she should slide down, enjoy the friction until their bodies separated. She rested her head against his instead.

"Abby?"

With all the stress and worry gone, exhaustion hit her. But her eyes popped open again just as they were beginning to close. "Yeah?"

"Next time, we use a bed."

It took another fifteen minutes for them to break apart. Spence couldn't stop kissing her while they straightened their clothes and cleaned up a bit. He didn't even try to hold back. The last one came as he pulled up the zipper to her dress. Before finishing the last inch, he leaned down and pressed a kiss on the bare skin of her shoulder. Tried to remember every scent and feeling so he could relive this moment later.

When she turned around to face him, he expected regret and maybe a little shyness. Instead, she smiled up at him. "Does my hair look like we just had sex?"

Every part of her did, but he figured that had more to do with his needs and his perception than with the state of her clothes and makeup. "You look amazing."

"We need to leave this room." She sighed. "I'm sure someone has been looking for us."

Knowing his family, many *someones* were. Maneuvering through the next twenty minutes might not be that easy. It would help if he could forget that he carried her ripped panties in his pocket. "I envy you being an only child at the moment."

She smiled and opened the door. Peeked out while he stole one last look at her perfect butt. The woman filled out a slim-fitting dress better than any woman he'd ever known. She was curvy and sleek…and he would have to concentrate very hard not to think about what she could do with that mouth.

They'd just stepped into the hall when Carter appeared in front of them. That grin. The way his gaze wandered over both of them.

This was not going to be good. Spence would bet money on that.

"Where were you two?" Carter asked as he glanced into the dark pantry behind them.

Abby's eyes widened. "What?"

"Hmm?" Spence asked at the same time.

Carter's grin only grew bigger. "Was that a hard question?"

Leave it to his baby brother to pick this moment to come home after months away. Now he was showing up everywhere. The guy's timing sucked. "Of course not."

Carter gestured for them to go into the library two doors down the hall. Since complying struck Spence as the quickest way through this situation, he followed. They all stepped inside and were immediately surrounded by walls of books. A desk sat in the corner by the large floor-to-ceiling window. There were a few other chairs scattered around the room but they stood there, with the door closed behind them.

Carter looked from Abby to Spence and back again. "You missed the toast to the happy couple."

"Well…" Yeah, that's all Spence had. His brain refused to jump-start after the mind-blowing sex.

"Ellie can't drink anyway," Abby said, piping up to fill the silence.

"Yes." Spence nodded. "Good. That's right."

Carter shook his head, looking far too amused by the stilted conversation. "Because that was my point."

"We're just…" It happened again. Spence started talking, then nothing. His mind went blank.

Abby touched the back of her hand against his chest. "Walking."

"Wow." Carter crossed his arms over his chest. Looked pretty impressed with himself, as if every minute was more fun than the last. "You two aren't very good at this. Maybe you need practice."

"What are you talking about?" Abby asked.

The door opened behind them and Jackson slipped inside, sparing Spence from whatever answer Carter might have come up with to Abby's question. Jackson's shoes clicked against the buffed hardwood floor as he walked. He'd picked up a piece of cake at some point and now balanced that plate along with his glass. With his fork raised halfway to his mouth he started talking.

"I heard you guys were in here. Where did you…" His gaze switched from Abby to Spence. "Oh."

Carter snorted. "Right?"

"I give up. Are we wearing a sign?" Abby finished the question by glaring at Spence.

He wasn't sure what he did to warrant that, or maybe he did, but he knew no matter what had happened in that pantry, this embarrassment was going to be his fault. No way would Carter let this opportunity pass.

"Kind of." Carter cleared his throat as he pointed at Spence's chest. "Your shirt is—"

"Buttoned wrong, genius." Jackson shook his head as he put his drink on the edge of the desk and scooped up a forkful of cake.

After a quick look at Spence, Abby rolled her eyes. "You had one job."

A guy could not catch a break around here. Spence went to work on fixing the misbuttoning. "Excuse me, but my brain is not working at top-speed right now."

No one said anything for a few seconds. Spence knew he should jump in and clean up his last comment but what the hell did he say?

When the quiet dragged on, Carter rubbed his hands together. "So, how do you want us to handle this?"

"With a little dignity would be nice," Abby mumbled as she threw them all a men-suck glance.

"We're all grown-ups." Jackson's gaze moved around the group before landing on Spence. "For the most part."

"Right. We've all had sex. Not together, of course." Carter was just revving up, speaking faster as he went when he glanced at Abby and his words sputtered out. "What? Are we dancing around the word? At least I hope it was good sex. You were both smiling a few minutes ago."

"I can think of a thousand places I'd rather be right now," Abby said in an emotionless voice.

"So that it's official and since I know introducing myself shouldn't get me in too much trouble compared to whatever else I might say, I'm Carter Jameson." He held out his hand to Abby.

She took it as she frowned at him. "We've actually met before."

Carter's eyes narrowed. "We have?"

Spence thought back to the calls he shared with Carter all those months ago. The complaints about Dad and his behavior. Talks about the kiss and how sick he felt at seeing it. He hoped Carter forgot every last word. "Be careful."

"I'm Abby Rowe." She finished shaking his hand, then dropped her arm to her side again. "I work for your company. On the management team, actually. We used to pass in the halls. Not often but sometimes when you were in the office visiting your brothers."

"I don't... Oh." Carter's eyes widened. "Okay, yeah."

Jackson nodded. "Subtle."

"You'd be less annoying if you didn't smile so big right now." Abby shot Carter her best watch-it look as she talked.

"Sorry." Carter had the grace to wince as he looked at Abby. Then he turned to Spence. "So, is she why you came back home so fast when Derrick called for help?"

This discussion just got worse and worse. It was as if Carter didn't have a filter. Spence wanted the talk before Abby unleashed and kicked them all. "Hey, Carter? Shut up."

The noise from the hallway grew louder right before the door pushed open. Spence's vision refused to focus...but then it did. He saw a couple—him in his sixties, tall with a regal look to him. Her in her forties with shoulder-length auburn hair and a smile that looked like it was plastered on her face against her will.

Eldrick and the newest missus. All dressed up with her in flowing off-white pants and a matching shirt, and him in navy pants and a blazer. The type of outfit that suggested he'd rather be on a boat.

The only thing that made the unwanted meeting tolerable was that Eldrick's newest wife looked even less excited to be there than any of his children. Spence almost felt sorry for her. Officially meeting the family for the first time like this couldn't be easy. Especially *this* family.

"I see your behavior has not improved since we last saw each other, Spencer." That familiar stern Dad voice floated through the room.

All of the amusement drained from Carter's face. "Dad."

"When did you get here?" Spence didn't mean for it to come out like an accusation but even he heard the edge to his tone.

"I just arrived. You remember Beth." Eldrick gestured toward his wife.

For a second, Spence thought he missed a marriage. They'd eloped and Derrick and Spence had only seen her once, even then only briefly and as she stepped on a private plane at the airport. Carter never had. But that wasn't the name Spence remembered. "I thought your name was Jackie."

She nodded. "Jacqueline Annabeth Winslow Jameson."

That was quite something. Spence felt a headache coming on.

"She prefers…" Eldrick smiled as he looked around the room, and then his mouth fell into a flat line. "Abigail."

Without a word, Abby picked up Jackson's glass and threw the contents in Eldrick's face. They all jumped back, and Beth or Jackie or whatever her name was this week gasped.

Abby didn't even blink. "Welcome home."

Eight

Abby's brain had clicked off. Just seeing Eldrick pushed her into a killing rage. He stood there, smiling while he acted as if everyone around him should jump to his command. When he said her name, her brain snapped. All those months of seething backed up on her and she grabbed the drink. Not her usual move but she refused to regret it.

She'd heard people whisper about his good looks. They hadn't faded as he'd aged. He still possessed that country-club air. The salt-and-pepper hair matched his trim frame. The Champagne dripping down his shirt and stuck in tiny droplets in his hair, not so much.

She hated every inch of his smug face.

She looked around the room. No one seemed angry, but Eldrick sputtered as he wiped his hands down his shirt. His wife patted her hand against his chest, as if that would somehow dry the material.

Well, they could all stare at her or be furious—even kick her out—Abby didn't care. Eldrick deserved to be drenched. That and so much more.

"What in the world was that about?" Jackie-Now-Beth asked.

"Ask him." Because Abby wanted to see if he would say it to her face. Spew his lies with her standing right there, ready to pounce.

"Okay." Jackson put out both hands as if trying to calm down the room. "Let's all relax for a second."

"Jackson is right. Let's not get excited. It isn't as if that's the first time someone doused Dad in a drink in this house." Carter shook his head. "I can think of at least two other wives who used that trick."

Abby liked him.

"Carter, not now." Spence issued the order without moving his gaze from her.

He still didn't get it. That realization moved through Abby, nailing her to the floor. After the sex and the flirting, even the fighting, he didn't see the truth. He still believed she was a willing participant in that kiss with his father back then.

Some of the fight ran out of her at the thought but she would not back down. Eldrick could not weasel out of this confrontation by throwing his weight around or running away to get married. She stood right in front of him because he needed to face her. He owed her this moment.

"That was unnecessary." Eldrick kept his voice even as he threw a scowl in Abby's general direction.

That ticked her off even more. "You made my life miserable."

"Who are you?" Beth asked. There wasn't any heat in her voice. More like a mix of confusion and concern.

Abby didn't know what to think about Beth. In her shoes, if she were married and in love, she'd go ballistic if someone attacked her husband. Then in private, she would shake him until he told her the truth.

But she asked, so... "I'm Abby. I work at Jameson Industries and—"

"Not if you keep behaving like that." The anger edged Eldrick's tone now. The threat hovered right there but he didn't drop it. "Do you understand me?"

He talked to her like she was a child. Dismissive. The man was completely annoying. She had no idea how he'd produced or had any part in raising his otherwise decent sons.

"No one is firing her." Spence's tone was clear and firm. The underlying beat of don't-test-me rang in his voice.

Abby couldn't figure out if that was aimed at her or his father...or both. She tried to ignore the part of her that cared what he thought. She had to block every memory of his touch and the way his mouth felt against her skin to get through this. Fury fueled her now and she couldn't back down. She needed all of her focus now. She'd waited for so long for this moment. It was happening.

She turned to Beth, not sure if the woman was an ally or not. "Your husband, on those occasions when he bothered to come into the office, would corner me. He talked about how we should have private dinners. Commented on my skirt length."

Carter's mouth dropped open. "What?"

"When was this?" Beth asked as she shifted a bit. One minute she was tight up against her husband's side. The next she put a bit of space between them.

Abby had expected the other woman to lash out and

aim all of her disbelief right at Abby, not believing any accusations. But Beth looked engaged. Maybe she'd always suspected her husband could cross the line. Abby wasn't sure. Beth's eyes had narrowed but she wasn't yelling or shouting about Eldrick's imaginary good points.

That was enough to encourage Abby to keep going. "It happened right up until the time he left to marry you."

"That's not true." Eldrick took a step in Abby's direction. "You stop this."

Spence blocked his path. "Let her talk."

That's exactly what she intended to do, with or without their permission. She'd laid this out for Human Resources at the office right after it happened. They'd called Derrick in and then she'd shut down. She knew she needed to own that piece, but back then the idea of going up against a wall of Jamesons had panicked her. She needed to hold on to her job, at least until she'd found something else.

It took her months to realize Derrick wasn't his father. Derrick would have believed her, but by then the damage had been done and Spencer was gone. She'd lost all she could tolerate losing and Eldrick was no longer around to cause trouble, so she let the complaint drop. But now he was back, and that meant he was fair game. She refused to let anyone else suffer because of him.

Which mentally brought her to the hardest part of her story. The part she once tried to tell Spence but he was too busy storming off to listen. "You kissed me. Grabbed me in my office and told me that Spence was wrong for me."

Carter moved then. He turned to face his father. "You did what?"

She couldn't stop now. The words spilled out of her. "He bragged about how Spence would never believe me. How he'd see us together and immediately blame me and bolt."

"Oh, man. That's messed up."

She was pretty sure that comment came from Jackson. She didn't look around to see, but Carter and Spence seemed frozen. Neither of them moved. The only sign of life she could pick up in Spence was the way his hands balled into fists at his sides.

"Okay, look." Eldrick held up his hand as he stepped into the center of the group. "You're exaggerating this a bit, don't you think?"

She refused to stop now or let this slide. This time he needed to face the consequences, even if they only amounted to her yelling at him. "You thought it was funny to see Spence back down."

When Eldrick took another step, Spence grabbed his arm and pulled him back. "Funny? How could you possibly think that?"

"I was saving you, as usual."

Spence made a choking sound. "You can't be serious."

"She worked for you. It was too risky for you to make a move. I was proving a point. It all worked out." Eldrick had the nerve to shake his head.

Between what he said and the patronizing tone in which he said it, Abby wanted to punch him. Worse, open that door and yell her accusations into the hall so that everyone in that big house, on that massive property, knew the kind of man Eldrick really was.

Eldrick stared down at Spence's hand on his arm. "It was a matter of containing the potential damage. We both know you weren't in it for the long term, so why endanger our position? Dating was too risky. The potential liability outweighed whatever feelings you thought you had."

Before Abby could say anything else, Beth turned to her husband. "Eldrick?"

Abby couldn't read the other woman. She stood tall and her voice never wavered. Abby knew almost nothing about her. No one at work talked about her. Jackson had said something about her being different from the other wives. Not as young. Not demanding or the type to run through money, except for her request that they move away and enjoy life on the beach.

One look from his wife and Eldrick's stern I'm-in-charge-here glare faltered. His tone morphed into a lighter, more cajoling sound. "Beth, it's not—"

"We were engaged when this happened. You hadn't announced it to your family, but you had asked. I wore the ring."

Eldrick shot a look in Abby's direction. She sensed a hint of desperation. He no longer stood there as if he could kick them all out at any minute, even though he likely could.

Good, let him squirm.

He shrugged. "Help me out here."

"You've got to be kidding." Abby crossed her arms in front of her to telegraph the very simple message that the man was on his own.

"She could have sued you." Beth took a step closer to Abby. "It sounds like she should have. And hurting your own son? Your behavior was appalling."

The move was so sudden that Abby lost her balance. She leaned against Beth for a second before straightening up again.

"I figured he was protected. It's his company, after all," Abby explained.

An odd sound escaped Spence. "Abby, you can't believe that his behavior would have been okay with us. With me."

She almost said words that would cut him down. The sentence was right there. *You were too busy running away to care.* The only thing that stopped her was Spence's pained expression. "He was in charge, Spence. He'd *been* in charge, had that big corner office that Derrick now uses. I didn't know how many other women—"

"None." Eldrick practically yelled the response.

Carter snorted. "That's doubtful."

Abby blew out a long breath and spilled the last of the truth as she looked at Spence. "I didn't know who to trust."

The hit didn't land any lighter because of her softer tone. She saw Spence wince. So did Jackson. But she wasn't aiming at either of them. Her target, the man she ached to hurt, stood right in front of her.

In the last few seconds he seemed to have lost some of his height. His shoulders fell and he stared at his wife as if he wasn't sure how to approach her.

"Beth, listen to me." Eldrick's hand brushed against Beth's arm.

"Did you really say those things to Abby?" When he didn't immediately answer her, Beth's eyebrow arched. "Well?"

She sounded like a mom now. A really ticked off one. Abby remembered that you're-in-trouble tone from her childhood.

Finally, Eldrick exhaled. "I don't remember exactly what I said."

Relief soared through Abby. Some of the tension eased from her body, leaving her feeling lighter. "Which means yes."

Eldrick snapped at her. "This isn't your business."

"How can you say that?" Carter asked in a voice that still sounded stunned and confused. "This is about her."

"And Spence is your son, Eldrick." Beth shook her head before glancing over at Abby. "Were you and Spence actually dating back then?"

Before she could answer, Spence jumped in. "We were starting to. I was hopeful."

Those words... Abby never expected to hear him admit that out loud, because that moment had passed. She'd spent so much time being angry and hurt because he didn't believe her. Because he didn't stick around long enough to listen to her. She'd never stopped to think about what he saw. That didn't forgive any of his behavior, but it meant something to see how broken he looked and sounded now that he knew the truth.

He did care.

Beth turned back to her husband. "What is wrong with you?"

"I've been asking that for years," Carter said half under his breath.

Eldrick shot Carter a withering look before answering. "Beth, this is a family matter."

"I am your wife now."

For once, Abby thought that was a good thing. This woman did not back down or buy into Eldrick's ramblings. But she clearly deserved a better husband.

After a few seconds, Eldrick seemed to mentally calm down. His shoulders relaxed and the ruddy color on his cheeks vanished. "We should talk in private."

Beth nodded. "Let's go."

"I haven't seen Derrick and his fiancée yet." One look at Beth's face and Eldrick nodded. "Fine."

Without another word, they walked across the library and opened the door. Eldrick didn't look back or say anything as they stepped into the hallway and closed the door behind them.

Abby didn't realize she'd been holding her breath until it seeped out of her. She suddenly felt dizzy and her throat ached. She'd been feeling off for a few days but chalked that up to all the energy she was using trying to tamp down on her attraction to Spence. Now she figured the draining fatigue came from finally letting all of her frustration out.

Carter smiled at her in a way that looked almost like an apology. "Happy?"

"I'm not unhappy." Tired and out of words, yes.

Spence stepped in front of her then. His face was pale and the sexy grin from the pantry was long gone. "Abby."

He probably wanted to talk it out, but she couldn't do it. She needed a break. A few minutes of quiet. "I want to go home."

He nodded as his voice stammered. "Of course. I'll take you."

"No, I will." Jackson backed Spence away. "You Jamesons probably need to talk this out."

"I don't—"

"Hey." Carter caught Spence's arm and pulled him back. "Give her a minute, Spence."

She appreciated the support. With her head spinning and her knees weak, she doubted she could get out of there without falling down. She'd never appreciated Jackson's supportive arm as much.

But a part of her did ache for Spence. For the grief

and pain she saw in his eyes. For the way his mouth dropped open and stayed there, as if he didn't know what to say.

She tried to smile at him but couldn't quite get there. "We'll talk soon."

She gave his arm a quick squeeze, and then she was gone.

Spence couldn't move. His brain screamed to go after her. Forget Carter's well-meaning warnings and Jackson's small head shake. He'd screwed this up in every way possible. Let his history with his father ruin his chance with Abby.

Back then it had seemed so simple. His father made moves on women all the time. Married or not, he was always looking for what else was out there. He'd flirted with women Spence dated until he learned never to bring them around the house or work. Having a thing for Abby, who was right there in the office, threw Spence's usual routine out of whack. He couldn't keep her away from his dad.

That was his one defense. He'd been using it since high school when Spence walked into the kitchen one night and saw his dad standing at the sink with his hand on Spence's then-girlfriend's lower back. They were whispering and laughing. He doubted anything actually happened, but it was so wrong. Dominating and sick.

Spence had been wary and on the lookout ever since. So, when he walked in on that kiss he thought… Bile rushed up the back of his throat at the memory.

"What is going on?" Derrick burst into the library, frowning and wide-eyed with confusion. "You all disappeared and Abby just ran out of here. Not actually, but she sure looked spooked."

Carter frowned. "Dad."

"Eldrick is here?" Derrick's mouth fell and his tone flattened. "Lucky us."

"He and Beth—"

"Wait." Derrick held up a hand. "Who is Beth?"

"Yeah, that's a confusing piece of the story. Apparently, we call his wife Beth now. Believe it or not, you'll like her." Carter shook his head. "But the point is Dad admitted to sexually harassing Abby and setting her up with that kiss to scare Spence off."

Spence appreciated Carter's explanation because he wasn't sure he could get one out right now. He wasn't sure of anything. He glanced at his watch, trying to calculate how much time he should wait before going to see Abby. Jackson might have the answer. Spence half hoped Jackson also would know what to say because Spence was clueless. There wasn't an apology big enough to handle this.

"I can't…" Derrick slipped his fingers through his hair. "I asked her back then, but…" He looked at Carter. "Is she okay?"

Carter shrugged. "She unloaded, so hopefully she will be."

"What about you?" Derrick glanced at Spence. "You okay?"

"No."

Carter gave him a reassuring pat on the shoulder. "You will be, too. Give it time."

Spence wasn't convinced.

Nine

Spence waited for two days. Sunday dragged by with him texting Abby and not receiving a response. Carter had convinced him to wait a little longer and Ellie agreed. Jackson fed him some updates. On Monday, she didn't show up for work and Spence's nerves were shot. He had this image of her packing and leaving town. That was his thing and he was desperate for her not to repeat his mistakes.

The sick thing sounded like subterfuge. Derrick said that never happened. He couldn't remember a day Abby had missed since starting with the company. And that did it. Spence spent the afternoon trying to come up with a plan that didn't come off controlling and rude like his father. Spence didn't want to be that guy. Ever.

But she was in hiding. Not her style and not something Spence had expected, but that's what he got. He had to deal with it. True, she deserved some peace and time to think. He tried to give it to her. He really did. But at seven on Monday night, he stepped into the lobby of her condo building and met up with Jackson.

"I hope I don't regret letting you in," Jackson said as they walked to the elevator.

Yeah, that made two of them. "Get in line."

The fact Jackson was comfortable there, that he got in and out and on the security-protected elevator without trouble had Spence's mind spinning. He grabbed on to the bar behind him in the elevator as the car started to move. He hoped the stranglehold would keep him from doing or saying something stupid.

After a few seconds of silence, he opened his mouth anyway. "She's—"

"Not expecting you," Jackson said.

Spence couldn't figure out if that was a good idea or not. Showing up unannounced might be a jerk move. Honestly, he'd pulled so many with her he couldn't tell where the line was anymore.

"Are you planning to stick around and referee?" Part of Spence didn't hate the idea. Strength in numbers and all that. Having reinforcements might not be bad, either, since he expected Abby to be furious.

The rest of him wanted Jackson out. The majority part. This was private, or it should be. The unloading, the telling of what happened back then, played out in front of an audience. She deserved an empty room for whatever else she needed to say. And he would take it. He owed her that much.

"You really have been gone a long time." A mass of keys and security fobs jangled in Jackson's hand.

"What?"

Jackson shook his head as he smiled. "I forgot we've

been hanging out over at Derrick's place or going out to eat since you've been back. So, you don't know."

The elevator bell dinged and the doors opened. Spence stepped out into the hall, not sure where to go or how to interpret Jackson's unusual ramblings.

"Any chance you're going to explain?" Spence asked.

Jackson nodded. "Follow me."

He turned left and started down the hall. Stopped in front of the first door and pointed at it. "She lives here."

Then he kept walking. Got to the next door and stopped. "This is mine."

Spence's heart stopped. For a second, he couldn't breathe. "You live in the same building? On the same floor?"

Next to each other. That struck Spence as convenient and frustrating, and his anxiety spun out of control inside him.

"Abby told me about a good deal. I jumped in, bought low and became her neighbor." Jackson winked at him. "But before you panic, and I can see it welling up in you already, I'm still only her good friend. Nothing more."

"Why?" Spence couldn't imagine another man not wanting her. Not making a move. Loyalty, sure, and none of the brothers or Jackson had ever tried to ask another's ex out, but still. The proximity, their clear chemistry.

"It was never going to happen." Jackson shook his head. "Because you love her."

There was that word again. Spence kept waiting for his brain to reject it, but it didn't happen.

The lock clicked and Jackson opened his door. "Don't mess this up."

When the bell bonged, Abby glared at the front door to her condo. She'd just sank down into the corner seat of her sectional. Arranged the blankets and pillows just right around her. Had a box of tissues on one side. The remote control on her lap. Medicine, water bottle and a cup of lemon tea right in front of her.

When the bell rang out a second time, she cursed under her breath. This could only be a handful of people. No one buzzed to come upstairs. The phone didn't ring from the front desk to ask her permission to send someone to her. Jackson had a key. That left someone in the building or maintenance.

She stomped across her living room, ignoring the way her bright purple slippers clapped against the hardwood floor. She wore sweatpants and a shirt. No bra. Someone was about to get a show.

She peeked in the peephole and froze. Clearly the bad cold or the medicine or just life in general was making her vision blur. There was no way Spence stood out there. None.

"What?" She shouted the question through the door.

"Abby, please let me in."

Yep, same silky voice. A defeated muffled tone, maybe, but that probably had something to do with him standing in the hallway.

But there was no use in ignoring him. That was easy on the phone. Harder when he hovered outside her door. She opened it and stared at him. "What?"

Whatever tough stance she was trying to take likely was ruined when she sniffled. Stupid cold.

He frowned at her. "You really are sick?"

Of all the things he could have said, that one was unexpected. "Of course. I don't hide. Like I'd give your father that satisfaction."

Oh, she'd wanted to. She'd even toyed with the idea. When the fever hit her on Saturday night after the big showdown with Eldrick, she'd chalked it up to frazzled nerves. By the next morning when she couldn't lift her head off the pillow, she realized it was something else.

Needing to sit down, she left Spence at the door and walked back to her sectional. The cushions had never looked so inviting. She flipped off the slippers and slid into her cocoon of covers. Didn't even look at him again until her head rested against the pillows propping her up from behind.

He stood over her, watching her. His gaze traveled over her. Not sexual. No, this felt like he was conducting an inventory. "When did you get sick?"

"I'd been fighting it off for about a week." She lifted her head in the direction of the pill bottle on the ottoman. "I took some medicine I happened to have here and thought I caught it in time, but no."

He sat on the edge of the couch. About a foot away from her. "It's not healthy to self-medicate."

"You sound like my doctor." She was kind of tired of men telling her she was wrong about things. Not a rational response, she knew. But still.

He looked around the condo. His gaze zipped to her modern kitchen and the sleek white quartz countertop. To the dishes piled in her sink. "Have you eaten?"

She cuddled deeper into the cushions and let his deep voice wash over her. "It's amazing what you can have delivered in this town."

"True."

That's all he said. He didn't move or try to get closer. She sensed he wanted to say something and she was not in the mood to make any of this easier on him. Now wasn't the right time and she didn't have the strength to carry on much of a conversation, but she could sit there and listen.

"I'll handle these." He stood up and stripped off his suit jacket. Threw it over her chair. The stupid thing hung there like it belonged in her condo.

She hated that.

"What are you talking about?" she asked as she watched those long legs carry him to the other side of the condo.

He stepped into the open kitchen and rolled up his shirtsleeves. "The dishes."

Did he just say… "Are you kidding?"

He shrugged. "Seems like the least I can do."

"You know how to do dishes?"

He looked up at her. "I'm not totally useless."

"No one said *totally*."

She thought she saw him smile at her joke as he went to work. Those long fingers soaped up the dishes. She considered reminding him she had a dishwasher, but it was right there. Surely he could see it.

No, she sensed this was something else. As if he were paying penance.

He cleaned in silence for the first five minutes. Then he started to talk. "I learned young to shut down. My dad would yell because nothing was ever good enough for him. I'd take myself out of the middle of it. Some days, he and Derrick would go at it." Spence shook his head as if he were reliving a memory in his mind. "Unbelievable."

She didn't say anything. The cadence of his voice comforted her. Getting a peek into his childhood seemed to chase some of the germs away.

"Eldrick Jameson is not a good man. He was a terrible, distant, mean father. Hell, he wasn't even much of a businessman. Derrick had to rescue the company from Dad's overspending and bad choices." Spence folded the towel and hung it on the bar on the stove. "Other kids had it much worse. I get that. We never wanted for anything. Dad kept up the outside appearances. Played the role of family man."

Abby thought about Eldrick's series of marriages. Of all the goodwill he'd run through in his life.

Spence walked back into the living room. She moved over a bit to silently tell him he could sit next to her.

He took the hint. Dropped into the cushions and snaked his arm along the back of the sectional. Didn't touch her. Didn't even come close, but having him near felt reassuring in an odd way.

"You weren't the first girlfriend he approached...and I know I'm taking liberties with that word." He waited until she nodded to continue. "But he'd made passes before. Sometimes the ploy worked, sometimes not. It chipped away at my trust of him and the women I was attracted to. Of myself."

Spence picked at a spot on the cushion. Sat in silence for a few seconds before continuing. "He knew I was likely to run if he pushed too hard and tested me all the time. Made it clear I didn't deserve anything in the company or in the way of a home life because I hadn't proven myself."

"He really was terrible." She hadn't meant to say that. It slipped out but it wasn't wrong.

"Still is, though Beth might turn out to be one of his better choices." Spence exhaled. "He's currently sending us through this list of tasks we have to perform in order for him to turn the company over."

"What's yours?"

"I don't know." Spence barked out a harsh laugh. "He gave Derrick an envelope for me but I never opened it. I was too busy trying to figure out where we stood."

We? She had no idea but she wasn't ready for this conversation either. "Spence, I—"

"I'm not asking. It was just an explanation." His hand dropped and his fingers moved closer to her shoulder, but he still didn't touch her.

She sensed he might not unless she gave permission. And that was not going to happen...yet.

"I learned this defense. Carter and I both did. We took off. Carter traveled. I tried to forget everything here and all my regrets."

She tipped her head back and looked at him. Let her gaze linger over his tired face and the dark circles under his eyes. "Am I a regret?"

"You are amazing. Smart and beautiful, funny and quick." He shot her a cute smile. "Sexy as hell. That pantry was basically every one of my fantasies brought to life." His smile faded. "But I messed up before. I do regret running out on you, not believing you. Breaking your trust before I really had a chance to earn it."

"I guess you had a reason not to trust so easily." She'd never admitted that before. Never even let it enter her head. In every scenario that ran through her mind, she was the sole victim in Eldrick's schemes. But now she saw that wasn't quite true.

"Don't give me an out, Abby." His fingers slipped lower then. Right next to her shoulder. Brushing against it in a soothing gesture. "I'm a grown man. I was done playing Eldrick's games but that doesn't excuse leaving you here to deal with him."

"He bolted soon after." She had been so happy that day. Happy every day since when he stayed gone.

Spence shook his head. "That's not my point."

She lifted her hand and covered his. Let their fingers tangle together. "I know."

They sat there in silence. Images ran across the television screen. She'd turned the sound off when the doorbell rang and hadn't turned it back on. Now they both watched the show, some detective thing with a lot of running, without any noise or talking.

She tugged him a bit closer. Felt the cushion dip when he slid over and wrapped an arm around her shoulders. The sex had been so good. Not smart, because she hadn't insisted on a condom and at some point they needed to talk about that, but hot and right and almost cleansing in the force of it. But this felt pretty great, too. The silence. The calm.

Her fingers slipped over the remote, but she still didn't turn on the sound. She didn't want to break the mood. Not when she could concentrate on the way his breath blew over her forehead, and how every now and then, he would turn his head to place a chaste kiss on her hair.

"I know I need to earn back your trust," he said into the quiet as darkness fell outside the windows behind the couch. "I just want you to think about giving me the chance to do that."

Hope soared inside her and her heartbeat kicked up. The traitorous thing. The answer *yes* screamed inside her head but she didn't say it out loud. Not yet. Not when Eldrick was still in town and Spence's propensity to flee hadn't been resolved. And she still needed to deal with Jeff Berger and whatever stupid thing he had planned for her.

She glanced up at Spence. Let her gaze wander over his lips. "I actually am hungry."

A smile broke out on his lips. This one genuine and warming. "What do you want?"

She turned just a bit under his arm so she could see him better. "You mean you can cook, too?"

"I order things." He suddenly looked so serious. "I'm really good at ordering."

The joking almost did her in, but she held on to her control. This would take time to fix. "You just ruined my image of you as this big domestic guy who could do anything in the house."

His eyebrow lifted. "Oh, I have skills. When you're feeling better, I'll show you."

Her heart jumped. "Interesting." Man, it so was.

"But for now..." He lifted his hips and slid his phone out of his back pocket. Started clicking on the keys. "You're getting soup."

It was the right answer but she wrinkled up her nose at the suggestion anyway. "I want a burger."

He shot her a side-eye. "I'll buy you as many as you want as soon as you're feeling better."

"That's a pretty good incentive to get well." So was he, but she didn't mention it.

"Then soup it is." He dropped a quick kiss on her forehead. "We'll get back to the good stuff soon enough."

For the first time in months she believed that. "You're on."

Ten

The next week passed by in a happy blur. They didn't get naked again, which Spence regretted, but it was the right answer. He was willing to give Abby as much time as she needed and hoped the answer wasn't forever.

She was feeling better and back to work, having missed only one day. Her so-called easier schedule quickly gave way to long meetings and even longer workdays. They went to dinner, talked, watched movies on her sectional, and then he went home each night after a lingering kiss. That was the new cycle.

Since Beth had dragged Eldrick right back out of town after the scene in the Virginia estate library, it was easy to ignore his calls. Even easier to ignore the stupid envelope with his To Do list for keeping the business. It sat unopened on the dresser in the bedroom Spence still used in Derrick and Ellie's house. She was still resting but up more. Keeping Carter entertained and Derrick smiling.

It was all so normal. Well, normal for other people. Spence didn't know what to do or what to think. He stayed on edge, waiting for the bad news to come. Because it always did.

In her second week back, they had a morning status meeting, covering several projects, and then Abby had a business lunch. Something she'd been putting off and moved on her calendar twice. He didn't know what it was but he trusted her. They were...*dating*. He guessed that was the right word, but who knew. He wasn't about to ask, because he didn't want to scare her away. Not when things were going well.

Right now she was sitting in a conference room chair, pummeling Rylan with questions. "When will the report be done?"

He shifted the papers around in front of him on the conference room table. Abby had insisted on scheduling them for the big room. The one with expensive artwork hanging on the walls and the blackout curtains. It spoke to the company's success and provided a level of intimidation.

The whole thing was wildly enjoyable for Spence to watch.

"I need—"

"Rylan, I am done playing with this." Abby leaned back in her chair. "You know I am."

Something had changed in the relationship between Abby and Rylan. It had always been professional, respectful and still was, but Abby's patience had seemingly expired. There was a charged energy in the room. Gone was Rylan's flirting and Abby's gentle coaxing. She was going in for the kill.

"I finished," Rylan said in a flat tone. "You set a deadline and I met it."

He pushed a report across the table. A letter attached to a thick binder with folded blueprints tucked inside.

Abby didn't touch it. "I thought so."

"The project has been approved. There are no more impediments to getting started on the work." Rylan couldn't have sounded less excited if he were talking about toothpaste.

Spence was pretty sure he'd missed a step. No question the Abby-Rylan dynamic had flipped. Rylan actually looked a little afraid of her, which was probably a wise choice. Abby walked into the meeting looking all professional and no-nonsense in her trim black suit. Rylan usually let his gaze travel a bit. He'd wait until she turned and would sneak a few peeks. Not today.

Spence found the outfit sexy as hell. That little bit of light blue stuck out from the top of her buttoned jacket had sent his control careening into a wall. He'd seen the jacket unbuttoned earlier in her office. He knew the shirt was silky and thin and all he wanted to do was get his hands under it.

He really hoped he earned that right back soon.

"If that's all?" Rylan stood up before he finished the sentence.

"You've signed everything?" Abby just stared at the man, still not touching the paperwork she'd pushed so hard to get completed. "I don't want any surprises."

"No, we're done."

She nodded. "Good answer."

A minute later, he was packed up and Spence showed him out the door. Handed him off to an assistant, then stepped back into the conference room. The satisfied grin on Abby's face suggested she liked how that battle ended.

"Want to clue me in?" he asked.

Her head jerked up. "What?"

"That was a big change in attitude. You were coddling him, letting him take the maximum time to ensure the project got approved. It's exactly what I would have done since Rylan seems like the type who craves attention." Minus the flirting, of course. Spence was pretty sure Rylan wouldn't have tried that tactic on him. Spence leaned against the table and faced her where she still sat in the chair. "He went from drooling over you and dragging his feet to jumping to your every demand."

She shrugged. "We had a chat and I made my position clear."

"Which means?"

"I told him he had misstepped if he thought he had a chance at something with me. Also made it clear I wanted the job done."

"Uh-huh." That sounded like half a story to Spence. "Did he actually make a pass at you?"

A week ago that question might have sent her temper spiking. It could have led to a fight, with one of them storming out. But that had changed, too. Spence no longer weighed every word. He was careful but not wary.

She stood up. Let her hand trail over his thigh. Low enough to be decent but with enough pressure to pull his mind away from the office. "Abby…"

"I made it clear that it would be stupid for him to try anything." She rubbed her thumb back and forth over a crease in his pants.

"Are you trying to prove to me that you can handle him?"

"Didn't I?"

"You did, but I already knew that you would." His hand went to her waist and he toyed with one of the buttons holding the sides of her jacket together. "Any chance I can convince you to skip your meeting and have lunch with me?"

By "lunch," he meant not eating. He'd settle for an actual meal, but his control was wavering. The more he watched her in action at work and cuddled with her on the couch at night, the more he wanted everything. And the more Jackson's use of the word *love* didn't seem so misplaced. Not that he was ready to talk about that, because he wasn't.

"Derrick would be impressed with your work ethic," she said.

Spence and Derrick had an understanding. Spence knew his strengths and Derrick didn't try to redirect those. "My skills tend to be best used in going out and getting us new projects to bid on, or better yet, just win outright."

"Always the salesman."

"It takes a lot of time and study." He stood up, letting his hand linger on her stomach. "Weeks, sometimes months, of reviewing everything to find the right course of action."

"Are we still talking about work?"

Not really. "Of course."

She tugged on the bottom of his tie. "How about this. We both be good employees this afternoon, then we'll meet up for dinner."

He liked the way her mind worked. "I can make a reservation."

"At my place." She skimmed a finger down the buttons of his shirt. "We'll stay in."

All the blood rushed from his head. The idea of a night with her, even just holding her, sounded so good. "You sure?"

"I hear you're very skilled at doing dishes."

He had to smile at that. She could charm and seduce him into just about anything. "Not to brag but I'm good at a lot of things."

"I plan to let you prove that to me."

With one battle done, Abby moved on to the next one. Last week, as soon as her bad cold passed, she'd called Rylan. Made it clear to him that passing notes to her from other businessmen was both juvenile and a move guaranteed to haunt him. She mentioned filing a complaint. Then she talked about telling Spence about what really happened and how Rylan let Jeff Berger use him.

She'd dropped every threat she could think of to teach him a lesson. Once she had his full attention, telling him he had exactly one week to finish his work and deliver his report had been easy, and he beat her deadline by a few days.

She suspected this meeting with Jeff would not run as smoothly.

They met in a noisy restaurant. One of those impossible-to-get-reservations type in a building that used to be a bank or a warehouse or something. It had soaring ceilings and the bar stretched out along one side with an open kitchen in the back.

The servers shared a similar look. She thought of it as unshaven, hair-in-a-bun male Pacific Northwest vibe. It fit with the decor and the all-black serving outfits. They seemed to know Jeff and hovered around the table, trying to please him. Even called him by name.

She wrote the whole scene off as more of his power-play antics. He wanted to impress her, make her think he controlled everything. Whatever.

What he didn't understand is she'd already taken on Eldrick and Rylan this week and somehow managed to tame Spence into potential boyfriend material at the same time. Whatever threats Jeff had planned would be just one in a long line she intended to bat down.

She ignored the menu in front of her and reached for the water glass. Taking a sip, she glanced around the main dining room. Saw the plates of salad and bottles of wine being delivered to tables. Heard the clink of silverware as she tried to decipher the mumble of conversation around her.

Jeff's heavy sigh broke through the action. He slipped an envelope across the table. "Here is an explanation of what we need and compensation for your time. Just as we discussed."

"We never discussed anything."

He frowned at her. "Don't play hard to get."

The man was savvy. Abby guessed there was a typed note and cash in there. Didn't matter because she didn't intend to open it and find out. She slid it back across the table in his direction. "Not interested."

Jeff made a big show of folding his menu and putting it aside. He leaned in with his elbows on the edge of the table. "Now, Abby. You don't even know what I'm offering."

Turned out this meal was exactly what she thought it was about—trying to get her to spy on Jameson Industries. She wasn't interested in anything from Jeff but she sure wasn't interested in that.

"A trip to nowhere." She looked around for the restroom. From there she could make an easy escape. That sounded smarter than risking Jeff making a scene. "No, thanks."

She turned in her chair and started to get up.

Jeff's hand clamped down on her wrist. "Sit down."

She didn't jerk back or start yelling. Didn't give him

the satisfaction of knowing his touch made her want to throw up the stale protein bar she'd choked down before coming into the restaurant fifteen minutes ago. "Amazing how you become less charming when you don't get what you want."

"I tried this the nice way. I offered you a job months ago, and you said no. I just offered you an easy way to make extra money and you pushed it away." He dropped her wrist and sat back again. "Do you see what I'm saying?"

She refused to rub her wrist to alleviate the burning sensation of his hold. "That you can't take no for an answer."

"You're the problem here, Abby."

She was just about done with overbearing businessmen. Seeing how others operated made her appreciate Derrick and Spence's style even more. No wonder Eldrick had thought he could get away with bullying. Apparently, it was the go-to move for many just like him.

But the comment did intrigue her. She gave in to her curiosity. Maybe this way she could prepare for whatever he had planned for the future. "How do you figure that?"

"I'm done losing to Derrick." Jeff shook his head. "All I need is some information. Not on every job, of course. That would look suspicious."

In other words, Jeff couldn't compete on a fair playing field. Good to know. "I work there. Screwing him screws me."

"You have a safety net in my office in the form of any managerial position you want. I'll make up a title for you."

Right, because that's how this worked. Once she broke the trust in one office, her reputation would be in shambles. No one would hire her, not even Jeff. But that didn't even matter because she wasn't tempted. Just because Jeff was that type didn't mean she was.

He'd made a similar offer at the lowest point in her business career. She'd been harassed and just lost Spence. Felt vulnerable and convinced she'd be fired. She guessed she'd given off a pathetic vibe. But still, she didn't bite then. She had no idea why Jeff thought she would now.

"You're asking the wrong person. I don't play like this." She had pride and integrity and didn't plan to forfeit either.

"You're going to regret this." Jeff stared at the untouched envelope then picked it up again. Slipped it in his jacket pocket.

"The lunch? I already do."

"We'll see how funny you think this is after…"

After what? She was dying to know. "Goodbye, Jeff."

She got up and forced her legs to move. Something about his tone and that last comment pulled at her as she walked away. The words could mean anything. But she'd learned early to expect the worst. Now she did.

Eleven

Spence followed her home that night. Abby left about fifteen minutes before he did because he got stuck on a phone call about a problem with a project at the University of Maryland. One of those calls he couldn't just jump off of because there were ten other bored people in on it who also wanted to get off the line.

The second after he hung up, he raced out of the office. Tried to act professional and nod and smile to everyone he passed in the office hallway but his insides churned. He'd heard the whispers about him dating Abby. Even spoke with Derrick about them. The conclusion was that Human Resources should talk to Abby to make sure she was okay. People dated. He and Abby knew the dangers because they'd already lived through them once. Mostly.

That left a clear line between him and Abby tonight. Except for the ongoing trust issues, his idiot father and the very real sense she was hiding something from him. All of those issues stayed stacked in a teetering tower between them, but Spence was ready to unpack.

He also ached to touch her again. Once had not been enough. The hurried sex in the pantry could only be described as explosive. He wanted to experience the joy of slowly getting to know her body. And that could happen tonight…unless he misread the cues, in which case dinner worked, too.

She'd slipped him a note with the security code for the garage and the number of the space to park in. Then, Abby being Abby, she re-sent the information by text. The numbers mixed with his memories of the pantry and clouded in his brain, but he managed to get inside the gate.

The elevator turned out to be tougher because it required the guy at the desk to call up and get permission from Abby to let him in. For one tense second, he worried she'd changed her mind and would say no, but the guy waved him up.

That was five minutes ago. Now he got off the elevator and shot Jackson's front door a quick look. Having him so close by rattled Spence but he pretended it wasn't a big thing.

He raised his hand to knock on Abby's door right as it opened. She stood there, hair falling over her shoulders and a welcoming smile on her face.

He almost lost it.

Somehow he managed to lean in for a quick kiss. Even the slight touch of their lips had his heart racing until the echo of it thumped in his ears. He stepped inside the condo and closed the door behind him. After turning the lock, he followed her inside the open space.

The condo was new, with top-end everything. Her

bedroom sat shadowed off to the right. He tried not to think about that room. Keeping his mind off the floor plan proved easy because he had something else—something much more interesting—to focus on right now.

Abby walked from the entryway through to the living room with those impressive hips swaying as she stepped. The drapes were drawn on the floor-to-ceiling windows behind her couch. Lamps lit the area in a soft glow. And she was wearing a dress. She'd been in a suit all day. He remembered because he'd thought about her skirt and the way it rode up her thighs, just a touch, as she walked.

The dress was solid red and bold. It wrapped around her with a same-color tie at her waist. He'd never seen it before but he was a fan.

As she stood there, her head tilted to the side and her hair cascaded over her shoulder. "Are you hungry?"

"Starving." He wasn't even sure if he could choke down food right now, but it seemed like a good answer. Logical in light of the time of night and the agreement they had to find food.

She made a humming sound. "That's a shame."

The list of take-out restaurants running through his brain slammed to a halt. "Excuse me?"

That smile, wide and inviting. Man, there was no way he was going to survive that. The seductive curve of her lips promised excitement. Or maybe he was still daydreaming. He honestly couldn't tell.

Reality blended with fantasy when he looked at her. Long legs and that face. Big eyes, full lips…yeah, he was lost. He had no defense against her.

She kept her hands at her side as she walked over to him. He would have moved but he was pretty sure his feet were welded to the floor. No part of him even flinched except the growing bulge in his pants. He really hoped that didn't make her twitchy. Another few minutes of her staring and she would notice. She couldn't *not* notice.

After a few yanks, she undid his tie and slipped it off his neck. Her fingers went to the buttons at the very top and opened two. When she slipped her hands inside the opening and placed her warm palm against his chest, he jumped. Couldn't help it.

"Are we eating?" The question sat out there. He sounded like he'd never had sex before, and he had. Plenty of times. But he didn't want to take a wrong turn here. He really wanted her to lead and take them down that hallway to her bedroom.

"You did say you were starving." She slipped her thumb up his throat to the bottom of his chin. Brushed it back and forth.

That touch fueled him. Spun him up and readied him for more.

"I can't remember what I said." He wasn't sure how he drove there without crashing the car.

"When?"

"Ever."

"That thing you do where you lose your speech when you touch me?" She leaned in and ran her tongue along the top of his ear then whispered, "Very sexy."

His cells caught on fire. He could smell her shampoo and feel her soft hair skim over his cheek. And that body. She leaned in, pressing her chest against his and his brain misfired.

"I don't want to misread…"

"I like when you're careful but you need to catch up

here." She bit down on his earlobe as she talked. Not hard but enough to get his attention.

The whisper of her voice echoed around him. He pulled back and looked at her. His gaze traveled over her face, looking for any sign of hesitancy. The blush on her cheeks and heat of her skin said yes. When her tongue peeked out, licked over his bottom lip, he may have said something. Who knew?

She shifted slightly and got a hand between them. With her fingers on that tie around her waist, she tugged. The belt came undone and the material keeping the dress closed slid open, revealing miles of perfect skin. She wore a pink bra that pushed her breasts up until they spilled over the tops of the cups and a tiny scrap that he guessed qualified as bikini bottoms.

It was a miracle his legs held him. Every thought about taking it slow left his head. Ran right out of there.

"I'm going to dream about this dress." He really wanted to buy her a thousand more like it. She could pick the colors. He did not care.

"About getting me out of it, I hope." With a shrug of her shoulders, she let the material slide off and fall to the floor with a swish. It pooled around her bare feet. Covered the soft purple polish covering her toes.

That choking sensation? He was pretty sure he swallowed his tongue. "Most definitely."

His words sounded garbled and a strange layer of fuzziness clogged his head. Whatever control he normally had he'd forfeited when he walked in the door.

A deep inhale didn't help. Neither did a silent count to ten. So, he gave in and touched her. Reached out and wrapped his arms around her. Lifted her off the floor and sighed in relief when her thighs clamped down against the outsides of his legs.

"It is unreal how sexy you are." Dabble filled his brain, so he wasn't a hundred percent sure what he'd said, but she smiled.

Fingers slipped through his hair as her other hand skimmed down his back. "Still hungry?"

The light bulb clicked on in his mind. He finally figured out she wasn't talking about food. "I'll show you in the bedroom."

Somehow he got them there. Walked backward for part of it. Knocked his arm against the door frame and bit back a curse. Once he righted himself, he started moving again. His elbow slammed into the wall as he searched for the light switch. Then it was on and all he could see was her face above him and the bedroom right behind her.

He didn't waste any time. He stepped up to the edge of the mattress and lowered her. Let her slip down his legs. As soon as she sat down, her fingers went to work on his belt then his zipper. He tried to breathe in, rushed to get air in his lungs as she lowered her head and took him in her mouth.

One swipe of her tongue. One press of her hand against him, fingers around him, and his control snapped. As gently as possible, he pulled her away from him. His hands shook with the need to throw her back on the bed, but she did it for him. With excruciating slowness, she leaned back. Pressed her back on the mattress and flung her arms out to her sides.

She winked at him. "Why are you still dressed?"

Good question. He nearly ripped his shirt off then yanked his pants down. Probably set a speed record in getting naked. Then he crawled up her body, rubbing against her, over her. The resulting friction had him gasping.

"Condom." He couldn't forget this time. He'd never gone without protection before her. Before Abby and that pantry.

He didn't regret it, but he could do better. He owed her that along with so many other things.

He scrambled off the bed as she called out his name. Man, he loved the sound of his full name on her lips.

"Spencer, what are you…" She smiled when she saw the condom in his hand. "Yes."

"We'll be more careful this time." While she was sick, he'd texted her about birth control and their failure to use any. She assured him she was on the Pill, but they'd agreed a repeat of that move was not smart.

"Why are you still talking?" she asked as she reached up and pulled him back on top of her.

He kissed her then. Let out all the pent-up need and desire and plowed them both under. Kissed her until the blood ran from his head and his lower half pulsed with the need to strip her underwear off and throw it on the floor.

When he lifted his head, she looked dazed. Smiling with swollen lips and big watchful eyes.

"You are so beautiful." He meant it. Every word.

He'd never had any woman break through his defenses and reach inside him like she had. Through everything, all the pain and distrust, he could never wipe her from his mind. Now he knew he didn't have to.

His hand slipped behind her back to unclip her bra. Peeling it off her was like unwrapping the best present. His breath caught in his throat as his mouth dipped to kiss her. He ran his tongue over her, around her nipples, and felt her fingers clench in his hair.

Slow. She deserved all of his attention for as long as he could handle it. But then her hand snaked down his body. Those fingers wrapped around his length. He had to rest his forehead against hers as he gulped in air and wrestled for control.

"Spencer." She brought her knees up until the inside of her thighs pressed against his sides. "Go faster."

The words pummeled him and the urge to give in grabbed him. But this was for her. Tonight, and for as many nights as she would give him. "Soon."

He moved down her body, kissing a trail over her bare skin. Loving every inch of her softness, each curve. He reached her stomach and pressed a kiss on the slight bump he found so sexy. When she gasped, he did it again.

Turning his head to the side, he rubbed his cheek against her bare skin. "You are perfect."

"You…" Her back arched off the bed and those heels dug into the mattress.

There, sprawled out with her chest rising and falling on harsh breaths, she silently called out to him. Looked so inviting.

His mouth dipped lower. A finger slipped inside her as she shifted on the bed. He circled and caressed until her thighs clenched against his shoulders. He would never get a clearer sign of how ready she was, and he didn't wait for one.

Up on his knees, he rolled on the condom. Then his body slid over hers again. He pressed inside. Keeping his thrust slow and steady, he pushed until her body tightened around his. His brain, his muscles—every part of him—begged for release. But he held back. He needed to know she'd gotten there before he let go.

Her breaths came in pants now. Her exposed neck enticed him as her head pressed deep into the pillows. She grabbed the comforter, balling it in her fists. With every second, her control slipped further away and it was amazing to watch.

Her skin glowed as sweat gathered on his forehead. Pressure built inside him, clawing at him. Still, he didn't give in. He slipped his hand between their bodies. Touched her as he pumped in and out.

The trembling started in her legs. He could feel the muscles vibrate against him as the pulses started moving through her. Her hips lifted and her hands grabbed on to his shoulder. He waited until the last second, until she gasped and her body bucked, before he gave in to his own orgasm. It rolled through him, wiping everything else out.

For those few minutes, it was just him and her and the rhythm pounding in his head as he pushed into her. When the explosion came, all he could do was ride it out. Hold on to her, wrap his body around hers and give himself over to it.

It took a bit more time for his body to calm and the pulsing to stop. Reality came back to him in pieces. Her fingers brushing over his shoulder lured him in. He buried his face in her shoulder and inhaled. He'd get up, move—do something. Soon. But not yet...

He didn't know how long he rested with her on the bed with his eyes closed. It really didn't matter since she'd curled into his side with her hand on his chest. He slipped his palm up and down the soft skin of her arm, loving the feel of her.

This felt right. He'd ached for this, dreamed about it, got angry that he couldn't stop thinking about what this might feel like when he left. Being away from her and adrift, not having any real direction, was the answer then. He'd needed to clear his head. Yeah, he got the facts wrong and blamed her instead of dumping it all on his father where it belonged. After those few stunned seconds, he'd been so willing to believe the man who raised him and always disappointed him. Spence knew now that he needed to break the habit.

He was about to drift off to sleep when she started talking. She leaned up on her elbow and stared down at him. "May I ask you a question?"

And that destroyed any chance of him sleeping, possibly ever. He couldn't think of a time when that question ended well. "Why do I think I should say no? I mean, I can only mess up from here, right?"

She smiled as her fingertip traced his lips. "You're not going to mess up."

"I like how much faith you have in me." He folded the arm that wasn't holding her behind his head. "Go ahead."

"What are we?"

The wording was strange but he knew exactly what she meant. They'd spent every evening together since she got over being sick. He planned to repeat that pattern next week and for many after that. "You sure know how to lead with the big questions."

"There's gossip at work and—"

"Does that bother you?" Maybe he'd been too casual about the boss thing. He'd taken himself off all of her projects. He would be there if she needed to consult but they restored Derrick as her direct line of supervision. It was neater that way. A separation of work and private life. Better for her in case she did have an issue.

"Not if whatever is between us is real."

The words beat back the anxiety welling inside of him. He had an easy answer for this. "It's real."

"Are you just saying that?" Her eyes narrowed but amusement still lingered in her voice.

Despite her light tone, he took the question very seriously. "Because we're naked and in your bed and I'm hoping I get to stay here? No. I'm saying the words because they're true. Because they've been true and probably were even back when I messed up and pushed you away."

She blew out a long breath as her hand came to rest on his chest again. "I hate what happened to us back then."

Now was the right time for the apology. Nothing fancy. Just the truth.

"I'm sorry. Sorry I didn't listen or trust you." He brushed her hair off her cheek. "Sorry I didn't punch my dad in the face."

"I don't want to come between you."

Spence almost laughed at that. Might have if she didn't look so serious. "Not possible. There's no relationship to ruin. Not anything meaningful."

"Don't say that."

Spence refused to get into that argument now. She was decent and loving and probably thought Eldrick might have some good hidden down deep inside him. Spence knew better. Even with Beth's coaxing, Eldrick would never be a guy Spence trusted around Abby. Not again.

He needed her to understand Eldrick wasn't between them. "But this—us—it is worth saving."

Her eyes got all shiny. "So, we're in this."

A lump clogged his throat, but he swallowed it down. "We're in it."

Her mood switched again. This time to playful as she climbed on top of him. Straddled his hips.

"Good. Now we can have dinner." She poked him in the chest. "I seem to remember you owing me a burger."

"At your service, ma'am."

Twelve

The next week passed in a haze of happiness. A voice in Abby's head told her to be careful, not to let herself enjoy it too much because it could be snatched away so quickly.

She'd never gone for long stretches without something going wrong. Like, spectacularly wrong. A bad boyfriend, a huge problem at work. Having to move. A huge expense she hadn't prepared for. Running out of money. Until she'd found stability with her job at Jameson, the last two years had been a constant strain.

Just to be safe, the only thing she'd spent any money on since she started receiving the big paycheck was her condo. She figured she always could sell it if finances grew tight again. It was her rainy-day fund, in a way.

Looking around the dining room table now, she couldn't call up any of those bad memories or nagging worries. Probably had something to do with how loud the Jameson family was. Man, they could talk about *anything*. Carter, specifically, was a pro at talking.

They'd all gathered to celebrate the news from Ellie's doctor that she could move around a bit more. She came back from her appointment two days ago and declared a family dinner was in order. Verbally walked all over Derrick's objections and made it happen. To make her happy, and everyone seemed determined to do that, they gathered.

Even now they passed a roast, vegetables and potatoes around the long rectangle table in Derrick and Ellie's dining room. Dishes clanked as Carter and Jackson argued about the benefits of mashed potatoes over all other potato dishes. Jackson's sister and Ellie's best friend, Vanessa, couldn't make it on short notice, and Ellie's brother was away at some computer seminar, but everyone else was there.

"Are you okay?" Spence whispered the question in Abby's ear as he leaned in closer.

She reached out and slid her hand over his thigh. Gave it a little squeeze. It was tempting to drive him a little mad under the table, but really, she wanted to keep the connection. After their week together, she'd been spoiled. She hated any distance between them outside of work.

This sensation of falling and being caught was new to her. So foreign but not unwelcome. Her young life centered on her and her mom. They had been an inseparable pair. Then she widened her circle to include a few friends. Now, with Spence, she opened it again for this makeshift family that joked with her while enveloping her in its incredible warmth.

He kissed her temple. "I know you're not used to so many people."

Carter snapped his fingers. He sat directly across from Abby and pointed at the dish next to Spence. "Stop licking your girlfriend and pass the peas."

Spence made a groaning sound. "Are you sad because you don't have a girlfriend?"

"We should find him one," Derrick said as he forked the meat off the tray then kept passing.

From his seat at one end of the table, he looked like a king presiding over his lands. Abby thought that might have been a scarier idea and his dominance might have carried more weight if he didn't spend half of the meal making lovey eyes at Ellie at the other end of the long table. He'd protested sitting so far apart but Ellie assured him he'd have the best view that way.

Honestly, Abby found the two of them adorable-bordering-on-annoying. Spence once talked about the bumpy road they had to engagement. She'd been in the office, but Derrick wasn't really one to drag his home life in. He hadn't before Ellie, anyway.

Not wanting to fall behind on the verbal poking going around the table, Abby leaned across Spence and looked at the one person at the table who seemed to keep eating no matter what happened around him. "Jackson, what's your sister's dating status?"

Jackson didn't even look up from his plate. "Nope."

"Come on." Carter laughed. "But she already loves me."

Jackson glared at Carter before glancing over at Abby. "I work with this crowd. Do you think I want to be related to them?" He froze for a second, then held up the hand that just happened to be holding his knife. "No offense."

Derrick snorted. "How could we possibly be offended by that?"

"I like them." Abby leaned in closer to Spence, soaking in his body heat. "You've all grown on me."

Spence slipped his hand around her and gave her lower back a gentle massage. "Thanks, babe. And the feeling is mutual."

Abby didn't know how he planned to eat with one hand attached to her, but that was his problem. She savored the touching and the food. She was about to ask Ellie how she'd made the meal when she was still confined to bed or sitting down for most of the day, but then common sense kicked in. The two women in the kitchen when they all arrived at the house likely did all the work. Clearly there were some benefits of eating at a Jameson home.

The money—the stunning breadth of it—still didn't sit right with Abby. She wasn't used to all that wealth. The Virginia house looked like a school when she'd driven up for the party. Derrick's town house was nothing short of spectacular but still managed to feel homey, which she credited to Ellie's handiwork.

Abby had been raised with so little. She appreciated every last shoe in her closet and can in her pantry. She'd picked each item out and purchased them. The only thing that kept her from fidgeting when she thought about the reality of Jameson money was that Spence never showed any sign of being impressed with his bank account. If he had, she would have balked.

"You have pet names for each other. Cute." Carter sent Spence a bug-eyed look. "The peas, Spence."

Spence didn't move. "You have legs."

"If I have to get up, I'm punching you."

"You're both annoying." Jackson picked up the bowl and passed it across the table to Carter.

He dug right in. "About time."

Through the controlled chaos, Derrick let out a loud exhale. Abby never knew her dad but she assumed this was the ultimate dad move. Make a noise and get everyone at the table listening. *Smooth.*

"This nonsense is going to stop when the baby comes," he said.

"We'll be too busy fighting over who gets to hold him to argue about anything else," Spence said as he tried to steal the bowl of peas back.

Carter moved it out of reach.

Ellie eyed them all over the top of her water glass. "Or her."

"Speaking of which—" Carter cut into his roast "—are you still trying to sell that faulty birth control story to explain your current state?"

"My pregnancy doesn't need to be explained," Ellie said, emphasizing each word.

"Carter." Abby was pretty sure Spence kicked his brother as he said his name.

Ellie wasn't quite as subtle. She fixed Carter with a you're-right-on-the-edge glare even though she looked like she was fighting back a smile. "Don't make me burn your clothes in the fireplace."

He winced. "Hormones?"

She waved a knife at him. "Don't test me."

Abby felt a fog roll over her. The conversation picked at a memory she'd shoved to the back of her brain. A piece of information she didn't want to deal with that now came screaming back to her.

The Pill. Sex. Antibiotics. She'd started taking the meds that were in her bathroom the second she started feeling sick. That happened before she had sex with Spence. Before, during and after.

Antibiotics and birth control pills were a bad combination. Still a long shot for getting pregnant, but it could happen. Some medications played with the effectiveness of the pill. When she climbed out of her sickbed and remembered that, she'd rechecked on the internet. The news was not as negative on the possibility of getting pregnant as she'd hoped.

Good grief. It wasn't possible…was it?

Abby tried to remember Ellie's list of pregnancy symptoms, all that she had to fight off and go through.

"Faulty birth control?" Abby didn't mean to say the words out loud, but they were the only ones in her mind right now.

"Is this appropriate dinner conversation?" Derrick asked.

"It is in this house." Spence shrugged as he made another grab for the peas and reached them this time.

His look of triumph over something so simple made Abby smile. Or it would have if she wasn't busy counting days on the calendar in her head.

"The pregnancy is high-risk because my IUD failed," Ellie explained. "It's still in there."

Carter whistled. "Damn, Derrick."

"I didn't do it."

Spence glanced at Derrick. "Well, technically…"

"It kind of depends what the 'it' is in that sentence." Jackson froze in the middle of moving the roast closer to him. "Is that the doorbell?"

The bell chimed a second time.

"Isn't everyone here?" Derrick asked the question to the room in general. He clearly didn't expect an answer because he was up and out of his chair, on the way to the door.

A terrible thought ran through Abby's head. She

leaned in to whisper it to Spence. "If your father is back in town—"

Carter nearly dropped his water glass. "Don't even joke about that."

Footsteps echoed on the hardwood floor as Derrick walked back in. He held an envelope. He dropped it on the sideboard that ran half of the length of the impossibly long room. Never looked at it again.

"What was it?" Spence asked even though he didn't sound that interested in the answer.

"Delivery of work documents." Derrick's gaze flicked to Ellie as he sat back down. "Don't glare. I didn't tell anyone to send stuff here."

"Yet, someone did. Gee, I wonder why they thought it was an okay thing to do." She did not sound pleased.

Derrick winked at her. "You forget how important I am."

"That ego." Carter shook his head. "Unbelievable."

Jackson scooped up more potatoes. "Try working with him."

Carter glanced at her. She could feel the heat of his stare as the conversation bounced around her. She tried to keep up but the idea of a baby was stuck in her head now. She wanted to kick it out but it had grabbed hold.

"Abby? Do you have an opinion on that?" Carter asked.

She couldn't stop looking at Spence, imagining what their children might look like. If a kid would have his stubbornness.

When she realized the table had gone unusually quiet and everyone stared at her, she struggled to mentally rewind the conversation and come up with an answer. "Uh, no. I'm taking the Fifth."

The talking picked back up again. About food. About

work. About anything Carter could think of, or so it seemed.

Spence leaned in closer, brushing her hair back behind her ear. "You sure everything is okay?"

"Just thinking." And panicking and generally kicking her own butt for being so careless. She'd never done that before. With her luck, it would only take one time.

He smiled at her. "You can concentrate on anything with all this noise?"

"It's called conversation, Spence," Jackson mumbled under his breath.

Ellie groaned. "Enough talking. Eat."

"The pregnant woman has spoken." Derrick picked up his glass in a toast.

"You know, for that power to keep working, you're going to have to be pregnant all the time." Jackson flinched, which must have meant Ellie kicked him. She was right there, after all. "Hey!"

"I'm up to the challenge," Derrick said.

Some of the color drained from Ellie's face. "Let's start with one first."

Abby looked down at her plate. She really hoped she wasn't the one saying that a month from now.

It took another half hour to finish up and move the conversation into the living room. On Ellie's orders, the men cleared the table and argued during every second of their work as if they'd been sent into the mines to dig for coal.

Spence didn't mind helping out. He'd do dishes, but he refused to do them alone. In Derrick's house, that usually wasn't necessary because family dinners meant he hired people to handle most of the work. With Ellie being less mobile. Derrick was interviewing for a full-time cook, but he had to do it behind her back because she was not comfortable with the idea.

Spence glanced into the great room next to where they'd eaten dinner and saw them all gathered around, lounging on sofas. Arguing, like they always did. He was pretty sure that was part of the Jameson gene pool. Jackson probably picked up the habit by association.

The only person not having coffee and debating dessert options was Abby. She stood in the doorway between the dining room and the great room, watching. He'd picked up on her mood change earlier. His family could be overwhelming. He got that. But he sensed something else was bothering her.

They'd been growing closer, spending more time together. Talking about things other than work. He didn't want her to shut down now.

"You sure you're okay?" He slipped his arms around her waist and pulled her body back against his. "You got quiet."

She sighed. "That was a lot of activity."

"Yelling. A meal with this group is a lot of yelling."

When she leaned against him, he put his chin on her shoulder. Breathed, letting this moment settle inside him. The comfort of it made him think he misread her earlier. The slight tension running through her had vanished. Now she relaxed.

She rubbed her hand over his arm. "You love it."

He couldn't deny it. Today was the kind of event that drew him back to DC. Being able to unwind with them. Joke and have fun without fear of someone losing their temper or their dad storming in. "I kind of do."

"Was it like that growing up?"

"Hell, no." He thought about the right way to explain it. He wasn't asking for pity or suggesting he had it bad, not compared to other people. But it hadn't been good, either. "We weren't allowed to talk at the table."

She turned around in his arms to face him, never breaking contact. "Are you kidding?"

The concern was evident in her eyes. Healthy concern. He could handle that.

He brushed his fingers through her hair, loving the feel of it. "Does Eldrick strike you as a guy who wanted to hear what his kids had to say?"

She rolled her eyes. "My mom would come home exhausted and still listen to me babble."

She shared so little about her past and her life before. From the few bits she'd dropped, Spence had an image in his mind. She liked solitude and trusted very few. That probably was a smart way to live. At least it seemed safer.

But he did miss having someone who knew more about her and might be able to offer some advice to him now and then. Ellie only offered up so much. "I'm sorry I never got a chance to meet your mom."

"Me, too."

He hugged her then. Pulled her in close and wondered how he'd ever let go of her in the past. That had been a terrible mistake, maybe his worst. And that was saying something.

He spied the envelope that was delivered earlier. He'd forgotten about it. Since it lay there untouched, he guessed Derrick had, too. Spence almost reached for it now. He had no idea what could be so important for a home delivery. Then he saw the return address. "Jeff Berger."

Abby froze in his arms. "What?"

Not wanting to let go of her, Spence nodded in the

direction of the envelope. "The delivery was from him. The guy has this weird competition thing with Derrick."

Her expression stayed unreadable. "Why?"

"When Derrick saved the company, he did it by grabbing a bunch of small jobs, then expanding the business into new areas, both geographic and different types of projects." Everything had been a struggle back then. Spence was relieved they'd moved past those days. "He cut right into Berger's business and Jeff took it personally and has been looking for revenge ever since."

Abby's hands slid down Spence's arms. Her fingers slipped through his. "Wow."

"It's a stupid guy thing. Jeff gets spun up even higher because Derrick won't engage."

She frowned. "Then why was Jeff at the party?"

"Keep your enemies close." At least that's what Spence assumed. He hadn't bothered to ask because he didn't care that much about Jeff.

"I hate that saying." An edge moved back into her voice.

He decided to let it go. She'd tell him when she was ready. "But it's smart."

"Unfortunately, yes."

She was frowning again but Spence had the perfect temporary solution. "We need cake."

"My hero."

Thirteen

The sun streamed through her bedroom windows early the next morning. The sheers blocked most of the harsh light, leaving the room bathed in a hazy glow. Shadows moved across her beige walls. She tried to concentrate, to keep her eyes open and watch the play of shape, but they kept drifting shut.

Blame Spence. His expert mouth and those hands were at fault. His fingertips slipped over her as he placed a trail of kisses over her inner thigh. When his mouth reached the very heart of her, her hips angled forward, giving him greater access.

Heat pounded her as she shifted on the mattress. Her skin felt tingly, as if every nerve ending had snapped to life. The coolness of the room blew over her bare skin but she barely felt it. Not while Spence's warmth surrounded her.

Her hand dropped down and her fingers tangled in

Spence's hair. She lifted her head to get a better view. The sight of him there, snuggled between her legs, had a breath stuttering in her chest. He was naked and confident. That finger worked magic as it slipped inside her.

"Spence…" she said his name on a soft puff of air.

Without breaking contact with her body, he glanced up. She could see those eyes as his mouth worked on her. The tightening inside her kept ratcheting up, bringing her closer to the edge. The orgasm hovered just out of reach. She tried to clamp down on those tiny inner muscles. Bring his finger in deeper and hold it there. But Spence had other ideas. He flipped her over until she landed on her stomach.

"Yes. Please." Her body begged for his touch. Forget playing games, she wanted more and depended on him to give it to her.

His hand smoothed down her back. Started at the base of her neck and traveled the whole way to the dip in the very small of her back. The trail sparked life into her exhausted body. Energy surged through her one more time. She separated her legs, hoping he'd get the hint, but he just kissed her. Pressed his lips to the base of her spine.

The touch was sexy. So seductive.

But enough. She twisted until her lower body stayed pressed to the mattress where he straddled her. Her top half turned to face him. "You are playing a dangerous game."

"Just enjoying a lazy morning." But that smile suggested he knew exactly what he was doing to her.

"Oh, really?" She pulled her legs up, tucking them close to her chest, and sat up.

His eyebrow lifted. "I thought you wanted to be touched."

"On your back."

Fire flashed in his eyes. His body practically pulsed with excitement. She was pretty sure she saw his hands shake as he lowered his body down. He rested on his back with his knees in the air and his feet flat against the bed.

"Well?" The challenge was right there in his voice.

Silly man. "Maybe I should take my time."

She sat next to him and dragged her finger up his thigh to his hip bone. Avoided the place he most obviously wanted to be touched. When he lifted his hips, pushing his growing length closer to her hand, she continued on to his stomach. Skimmed her palm over the firm muscles there. The ridges were so pronounced. So sexy.

"Abby, I'm dying here." His voice sounded strained.

She loved that reaction.

Making sure to brush her body against his, she reached over him. Dipped down so her breasts pressed against him, but only for a second. He reached for her, but she'd grabbed the condom off the nightstand and sat back up.

Holding the packet, she hesitated. Memories of the dinner and the medication issue came rushing back at her. She thought about what could be and the decisions they'd have to make.

Then his thumb trailed over her thighs and slipped between her legs. "Hey, you okay?"

She heard the note of concern in his voice. Saw his eyes start to narrow. They would talk, but not now. She bent over him and pressed her mouth against his in a kiss that reassured him everything would be fine. In that moment, she believed it.

She opened the packet and unrolled the condom over him. Didn't waste another second thinking or debating. Not when he was right there and so ready.

She lifted one leg and straddled his hips. Pressed her palm against his chest. Her other hand went to his length. The slightest touch had his hips lifting, as if seeking out more. And she gave it to him.

She pushed up on her knees and fitted her body to his. Relaxing down, she let him slide into her. The connection, that friction had her heartbeat skipping again. Pressing on his chest, she lifted her body again. Slow and deliberate, she pulled up until they almost separated, and then she plunged down again.

The movement, the up and down, had her breath hitching in her chest. She squeezed her thighs together and heard him moan. With their bodies wrapped around each other, touching in so many places, every shift she made sent a vibration racing through him. She welcomed the surge of power that moved through her.

His hands slipped to the back of her thighs. His fingers clenched against her skin. "I need you to move."

It was so tempting to draw out the sweet torture. She tried for a few more seconds, but got caught in her own trap. Her heartbeat thundered in her ears and their joint breathing echoed around the room. The heated skin and slow thrust of his body into hers had that tension winding inside her again. Every muscle tightened as her head fell back.

She let her hair drop down her back. Dug her fingernails into his skin, imprinting marks on his chest. A wild need fueled her now. An almost primal need to get closer, to feel his body buck under hers.

His hands settled on her hips and he held her there. Kept her suspended on her knees as he lifted his hips up and down. That final move had her head spinning. The building inside her spilled over. The orgasm hit her before she was ready but right when she needed it. Raw and pulsing, her body let go.

She closed her eyes, enjoying the sensations riding her. Feeling him tense under her. She knew he was close and tightened her thighs on either side of his waist to make it happen. Then they both lost it. Their breaths mixed and their muscles shook. She came and he got there right after her.

There were words she needed to say. But her mind couldn't hold a thought. Whatever it was would have to wait until breakfast, or at least until her brain restarted. Until then she could close her eyes again.

She sank down, curling up on his chest. Loving the feel of his strong arms as they wrapped around her. Their bodies were joined and hot. They should head for the shower. That needed to happen…

She drifted off to sleep.

Two hours later, he walked around her kitchen, cursing her for not having milk in the house. She drank her coffee black and professed a general disdain for milk. She insisted adults didn't have a big glass of the stuff with any meal. She wasn't wrong about that part, but a guy needed certain things in his morning beverage.

Thanks to the sex, he was willing to let the oversight slide this time. Probably every time.

He turned around and leaned against the cabinet next to the stove. His gaze moved over the condo. From here, he could see the living area and catch a peek of the unmade bed they just crawled out of down the hall to the left. Another bathroom and bedroom sat on the right side of the condo. He barely ventured over there because he had no intention of sleeping separate from her.

The sectional caught his attention. The thing was not small. She mentioned something about wanting a couch that could function as a bed when she was too lazy to get up. A place she could curl up and watch movies. He wasn't entirely sure what that meant but from the pillows stacked on it and on the floor around it, and that blanket rolled up in a ball, he couldn't deny his love of relaxing on it with her.

"Good morning." She walked into the kitchen wearing a pair of shorts and a slim-fitting T-shirt. It had a tiny dog with big eyes on it.

He appreciated the outfit. It might be his second favorite, next to that red wrap dress. That thing went in his clothing Hall of Fame. He seriously considered wading into her walk-in closet to find it and move it to the front as a hint.

She was barefoot and those legs went on forever. Much more of this and they'd be back in that bedroom for round three.

She took his mug and grabbed a quick sip. "Have you finally come to your senses and started drinking your coffee black?"

"You're out of milk."

"I don't buy it."

"Which should be illegal."

She took another sip. "I have that stuff you don't need to refrigerate."

She had to be kidding with that. "Woman, no."

"Fine." She smiled as she poured her own cup and joined him in leaning against the cabinets.

They both surveyed the condo. It was a quiet, relaxing morning. Not the way he was used to getting up but he hoped it became a habit.

"I need to ask you a weird question."

And then she ruined the peace with that comment.

"You have got to stop beginning conversations with that sort of phrase." He pretended to wipe his forehead. "I'm already sweating."

"The topic won't help."

Yeah, he needed to put down the breakable mug. He set it on the counter and faced her, not sure what was about to hit him. "And?"

"We didn't use a condom the first time."

He let out some of the breath he'd been holding. They'd already been through this, but maybe she forgot because she was sick with a fever at the time. "I'm sorry. That was my fault."

She shook her head. "We were both there. We're both responsible for being...irresponsible."

That all sounded reasonable. "Okay. That's nice to hear but I admit I'm a bit lost because you're frowning and looking serious."

"What if I got pregnant?" The question rushed out of her.

He was happy he had a hold on the edge of the counter or he might have fallen to the floor. "Uh...is this hypothetical?"

"I'm serious."

He was terrified and his tongue might have gone numb. "I am, too."

"So?"

"Do you think you're pregnant?" He reached for her then. Put his hands on her waist and turned her until they stood only a few inches apart, facing each other head-on.

She put her mug down and rested her hands on his chest. "I don't know."

Not the answer he wanted…or maybe it was. He was new at this.

"Okay. Why do you think it's a possibility?" Because that had never entered his mind. They had sex without the condom and talked about it. About her being on the Pill and both of them always being careful until right then.

A new phase, a more responsible one, started. Now this.

"I was on antibiotics." She must have seen the confusion on his face because after a few beats of silence she continued talking. "The meds can mess with the Pill."

The comment triggered a memory. He'd known that. Somewhere in the back of his mind, he'd filed that information away, hoping never to need to use it.

He swallowed as he forced his voice to stay calm. Inside him was a wild frenzy. His brain skipped from question to question. His knees tried to fold. He wasn't completely sure he was still breathing. "Do you want to take a test?"

"We should."

She sounded so calm. How the hell was that possible?

"If you are…" He had no idea what to say next.

"Is that panic I hear in your voice?" A slight bit of anger vibrated in hers.

"No." Yes. Absolutely, yes. But they would get through it. "We'll handle it."

Her eyes narrowed and her body stiffened. "What does that mean?"

This was the one question he had the answer to. "We will do whatever you want us to do."

"Even if that means having the baby?"

His vision blinked out for a second. He looked at his life as it stretched out in front of him. He'd never seen an image that included kids. For Derrick, sure. The guy was a born father. He was even great with Ellie's grown brother. But Spence wasn't convinced he possessed the skills. Looked like he'd be taking every class available to try to get up to speed.

Somehow, he would manage. That's what he did. That's what she and a baby would deserve. No matter how limited he might be, she would be great. And he could learn to be better than his father ever was.

He nodded. "Even then. We'll have the baby."

She still hadn't moved. "Get married?"

He had no idea where that came from, but as he stood there, he realized he viewed that as a package. "Yes."

She touched a finger to the corner of his mouth. "You look a little green."

Of course he did. Anyone would. No one should waltz into parenthood without at least a little panic. "Didn't you when you first realized this was a possibility?"

For a few more seconds, she just stood there, staring at him in silence. Finally, a small smile broke out on her lips. Some of the tension strangling the kitchen evaporated as she nodded. "Fair enough."

Not the words he'd use, but okay. "Abby, you can count on me."

He hoped that was true. He wasn't the guy who stuck around, but he would. They may have stumbled through their relationship so far, and still kind of were, but they would resolve all of their issues and concerns. And fast. He'd make her happy and do what they needed to do. But they were dealing in ifs and not facts.

"We definitely should take the test." *We* being her,

and *test* meaning as many as he could find. There was no reason to believe one.

"Tomorrow."

He didn't understand the delay. "Why wait?"

"We're going to enjoy one more day of not knowing."

It hit him then. She really thought she was. She denied having symptoms...or had he asked that? The whole conversation was a blur. It would take days for him to unravel it and get his mind working again.

"If you want us to wait, we wait." It couldn't hurt anything. They would be so early. Not that he knew anything about babies or timing, because he didn't.

"You're a good man, Spencer Jameson."

He wasn't, but he was trying. For her. "Because of you."

"You give me too much credit." Her arms wound around his neck. The lightness in her voice suggested she'd dealt with the pregnancy information and had mentally moved on to the next topic.

He was not so lucky.

"You're the best thing that's ever happened to me." As he said the words, he realized he meant them. Without the pregnancy news, this is where he'd tell her he loved her. Because he did. He hadn't needed Jackson to tell him. Not really. The sensation that moved through him when he saw her, or even just heard her voice in the hallway, wasn't like anything he'd ever experienced. It filled him, made him feel whole.

But there was too much going on to say the words now. He didn't want one thing messed up with the other. When he said the words, he didn't want there to be any doubt why he did. That meant waiting, holding it inside for another few days, which was safer anyway. Once he said them, he wouldn't be able to call them back.

Her smile grew. "I am pretty great."

"And so modest."

She kissed him. Short and sweet. "And hungry."

"For food this time, right? I can fix that one right now." He pulled back, thinking to raid the refrigerator even though the idea of stepping outside for a few gulps of fresh air sounded good.

She caught his arm as he brushed past her. "Thank you."

Gratitude. He wasn't sure how he felt about that. Then again, he didn't feel much of anything at the moment. He was numb. "For?"

"Everything."

Fourteen

Abby didn't often get a summons to come to Derrick's office in the middle of the afternoon. He called her or sent a message. That worked best since she had a calendar full of meetings and phone calls, but she pushed everything for this meeting.

Now that the school renovation project was a go, she had about a hundred deadlines to set and people she needed to corral. Not that she minded. This was her favorite part, setting everything down and seeing the hard work turn into something real.

That's kind of how she thought of Spence. He'd stayed at her house for a string of nights. Settled in and looked right at home there on her couch. He'd even survived the baby talk this morning. She almost didn't. Her emotions had roller-coastered all over the place as she watched his facial expression change. Surprise to panic to should-I-run. The good news is that last one only came in a flash then was gone again.

But they needed to know the truth in case they had to make plans. No more guessing. She had two tests in her bag. Tonight they would have the answer.

Her stomach flipped at the thought. She'd held it together so far, but she was pretty sure she'd be bent over blowing into a paper bag no matter what the result was. The anxiety growing inside her guaranteed that.

Speaking of the possible future daddy...she looked up right as she turned the corner to the hallway leading to Derrick's office. Spence stood there. Tall and confident. The unexpected sight of him made her steps falter, but she quickly regained her balance.

"What are you doing?" She put her hand on his arm. Even thought about kissing him.

Despite the lack of traffic in this hall, she refrained from the public display of affection. It wasn't really her thing. They needed to keep a work–home life separation anyway. Human Resources had suggested a list of things they should do and not do. French kissing in the hallway had to be on there somewhere.

"Derrick asked to see me," Spence said.

Her hand tightened on Spence's arm. She didn't notice until his shirtsleeve bunched in her palm. "Me, too."

He frowned at that information. "Maybe Ellie?"

The thought tumbled in Abby's head. Her mind raced to the worst scenario. Just when she thought she'd stumbled on the worst, she came up with another. "Oh, no."

"It's okay." Spence put his hand over hers. The warmth on his skin seeped into hers. "He wouldn't be at work if something was wrong with her at home."

"Right." Derrick would burn marks in the carpet getting out of there and to Ellie. That's who he was.

But Abby got back to walking, just in case. Even picked up the pace a bit.

They passed by Jackson's office. His phone rang. The door was open but he wasn't at his desk. Not an unusual occurrence since he seemed to answer to everyone in the building. People called him for help and advice.

Derrick's door was open and she heard voices, both of them familiar. Carter mumbled something in an unusually serious tone. It was enough to get the worry churning inside her again.

Spence pushed open the door and they stepped inside. "What's going on?"

"We have a problem." Carter's gaze slipped to her as he spoke. "Close the door."

This couldn't be good. Closed-door meetings sometimes meant nothing, but the look on Carter's face—drawn and a bit pale—suggested this was big.

Spence shook his head. "What did Dad do now?"

Just the mention of him touched off a new bout of frustration inside her. Anger welled, ready to boil up and spill over. Eldrick had that effect on her and likely always would.

Carter continued to stare. A strange coldness washed over Abby. She was so used to his smile and joking. From the minute she met him, she'd been struck by his genuine warmth. Derrick had to work at it. Spence tried to hide his. Carter was open and out there…but right now, he held his jaw stiff enough to crack.

Derrick dropped a large envelope on his desk. It had been opened and there was a note on top and photos spilled out. "It's not Dad."

Now he looked at Abby, too. The joint force of Derrick and Carter's angry attention only upped her anxiety levels. She handled stress fine but this crashed over her.

She mentally raced through every project, trying to

think of what might have happened or gone wrong. It couldn't be the possibility of a new baby because she doubted Spence would have told them without knowing for sure or talking to her first. And she couldn't imagine either one of Spence's brothers having this reaction.

No, this was something else. Something fundamental that drove right to the heart of their loyalty to her and trust in her.

She looked at the familiar envelope. She couldn't place it, and then it hit her. The delivery at the family dinner. Jeff Berger, the big jerk.

"I don't understand what's going on," Spence said as he took a step toward Derrick's desk.

Carter kept his focus solely on her as he spoke. "Look at the photos."

Spence picked them up, filed through them, hesitating on the second before looking at them all again. With every movement, every shift, Abby felt her happiness drift away. Jeff had set her up. Somehow, he figured out how to get to Derrick. Worse, to Spence.

"What am I looking at?" Spence turned to her. "What are these?"

She couldn't avoid taking a turn now. She stepped up beside Spence and reached for the photos. Nothing in them proved to be much of a surprise. Her at the restaurant with Jeff. Jeff leaning in. His smile. It all looked intimate, so completely wrong and out of context to what really happened.

Never mind that she hadn't done anything wrong. That she'd turned Jeff down not once but twice. Several times, actually. She could feel the collective heat from the Jameson men's stares. It pounded down on her as she focused on the photos.

Jeff Berger was a piece of garbage. And he was determined to ruin her because she refused to dance at his command.

"There's a note." Derrick's voice sounded flat as he handed the sheet over to Spence then turned to her. "He says you approached him about working in his company. Offered proprietary information to him, saying he could expand and take us out of the market. He says he's warning me as a favor."

Her stomach dropped. She literally expected to see it hit the floor.

Her hands shook as she let the photos slip onto the desk. Denials and defenses crashed through her brain. She wrestled with the right thing to say, with how to explain what happened.

A warning as a favor. She wondered how long it took Jeff to come up with that gem. The man was a complete liar.

"Are you going to say anything?" Carter asked.

Derrick held up a hand. "Give her a second."

This time Carter snorted. "For what? She either has answers or she doesn't."

They were talking around her, over her. Derrick and Carter, but not Spence. All she cared about was his reaction. It took all of her strength to look at him.

She glanced over. Saw his wrinkled brow and eyes filled with confusion. Not hate or hurt, or anything like what seemed to simmer under the surface with Carter. No, Spence was struggling. She could see it on his face.

"It's not what you think." That wasn't the right thing to say but her brain refused to function. Her skin itched from being on display. Standing there in the middle of all of them having to defend herself...she hated Jeff for that. She would always hate him for that.

Spence hesitated for a second before he said anything. "Well, I think Jeff Berger is an ass."

Relief surged through her, but she tamped it down. She refused to get excited or believe that he wouldn't turn on her again. They had been through this sort of thing before. Denial mixed with disbelief.

"He insisted we meet." She left out the part about Rylan's role in all of this. He'd been complicit, but this part—all the trauma of this moment—was all on Jeff. This was about his vendetta against Derrick. The one she'd been dragged into the middle of and now had to fight her way back out of again.

"*He* did." Carter repeated.

She couldn't tell whether he believed her or not. Right now, the only thing that mattered was that they all listened. She needed Spence to step up and believe her. "Around the time you left, after the kiss and the mess with your father, Jeff contacted me. I was upset and frustrated and half convinced I was going to get fired…"

She stopped to catch her breath. She expected them to jump in and start firing questions at her, but they stayed quiet. They watched. Stood there taking it in with those matching blank expressions on their faces.

With no other choice, she pushed ahead. "I agreed thinking I might need to find another job."

Derrick frowned. "That was never a possibility. I begged you to stay."

"I know that now, but put yourself in my position. I'd fallen for a Jameson brother and now he hated me—"

Spence shook his head. "Abby, no. That was never true."

"Let her finish." Carter issued the order in a strangely soft voice as he sat on the edge of Derrick's big desk.

"It made sense that in a choice between me and Spence—worse, between me and Eldrick—that I would lose. So, I was looking at other options."

"I would have done the same." It was the first positive thing Carter had said.

That glimmer of support spurred her on. "Well, Jeff did offer but he wanted business secrets and information on Derrick. I said no. I stopped taking his calls. Made every contact from his office run through my assistant first to make sure it was legitimate and work-related. He kept at it, checking in now and then. I ignored it all."

"But not forever." Spence pointed at the photos. "You wore that suit to work not too long ago. That restaurant is new. This is a recent meeting."

The accusation hung right there. There was nothing subtle about what Spence was saying. But he wasn't wrong, either. Denying the reality would only make things worse. Plus, she wanted to be honest.

She never intended to hide and sneak around with Jeff. He made that happen and she got pulled in. She'd take responsibility for not going to Derrick about the contacts, but the rest of this was a battle that wasn't even about her.

"He recently sent me a note demanding that we meet again. It had been months, so the contact didn't make sense. I ignored him again, but he was persistent. A bit threatening."

Carter slipped off the desk to stand again. "What?"

She rushed to explain. "Not physically. I never felt that."

"He cornered you at the engagement party." Spence exhaled. "You two were on the balcony."

She wasn't sure what the extra fact added. Spence's voice, his expression…he didn't give anything away.

Doubts and concerns had to be spinning around inside him but he kept them all bottled up. Like the old Spence, he projected an outward calm while the storm raged.

That terrified her. Repressing could only mean bad things for them, for their future.

"He made it clear that our meeting would happen. Rather than fight it, I gave in." Her gaze traveled over them as she rubbed her hands together. Her skin was deathly cold. "Because I knew whatever he said wouldn't matter. I was never going to give him those secrets or work for him."

"What exactly did he want?" Derrick asked as he picked up his pen then put it down again.

"He didn't give specifics. He had an envelope for me but I refused to take it. I didn't even touch it because the whole meeting, the setup and nasty words, clearly were about wanting to get at Derrick and the company, and have an advantage in bidding. About winning contracts away from *us*." She added the emphasis to telegraph that they were in this together. Her loyalty stayed firmly with this company. Always. Even if she left, she'd never endanger what they'd built here.

"He's got a thing about Derrick." Carter shot his older brother an odd look. "You are going to have to confront him eventually."

Derrick nodded but didn't say anything.

"These photos." Spence fingered each one. "They look—"

"Staged." That was the right answer. She filled in the blank because if he suggested any other option she would lose it.

Her control hovered right on the edge. She wanted to open her mouth and yell at them. Surely they could see she'd been set up.

Spence nodded but his focus stayed on the photos. He paged through them one by one. Got to the last one then went back again. With every swipe of his hand, her fury built. It raced through her, fueling her.

"Clearly he had a photographer waiting." Anger vibrated in her voice.

Both Carter and Derrick watched her. Whatever they heard or saw had them both staring. Neither looked upset. It was more like they were analyzing her, testing her mood. Well, they didn't need to guess because she had every intention of unloading right now.

She slapped her hand over the photos, forcing Spence to look at her. "I have zero interest in Jeff and his bargains."

Spence nodded. "Okay."

Okay? "I said no because of you." She looked around at Carter and Derrick, too. "Because of all of you. Because I love this job, and I'm starting to love this family. And because being disloyal is not who I am. I can't believe I have to explain that to you."

Carter shook his head. "You don't."

For some reason that sent her temper flaring. "You believed the photos. When I walked in here, you thought I cheated on Spence or screwed over the company. Something."

"I read a note and saw some photos."

"And blamed me."

"Okay, hold it." Derrick held up both hands. "No one thinks you did anything. We wanted an explanation. It's clear this is Jeff being Jeff. I'm just sorry you got dragged into the middle of my garbage."

Her heartbeat still drummed in her ears. She wanted to believe that they saw the truth immediately. The rational part of her brain recognized that they had to go into this conversation wary and ask questions. But she was so tired of fighting. "I would never betray you."

Spence looked at her then. "Why didn't you tell me?"

The relief that had just started swirling through her petered out. "What?"

"We've been together nonstop. We've talked about other topics, very personal things. You never bothered to tell me about what Jeff did back then or what he was threatening you with now."

"So, this is my fault?"

The loudness of Spence's voice now matched hers. "I'm asking a simple question."

One that made her temper soar. He had a right to question. They did need to talk this through. She got all of that. But standing there, right then, in the middle of it all, she felt nothing but raw and hollowed out. Instead of leaping to her defense along with Derrick and Carter, Spence was still doubting her.

"He told me you wouldn't believe me."

"No, he's wrong." Spence shook his head. "I never said that."

He didn't have to. She heard the words so clearly in her head. "First your dad. Now Jeff. You never believe me."

Spence reached out and held her arm by the elbow. "Hey, that's not fair."

"When will I learn?" She pulled out of his grip. "You know when? Right now. I'm going to finally learn the lesson now."

The whole room vibrated from the force of her slamming Derrick's office door as she stormed out. Spence watched her go without saying a word. Speech failed him. He didn't understand what just happened. He'd been trying to reason it all out in his mind, every step. The idea that Jeff Berger was trying to push her around and she didn't tell him…it made Spence sick. What kind of trust was that?

He took a step, thinking to go after her. Carter blocked his path.

He loomed there. "You have a couple of choices about what you do next."

One. There was only one choice and Spence was about to do it. "I'm going to talk with her."

"Wrong one," Derrick said as he walked out from behind his desk to stand beside Carter.

They formed a wall in front of Spence. He would have to get around both of them to get out of there.

"What is this?" Spence looked back and forth between his two brothers. "You can't believe she's working with Jeff."

Derrick scoffed. "Of course not."

"She's not the type," Carter added as he shook his head.

Some of the indignation ran out of Spence then. He thought he was going to have to come to her defense, explain it to them. There was no way she would do what Jeff suggested. She'd had multiple chances to screw them all over and never took one. That's not how she operated. When she was ticked off, she fought the battle head-on. Spence knew because he'd gone more than a few rounds with her.

One of the things he loved about her was her refusal to back down. She fought for what she believed in and refused to be shoved around or forgotten. He found that drive, that will, so sexy.

"Then what's the problem with me going after her?" Spence asked because he really didn't get it.

Carter made a hissing sound. "See, you questioned her."

"No…"

Derrick nodded. "You did."

That didn't happen. "I never believed the note from Jeff."

"I wanted an explanation, which is fine. I'm not sleeping with her. But once she gave it, I was all in on her side." Carter winced. "But you questioned why she didn't let you rescue her."

"Women hate that sort of thing where you rush in and try to save the day without talking to them first." Derrick shrugged. "Or so I've been told by Ellie about a thousand times."

They had both lost it. Spence didn't understand what they didn't get about this situation. "We're dating."

Carter nodded. "Uh-huh."

"I'm in love with her."

Derrick clapped Spence on the back. "There it is."

Carter whistled. "Finally."

It was as if they had the code to some secret language he didn't have. "I hate you both right now."

"You and Abby need to learn how to communicate." Derrick made that pronouncement as he returned to his oversize desk chair and sat down.

"If you're ready to do that, you should go find her. If not…" Carter shook his head. "I'd wait until I had an epiphany."

"I don't know what either of you are talking about." Spence didn't. Advice swam around in his head. Competing feelings of frustration and desperation battled inside him. He didn't want the rift between them to grow. But he wasn't quite sure what he needed to do, either.

Then there was the baby. That issue never left his

mind. Bringing the possibility up now to Abby might get him punched. Even he was smart enough to know he needed to keep whatever was brewing between them separate from family talk.

He tried to come up with the right question to ask as Derrick picked up the phone. "Who are you calling?"

"It's time Jeff Berger and I meet."

"Do it in public and don't run him over with a car," Carter said. "If you do, make it look like an accident."

Through the haze of confusion one thought settled in Spence's mind. His brothers really did trust and believe Abby. She told her side and they fell into line.

Maybe now it was his turn.

Forget waiting. Now was the right time. He headed for the door.

Derrick hung up the phone again without dialing. "Where are you going?"

"To find Abby."

"I guess that means you've had that epiphany," Carter said, sounding pretty pleased with himself.

"No, but I'm hoping it will hit me on the way." Spence's fingers touched the door handle before he glanced back at Derrick. "I'll leave Jeff to you. If I confront him right now, I might kill him."

"Consider him handled."

One problem down. Now Spence had the bigger one to conquer.

Fifteen

Abby paced back and forth in her office. It felt as if hours had passed, but she knew that wasn't true. She couldn't see the clock or hear any noise. Her curt order to her assistant to hold all of her calls and visitors—something she'd apologize for later—probably said enough for the people outside her door to scurry away.

She wasn't one to close the door and demand peace. When she did, people knew it meant something. Since the gossip about her love life and dating Spence swirled around the office, some might even figure out the source of her frustration.

The chill refused to leave her bones. She had no idea how it was possible to feel hot and ice-cold at the same time, but there she was. The pain in her stomach and her head. Both thumped, demanding attention.

She didn't even hear the door open. She turned, thinking to go in search of something for the headache, and ran right into Spence's broad chest. He reached for her arms and held her, more to keep her from falling than anything else. This wasn't a hug. There was nothing intimate about it. More of a safety-first sort of thing.

He steadied her then reached back to close the door. There, that would stop the gossip. Abby almost rolled hers eyes at the novice move.

"What are you doing here?" She thought for sure he'd hide in Derrick's office all day. If he had a home, he might go there but he didn't. And that bothered her, too.

All of her confusion and questions balled up together. He'd left the last time. There was nothing stopping him from going again. His reaction to the baby had been almost perfect. Sure, he wavered a bit at first but so did she. But she sensed he was waiting to see if this whole visit-home-to-Derrick thing worked out.

His hands dropped to his sides as he looked down at her. "This time you ran."

She searched his face for any sign that they were going to be okay. Not that she wanted a handwritten agreement signed in blood. She didn't even require some sort of long-term commitment, though her heart begged for one. But everything about him, from the fact he lived out of a bag to his office that still looked like no one had been assigned there, showed that he lived his life in a temporary fashion. She didn't know why the Jeff Berger situation drove that point home, but it did.

Now what?

"I needed space," she said, knowing it sounded trite and was only half-correct.

He nodded. "I get it."

That just made the confusion inside her spin faster. "Do you?"

When he frowned at her, she decided to take hold of the conversation. That might be the only way to get through this. Then she could go home and curl up on the couch and forget everything about the last few weeks. Go back to building emotional walls and burying herself in projects in the office.

"Why haven't you started any new projects at work?" It was so simple that she wondered why she hadn't seen it before.

His eyes widened. "What?"

The response was fair. She hadn't exactly built up to it, but the topic was not going away. It had taken hold in her head and she had to ride it out now. "You're the head of new acquisitions. I think that's the fancy title, right? But I haven't seen you do one lick of work on anything but projects already in progress."

His hands went to his hips and a look of pure disbelief crossed his face. He looked ten seconds from exploding. "You're giving me a work evaluation?"

She couldn't tell if he was stalling while his mind came up with a snappy answer or if he really didn't understand how he came off to the world. "You're great at the job. I doubt you even realize how good you are. It's a natural skill for you. People listen to you. You're organized. You can get things moving and straightened out. You've been the perfect closer."

He shook his head. "What does any of this have to do with Jeff Berger?"

Nothing, everything. She wasn't sure how to explain how it all came together in her head, so she didn't even try.

She moved away from him, slipped behind her desk. Stood with her hands on the back of her chair. It provided a wall of sorts, a shield for what she feared was to come. "This issue is so much bigger than him."

He threw his hands up. "Fill me in because I'm lost."

But that tone. He wasn't engaged and listening, wanting to get it. That tone was defensive. It was the one he used as he prepared for verbal battle. She'd heard it before. He used it on business associates and on her.

It meant he was already closing a door. She could almost feel it slam shut on her.

"You're a good closer because what's required of that job is wrapping up and moving on. Your specialty area." It seemed so clear to her now. No wonder he volunteered to handle those tasks for Derrick while Ellie was on bed rest.

"We're back to talking about my dad and what happened back then?" Spence rested his palms against her desk. Leaned down and faced off with her right over her desk. "Are you kidding me? I thought we moved forward."

"When?"

"Isn't that what the sex was about?"

The walls shook from the force of his voice. She glanced at the door, happy that it was closed. But people walking by had to know a fight waged in her office.

Let them listen.

She struggled to keep her voice calm. Did not let him see that the sex comment slashed through her. "Have we ever dealt with the underlying issue?"

"That you're afraid of commitment."

Her mouth dropped open. She felt it go. "Me?"

He pushed off the desk and stood up straight again. "You are so sure people are going to leave you."

The comment hit its mark. She felt it right to the center of her chest. But he was missing a very important piece of this puzzle. "You did leave me."

"I messed up, Abby. I am sorry." He turned away from her for a second and wiped a hand through his hair. When he looked at her again, his eyes were wild. It was as if the warring inside him was tearing him apart. "I will say it to you however many times it takes to make it better for you. Just tell me."

It was so tempting to drop the subject. Go to him, hug it out. Pretend that this subject and the worry wouldn't haunt her nights…but it would.

"Promise me you won't do it again." It was an impossible request. So unfair of her, and she knew that. She just didn't know how else to say what she needed.

She'd spent a lifetime losing the people she loved. She closed the circle, only let a few in. But the point was she *had* let him in. Now she worried he was clawing against the walls to get out again.

"I…what are you talking about?" His voice came out as a ragged whisper.

"Jeff's stuff was another hole you could slip through. An excuse you could use to go."

Spence shook his head. His voice carried a pleading tone now. "I didn't. I stood in that office and defended you."

"You wanted to know why I didn't tell you about Jeff and his threats." The words stuck in her throat but she pushed them out. She'd only just figured out half of this herself, and it sucked to dump it on him. But it was about him. "In part, I wanted to handle it. Not give Derrick another burden. Back then, not give him a reason to doubt me because he was my boss and you were gone."

"Sure, that makes sense."

"This time, I kept it quiet so *you* wouldn't have a reason to doubt me."

His shoulders fell, as if the will had run right out of him. "You are confusing all of these things. They aren't related to each other."

"I can't wait around for you to leave me again." She almost sobbed when she said it, but there it was. The real fear. The one that spun around inside her, getting bigger, grabbing on to everything. It tainted the good times and made the idea of being pregnant almost impossible to bear.

His eyes looked empty now. The voice, the way he stood there, as if his muscles had stopped working. It all suggested that he was lost. She would do anything to lead him back to her, but he had to help her. He needed to recognize that this was an issue and fight with her.

"How about trusting me enough to know I'm going to stay."

The words pummeled her. "Trust is earned."

"You're saying I don't deserve it." It wasn't a question. He said it as a statement of fact.

That's not how she meant it. She did not see him as a lost cause. He was smart and funny, charming and sexy. He had a bone-deep loyalty, because that is why he came back to help Derrick. Not out of curiosity.

He was her everything and could be all she ever wanted. When she looked at him she knew she'd love him forever.

That realization had her pressing her hand against her chest. "I haven't seen many clues that you intend to put down roots. No house. No new work."

He made a strangled sound. "You and the baby. The *maybe* baby."

All the hope ran out of her then. She leaned harder

against the chair to keep from falling to the floor. "That's exactly the wrong answer."

"Why?"

"I need you to stay because you want to, not because you have to." It was just that simple. After a lifetime of settling for limited friendships and not going too deep, she wanted it all. "Until you make a decision about that, you need to stay away."

"Abby." He reached for her.

She was already moving. She held open the door, knowing he would go. He should. The things he needed to decide had to be done without her. All she could do was hope he'd come back. "The choice is yours."

Later that night, after ignoring a series of Jameson-related calls and Jackson's knock at the door, Abby sat on her couch. She'd put on her sweatpants and curled up in the corner. The move usually made her feel better, but not this time.

She wasn't alone, but she didn't blame the company. It was hard to get angry with a pregnant woman who refused to leave the hallway until Abby let her in. Stubbornness ran deep in Ellie.

"Are you supposed to be out of bed?" Abby asked for the third time.

Ellie didn't take the hint. She leaned into the cushions and rubbed her nonexistent belly. "This sounded like an emergency."

Not that Abby had thrown up the white flag. She'd purposely not bothered Ellie because she didn't want to upset her. She also didn't want Ellie getting together with another Jameson and ganging up on Spence. He needed to come to whatever conclusion he came to on his own.

Just thinking about that sent a new wave of sadness crashing through Abby. Spence was the type who did better with a little guidance. He was someone her grandmother would say *needed a good woman*. Abby really wanted to be that.

Since she didn't squeal, Abby knew that left a few suspects. "Derrick told you about what happened in the office."

Abby was pretty sure her fight with Spence had already made the rounds at the company. They hadn't been quiet. And the look on his face as he walked out of her office. She felt like she'd kicked a puppy.

"Derrick and Carter told Jackson, who called me. Then Derrick texted. Carter came by the house." Ellie cited the list in a singsongy voice. "Honestly, it was this weird chain of communication from Jameson men."

Abby noticed one name was missing. "Not all of them."

"No, Spence is likely afraid of me right now, which is not a bad thing."

Ellie's smile was almost chilling. Abby hated to think what that meant. "What did you do?"

"Told him to stop being a—" Ellie's voice cut off as she waved a hand in the air. "That's enough about him. How are you?"

Nice try. "A mess."

Ellie put a pillow in front of her and held on to it like a life jacket. "I can see that."

"Thanks." She owned a mirror. She knew.

"But the look is familiar. I had it when I thought Derrick and I were over."

Abby still couldn't believe that happened. "You two are so obviously perfect for each other."

Ellie snorted. "So, you can see it in others just not in your own life."

They'd circled right back to Spence. No surprise there. Abby was impressed with how quickly Ellie managed it. "You're lucky you're pregnant."

"Spill." Ellie threw the pillow to the side and shifted so that she sat sideways on the couch, facing Abby. "Now. I have a ticking clock here. Jackson brought me over. Once Derrick figures that out, he'll yell this building down."

Rather than debate about where she should be, Abby dove in. What was the harm in reliving this disaster one more time? "You heard about Jeff Berger."

Ellie nodded. "Yep, unfortunately. And if I never hear his name again, I'll be thrilled."

"Same here." Some of the energy ran out of Abby there. She'd been holding it together, but only by a thread. When she looked at Ellie's face now, she wanted to just get the rest out. "He's a runner, Ellie."

Ellie frowned. "This Berger guy?"

"You know who I'm talking about. He hasn't settled in. He's living out of your house and mine. His workload is a mix of odds and ends, other people's stuff." Abby cut off the list before it got so long that it strangled the last little bit of hope inside her. "You know he could pick up again."

"You're jumping around. First, this Berger guy. Now the running thing."

"It's all part of the same problem." At least it was in Abby's head. "He's looking for reasons to go. I tie him here. Other things tie him here. But does he really want to be here? I just feel like he's hiding things."

Ellie made a humming sound. "Like you did when you withheld the details of this Berger guy's threats."

Okay...well that was an annoying comparison. "It's not the same thing."

"Sure it is. It's all about trust. Neither of you have moved past what happened before and forgiven each other."

Abby got stuck on the "neither" part. "What did I do?"

"Oh, most of the blame goes to Spence and his father. But how much of a fight did you put up?" Ellie's eyebrow lifted. "I'm betting you assumed Spence would leave, because your life is easier when you don't connect with people all that much. Then he confirmed your worst fears. Rather than yelling at him like he deserved, you retreated."

That was ridiculous...wasn't it? "I don't retreat."

Ellie let out an annoying snort. A pretty loud one, too. "Do you love him?"

Abby didn't stall or gloss over the question. She hit it head-on. "More than anything."

It felt weird to say the words. To hear them out there. She did love him. Like, couldn't-think-straight love him.

"Then let him in and insist he do the same with you." Ellie smiled as if she'd solved all the world's problems. "As an objective observer, neither of you is going anywhere."

"I'm not." Abby was hoping he wasn't. Which meant only one thing. Ellie was right. "You sort of make some sense. Kind of."

"That must have hurt to admit."

Abby made a face. "A little."

"Good." When Abby started to say something, Ellie held up her hand. "I mean it's good because the rest of the family is exhausted by the inability of both of you otherwise very smart people to figure this out."

This was the lecture Abby never expected to hear, but it made her feel better. She'd been blaming him and waiting for him to step up. Maybe she needed to make it clear that she could take a step, too. "Nice delivery."

Ellie's demeanor changed. She grew serious as she reached out and grabbed Abby's hand. "Trust him, Abby. Then maybe leave a little room to trust yourself."

Abby realized that for a person who didn't have many friends, she sure did pick the right ones. "Thanks."

Ellie gave Abby's hand another squeeze before she let go. "Before you do anything, do you think we can convince Jackson to get us some food?"

"It is one of his many skills."

"Good man."

Sixteen

Spence sat on the edge of his bed at Derrick's place, trying to reason out what Abby had said. He still thought she'd mixed up events and created a big thing that didn't exist. The running away issue…he had to own up to that. It was his go-to move and giving it up would take everything he had.

But he'd do it for her. He'd do almost anything for her.

"Why are you here?"

Spence looked up to find Derrick leaning in the doorway. He looked comfortable. Like a man who had finally found some peace At least until the screaming baby came.

"That's welcoming." Spence didn't bother to get up or move over. He knew Derrick would loom there, waiting for the right time to impart some wisdom. That was *his* go-to move.

Derrick let out a long and very loud exhale. "You

should be at Abby's, insisting you two can work things out."

"Can we?" That was the question that kept bouncing around in Spence's head. He'd never wanted anything this much.

"You know the answer. You're just feeling sorry for yourself."

As pep talks went, this was not one of Derrick's better ones. Spence was hoping for more. "Thanks, man."

"You have a right to. Your life is a mess." Derrick did step inside then. He walked over and sat next to Spence. "But she's the right one for you and you know that. Put away the fear and set down roots. You belong here. You belong with her."

He sounded like Abby. Their comments mirrored each other. Apparently, everyone else could see his fear. So much for the theory he did a good job of hiding it. "You make it sound easy."

Derrick laughed. "Oh, it's scary as hell. I know."

"And I have this." Spence reached beside him and picked up the unopened envelope from Eldrick. This was part of the requirements that would allow Derrick to take over the business. What needed to be done to make Eldrick slip away permanently, because Spence knew Derrick feared Dad would just walk into the office one day and try to run things again. The ownership percentages allowed him to do it.

"Open it." Derrick shrugged, acting as if his entire business future didn't ride on whatever was inside. "You may as well face everything at once. Let's see if you balk."

Spence ripped the top open. "And my list of requirements is…wait."

The air punched out of his lungs. Spence blinked

a few times, trying to bring the simple sentences into focus. This wasn't a legal document; it was...he didn't know what it was.

Derrick frowned as he grabbed the paper out of Spence's hands. "What?"

Go find Abigail. Beg her to take you back. She never betrayed you.

"Come on. Is our dad taking responsibility for something? That can't be right." It seemed impossible. Spence couldn't even get the words to register in his brain.

"Yes, but even weirder, I think he's matchmaking." Derrick turned the paper over then flipped it back again. "This can't be from Beth or her doing. The envelope was here long before the engagement party, and that's where she found out. That's all Dad."

"Our dad?" The one who harassed Abby and kissed her. The one who sent them down this awful road. "No way."

"Apparently people can change." Derrick handed the paper back to Spence. "Your turn."

An hour later, Spence stood at Abby's door. Without saying a word, she gestured for him to step inside. Didn't slam the door on his face.

That alone seemed like a step forward. "Thanks for letting me come in."

"You still have the key and the security codes."

Some of the hope inside him died. Her voice sounded flat and there was nothing welcoming about a conversation about security codes. "Is that why you agreed to see me?"

She stopped in the middle of her living room and faced him. She wore oversize sweatpants and a T-shirt with a rip along the shoulder seam. Her hair was half in and half out of a ponytail holder.

She had never looked more beautiful to him.

She sighed. "No, I agreed because I love you."

His mind went blank and his mouth went dry. He was pretty sure he made that up in his head. There was no way she said those words. "What?"

"There, I said it. I love you." She threw up her hands then let them drop to her sides again. "You ran out on me, and I am terrified you will do it again, but that's the truth. I love you, you big moron."

He was even fine with the last part. "Abby—"

"I believe in you even though you don't believe in yourself."

His brain finally signaled his legs to move. In a few steps, he was in front of her, had his hands on her waist and pulled her in closer to him. "Don't stop."

She frowned at him. "What?"

They *really* did need to work on their communication skills. He decided to start now. "I can't deny that there's this whirling sensation inside me. When things blow up and a fight that could shred everything looms, I go. It stops the arguing and I can catch my breath. I've been using that defense mechanism since I was a kid."

She started to pull away. "Right."

"Not with you." He hugged her even tighter. Pressed his lips against her eyebrow in a kiss that was meant mostly to soothe her but ended up calming him. When he pulled back, some of the wariness had left her eyes. "See, every other time, I walked away and the feelings, the churning, the reason I fled in the first place, disappeared. With you, the need only got stronger."

Her fingers clenched against his forearms. "You didn't come back to me. I waited for some sign. Any sign."

"I felt broken, Abby. I knew I had already fallen for you and then my dad…" Mentioning him could ruin everything. He wasn't the problem between them now. Not really. "Forget that. This was my fault. I left and I missed you every single day. I couldn't visit my brother because I worried I would see you."

She nibbled on her bottom lip. For a few seconds, she didn't say anything and he held his breath…waiting.

When nothing happened, he tried again. "It was a crappy thing to leave and then to make you wait. You suffered. I suffered. I don't want to do it anymore."

She brushed her fingertip over his bottom lip. "Can you break the cycle?"

She'd asked the question but he sensed she was starting to believe. To hope.

"Before you told me about the possible pregnancy, I wanted to tell you how I felt." He nodded toward the living room. "Sitting right there on that couch, I was going to tell you I loved you. That I'd figured out I would always love you. That you were worth sticking around and fighting through the mess."

Tears gathered in her eyes. "Spence."

He rushed to get the rest out. "I didn't tell you then because I didn't want you to think I did it because I had to, but I'll tell you now." He rested his forehead against hers and inhaled. "Baby or not, I want to build a life with you. That gnawing sense of wanting to bolt will likely always be with me, but I don't want to leave you. Ever."

She wrapped her arms around his neck. "Sounds like I'd have to go with you then."

The words were muffled in his neck, but he heard them. Also picked up on the happiness in her tone. How much lighter she sounded.

"That also works." He lifted her head and stared down into her eyes. "But really, I love my brothers. I've even gotten used to the office, which is nothing short of a miracle."

She smiled. "What are you saying?"

He recognized hope when he saw it. It soared through him, too. "Take a chance on me. I know I'm a risk, but—"

"Stop." She shrugged as she hugged him close. "It's too late. My life is already bound up with yours. I'm afraid you're stuck with me."

"I love the sound of that." He kissed her. Let his lips linger over hers, loving the feel of her body pressed against his.

"Good, because I plan on making it a requirement for the next fifty years or so."

He didn't try to fight the smile. "Then we should start now."

"I like your style."

It was well past two in the morning. They were in bed, lying side by side, recovering from what she might call the greatest make-up sex of all time. She'd mentioned that to him and he hadn't stopped smiling. Until right now.

She looked at his hands, those long fingers. Saw the white stick he held in a death grip. "You keep staring at it."

"It's so little and has the power to change everything with a plus sign."

He'd insisted on the pregnancy test after their last

round. She'd wanted cake, but he won the argument. Now, if only the panic screaming through her would stop.

"I could make a joke about how babies disrupt lives, but I'm not sure you're ready for that." She also wanted to point out that the Jameson men were pretty fertile and warn Carter, but the timing seemed wrong for that, too.

Spence shook the stick. "It should do something."

"Like?"

He shrugged. "Balloons should pop out of it. Maybe play music."

"It's not a magic stick."

He snorted as his head turned and he faced her. "It kind of is. We wave it and it changes everything about our lives together."

Skipping the cake might have been smart. Her stomach wouldn't stop dancing. "Well, that's true."

His eyes narrowed just a fraction. "You okay?"

"Scared." It would take her a while to figure out how to deal with this news. They'd have to make plans, but she knew they would do it together. He'd made that clear. "Not about us. Not about how much I love you."

He turned over and faced her. Wrapped an arm around her waist as he watched her. "But?"

"This is going to be hard. We're still trying to sort ourselves out as a couple and now we'll have this." A few hours ago, that would have terrified her, but not as much now. She just needed to make sure he agreed with her. "Spence, this is—"

"I'm going to get angry if you offer me an out."

"Six weeks ago, when you stepped back into my life, I knew you as the guy who bolted when everything got to be too much." She winced as she pointed that out. She didn't want to start another fight.

"Didn't we settle this?" But he didn't sound angry. Instead, he rolled her onto her back and balanced his body over hers.

She ran a hand up and down his bare arm, loving the feel of his sleek muscles under her fingertips. "I trust you to stay. The point is I want you to."

"Leaving you, losing you, ripped me apart." He pressed a quick kiss on the tip of her nose. "It was a wake-up call for me to get my act together."

She let the words settle in her head. Yeah, she liked the sound of that. A lot. "And I'm part of that act?"

He snorted. "You have the main role in it."

The last of her defenses crumbled. The walls came roaring down and took her doubts with them. In a few short hours, with a couple of words, he brought her peace. It would not be easy. Knowing the two of them, life would not be quiet or simple. It would be loud and loving and perfectly imperfect, and that sounded pretty great to her.

"I love you. You and your big messy family." Because when she claimed him, she decided she'd claim them, too. "Okay, not your dad."

"Remind me to show you something later." His smile was downright mysterious. "A letter."

She didn't want to know, yet part of her did. She guessed he did that on purpose. Reeled her in and made her care about Eldrick, which should have been an impossible feat.

"I hate letters right now." They reminded her of Jeff and no matter how tonight turned out, she still despised that guy.

Spence's smile only grew wider. "This one may surprise you."

"I'm intrigued." She was about to pepper him with

questions, but his hand slipped under the covers. Right down to her thigh. "Oh, yeah. There." Then those expert fingers traveled a big higher. "The letter can wait."

"Yes, it can."

"I'm going to let you show me how much you love me."

He rolled over her then. "Again?"

"I'm sure you can handle it."

He lowered his mouth until it hovered right above hers. "I can handle you."

"Show me."

* * * * *

MILLS & BOON

THE HEART OF ROMANCE

A ROMANCE FOR EVERY READER

MODERN

Prepare to be swept off your feet by sophisticated, sexy and seductive heroes, in some of the world's most glamourous and romanti locations, where power and passion collide.

HISTORICAL

Escape with historical heroes from time gone by. Whether your passion for wicked Regency Rakes, muscled Vikings or rugged Highlanders, aw the romance of the past.

MEDICAL

Set your pulse racing with dedicated, delectable doctors in the high-pres sure world of medicine, where emotions run high and passion, comfort a love are the best medicine.

True Love

Celebrate true love with tender stories of heartfelt romance, from the rush of falling in love to the joy a new baby can bring, and a focus on th emotional heart of a relationship.

Desire

Indulge in secrets and scandal, intense drama and plenty of sizzling hot action with powerful and passionate heroes who have it all: wealth, status good looks…everything but the right woman.

HEROES

Experience all the excitement of a gripping thriller, with an intense ro mance at its heart. Resourceful, true-to-life women and strong, fearless m face danger and desire - a killer combination!

To see which titles are coming soon, please visit

millsandboon.co.uk/nextmonth

JOIN US ON SOCIAL MEDIA!

Stay up to date with our latest releases, author news and gossip, special offers and discounts, and all the behind-the-scenes action from Mills & Boon...

 millsandboon

 millsandboonuk

f millsandboon

It might just be true love...